Ruth Miller 1969.

KT-218-111

THAT HIDEOUS STRENGTH

'As a thriller it makes good reading, for Dr Lewis writes with scholarly ease, and he has a fertile imagination. But, like a good fairy story, it has moral significance: it suggests the dangers that beset humanity, and the whole terrifying vastness and depth of the universal conflict that lies beneath the surface of visible reality.'—*Scotsman*.

By the same author in PAN Books

OUT OF THE SILENT PLANET
VOYAGE TO VENUS

CONDITIONS OF SALE

This book shall not, by way of trade or otherwise, be
lent, re-sold, hired out or otherwise circulated without
the publisher's prior consent in any form of binding or
cover other than that in which it is published and without a similar condition including this condition being
imposed on the subsequent purchaser

THAT HIDEOUS STRENGTH

C. S. LEWIS

PAN BOOKS LTD : LONDON

First published 1945 by John Lane the Bodley Head Ltd.
This edition, abridged by the author, published 1955 by
Pan Books Ltd., 33 Tothill Street, London, S.W.1

330 02170 2

2nd Printing 1956
3rd Printing 1960
4th Printing 1962
5th Printing 1963
6th Printing 1965
7th Printing 1968

All rights reserved

The Shadòw of that hyddeous strength
Sax myle and more it is of length.

SIR DAVID LINDSAY: from
Ane Dialog (describing the
Tower of Babél)

Printed in Great Britain by Richard Clay (The Chaucer Press), Ltd.,
Bungay, Suffolk

PREFACE

THIS is a ' tall story ' about devilry, though it has behind it a serious ' point ' which I have tried to make in my *Abolition of Man*. In the story the outer rim of that devilry had to be shown touching the life of some ordinary and respectable profession. I selected my own profession, not, of course, because I think Fellows of Colleges more likely to be thus corrupted than anyone else, but because my own profession is naturally that which I know best. A very small university is imagined because that has certain conveniences for fiction. Edgestow has no resemblance, save for its smallness, to Durham—a university with which the only connection I have ever had was entirely pleasant.

In reducing the original story to a length suitable for this edition, I believe I have altered nothing but the *tempo* and the manner. I myself prefer the more leisurely pace—I would not wish even *War and Peace* or *The Faerie Queene* any shorter—but some critics may well think this abridgment is also an improvement.

C. S. L.

CHAPTER ONE

SALE OF COLLEGE PROPERTY

I

" Matrimony was ordained, thirdly," said Jane Studdock to herself, " for the mutual society, help, and comfort that the one ought to have of the other." She had not been to church since her schooldays until she went there six months ago to be married, and the words of the service had stuck in her mind.

Through the open door she could see the tiny kitchen of the flat and knew how tidy it was. The beds were made and the rooms " done ". There was nothing that had to be done till six o'clock, even supposing that Mark was really coming home for dinner. But there was a College meeting to-day. Almost certainly Mark would ring up about tea-time to say that the meeting was taking longer than he had expected and that he would have to dine in College.

" Mutual society, help, and comfort," said Jane bitterly. In reality marriage had proved to be the door out of a world of work and comradeship and laughter and innumerable things to do, into something like solitary confinement.

" Here I am, starting to waste another morning, mooning," said Jane to herself sharply. " I *must* do some work." By work she meant her doctorate thesis on Donne. She still believed that if she got out all her note-books and editions and really sat down to the job she could force herself back into her lost enthusiasm for the subject. But before she did so she turned over a newspaper which was lying on the table and glanced at a picture on the back page.

The moment she saw the picture, she remembered her dream; not only the dream but the time after she had crept out of bed and sat waiting for the morning, afraid to put on the light for fear Mark should wake up and fuss, yet feeling offended by the sound of his regular breathing. He was an excellent sleeper. Only one thing ever seemed able to keep him awake after he had gone to bed, and even that did not keep him awake for long.

7

She had begun by dreaming simply of a face. It was a foreign-looking face, bearded and rather yellow, with a hooked nose. It was frightened. The mouth sagged open and the eyes stared as she had seen other men's eyes stare for a second or two when some sudden shock had occurred. But this face seemed to be meeting a shock that lasted for hours. Then gradually she became aware of more. The face belonged to a man who was sitting hunched up in one corner of a little square room with white-washed walls. At last the door was opened and a rather good-looking man with a pointed grey beard came in. The prisoner seemed to recognise him as an old acquaintance and they began to talk. In all the dreams which Jane had hitherto dreamed, one either understood what the dream-people were saying or else one did not hear it. But in this dream—and that helped to make its extraordinary realism—the conversation was in French, and Jane understood bits of it, but by no means all, just as she would have done in real life. The visitor was telling the prisoner something which he apparently intended him to regard as good news. And the prisoner at first looked up with a gleam of hope in his eye and said "*Tiens . . . ah . . . ça marche*": but then he wavered and changed his mind. The visitor continued in a low, fluent voice to press his point. He was a good-looking man in his rather cold way, but he wore pince-nez, and these kept on catching the light so as to make his eyes invisible. This, combined with the almost unnatural perfection of his teeth, gave Jane a disagreeable impression. She could not make out what it was that the visitor was proposing. At this point the dream became nightmare. The visitor, still smiling his cold smile, seized the prisoner's head between his hands. He gave it a sharp turn—just as Jane had last summer seen men give a sharp turn to the helmet on a diver's head. The visitor unscrewed the prisoner's head and took it away. Then all became confused. The head was still the centre of the dream, but it was a different head now—a head with a reddish-white beard all covered with earth. It belonged to an old man whom some people were digging up in a kind of churchyard—a sort of ancient British, druidical kind of man, in a long mantle. This ancient thing was coming to life. "Look out!" she cried in her dream. "He's alive. Stop! stop! You're waking him." But they did not stop. The old, buried man sat up and began talking in something that sounded vaguely like Spanish. And this frightened Jane so badly that she woke up.

But it was not the mere memory of a nightmare that made the room swim before Jane's eyes. There, on the back page of the newspaper, was the head she had seen in the nightmare: the first head (if there had been two of them)—the head of the prisoner. She took up the paper. EXECUTION OF ALCASAN was the headline, and beneath it, SCIENTIST BLUEBEARD GOES TO GUILLOTINE. She remembered having vaguely followed the case. Alcasan was a distinguished radiologist in a neighbouring country—an Arab by descent, they said—who had cut short a brilliant career by poisoning his wife. So that was the origin of her dream. She must have looked at this photo in the paper before going to bed. But that couldn't be it. It was this morning's paper. But of course there must have been some earlier picture which she had seen and forgotten—weeks ago when the trial began. And now for Donne.

" I *must* get back my power of concentrating," said Jane: and then, " Was there a previous picture of Alcasan? Supposing . . ."

Five minutes later she swept all her books away, went to the mirror, put on her hat, and went out. She was not sure where she was going. Anywhere, to be out of that flat, that whole house.

II

Mark, meanwhile, was walking down to Bracton College. Edgestow is the smallest of universities. Apart from Bracton and from the new women's college beyond the railway, there are only two colleges; Northumberland, below Bracton on the River Wynd, and Duke's opposite the Abbey. Bracton takes no undergraduates. It was founded in 1300 for the support of ten learned men whose duties were to pray for the soul of Henry de Bracton and study the laws of England. The number of Fellows has gradually increased to forty, of whom only six now study Law and of whom none, perhaps, prays for the soul of Bracton. Mark Studdock was a Sociologist and had been elected five years ago. He was beginning to find his feet. If he had felt any doubt on that point (which he did not) it would have been laid to rest when he found himself meeting Curry just outside the post office, and seen how natural Curry found it that they should walk to College together and discuss the agenda for the meeting. Curry was the sub-warden of Bracton.

"Yes," said Curry. "It will take the hell of a time. Probably go on after dinner. We shall have the obstructionists wasting time. Luckily that's the worst they can do."

You would never have guessed from the tone of Studdock's reply what intense pleasure he derived from Curry's use of the pronoun " we ". So very recently he had been an outsider, watching the proceedings of what he then called " Curry and his gang " with awe and with little understanding. Now he was inside, and " the gang " was " we " or " the progressive element in College ". It had happened quite suddenly and was still sweet in the mouth.

"You think it'll go through, then? " said Studdock.

"Sure to," said Curry. "We've got the Warden, and the Bursar, and all the chemical and biochemical people for a start. Bill the Blizzard will probably do something pretty devastating, but he's bound to side with us if it comes to a vote. Besides: I haven't yet told you. Dick's going to be there. He came up in time for dinner last night."

Studdock's mind darted hither and thither in search of some safe way to conceal the fact that he did not know who Dick was. In the nick of time he remembered a very obscure colleague whose Christian name was Richard.

"Telford? " said Studdock in a puzzled voice. He knew very well that Telford could not be the Dick that Curry meant.

"Good Lord! Telford! " said Curry with a laugh. "No. I mean Lord Feverstone—Dick Devine as he used to be."

"I *was* a little baffled by the idea of Telford," said Studdock, joining in the laugh. "I'm glad Feverstone is coming. I've never met him you know."

"Oh, but you must," said Curry. "Look here, come and dine in my rooms to-night. I've asked him."

"I should like to very much," said Studdock quite truly. And then, after a pause, "By the way, I suppose Feverstone's own position is quite secure? "

"How do you mean? " asked Curry.

"Well, there was some talk, if you remember, as to

whether someone who was away quite so much could go on holding a Fellowship."

"Oh, you mean Glossop and all that ramp. Nothing will come of that. Didn't you think it absolute blah?"

"As between ourselves, yes. But I confess if I were put up to explain *in public* exactly why a man who is nearly always in London should go on being a Fellow of Bracton, I shouldn't find it altogether easy. The real reasons are the sort that Watson would call imponderables."

"I don't agree. Isn't it important to have influential connections with the outer world? It's not in the least impossible that Dick will be in the next Cabinet. Even already Dick in London has been a damn sight more use to the College than Glossop and half a dozen others of that sort have been by sitting here all their lives."

"Yes. Of course that's the real point. It would be a little difficult to put in that form at a College meeting, though!"

"There's one thing," said Curry in a slightly less intimate tone, "that perhaps you ought to know about Dick."

"What's that?"

"He got you your Fellowship."

Mark was silent. He did not like things which reminded him that he had once been not only outside the progressive element but even outside the College. He did not always like Curry either. His pleasure in being with him was not that sort of pleasure.

"Yes," said Curry. "Denniston was your chief rival. Between ourselves, a good many people liked his papers better than yours. It was Dick who insisted all through that you were the sort of man we really wanted. And I must say he turned out to be right."

"Very kind of you," said Studdock with a little mock bow. He was surprised at the turn the conversation had taken. It was an old rule at Bracton that one never mentioned in the presence of a man the circumstances of his own election, and Studdock had not realised till now that this also was one of the traditions the Progressive Element was prepared to scrap.

"I'm glad you're going to meet Dick," said Curry. "We haven't time now, but there's one thing about him I wanted to discuss with you."

Studdock looked enquiringly at him.

"James and I and one or two others," said Curry in a somewhat lower voice, "have been thinking he ought to be the new warden. But here we are."

"It's not yet twelve," said Studdock. "What about popping into the Bristol for a drink?"

Into the Bristol they accordingly went. It would not have been easy to preserve the atmosphere in which the Progressive Element operated without a good many of these little courtesies. This weighed harder on Studdock than on Curry, who was unmarried and had a sub-warden's stipend.

III

The only time I was a guest at Bracton I persuaded my host to let me into the Wood and leave me there alone for an hour.

Very few people were allowed into Bragdon Wood. If you came in from the street and went through the College to reach it, the sense of gradual penetration into a holy of holies was very strong. First you went through the Newton quadrangle, which is dry and gravelly. Next you must enter a cool, tunnel-like passage, nearly dark at midday unless either the door into Hall should be open on your right or the buttery hatch on your left, giving you a glimpse of indoor daylight falling on panels and a whiff of the smell of fresh bread. When you emerged from this tunnel you would find yourself in the cloister of the much smaller quadrangle called Republic. Chapel is not far off: the hoarse, heavy noise of the works of a great and old clock comes to you from somewhere overhead. You went along this cloister, past slabs and urns and busts that commemorate dead Bractonians, and then down shallow steps into the full daylight of the quadrangle called Lady Alice. There were no buildings straight ahead on the fourth side of Lady Alice: only a row of elms and a wall; and here first one became aware of the sound of running water and the cooing of wood pigeons. In the wall there was a door. It led you into a covered gallery pierced with narrow windows on either side. Looking out through these, you discovered that you were crossing a bridge and the dark-brown dimpled Wynd was flowing under you. Now you were very near your goal. A wicket at the far end of the bridge brought you out on the Fellows' bowling-green, and across that you saw the high wall of the Wood, and through the Inigo Jones gate you caught a glimpse of sunlit green and deep shadows.

Half a mile is a short walk. Yet it seemed a long time before I came to the centre of the Wood. I knew it was the centre, for there was the thing I had chiefly come to see. It was a well: a well with steps going down to it and the remains of an ancient pavement about it. It was very imperfect now. This was the heart of Bracton or Bragdon Wood: out of this all the legends had come. The archaeologists were agreed that the masonry was very late British-Roman work, done on the very eve of the Anglo-Saxon invasion.

There is good evidence that the well with the British-Roman pavement was already " Merlin's Well " in the fourteenth century, though the name is not found till Queen Elizabeth's reign.

IV

The most controversial business before the College meeting was the question of selling Bragdon Wood. The purchaser was the N.I.C.E., the National Institute of Co-ordinated Experiments. They wanted a site for the building which would worthily house this remarkable organisation. The N.I.C.E. was the first-fruit of that constructive fusion between the state and the laboratory on which so many thoughtful people base their hopes of a better world. It was to be free from almost all the tiresome restraints—" red tape " was the word its supporters used—which have hither-to hampered research in this country. It was also largely free from the restraints of economy. Persistent pressure and endless diplomacy on the part of the Senate of Edgestow had lured the new Institute away from Oxford, from Cambridge, from London. It had thought of all these in turn as possible scenes for its labours. At times the Progressive Element in Edgestow had almost despaired. But success was now practically certain. If the N.I.C.E. could get the necessary land, it would come to Edgestow.

Three years ago, if Mark had come to a College meeting at which such a question was to be decided, he would have expected to hear the claims of sentiment against progress and beauty against utility openly debated. He knew now that that was not the way things are done.

The Progressive Element managed its business really very well. Most of the Fellows did not know that there was any question of selling the Wood. They saw, of course, from their agenda paper that Item 15 was " Sale of College Land ", but as that appeared at every College meeting, they were not very interested. They also saw that Item 1 was " Questions about Bragdon Wood ". These were not concerned with the proposed sale. Curry, as sub-warden, had some letters to read. The first was from a society concerned for the preservation of ancient monuments. I think myself that this society had been ill-advised to make two complaints. It would have been wiser if they had confined themselves to drawing the College's attention to the disrepair of the wall round the Wood. When they went on to urge the desirability of building some protection over the Well itself the College began to be restive. Before Curry sat down, everyone in the room desired strongly to make the outer world understand that Bragdon Wood was the private property of Bracton College. Then he rose again to read another letter. This was from a society of Spiritualists who wanted leave to investigate the " reported phenomena " in the Wood—a letter " connected," as Curry said, " with the next, which, with the Warden's permission, I will now read to you." This was from a firm who had heard of the Spiritualists' proposal and wanted permission to make a film of the Spiritualists looking for the phenomena. Curry was directed to write short refusals to all three letters.

Then came a new voice. Lord Feverstone had risen. He agreed with the action taken about these letters from busybodies outside. But was it not, after all, a fact that the wall of the Wood *was* in a very unsatisfactory condition? At once the Bursar, James Busby, was on his feet. He welcomed Lord Feverstone's question. He had recently taken expert advice about the wall of the Wood. " Unsatisfactory " was too mild a word. Nothing but a complete new wall would meet the situation. With great difficulty the probable cost of this was elicited from him: and when the College heard the figure it gasped. Lord Feverstone enquired whether the Bursar was seriously proposing that the College should undertake such an expense. Busby (a large ex-clergyman with a bushy black beard) replied with some temper that if he *were* to make a suggestion it would be that the question could not be treated in isolation from some important financial considerations which it would become his duty to lay before them later in the day. There was a pause at this ominous statement, until gradually, one by one, the " outsiders " and " obstructionists ", the men not included in the Progressive Element, began coming into the debate. The Progressive Element let them talk for nearly ten minutes. Then Lord Feverstone wanted to know whether it was possible that the Bursar and the Preservation Committee could really find no alternative between building a new wall and allowing Bragdon Wood to degenerate into a common. The Bursar answered in a low voice that he *had* in a purely theoretical way got some facts about possible alternatives. A barbed-wire fence—but the rest was drowned in a roar of disapproval. Finally, the matter was postponed for consideration at the next meeting.

During this item the thoughts of more than one Fellow had turned to lunch, and attention had wandered. But when Curry rose at five minutes to one to introduce Item 2, there was a sharp revival of interest. It was called " Rectification of an Anomaly in the Stipends of Junior Fellows ". I would not like to say what the junior Fellows of Bracton were getting at this time, but I believe it hardly covered the expenses of their residence in College. Studdock, who had recently emerged from this class, understood the look in their faces. The Bursar rose to reply to Curry's proposal. He hoped that no one would imagine he approved the anomaly which had, in 1910, excluded the lowest class of the Fellows from the new clauses in the eighteenth paragraph of Statute 17; but it was his duty to point out that this was the second proposal involving heavy expenditure which had come before them that morning. It could not be isolated from the whole problem of the financial position of the College which he hoped to lay before them during the afternoon. A great deal more was said, but when, at quarter to two, the meeting adjourned for lunch, every junior had it fixed in his mind that a new wall for the Wood and a rise in his own stipend were strictly exclusive alternatives.

In this frame of mind the College returned after lunch to consider its finances. It was a sunny afternoon; and the smooth flow of the Bursar's exposition had a sort of hypnotic power. Fellows of colleges do not always find money matters easy to understand. They gathered that the situation was bad; very bad indeed. It is very seldom that the affairs of a large corporation, indefinitely committed to the advancement of learning, can be described as being, in a quite unambiguous sense, satisfactory. Some minor re-trenchments and re-investments were approved, and the College adjourned for tea in a chastened mood. Studdock rang up Jane and told her he would not be home for dinner.

It was not till six o'clock that all the converging lines of thought and feeling aroused by the earlier business came together upon the question of selling Bragdon Wood. It was not called the sale " of Bragdon Wood ", but " of the area coloured pink on the plan which, with the Warden's permission, I will now pass round the table ". Curry admitted that this involved the loss of *part* of the Wood. In fact, the proposed N.I.C.E. site still left to the College a strip about sixteen feet broad along the far half of the south side. In answer to questions he admitted that unfortunately —or perhaps fortunately—the Well itself was in the area which the N.I.C.E. wanted. The rights of the College to access would, of course, be guaranteed: and the Well and its pavement would be preserved by the Institute. He refrained from advice and merely mentioned the quite astonishing figure which the N.I.C.E. was offering. After that, the meeting became lively. The advantages of the sale discovered themselves one by one like ripe fruit drop-ping into the hand. It solved the problem of the wall: it solved the problem of protecting ancient monuments: it solved the financial problem: it looked like solving the problem of the junior Fellows' stipends.

The few real " Die-hards " present, to whom Bragdon Wood was almost a basic assumption of life, could hardly bring themselves to realise what was happening. When at last old Jewel, blind and shaky, rose to his feet, his voice was hardly audible. At this moment Lord Feverstone folded his arms, and looking straight at the old man said in a very loud, clear voice:

" If Canon Jewel wishes us *not* to hear his views, I suggest that his end could be better attained by silence."

Jewel had been already old in the days before the first war when old men were treated with kindness, and he had never succeeded in getting used to the modern world. He stared with puzzled eyes.

The motion was carried.

V

After leaving the flat that morning Jane also had gone down to Edgestow and had bought a hat, when Mrs. Dimble met her coming out of Sparrow's and said: " Hullo, dear! Been buying a hat? Come home to lunch and let's see it. Cecil has the car just round the corner."

Cecil Dimble, a Fellow of Northumberland, had been Jane's tutor for her last years as a student, and Mrs. Dimble (one tended to call her " Mother Dimble ") had been a kind of universal aunt to all the girls of her year. A liking for the female pupils of one's husband is not, perhaps, so common as might be wished among dons' wives: but Mrs. Dimble appeared to like all Dr. Dimble's pupils.

They drove over the bridge to the north of Bracton and then south along the bank of the Wynd to the Dimbles' front door.

" How lovely it's looking! " said Jane as she got out of the car. The Dimbles' garden was famous.

" You'd better take a good look at it then," said Dr. Dimble.

" What do you mean? " asked Jane.

" Haven't you told her? " said Dr. Dimble to his wife.

" I haven't screwed myself up to it yet," said Mrs. Dimble. " Anyway, I expect she knows. Your own college is being so tiresome, dear. They're turning us out. They won't renew the lease."

" Oh, Mrs. Dimble! " exclaimed Jane. " And I didn't even know this was Bracton property. Mark never talks about College business."

" Good husbands never do," said Dr. Dimble. " At least only about the business of other people's colleges. Is no one coming in to have lunch? "

Dimble guessed that Bracton was going to sell the Wood and everything else it owned on that side of the river, and felt too strongly on the subject to wish to talk about it before the wife of one of the Bracton men.

" You'll have to wait for your lunch till I've seen Jane's new hat," said Mother Dimble, and forthwith hurried Jane upstairs.

17

Then followed some minutes of conversation which was strictly feminine in the old-fashioned sense. Jane, while preserving a certain sense of superiority, found it indefinably comforting. When the hat was being put away again Mrs. Dimble suddenly said:

"There's nothing wrong, is there?"

"Wrong," said Jane. "Why? What should there be?"

"You're not looking yourself."

"Oh, I'm all right," said Jane, aloud. Mentally she added: "She's dying to know whether I'm going to have a baby. That sort of woman always is."

"Do you hate being kissed?" said Mrs. Dimble unexpectedly.

"Do I hate being kissed?" thought Jane to herself. "That indeed is the question. Hope not for mind in women——" She had intended to reply "Of course not," but inexplicably, and to her great annoyance, found herself crying instead. And then, for a moment, Mrs. Dimble became simply a grown-up as grown-ups had been when one was a very small child. Not to detest being petted and pawed was contrary to her whole theory of life: yet before they went downstairs she had told Mrs. Dimble that she was not going to have a baby but was a bit depressed from being very much alone and from a nightmare.

During lunch Dr. Dimble talked about the Arthurian legend. "It's really wonderful," he said, "how the whole thing hangs together, even in a late version like Malory's. You've noticed how there are two sets of characters? There's Guinevere and Launcelot and all those, all very courtly and nothing particularly British about them. But then in the background there are all those *dark* people like Morgan and Morgawse, who are very British indeed and usually more or less hostile. Mixed up with magic. Merlin too, of course, is British. Doesn't it look very like a picture of Britain as it must have been on the eve of the invasion?"

"How do you mean, Dr. Dimble?" said Jane.

"Well, wouldn't there have been one section of society that was almost purely Roman? People talking a Celticised Latin—something that would sound to us rather like Spanish: and fully Christian. But farther up country, in the out-of-the-way places, there would have been little courts ruled by real old British under-kings, talking something like Welsh, and practising a certain amount of the Druidical religion."

"And which would Arthur himself have been?" said Jane.

"One can imagine a man of the old British line, but a Christian and a fully-trained general with Roman technique, trying to pull this whole society together. There'd be jealousy from his own British family. And always that under-tow, that tug back to Druidism."

"And where would Merlin be?"

"Yes. . . . He's the really interesting figure. Did the whole thing fail because he died so soon? Has it ever struck you what an odd creation Merlin is? He's not evil: yet he's a magician. He is obviously a druid: yet he knows all about the Grail."

"It *is* rather puzzling. I hadn't thought of it before."

"I often wonder," said Dr. Dimble, "whether Merlin doesn't represent the last trace of something that became impossible when the only people in touch with the supernatural were either white or black, either priests or sorcerers."

"What a horrid idea," said Mrs. Dimble. "Anyway, Merlin happened a long time ago if he happened at all, and he's safely dead and buried under Bragdon Wood as we all know."

"Buried but *not* dead, according to the story," corrected Dr. Dimble.

"Ugh!" said Jane involuntarily.

"I wonder what they *will* find if they start digging up that place for the foundations of their N.I.C.E.," said Dr. Dimble.

"First mud and then water," said Mrs. Dimble. "That's why they can't really build it there."

"So you'd think," said her husband. "And if so, why should they want to come here at all? They're not likely to be influenced by any poetic fancy about Merlin's mantle having fallen on them!"

"Merlin's mantle indeed!" said Mrs. Dimble.

"Yes," said the Doctor. "It's a rum idea. I dare say some of his set would like to recover the mantle well enough. I don't think they'd like it if the old man himself came back to life along with it."

"That child's going to faint," said Mrs. Dimble suddenly.

19

" Hullo! What's the matter? " said Dr. Dimble, looking with amazement at Jane's face. " Is the room too hot for you? "

" Oh, it's too ridiculous," said Jane.

" Let's come into the drawing-room," said Dr. Dimble. " Here. Lean on my arm."

In the drawing-room Jane attempted to excuse her behaviour by telling the story of her dream. " I suppose I've given myself away dreadfully," she said. " You can both start psycho-analysing me now."

From Dr. Dimble's face Jane might have indeed conjectured that her dream had shocked him exceedingly. " Extraordinary thing . . ." he kept muttering. " *Two* heads. And one of them Alcasan's. Now is that a false scent? "

" Don't, Cecil," said Mrs. Dimble.

" Do you think I ought to be analysed? " said Jane.

" Analysed? " said Dr. Dimble, as if he had not quite understood. " Oh, I see. You mean going to Brizeacre or someone? "

Jane realised that her question had recalled him from some quite different train of thought. The telling of her dream had raised some other problem, though what this was she could not even imagine.

Dr. Dimble looked out of the window. " There is my dullest pupil just ringing the bell," he said. " I must go to the study." He stood for a moment with his hand on Jane's shoulder. " Look here," he said, " I'm not going to give any advice. But if you do decide to go to anyone about that dream, I wish you would *first* consider going to someone whose address Margery or I will give you."

" You don't believe in Mr. Brizeacre? " said Jane.

" I can't explain," said Dr. Dimble. " Not now. Try not to bother about it. But if you *do*, just let us know first. Good-bye."

Almost immediately after his departure some other visitors arrived, so that there was no opportunity of further private conversation between Jane and her hostess. She left the Dimbles about half an hour later and walked home.

CHAPTER TWO

DINNER WITH THE SUB-WARDEN

I

" This is a blow! " said Curry.

" Something from N.O.? " said Busby. He and Lord Feverstone and Mark were all drinking sherry before dining with Curry. N.O., which stood for *Non Olet*, was the nickname of Charles Place, the Warden of Bracton.

" Yes, blast him," said Curry. " Wishes to see me on a most important matter after dinner."

" That means," said the Bursar, " that Jewel and Co. have been getting at him and want to find some way of going back on the whole business."

" Jewel! Good God! " said Busby, burying his left hand in his beard.

" I was rather sorry for old Jewel," said Mark.

" Sorry for Jewel? " said Curry, wheeling round. " You wouldn't say that if you knew what he was like in his prime."

" I agree with you," said Feverstone to Mark, " but then I take the Clausewitz view. Total war is the most humane in the long run. I shut him up instantaneously. He'll be enjoying himself, because I've confirmed everything he's been saying about the younger generation for forty years. What was the alternative? To let him drivel on until he'd worked himself into a coughing fit or a heart attack, and give him in addition the disappointment of finding that he was treated civilly."

" That's a point of view, certainly," said Mark.

" Damn it all," continued Feverstone, " no man likes to have his stock-in-trade taken away. What would poor Curry, here, do if the Die-hards one day all refused to do any die-harding? "

" Dinner is served, sir," said Curry's " Shooter "—for that is what they call a college servant at Bracton.

" That's all rot, Dick," said Curry as they sat down. " There's nothing I should like better than to see the end of all these Die-hards and be able to get on with the job. You don't suppose I *like* having to spend all my time merely getting the road clear?" Mark noticed that his host was a little nettled at Lord Feverstone's banter. The latter had an extremely virile and infectious laugh. Mark was beginning to like him.

"The job being . . .?" said Feverstone.

"Well, some of us have got work of our own to do," replied Curry.

"I never knew you were *that* sort of person," said Feverstone.

"That's the worst of the whole system," said Curry. "In a place like this you've either got to be content to see everything go to pieces or else to sacrifice your own career as a scholar to all these infernal college politics. One of these days I *shall* chuck that side of it and get down to my book."

"I see," said Feverstone. "In order to keep the place going as a learned society, all the best brains in it have to give up doing anything about learning."

"Exactly!" said Curry. "That's just—— " and then stopped, uncertain whether he was being taken quite seriously.

"All that's very well in theory," said Busby, "but I think Curry's quite right. Supposing he resigned his office as sub-warden and retired into his cave. He might give us a thundering good book on economics—— "

"Economics?" said Feverstone, lifting his eyebrows.

"I happen to be a military historian, James," said Curry. He was often annoyed at the difficulty which his colleagues seemed to find in remembering what particular branch of learning he had been elected to pursue.

"Military history, of course," said Busby. "As I say, he might give us a thundering good book on military history. But it would be superseded in twenty years. Whereas the work he is actually doing for the College will benefit it for centuries. This whole business, now, of bringing the N.I.C.E. to Edgestow. Think of the new life, the stirring of dormant impulses. What would any book on economics——?"

"Military history," said Feverstone gently, but Busby did not hear.

"What would any book on economics be, compared with a thing like that?" he continued. "I look upon it as the greatest triumph of practical idealism that this century has yet seen."

22

The good wine was beginning to do its good office. We have all known the kind of clergyman who tends to forget his clerical collar after the third glass: but Busby's habit was the reverse. As wine loosened his tongue, the parson, still latent within him after thirty years' apostasy, began to wake into a strange galvanic life.

"I make no claim to orthodoxy," he said. "But if religion is understood in the deepest sense, I say that Curry, by bringing the N.I.C.E. to Edgestow, has done more for it in one year than Jewel has done in his whole life."

"Has anyone discovered," asked Feverstone, "what, precisely, the N.I.C.E. is, or what it intends to do?"

"That comes oddly from you, Dick," said Curry. "I thought you were in on it yourself."

"Isn't it a little naïve," said Feverstone, "to suppose that being in on a thing involves any distinct knowledge of its official programme?"

"Oh well, if you mean *details*," said Curry, and then stopped.

"Surely, Feverstone," said Busby, "you're making a great mystery about nothing. I should have thought the objects of the N.I.C.E. were pretty clear. It's the first attempt to take applied science seriously from the national point of view. Think how it is going to mobilise all the talent of the country: and not only scientific talent in the narrower sense. Fifteen departmental directors at fifteen thousand a year each! Its own legal staff! Its own police, I'm told!"

"I agree with James," said Curry. "The N.I.C.E. marks the beginning of a new era—the *really* scientific era. There are to be forty interlocking committees sitting every day, and they've got a wonderful gadget by which the findings of each committee print themselves off in their own little compartment on the Analytical Notice-Board every half-hour. Then that report slides itself into the right position where it's connected up by little arrows with all the relevant parts of the other reports. It's a marvellous gadget. The different kinds of business come out in different coloured lights. They call it a Pragmatometer."

"And there," said Busby, "you see again what the Institute is already doing for the country. Pragmatometry is going to be a big thing. Hundreds of people are going in for it."

" And what do you think about it, Studdock? " said Feverstone.

" I think," said Mark, " that James touched the important point when he said that it would have its own legal staff and its own police. I don't give a fig for Pragmatometers. The real thing is that this time we're going to get science applied to social problems and backed by the whole force of the state, just as war has been backed by the whole force of the state in the past."

" Damn," said Curry, looking at his watch. " I'll have to go and talk to N.O. now. If you people would like any brandy when you've finished your wine, it's in that cupboard. You're not going, James, are you? "

" Yes," said the Bursar. " I'm going to bed early. Don't let me break up the party for you two. I've been on my legs nearly all day, you know. A man's a fool to hold any office in this College. Continual anxiety. Crushing responsibility."

As soon as the two men had got out of the room Lord Feverstone looked steadily at Mark for some seconds. Then he chuckled. Then he threw his lean, muscular body well back into his chair and laughed louder and louder. He was very infectious in his laughter, and Mark found himself laughing too. " Pragmatometers—practical idealism," gasped Feverstone. It was a moment of extraordinary liberation for Mark. All sorts of things about Curry and Busby which he had not previously noticed came to his mind. He wondered how he could have been so blind to the funny side of them.

" It really is rather devastating," said Feverstone when he had partially recovered, " that the people one has to use for getting things done should talk such drivel about the things themselves."

" And yet they *are*, in a sense, the brains of Bracton," said Mark.

" Good Lord, no! Glossop and Bill the Blizzard and even old Jewel have ten times their intelligence."

" I didn't know you took that view."

" I think Glossop etc. are quite mistaken. I think their idea of culture and knowledge and what not is unrealistic. But it is quite a clear idea and they follow it out consistently. They know what they want. But our two poor friends haven't a ghost of a notion where they're going.

They'll sweat blood to bring the N.I.C.E. to Edgestow: that's why they're indispensable. But what the point of the N.I.C.E. is, what the point of anything is—ask them another. Pragmatometry! Fifteen sub-directors!"

"Well, perhaps I'm in the same boat myself."

"Not at all. You saw the point at once."

Mark was silent. The giddy sensation of being suddenly whirled up from one plane of secrecy to another prevented him from speaking.

"I want you to come into the Institute," said Feverstone.

"You mean—to leave Bracton?"

"That makes no odds. Anyway, I don't suppose there's anything you want here. We'd make Curry warden when N.O. retires and——"

"They were talking of making you warden."

"God!" said Feverstone, and stared.

Mark realised that from Feverstone's point of view this was like the suggestion that he should become Headmaster of a small idiots' school.

"You," said Feverstone, "would be absolutely wasted as warden. That's the job for Curry. You want a man who loves business and wire-pulling for their own sake and doesn't really ask what it's all about. We've only got to tell him that he thinks so-and-so is a man the College wants, and then he'll never rest till so-and-so gets a Fellowship. That's what we want the College for: a drag net, a recruiting office."

"A recruiting office for the N.I.C.E., you mean?"

"Yes, in the first instance. But it's only one part of the general show."

"I'm not sure that I know what you mean."

"You soon will. It sounds rather in Busby's style to say that humanity is at the cross-roads. But it is the main question at the moment: which side one's on—obscurantism or order. If Science is really given a free hand it can now take over the human race and recondition it: make man a really efficient animal. If it doesn't—well, we're done."

"Go on."

"There are three main problems. First, the inter-planetary problem."

"What on earth do you mean?"

"We can't do anything about that at present. The only man who could help was Weston."

25

" He was killed in a blitz, wasn't he? "

" He was murdered, and I've a shrewd idea who the murderer was."

" Good God! Can nothing be done? "

" There's no evidence. The murderer is a respectable Cambridge don with a game leg and a fair beard. He's dined in this College."

" What was Weston murdered for? "

" For being on our side. The murderer is one of the enemy."

" You don't mean to say he murdered him for that? "

" Yes," said Feverstone, bringing his hand down smartly on the table. " That's just the point. People like Curry or James think the violent resistance of the other side ended with the persecution of Galileo and all that. But don't believe it. It is just beginning. They know now that we have at last got *real* powers. They're going to fight every inch. They'll stop at nothing."

" They can't win," said Mark.

" We'll hope not," said Lord Feverstone. " That is why it is of such immense importance to each of us to choose the right side."

" Oh, I haven't any doubt which is *my* side," said Mark. " Hang it all—the preservation of the human race—it's a pretty rock-bottom obligation."

" Well, personally," said Feverstone, " I'm not indulging in any Busbyisms about that. The practical point is that you and I don't like being pawns, and we do rather like fighting—specially on the winning side."

" And what is the first practical step? "

" Yes, that's the real question. As I said, the inter-planetary problem must be left on one side for the moment. The second problem is our rivals on this planet. I don't mean only insects and bacteria. There's far too much life of every kind about, animal and vegetable. We haven't really cleared the place yet. All that is to be gone into. The third problem is man himself."

" Go on. This interests me very much."

" Man has got to take charge of man. That means, re-member, that some men have got to take charge of the rest."

" What sort of thing have you in mind? "

" Quite simple and obvious things, at first—sterilisation

26

of the unfit, liquidation of backward races, selective breeding. Then real education, including pre-natal education. By real education I mean one that makes the patient what it wants infallibly: whatever he or his parents try to do about it. Of course, it'll have to be mainly psychological at first. But we'll get on to biochemical conditioning in the end and direct manipulation of the brain. A new type of man: and it's people like you who've got to begin to make him."

"That's my trouble. Don't think it's false modesty: but I haven't yet seen how I can contribute."

"No, but *we* have. You are what we need; a trained sociologist with a radically realistic outlook, not afraid of responsibility. Also, a sociologist who can write."

"You don't mean you want me to write up all this?"

"No. We want you to write it *down*—to camouflage it. Only for the present, of course. Once the thing gets going we shan't have to bother about the great heart of the British public. But in the meantime it *does* make a difference how things are put. For instance, if it were even whispered that the N.I.C.E. wanted powers to experiment on criminals, you'd have all the old women of both sexes up in arms and yapping about humanity: call it re-education of the maladjusted and you have them all slobbering with delight. Odd thing it is—the word 'experiment' is unpopular, but not the word 'experimental'. You mustn't experiment on children: but offer the dear little kiddies free education in an experimental school attached to the N.I.C.E. and it's all correct!"

"You don't mean that this—er—journalistic side would be my main job?"

"It's nothing to do with journalism. Your readers in the first instance would be committees of the House of Commons, not the public. But that would only be a sideline. As for the job itself—why, it's impossible to say how it might develop. Talking to a man like you, I don't stress the financial side."

"I wasn't thinking about that," said Mark, flushing with pure excitement.

"Look here," said Feverstone. "Let me run you across to-morrow to see John Wither. You'll meet all the important people there, and it'll give you a chance to make up your mind."

"How does Wither come into it? I thought Jules was

the head of the N.I.C.E." Jules was a distinguished nove-
list and scientific populariser whose name always appeared
before the public in connection with the new Institute.

"Jules! Hell's bells!" said Feverstone. "He's all right
for selling the Institute to the great British public in the
Sunday papers and he draws a whacking salary. He's no
use for work."

"Oh quite," said Mark. "I was always rather puzzled
at his being in the show. Do you know, since you're so
kind, I think I'd better accept your offer and go over to
Wither for the week-end. What time would you be
starting?"

"About quarter to eleven. They tell me you live out
Sandown way. I could call and pick you up."

"Thanks very much. Now tell me about Wither."

"John Wither," began Feverstone, but suddenly broke
off. "Damn!" he said. "Here comes Curry."

II

Mark walked home. Something happened to him the
moment he had let himself into the flat which was very
unusual. He found himself, on the door-mat, embracing a
frightened, half-sobbing Jane—even a humble Jane, who
was saying, "Oh, Mark, I've been so frightened."

There was a quality in the very muscles of his wife's body
which took him by surprise. A certain indefinable defensiveness had momentarily deserted her. He had known
such occasions before, but they were rare. And they
tended, in his experience, to be followed next day by
inexplicable quarrels.

But the reasons for her unusual behaviour on this particular evening were simple enough. She had got back from
the Dimbles at about four, and had had to light up and
draw the curtains before she had finished tea. The thought
had come into her mind that her fright at the dream, at the
mention of a mantle, an old man, an old man buried but
not dead, and a language like Spanish, had been as irrational as a child's fear of the dark. This had led her to
remember moments when she had feared the dark. She
allowed herself to remember them too long. The evening
somehow deteriorated. She was restless. From being restless she became nervous. Then came a curious reluctance

to go into the kitchen to get herself some supper. And now there was no disguising the fact that she was frightened. In desperation she rang up the Dimbles. " I think I might go and see the person you suggested, after all," she said. Mrs. Dimble's voice came back, after a curious little pause, giving her the address. Ironwood was the name, Miss Ironwood, who lived out at St. Anne's on the Hill. Jane asked if she should make an appointment. " No," said Mrs. Dimble, " they'll be—you needn't make an appointment." Jane kept the conversation going as long as she could. Secretly she had had a wild hope that Mother Dimble would recognise her distress and say at once, " I'll come straight up to you by car." Instead, she got the mere information and a hurried " Good night." It seemed to Jane that by ringing up she had interrupted a conversation about herself: or about something else more important, with which she was somehow connected. And what had Mrs. Dimble meant by " They'll be——" " They'll be expecting you "?

" Damn the Dimbles! " said Jane to herself. And now that the life-line had been used and brought no comfort, the terror, as if insulted by her futile attempt to escape it, rushed back on her and she could never afterwards remember whether the horrible old man and the mantle had actually appeared to her in a dream or whether she had merely sat there hoping that they would not.

And that is why Mark found such an unexpected Jane on the door-mat. It was a pity, he thought, that this should have happened on a night when he was so late and so tired and, to tell the truth, not perfectly sober.

III

" Do you feel quite all right this morning? " said Mark.

" Yes, thank you," said Jane shortly.

Mark was lying in bed and drinking a cup of tea. Jane was seated at the dressing-table, partially dressed, and doing her hair.

Jane thought she was annoyed because her hair was not going up to her liking and because Mark was fussing. She also knew, of course, that she was angry with herself for the collapse which had betrayed her last night into being what she detested—the " little woman " of sentimental fiction

29

running for comfort to male arms. But she thought this anger was only in the back of her mind, and had no suspicion that it was pulsing through every vein and producing the clumsiness in her fingers which made her hair seem intractable.

"Because," continued Mark, "if you felt the least bit uncomfortable, I *could* put off going to see this man Wither."

Jane said nothing.

"Supposing I did," said Mark, "you wouldn't think of asking Myrtle over to stay?"

"No thank you," said Jane emphatically; and then, "I'm quite accustomed to being alone."

"I know," said Mark in a defensive voice. "That's the devil of the way things are in College at present. That's one of the chief reasons I'm thinking of another job."

Jane was still silent.

"Look here, old thing," said Mark. "There's no good beating about the bush. I don't like going away while you're in your present state——"

"What state?" said Jane.

"Well—I mean—just a bit nervy—as anyone may be temporarily."

"Because I happened to be having a nightmare when you came home last night—or rather this morning—there's no need to talk as if I was a neurasthenic." This was not in the least what Jane had intended or expected to say.

"Now there's no good going on like that . . ." began Mark.

"Like what?" said Jane loudly, and then, before he had time to reply, "If you've decided that I'm going mad you'd better get Brizeacre to come down and certify me. It would be convenient to do it while you're away. I'm going to see about the breakfast now. If you don't dress pretty quickly, you'll not be ready when Lord Feverstone calls."

Mark gave himself a bad cut while shaving (and saw, at once, a picture of himself talking to the all-important Wither with a great blob of cotton-wool on his lip), while Jane decided, from a mixture of motives, to cook Mark an unusually elaborate breakfast, and upset it all over the new stove at the last moment. They were still at the table and both pretending to read newspapers when Lord Feverstone arrived. Unfortunately Mrs. Maggs arrived at the same moment. Mrs. Maggs was that element in Jane's economy represented by the phrase " I have a woman who comes in twice a week." They were about the same age and to a bachelor's eye there was no very noticeable difference in their clothes. It was therefore perhaps excusable that when Mark attempted to introduce Feverstone to his wife Feverstone should have shaken Mrs. Maggs by the hand : it did not sweeten the last few minutes before the two men departed.

Jane left the flat under pretence of shopping almost at once. " I really couldn't stand Mrs. Maggs to-day," she said to herself. " She's a terrible talker." So that was Lord Feverstone—that man with the loud, unnatural laugh and the mouth like a shark. Apparently a fool, too! Jane had distrusted his face. Probably he was making a fool of Mark. Mark was so easily taken in. If only he wasn't at Bracton ! It was a horrible college. And meanwhile, what of the day that awaited her, and the night, and the next night?

She must do something. She even thought of following Mark's advice and getting Myrtle to come and stay. But Myrtle was Mark's twin sister, with much too much of the adoring sister's attitude to the brilliant brother. Then she thought of going to see Dr. Brizeacre as a patient. But when she came to think of answering the sort of questions which Brizeacre would ask, this turned out to be impossible. In the end, somewhat to her own surprise, she found that she had decided to go out to St. Anne's and see Miss Ironwood. She thought herself a fool for doing so.

IV

Mark Studdock was being driven to the Blood Transfusion Office at Belbury, where the nucleus of the N.I.C.E. had taken up its temporary abode. The very size and style of Feverstone's car had made a favourable impression on him the moment he saw it. And what fine, male energy (Mark felt sick of women at the moment) revealed itself in the very gestures with which Feverstone settled himself at the wheel and clasped his pipe firmly between his teeth ! The speed of the car, even in the narrow streets of Edgestow, was impressive, and so were the laconic criticisms of Feverstone on other drivers and pedestrians. Once over the level crossing and beyond Jane's old college (St. Elizabeth's), he began to show what his car could do. Telegraph posts raced by, bridges rushed overhead with a roar, villages streamed backward to join the country already devoured, and Mark, at once fascinated and repelled by the insolence of Feverstone's driving, sat saying " Yes " and " Quite " and " It was *their* fault ", and stealing sidelong glances at his companion. The long, straight nose and the clenched teeth, the hard, bony outlines beneath the face, the very clothes, all spoke of a big man driving a big car to somewhere where they would find big stuff going on. And he, Mark, was to be in it all.

Jane Studdock meanwhile was progressing slowly towards the village of St. Anne's. The train, which started at half-past one, jerked and rattled along an embankment whence she looked down through bare branches and branches freckled with yellow leaves into Bragdon Wood itself and thence along the edge of Brawl Park and so to the first stop at Duke's Eaton. Here, as at Woolham and Cure Hardy and Fourstones, the train settled back, when it stopped, with a little jerk and something like a sigh. And then there would be a noise of milk cans rolling and coarse boots treading on the platform and after that a pause while the autumn sunlight grew warm on the window-pane and smells of wood and field from beyond the tiny station floated in. At quarter-past two she came to St. Anne's, which was the terminus of the branch, and the end of everything. The air struck her as cold and tonic when she left the station.

There was still a climb to be done on foot, for St. Anne's is perched on a hilltop. A winding road between high banks led her up to it. As soon as she had passed the church she turned left, as she had been instructed, at the Saxon Cross. Presently she came to a high wall on her right that seemed to run on for a great way. There was a door in it and beside the door an old iron bell-pull. She felt sure she had come on a fool's errand: nevertheless she rang. When the jangling noise had ceased there followed a silence so long, and so chilly, that Jane began to wonder whether the house were inhabited. Then, just as she was debating whether to ring again or to turn away, she heard the noise of someone's feet approaching on the inside of the wall.

Meanwhile Lord Feverstone's car had long since arrived

at Belbury—a florid Edwardian mansion which seemed to have sprouted into a widespread outgrowth of newer and lower buildings in cement, which housed the Blood Transfusion Office.

CHAPTER THREE

BELBURY AND ST. ANNE'S-ON-THE-HILL

I

ON his way up the wide staircase Mark caught sight of himself in a mirror. The blob of cotton-wool on his lip had been blown awry during the journey and revealed a patch of blackened blood beneath it. A moment later he found himself in a room with a blazing fire, being introduced to Mr. John Wither, Deputy Director of the N.I.C.E.

Wither was a white-haired old man with a courtly manner. His face was clean-shaven and very large indeed, with watery blue eyes and something rather vague and chaotic about it. He did not appear to be giving them his whole attention, though his actual words and gestures were polite to the point of effusiveness. He said it was a great, a very great, pleasure to welcome Mr. Studdock among them. It added to the deep obligations under which Lord Feverstone had already laid him. He hoped they had had an agreeable journey. Mr. Wither appeared to be under the impression that they had come by air and, when this was corrected, that they had come from London by train. Then he began enquiring whether Mr. Studdock found his quarters perfectly comfortable and had to be reminded that they had only that moment arrived. "I suppose," thought Mark, "the old chap is trying to put me at my ease." In fact, Mr. Wither's conversation was having precisely the opposite effect. Mark wished he would offer him a cigarette. His growing conviction that this man knew nothing about him, and that all the schemes and promises of Feverstone were dissolving into mist, was uncomfortable. At last he endeavoured to bring Mr. Wither to the point by saying that he was still not quite clear in what capacity he would be able to assist the Institute.

" I assure you, Mr. Studdock," said the Deputy Director with an unusually far-away look in his eye, " that you needn't anticipate the slightest . . . er . . . the slightest difficulty on that point. There was never any idea of circumscribing your activities and your general influence on policy, much less your relations with your colleagues and what I might call in general the terms of reference under which you would be collaborating with us, without the fullest possible consideration of your own views and, indeed, your own advice. You will find us, Mr. Studdock, if I might express myself in that way, a very happy family."

" Oh, don't misunderstand me, sir," said Mark. " I only meant that I felt I should like some sort of idea of what exactly I should be doing if I came to you."

" Well now, when you speak of coming to us," said the Deputy Director, " that raises a point on which I hope there is no misunderstanding. I think we all agreed that no question of residence need be raised—I mean, at this stage. We thought, we all thought, that if you cared to live in Cambridge——"

" Edgestow," prompted Lord Feverstone.

" Ah yes, Edgestow," here the Deputy Director turned round and addressed Feverstone. " I was just explaining to Mr. . . . er . . . Studdock, and I feel sure you will fully agree with me, that nothing was farther from the mind of the committee than to dictate in any way, or even to advise, where Mr. ——, where your friend should live. Of course, wherever he lives we should place air and road transport at his disposal. I dare say you have already explained to him that all questions of that sort will adjust themselves without the smallest difficulty."

" Really, sir," said Mark, " I wasn't thinking about that. I haven't—I mean I shouldn't have the smallest objection to living anywhere; I only——"

" But I assure you, Mr. . . . er . . . I assure you, sir, that there is not the smallest objection to your residing wherever you may find convenient. There was never, at any stage, the slightest suggestion——" but here Mark, in desperation, ventured to interrupt himself.

" It is the exact nature of the work," he said, " and of my qualifications for it that I wanted to get clear."

" My dear friend," said the Deputy Director, " you need

34

not have the slightest uneasiness in that direction. As I said before, you will find us a very happy family, and may feel perfectly satisfied that no questions as to your entire suitability have been agitating anyone's mind in the least. I should not be offering you a position among us if there were the slightest danger of your not being completely welcome to all, or the least suspicion that your very valuable qualities were not fully appreciated. You are—you are among *friends* here, Mr. Studdock. I should be the last person to advise you to connect yourself with any organisation where you ran the risk of being exposed . . . er . . . to disagreeable personal contacts."

Mark did not ask again in so many words what the N.I.C.E. wanted him to do; partly because he began to be afraid that he was supposed to know this already, and partly because a perfectly direct question would have sounded a crudity in that room—a crudity which might suddenly exclude him from the warm and almost drugged atmosphere of vague, yet heavily important, confidence.

" You are very kind," he said. " The only thing I should like to get just a little clearer is the exact—well, the exact scope of the appointment."

" Well," said Mr. Wither in a voice so low and rich that it was almost a sigh. " I am very glad you have raised that issue now in a quite informal way. Obviously neither you nor I would wish to commit ourselves, in this room, in any sense which was at all injurious to the powers of the committee. We do not really think, among ourselves, in terms of strictly demarcated functions, of course. Everyone in the Institute feels that his own work is not so much a departmental contribution as a moment or grade in the progressive self-definition of an organic whole."

And Mark said—for he was young and shy and vain and timid—" I do think that is so important. The elasticity of your organisation is one of the things that attracts me." After that, he had no further chance of bringing the Director to the point, despite the torturing recurrence of the question, " What are we both talking *about*? "

At the very end of the interview there came one moment of clarity. Mr. Wither supposed that he, Mark, would find it convenient to join the N.I.C.E. club: even for the next few days he would be freer as a member than as someone's guest. Mark agreed and then flushed crimson on learning

35

that the easiest course was to become a life member at the cost of £200.

"How silly," he said aloud, "I haven't got my cheque-book with me."

A moment later he found himself on the stairs with Feverstone.

"Well?" asked Mark eagerly.

Feverstone did not seem to hear him.

"Well?" repeated Mark. "When shall I know my fate? I mean, have I got the job?"

"Hullo, Guy!" bawled Feverstone suddenly to a man in the hall beneath. Next moment he had trotted down to the foot of the stairs, grasped his friend warmly by the hand, and disappeared. Mark, following him more slowly, found himself in the hall, among the groups and pairs of chattering men, who were all crossing it towards the big folding doors on his left.

II

The agreeable smells which came from the folding doors made it obvious that people were going to lunch. In the end he decided that he couldn't stand there looking like a fool any longer, and went in.

There was a single long table, already so nearly filled that, after looking in vain for Feverstone, he had to sit down beside a stranger. "I suppose one sits where one likes?" he murmured as he did so; but the stranger apparently did not hear. He was eating very quickly and talking at the same time to his neighbour on the other side.

"That's just it," he was saying. "As I told him, it makes no difference to me which way they settle it. I've no objection to the I.J.P. people taking over the whole thing if that's what the D.D. wants, but what I dislike is three H.D.s all tumbling over one another about some job that could really be done by a clerk. It's becoming ridiculous."

It was a relief to Mark when people began getting up from table. Following the general movement, he recrossed the hall and came into a large room where coffee was being served. Here at last he saw Feverstone. Mark wished to approach him, if only to find out whether he were expected to stay the night, but the knot of men round Feverstone was of that confidential kind which it is difficult to join. He moved towards one of the many tables and began turning over the pages of an illustrated weekly. When he looked up he found himself face to face with one of his own colleagues, a Fellow of Bracton, called Hingest. The Progressive Element called him Bill the Blizzard.

Hingest had not been at the College meeting, and was hardly on speaking terms with Feverstone. Mark realised with a certain awe that here was a man *directly* in touch with the N.I.C.E.—one who started at a point beyond Feverstone. Bill the Blizzard had an old-fashioned curly moustache in which white had almost triumphed over yellow, a beak-like nose, and a bald head.

" This is an unexpected pleasure," said Mark with a hint of formality. He was always a little afraid of Hingest.

" Huh? " grunted Bill. " Eh? Oh, it's you, Studdock? Didn't know they'd secured your services here."

" I was sorry not to see you at the College meeting yesterday," said Mark.

This was a lie. The Progressive Element always found Hingest's presence an embarrassment. As a scientist—and the only really eminent scientist they had—he was their rightful property; but he was that hateful anomaly, the wrong sort of scientist. Glossop, who was a classic, was his chief friend in College. He had the air of not attaching much importance to his own revolutionary discoveries in chemistry and of valuing himself much more on being a Hingest: the family was of almost mythical antiquity.

" Eh? What's that? College meeting? " said the Blizzard. " What were they talking about? "

" About the sale of Bragdon Wood."

" All nonsense," muttered the Blizzard.

" I hope you would have agreed with the decision we came to."

" It made no difference what decision they came to."

" Oh ! " said Mark with some surprise.

" It was all nonsense. The N.I.C.E. would have had the Wood in any case. They had powers to compel a sale."

" What an extraordinary thing ! I was given to understand they were going to Cambridge if we didn't sell."

" Not a word of truth in it. And there's nothing extraordinary in the fact that the N.I.C.E. should wish to hand over to Bracton the odium of turning the heart of England

37

into a cross between an abortive American hotel and a glorified gas-works. The only puzzle is why the N.I.C.E. should want that bit of land."

"I suppose we shall find out as things go on."

"You may. I shan't."

"Oh?" said Mark interrogatively.

"I've had enough of it," said Hingest, lowering his voice, "I'm leaving to-night. I don't know what you were doing at Bracton, but if it was any good I'd advise you to go back and stick to it."

"Really!" said Mark. "Why do you say that?"

"Doesn't matter for an old fellow like me," said Hingest, "but they could play the devil with *you*."

"As a matter of fact," said Mark, "I haven't fully made up my mind. I don't even know yet what my job would be if I stayed."

"What's your subject?"

"Sociology."

"Huh!" said Hingest. "In that case I can soon point you out the man you'd be under."

"Perhaps you could introduce me."

"All right," said Hingest. "No business of mine." Then he added in a louder voice, "Steele!"

Steele turned round. He was a tall, unsmiling man with that kind of face which, though long and horse-like, has nevertheless rather thick and pouting lips.

"This is Studdock," said Hingest. "The new man for your department." Then he turned away.

"Oh," said Steele. Then after a pause, "Did he say *my* department?"

"That's what he *said*," replied Mark. "I'm a sociologist—if that throws any light on it."

"I'm H.D. for sociology all right," said Steele. "But this is the first I've heard about you. Who told you you were to be there?"

"Well," said Mark, "the thing is rather vague. I've had a talk with the Deputy Director, but we didn't go into details."

Steele whistled. "I say, Cosser," he called out to a freckle-faced man who was passing by, "listen to this. Feverstone has just unloaded this chap on our department without a word to me about it. What do you think of that?"

" Well I'm damned ! " said Cosser.

" I'm sorry," said Mark, a little stiffly.   " I seem to have been put in a false position.   I only came over as an experiment.   It is a matter of indifference to me whether I take a job in the N.I.C.E. or not."

" You see," said Steele to Cosser, " there isn't really any room for a man in our show—specially for someone who doesn't know the work.   Unless they put him on the U.L."

" That's right," said Cosser.

" Mr. Studdock, I think," said a new voice at Mark's elbow, a treble voice which seemed disproportionate to the huge hill of a man whom he saw when he turned his head. He recognised the speaker.   His dark, smooth face and black hair were unmistakable, and so was the accent.   This was Professor Filostrato, the physiologist, whom Mark had sat next to at a dinner two years before.   Mark was charmed that such a man remembered him.

" I am very glad you have come to join us," said Filostrato, taking hold of Mark's arm and gently piloting him away from Steele and Cosser.

" To tell you the truth," said Mark, " I'm not sure that I have.   I was brought over by Feverstone but he has disappeared, and Steele——"

" Bah !   Steele ! " said the Professor.   " That is all a bagatelle.   He get too big for his boots.   He will be put in his place one of these days.   It may be you who will put him."

" I have a strong objection to being put in a false position——" began Mark.

" Listen, my friend," interrupted Filostrato.   " The first thing to realise is that the N.I.C.E. is serious.   It is nothing less than the existence of the human race that depends on our work : our *real* work, you comprehend ?   You will find frictions and impertinences among this *canaglia*, this rabble. They are no more to be regarded than your dislike of a brother officer when the battle is at his crisis."

" As long as I'm given something to do that is worth doing," said Mark, " I shouldn't allow anything of that sort to interfere with it."

" Yes, yes, that is right.   These Steeles and Feverstones— they are of no consequence.   As long as you have the good will of the Deputy Director you snap your fingers at them. You need listen to no one but him, you comprehend ?   Ah—

39

and there is one other. Do not have the Fairy for your enemy."

" The Fairy? "

" Yes. Her they call the Fairy. Oh, my God, a terrible *Inglesaccia*! She is the head of our police, the Institutional Police. *Ecco*, she come. I will present you. Miss Hardcastle, permit that I present to you Mr. Studdock."

Mark found himself writhing from the stoker's or carter's hand-grip of a big woman in a black, short-skirted uniform. Despite a bust that would have done credit to a Victorian barmaid, she was rather thickly built than fat and her iron-grey hair was cropped short. Her face was square, stern, and pale, and her voice deep. A smudge of lip-stick laid on with violent inattention to the real shape of her mouth was her only concession to fashion, and she rolled or chewed a long black cheroot, unlit, between her teeth. As she talked she had a habit of removing this, staring intently at the mixture of lip-stick and saliva on its mangled end, and then replacing it more firmly than before. She sat down immediately in a chair close to where Mark was standing, flung her right leg over one of the arms, and fixed him with a gaze of cold intimacy.

III

Click—clack, distinct in the silence, where Jane stood waiting, came the tread of the person on the other side of the wall. Then the door opened and Jane found herself facing a tall woman of about her own age.

" Does a Miss Ironwood live here? " said Jane.

" Yes," said the other girl, neither opening the door any farther nor standing aside.

" I want to see her, please," said Jane.

" Have you an appointment? " said the tall woman.

" Well, not exactly," said Jane. " Dr. Dimble said I shouldn't need an appointment."

" Oh, if you're from Dr. Dimble," said the woman, " come in. There's not room for two on this path, so you must excuse me if I go first."

The woman led her along a brick path beside a wall on which fruit trees were growing, and then to the left along a mossy path with gooseberry bushes on each side. Presently they found themselves at a small side door, flanked

40

by a water butt, in the long wall of a large house. Just as they did so a window clapped shut upstairs.

A minute or two later Jane was sitting waiting in a large sparely furnished room with a shut stove to warm it. The tall woman's tread died away in the passages and the room became very quiet when it had done so. Occasionally the cawing of rooks could be heard. A long time passed.

When at length the other girl returned Jane now conceived for her that admiration which women, more often than is supposed, feel for other women. It would be nice, Jane thought, to be like that—so straight, so fit to be mounted on a horse, and so tall.

" Is . . . is Miss Ironwood in? " said Jane.

" Are you Mrs. Studdock? " said the girl.

" Yes," said Jane.

" I will bring you to her at once," said the other. " We have been expecting you. My name is Camilla Denniston."

Jane followed her. They went a long way before Camilla knocked at a door and stood aside for Jane to enter, saying " She has come." And Jane went in; and there was Miss Ironwood dressed all in black and sitting with her hands folded on her knees.

The hands were big and boney, though they did not suggest coarseness. She was perhaps nearer sixty than fifty.

" What is your name, young lady? " said Miss Ironwood, taking up a pencil and a note-book.

" Jane Studdock."

" Are you married? "

" Yes."

" Does your husband know you have come to us? "

" No."

" And your age, if you please? "

" Twenty-three."

" And now," said Miss Ironwood, " what have you to tell me? "

Jane took a deep breath. " I've been having bad dreams and—and feeling depressed lately."

Jane's narrative—she did not do it very well—took some time. While she was speaking she kept her eyes fixed on Miss Ironwood's large hands and her black skirt and the pencil and the note-book. As she proceeded she saw Miss Ironwood's hand cease to write and the fingers

41

wrap themselves round the pencil: immensely strong fingers they seemed. And they tightened, as if under the influence of some stifled emotion, and broke the pencil in two. Jane stopped and looked up at Miss Ironwood's face. The grey eyes were still looking at her with no change of expression.

" Pray continue, young lady," said Miss Ironwood.

Jane resumed her story. When she had finished, Miss Ironwood put a number of questions. After that she became silent for so long that Jane said:

" Is there, do you think, anything very serious wrong with me? "

" There is nothing wrong with you," said Miss Ironwood.

" You mean it will go away? "

" I should say probably not."

" Is it something that can't be cured? "

" The reason you cannot be cured is that you are not ill."

" But there must be something wrong. It's surely not natural to have dreams like that."

There was a pause. " I think," said Miss Ironwood, " I had better tell you the whole truth."

" Yes, do," said Jane in a strained voice.

" And I will begin by saying this," continued Miss Ironwood. " You are a more important person than you imagine."

Jane said nothing, but thought inwardly, " She is humouring me. She thinks I am mad."

" What was your maiden name? " asked Miss Ironwood.

" Tudor," said Jane.

" The Warwickshire branch of the family? "

" Yes."

" Did you ever read a little book by an ancestor of yours about the Battle of Worcester? "

" No. Father had a copy—the only copy, I think."

" There are at least two others: one is in this house. Your ancestor gave a full and, on the whole, correct account of the battle, which he says he completed on the same day on which it was fought. But he was not at it."

Jane, who had not really been following this, looked at Miss Ironwood.

" If he was speaking the truth," said Miss Ironwood, " and we believe that he was, he dreamed it. Do you understand? "

" Dreamed about the battle? "

" Yes. But dreamed it right. He saw the real battle in his dream."

" I don't see the connection."

" Vision—the power of dreaming realities—is sometimes hereditary," said Miss Ironwood.

Something seemed to be interfering with Jane's breathing. She felt a sense of injury—this was just the sort of thing she hated.

" Can it be proved? " she asked. " I mean; we have only his word for it."

" We have your dreams."

" What do you mean? "

" My opinion is that you have seen real things in your dreams. You have seen Alcasan as he really sat in the condemned cell: and you have seen a visitor whom he really had."

" But—but—oh, this is ridiculous," said Jane. " *That* part was a mere coincidence. The rest was just nightmare. It was all impossible. He screwed off his head, I tell you. And they . . . dug up the horrible old man. They made him come to life."

" There are some confusions there, no doubt. But in my opinion there are realities behind even those episodes."

" I am afraid I don't believe in that sort of thing," said Jane coldly.

" Your upbringing makes it natural that you should not," replied Miss Ironwood.

" Can you, then, do nothing for me? I mean, can you not stop it—cure it? "

" Vision is not a disease."

" But I don't *want* it," said Jane passionately.

" If you go to a psychotherapist," said Miss Ironwood, " he will proceed on the assumption that the dreams reflect your own subconscious. He would try to treat you. It would certainly not remove the dreams."

" But what is this all about? " said Jane. " I want to lead an ordinary life. I want to do my own work. Why should I be selected for this horrible thing? "

There was a short silence. Jane made a vague movement and said, rather sulkily, " Well perhaps I'd better be going . . ." Then suddenly, " But how can you *know* all this? "

"We know your dreams to be partly true because they fit in with information we already possess. It was because he saw their importance that Dr. Dimble sent you to us."

"Do you mean he sent me here not to be cured but to give information?" said Jane.

"Exactly."

"I wish I had known that a little earlier," said Jane coldly, getting up to go. "I had imagined Dr. Dimble was trying to help me."

"He was. But he was also trying to do something more important at the same time."

"I suppose I should be grateful for being considered at all," said Jane dryly.

"Young lady," said Miss Ironwood. "You do not at all realise the seriousness of this matter. The things you have seen concern something compared with which the happiness, or even the life, of you and me *is* of no importance. You cannot get rid of your gift. You can try to suppress it, but you will fail, and you will be badly frightened. On the other hand, you can put it at our disposal. If you do, you will be less frightened in the long run and you will be helping to save the human race from a very great disaster. Or thirdly, you may tell someone else about it. If you do that, you will almost certainly fall into the hands of other people who are at least as anxious as we to make use of your faculty and who will care no more about your life and happiness than about those of a fly. The people you have seen in your dreams are real people. It is not at all unlikely that they know you have, involuntarily, been spying on them. I would advise you, even for your own sake, to join our side."

"You keep on talking of *we* and *us*. Are you some kind of company?"

"Yes. You may call it a company."

Jane had been standing for the last few minutes: and she had almost been believing what she heard. Then suddenly all her repugnance came over her again—all her wounded vanity, and her general dislike of the mysterious and the unfamiliar. "She's made me worse already," thought Jane, still regarding herself as a patient. Aloud, she said:

"I must go. I don't know what you are talking about. I don't want to have anything to do with it."

Mark discovered in the end that he was expected to stay, at least for the night, and when he went up to dress for dinner he was feeling more cheerful. This was partly due to a whisky-and-soda taken with " Fairy " Hardcastle immediately before. The bedroom with its bright fire and its private bathroom attached had also something to do with it. Thank goodness he had allowed Jane to talk him into buying that new dress-suit! But what had reassured him most of all was his conversation with the Fairy.

It would be misleading to say that he liked her. She had indeed excited in him all the distaste which a young man feels at the proximity of something rankly, even insolently, sexed and at the same time wholly unattractive. And something in her cold eye had told him that she was well aware of this reaction and found it amusing. She had drifted into police reminiscences. In spite of some initial scepticism, Mark was gradually horrified by her assumption that about thirty per cent of our murder trials ended by the hanging of an innocent man. There were details, too, about the execution shed which had not occurred to him before.

All this was disagreeable. But it was made up for by the deliciously esoteric character of the conversation. Several times that day he had been made to feel himself an outsider : that feeling completely disappeared while Miss Hardcastle was talking to him. She had apparently lived an exciting life. She had been, at different times, a suffragette, a pacifist, and a British Fascist. She had been manhandled by the police and imprisoned. On the other hand, she had met Prime Ministers and Dictators, and all her history was secret history. She knew from both ends what a police force could do and what it could not, and there were in her opinion very few things it could not do.

For the Fairy, the police side of the Institute was the really important side. It existed to relieve the ordinary executive of what might be called all sanitary cases—a category which ranged from vaccination to charges of unnatural vice—from which it was only a step to bringing in all cases of blackmail. As regards crime in general, they had already popularised in the Press the idea that the Institute should be allowed to experiment largely in the hope of discovering how far humane, remedial treatment could be substituted for the old notion of " retributive " punishment. That was where legal Red Tape stood in their way. " But there are only two papers we don't control," said the Fairy. " And we'll smash them." And then one would have *carte blanche*. Mark did not immediately follow this. But the Fairy pointed out that what had hampered every English police force up to date was precisely the idea of deserved punishment. For desert was finite: you could do so much to the criminal and no more. Remedial treatment, on the other hand, need have no limit; it could go on till it had effected a cure, and those who were carrying it out would decide when *that* was. And if cure were humane and desirable, how much more prevention? Soon anyone who had ever been in the hands of the police at all would come under the control of the N.I.C.E.; in the end, every citizen. " And that's where you and I come in," added the Fairy.

This had brought Mark back to his doubts whether he were really being given a job and, if so, what it was. But she had laughed at his fears. " You're in all right, sonny," she said. " Only don't be too particular about what exactly you've got to do. Wither doesn't like people who try to pin him down. And don't believe everything you're told."

At dinner Mark found himself next Hingest.

" Well," said Hingest, " have they finally roped you in, eh? Because if you thought the better of it I'm motoring back to-night and I could give you a lift."

" You haven't yet told me why you are leaving us yourself," said Mark.

" Oh, well, it all depends what a man likes. If you enjoy the society of that Italian eunuch and the mad parson and that Hardcastle girl—her grandmother would have boxed her ears if she were alive—of course there's nothing more to be said."

" I suppose it's hardly to be judged on purely social grounds—I mean, it's something more than a club."

" Eh? Judged? Never judged anything in my life, except at a flower show. I came here because I thought it had something to do with science. Now that I find it's something more like a political conspiracy, I shall go home."

" You mean, I suppose, that the social planning doesn't

46

appeal to you? I can understand that it doesn't fit in with your work as it does with sciences like sociology, but——"

" There *are* no sciences like sociology. And if I found chemistry beginning to fit in with a secret police run by a middle-aged virago who doesn't wear corsets and a scheme for taking away his farm and his shop and his children from every Englishman, I'd let chemistry go to the devil and take up gardening again."

" Bill ! " said Fairy Hardcastle suddenly, from the far side of the table.

Hingest fixed his eyes upon her and his face grew a dark red.

" Is it true," bawled the Fairy, " that you're off by car after dinner? "

" Yes, Miss Hardcastle, it is."

" I was wondering if you could give me a lift."

" I should be happy to do so," said Hingest in a voice not intended to deceive, " if we are going in the same direction."

" Will you be passing Brenstock? "

" No, I go down Potter's Lane."

" Oh, damn ! No good to me. I may as well wait till the morning."

After this Mark found himself engaged by his left-hand neighbour and did not see Bill the Blizzard again until he met him in the hall after dinner. He was in his overcoat and just ready to step into his car.

He began talking as he opened the door, and Mark was drawn into accompanying him across the gravel sweep to his car.

" Take my advice, Studdock," he said. " You'll do yourself no good by getting mixed up with the N.I.C.E.—and, by God, you'll do nobody else any good either."

" I suppose there are two views about everything," said Mark.

" Eh? Two views? There are a dozen views about everything until you know the answer. Good night."

He started up the car and drove off.

v

Jane came back from St. Anne's very little pleased with her interview, and had no sooner reached the flat than the telephone went. " Is that you, Jane? " came a voice. " It's me, Margaret Dimble. Such a dreadful thing's happened. I'll tell you when I come. I'm too angry to speak at the moment. Have you a spare bed by any chance? What? Mr. Studdock's away? Not a bit, if *you* don't mind. I've sent Cecil to sleep in College. You're sure it won't be a nuisance? Thanks most awfully. I'll be round in half an hour."

CHAPTER FOUR

THE LIQUIDATION OF ANACHRONISMS

I

ALMOST before Jane had finished putting clean sheets on Mark's bed, Mrs. Dimble arrived. " You're an angel to have me," she said. " We'd tried every hotel in Edgestow I believe. All full up with the hangers-on and camp followers of this detestable N.I.C.E. Secretaries here— typists there—commissioners of works—the thing's out- rageous. If Cecil hadn't had a room in College I really believe he'd have had to sleep in the waiting-room at the station. I only hope that man in College has aired the bed."

" But what on earth's happened? " asked Jane.

" Turned out, my dear! "

" But it isn't possible, Mrs. Dimble. I mean, it can't be legal."

" That's what Cecil said. . . . Just think of it, Jane. The first thing we saw when we poked our heads out of the window this morning was a lorry on the drive and a small army of what looked like criminals with picks and spades. There was an odious little man in a peaked cap who said they'd have no objection to our remaining in possession (of the *house*, mind you, not the garden) till eight o'clock to-morrow morning. No objection! "

" But surely—surely—it must be some mistake."

" Of course Cecil rang up your Bursar. And of course your Bursar was out, and by that time the big beech had been cut down. At last Cecil did get Mr. Busby, who said

48

there must be some misunderstanding, but it was out of his hands now, and we'd better get on to the N.I.C.E. at Belbury. Of course it turned out to be quite impossible to get *them*. But by lunch-time we saw that one simply *couldn't* stay there."

" Why not? "

" My dear, you've no conception what it was like. Great lorries and traction engines roaring past all the time. Why, our own tradesmen couldn't get through it. The milk didn't arrive till eleven o'clock. We'd the greatest difficulty in getting into town ourselves. Flares and noise everywhere and the road practically ruined. And the people! Such horrid men. I didn't know we *had* workpeople like that in England."

" And what are you going to do? " asked Jane.

" Heaven knows! " said Mrs. Dimble. " Cecil has been at Rumbold the solicitor's. Rumbold doesn't seem to know where he is. He keeps on saying the N.I.C.E. are in a very peculiar position legally. There's no question of trying to live on the far side of the river any longer, even if they'd let us. All the poplars are going down. All those nice little cottages by the church are going down. I found poor Ivy—that's your Mrs. Maggs, you know—in tears. Poor things! They do look dreadful when they cry on top of powder. She's being turned out too; she's had enough troubles in her life without this. I was glad to get away. The men were so horrible. Three big brutes came to the back door asking for hot water and went on so that they frightened Martha out of her wits. A sort of special constable sent them away. What? Oh yes, there are dozens of what look like policemen all over the place, and I didn't like the look of *them* either. Cecil and I both thought the same thing: we thought, it's almost as if we'd lost the war. Oh, good girl, tea! That's just what I wanted."

" You must stay here as long as you like, Mrs. Dimble," said Jane. " Mark'll just have to sleep in College."

" Well, really," said Mother Dimble, " I feel at the moment that no Fellow of Bracton ought to be allowed to sleep anywhere! As a matter of fact, I shan't have to. Cecil and I are to go out to the Manor at St. Anne's. We have to be there so much at present, you see."

" Oh," said Jane involuntarily, as her own story flowed back on her mind.

"Why, what a selfish pig I've been," said Mother Dimble. "Here have I been quite forgetting that you've been out there and are full of things to tell me. Did you see Grace? And did you like her?"

"Is 'Grace' Miss Ironwood?" asked Jane.

"Yes."

"I saw her. I don't know if I liked her or not. But I don't want to talk about all that. I can't think about anything except this outrageous business of yours. It's you who are the real martyr, not me."

"No, my dear," said Mrs. Dimble, "I'm not a martyr. I'm only an angry old woman with sore feet and a splitting head (but that's beginning to be better). After all, Cecil and I haven't lost our livelihood as poor Ivy Maggs has. It doesn't *really* matter leaving the old house, all those big rooms which we thought we should want because we were going to have lots of children, and then we never had. Jane, that's the third time you've yawned. You're dropping asleep and I've talked your head off. It comes of being married for thirty years. Husbands were made to be talked to. It helps them to concentrate on what they're reading."

Jane found Mother Dimble an embarrassing person to share a room with because she said prayers. One didn't know where to look.

II

"Are you awake now?" said Mrs. Dimble's voice, quietly, in the middle of the night.

"Yes," said Jane. "I'm so sorry. Did I wake you up? Was I shouting?"

"Yes. You were shouting out about someone being hit on the head."

"I saw them killing a man . . . a man in a big car driving along a country road. Then he came to a cross-roads and there was someone standing in the middle of the road waving a light to stop him. I couldn't hear what they said; I was too far away. They must have persuaded him to get out of the car somehow, and there he was talking to one of them. The light fell full on his face. He wasn't the same old man I saw in my other dream. He hadn't a beard, only a moustache. And he had a very quick, kind of proud, way. He didn't like what the man said to him and presently he put up his fists and knocked him down. Another man behind him tried to hit him on the head with something, but the old man was too quick and turned round in time. Then it was rather horrible, but rather fine. There were three of them at him and he was fighting them all. I've read about that kind of thing in books, but I never realised how one would feel about it. Of course they got him in the end."

III

"Without a doubt," thought Mark, "this must be the Mad Parson that Bill the Blizzard was talking of." The committee at Belbury did not meet till 10.30, and ever since breakfast he had been walking with the Reverend Straik in the garden, despite the raw and misty weather of the morning. At the very moment when the man had first buttonholed him, the threadbare clothes and clumsy boots, the frayed clerical collar, the dark, lean, tragic face, gashed and ill-shaved and seamed, and the bitter sincerity of his manner, had struck a discordant note. It was not a type Mark had expected to meet in the N.I.C.E.

"Do not imagine," said Mr. Straik, "that I indulge in any dreams of carrying out our programme without violence. There will be resistance. They will gnaw their tongues and not repent. We face these disorders with a firmness which will lead traducers to say that we have desired them. In a sense we have. It is no part of our witness to preserve that organisation of ordered sin which is called Society."

"Now that is what I meant," said Mark, "when I said that your point of view and mine must, in the long run, be incompatible. The preservation, which involves the thorough planning, of society is just precisely the end I have in view. I do not think there is or can be any other end. The problem is quite different for you because you look forward to something better than human society, in some other world."

"With every thought and vibration of my heart," said Mr. Straik, "I repudiate that damnable doctrine. The Kingdom of God is to be realised here—in this world. And it will be. At the name of Jesus every knee shall bow. In

51

that name I dissociate myself completely from all the organised religion that has yet been seen in the world."

And at the name of Jesus, Mark, who would have lectured on abortion or perversion to an audience of young women without a qualm, felt himself so embarrassed that he knew his cheeks were slightly reddening.

"You mean," said he, "that as far as immediate practice is concerned, there are no limits to your co-operation with the programme?"

"Sweep away all idea of co-operation!" said the other. "Does clay *co-operate* with the potter? You have no choice whether you will be used or not. There is no turning back. No one goes *out* of the N.I.C.E. Those who try to turn back will perish. For it's all true, you know. It is the saints who are going to inherit the earth—here in England, perhaps within the next twelve months." Then, suddenly lowering his voice, Straik added, "The *real* resurrection is even now taking place. The real life everlasting. Here in this world. You will see it."

"I say," said Mark, "it's nearly twenty past. Oughtn't we to be going to the committee?"

Straik turned with him in silence. Partly to avoid further conversation, Mark said presently:

"A rather annoying thing has happened. I've lost my wallet. There wasn't much in it, but it's a nuisance. Ought I to tell someone?"

"You could tell the steward," said Straik.

IV

The committee sat for about two hours and the Deputy Director was in the chair. His method of conducting business was slow and involved, and to Mark it soon became obvious that the real work of the N.I.C.E. must go on somewhere else. This, indeed, was what he had expected, and he was too reasonable to suppose that he should find himself, at this early stage, in the Inner Ring or whatever at Belbury corresponded to the Progressive Element at Bracton. This morning the business mainly concerned the details of the work already begun at Edgestow. It was only at the end of the meeting that Wither opened a much more sensational subject. He believed that most of those present had already heard the very distressing piece of news which it was, never-

theless, his duty now to communicate to them in a semi-
official manner. He was referring, of course, to the
murder of Mr. William Hingest. As far as Mark could discover Bill the Blizzard had been discovered with his head
beaten in by some blunt instrument, lying near his car in
Potter's Lane at about four o'clock that morning. He had
been dead for several hours. Mr. Wither ventured to
suppose that it would be a melancholy pleasure to the committee to know that N.I.C.E. police had been on the scene
of the crime before five, and that neither the local authorities
nor Scotland Yard were making any objections to the fullest
collaboration. He felt that if the occasion were more
appropriate he would have welcomed a motion for some
expression of the gratitude they must all feel to Miss Hardcastle and possibly of congratulations to her on the smooth
interaction between her own forces and those of the state.
This was a most gratifying feature in the sad story and, he
suggested, a good omen for the future. He concluded by
suggesting that they should all stand in silence for one
minute as a token of respect for the memory of William
Hingest.

And they did—a world-without-end minute in which odd
creakings and breathings became audible, and behind the
mask of each glazed and tight-lipped face, shy, irrelevant
thoughts of this and that came creeping out.

Then there was a stir and a bustle and the committee
broke up.

v

The whole process of getting up and doing the " morning jobs " was more cheerful, Jane found, because she had
Mrs. Dimble with her. It was a bright sunny morning, and
as they sat down to breakfast in the kitchen Jane was feeling
bright herself. During the night her mind had evolved a
comfortable theory that the mere fact of having seen Miss
Ironwood and " had it all out " would probably stop the
dreams altogether.

She glanced at the clock and wondered why Mrs. Maggs
hadn't yet turned up.

" My dear, I'm afraid you've lost Ivy Maggs," said
Mrs. Dimble. " Didn't I tell you they'd taken her house
too? There's nowhere for her to live in Edgestow."

53

" Bother ! " said Jane : and added, without much interest in the reply, " What is she doing, do you know? "

" She's gone out to St. Anne's."

" Has she got friends there? "

" She's gone to the Manor, along with Cecil and me."

" Do you mean she's got a job there? "

" Well, yes. I suppose it is a job."

Mrs. Dimble left at about eleven. She also, it appeared, was going to St. Anne's, but was first to meet her husband and lunch with him at Northumberland. Jane walked down to the town with her and they parted at the bottom of Market Street. It was just after this that Jane met Mr. Curry.

" Have you heard the news, Mrs. Studdock? " said Curry.

" No. What's wrong? " said Jane. She thought Mr. Curry a pompous fool and Mark a fool for being impressed by him. But as soon as Curry began speaking her face showed all the wonder and consternation he could have wished. The murder of Hingest had already become Curry's property. The " matter " was, in some indefinable sense, " in his hands ", and he was heavy with responsibility. At another time Jane would have found this amusing. She escaped from him as soon as possible and went into Blackie's for a cup of coffee. She felt she must sit down.

The death of Hingest in itself meant nothing to her. But the certainty that she herself in her dream had witnessed a real murder shattered the consoling pretences with which she had begun the morning. It came over her with sickening clarity that the affair of her dreams, far from being ended, was only beginning. It would drive her mad, she thought, to face it alone. The other alternative was to go back to Miss Ironwood. But that seemed to be only a way of going deeper into all this darkness. She didn't want to get drawn in. It was unfair. It wasn't as if she had asked much of life. All she wanted was to be left alone.

VI

Cosser—the freckle-faced man with the little wisp of black moustache—approached Mark as he was coming away from the committee.

" You and I have a job to do," he said. " Got to get out a report about Cure Hardy."

54

Mark was very relieved to hear of a job. But he was a little on his dignity.

" Does that mean I *am* to be in Steele's department after all ? "

" That's right," said Cosser.

" The reason I ask," said Mark, " is that neither he nor you seemed particularly keen on having me. I don't want to push myself in, you know. I don't need to stay at the N.I.C.E. at all if it comes to that,"

" Well, don't start talking about it here," said Cosser. " Come upstairs."

They were in the hall and Mark noticed Wither pacing thoughtfully towards them. " Wouldn't it be as well to speak to *him* ? " he suggested. But the Deputy Director, after coming within ten feet of them, had turned in another direction. He was humming to himself under his breath and seemed so deep in thought that Mark felt the moment unsuitable for an interview. Cosser apparently thought the same, and Mark followed him up to an office on the third floor.

" It's about the village of Cure Hardy," said Cosser, when they were seated. " You see, all that land at Bragdon Wood is going to be little better than a swamp once they get to work. Why the hell we wanted to go there I don't know. Anyway, the latest plan is to divert the Wynd : block up the old channel through Edgestow altogether. Look. It's to be diverted and brought down an artificial channel—here, to the east, where the blue line is—and rejoin the old bed down here."

" The university will hardly agree to that," said Mark.

" We've got the university by the short hairs," said Cosser. " The point is that the new Wynd must come right through Cure Hardy in this narrow little valley. The idea is to dam the valley at the southern end and make a big reservoir."

" But what happens to Cure Hardy ? "

" That's another advantage. We build a new model village four miles away."

" I say, there'll be the devil of a stink about this. Cure Hardy is famous. It's a beauty spot."

" That's where you and I come in. We've got to make a report on Cure Hardy. We'll run out and have a look round to-morrow, but we can write most of the report today. It ought to be pretty easy. If it's a beauty spot, you can bet it's insanitary. Then we've got to get out some facts about the population. I think you'll find it consists chiefly of undesirable elements—small *rentiers* and agricultural labourers."

"That's easy enough," said Mark, "but before I get down to it I'd like to be a bit clearer about my position. Oughtn't I to go and see Steele?"

"I wouldn't do that," said Cosser.

"Why not?"

"Well, for one thing, Steele can't prevent you if the D.D. backs you up. For another, Steele is rather a dangerous man. There's another thing, too. I don't think things can go on in this department in the way they are at present."

Mark understood. Cosser was hoping to get Steele out of the department altogether.

"I got the impression," said Mark, "that you and Steele hit it off together rather well."

"The great thing here," said Cosser, "is never to quarrel with anyone."

"Of course," said Mark. "By the way, if we go to Cure Hardy to-morrow I might as well run in to Edgestow and spend the night at home."

For Mark a good deal hung on the answer to this. But Cosser merely said, "Oh," leaving Mark in doubt whether no one needed leave of absence or whether Mark was not sufficiently established as a member of the Institute for his absence to be of any consequence. Then they went to work on their report.

Next day they drove to Cure Hardy, and walked about the village for two hours and saw all the abuses and anachronisms they came to destroy. They saw the backward labourer and heard his views on the weather. They met the wastefully supported pauper shuffling across the courtyard of the alms-houses to fill a kettle, and the elderly *rentier* in conversation with the postman. It did not quite escape Mark that the face of the labourer was rather more interesting than Cosser's and his voice a great deal more pleasing to the ear. But all this did not influence his sociological convictions, for his education had had the effect of making things that he read and wrote more real to him than things he saw. Statistics about agricultural labourers were the substance: any real ditcher, ploughman, or farmer's boy, was the shadow. In his own way, he believed as firmly as any mystic in the superior reality of the things that are not seen.

On their way back Cosser dropped him near Edgestow station, and as he walked home Mark began to think of what he would say to Jane about Belbury. You will misunderstand him if you think he was consciously inventing a lie; his misgiving and uneasiness quickened his desire to cut a good figure in the eyes of his wife. Almost without noticing it, he decided not to mention Cure Hardy; Jane cared for old buildings and all that sort of thing. When Jane heard the door opening and looked round and saw Mark, she saw a rather breezy Mark. Yes, he was almost sure he'd got the job. The salary wasn't fixed, but he'd be going into that to-morrow. But he had already got on to the real people there.

Jane decided to tell him nothing about the dreams or St. Anne's. Men hated women who had things wrong with them, specially queer, unusual things. Her resolution was easily kept, for Mark full of his own story, asked her no questions. She was not, perhaps, entirely convinced by what he said. Very early in the conversation she said in a sharp, frightened voice (she had no idea how he disliked that voice), "Mark, you haven't given up your Fellowship at Bracton?" He said No, of course not, and went on.

VII

That evening the Fellows of Bracton sat in Common Room over their wine and dessert. Feverstone and Curry were sitting together. Until that night for about three hundred years this Common Room had been one of the pleasant quiet places of England, and at this hour and season the windows were, of course, shut and curtained. But from beyond them came such noises as had never been heard in that room before—shouts and curses and the sound of lorries heavily drumming past or harshly changing gear, rattling of chains, drumming of mechanical drills, clanging of iron, whistles, thuddings, and an all-pervasive vibration. Beyond those windows, scarcely thirty yards away on the other side of the Wynd, the conversion of an ancient woodland into an inferno of mud and steel and concrete was already going on. Several members even of the Progressive Element had already been grumbling about it. Curry was doing his best to brazen it out, and though his conversation with Feverstone had to be conducted at the top of their voices, he made no allusion to this inconvenience.

"It's quite definite, then," he bawled, "that young Studdock is not coming back?"

"Oh, quite," shouted Feverstone.

"When will he send a formal resignation?"

"Haven't an earthly!"

"We must begin thinking about the vacancy at once."

"Does his successor have to be a sociologist? I mean is the Fellowship tied to the subject?"

"Oh, not in the least. I say, Feverstone, oughtn't we to give this new subject a leg up?"

"What new subject?"

"Pragmatometry."

"Well, now, it's funny you should say that, because the man I was beginning to think of has been going in a good deal for pragmatometry. One could call it a fellowship in social pragmatometry, or something like that."

"Who is the man?"

"Laird—from Leicester, Cambridge."

It was automatic for Curry, though he had never heard of Laird, to say "Ah, Laird. Just remind me of the details."

"Well," said Feverstone, "as you remember, he was in bad health at the time of his finals, and came rather a cropper. The Cambridge examining is so bad nowadays that one hardly counts that. He used to edit *The Adult*."

"Yes, to be sure. That Laird. But I say, Dick . . ."

"Yes?"

"I'm not quite happy about his bad degree. Of course I don't attach a superstitious value to examination results any more than you do. Still . . . we have made one or two unfortunate elections lately."

"I'm going to be at Cambridge next week," Feverstone said, "in fact I'm giving a dinner. I'd as soon it wasn't mentioned here, because, as a matter of fact, the P.M. may be coming, and one or two big newspaper people and Tony Dew. What? Oh, of course you know Tony. That little dark man from the Bank. Laird is going to be there. He's some kind of cousin of the P.M.'s. I was wondering if you could join us."

" Well, it would be very difficult. It rather depends on when old Bill's funeral is to be. Was there anything about the inquest on the six-o'clock news? "

" I can't hear," yelled Feverstone. " Is this noise getting worse? Or am I getting deaf? "

" I say, Sub-Warden," shouted Ted Raynor from beyond Feverstone, " what the devil are your friends outside doing? "

" Listen! " said Glossop suddenly, " that's not work. Listen to the feet."

Next moment nearly everyone in the room was on his feet. " They're murdering someone," said Glossop, " There's only one way of getting a noise like that out of a man's throat." " Where are you going? " asked Curry. " I'm going to see what's happening," said Glossop. " I shouldn't go out if I were you," said Feverstone, " it sounds as if the police, or something, was there already."

" What do you mean? "

" Listen. There! "

" I thought that was their infernal drill."

" Listen! "

" My God . . . you really think it's a machine-gun? "

" Look out! Look out! " said a dozen voices, as a splintering of glass became audible and a shower of stones fell on to the Common Room floor. A moment later several of the Fellows had made a rush for the windows and put up the shutters. Glossop had a cut on the forehead, and on the floor lay the fragments of that famous east window on which Henrietta Maria had once cut her name with a diamond.

CHAPTER FIVE

ELASTICITY

I

Next morning Mark went back to Belbury by train. This return—just sauntering in and hanging up his hat and ordering a drink—was a pleasant contrast to his first arrival. The servant who brought the drink knew him. Filostrato nodded to him. After the drink he strolled upstairs to Cosser's office.

Steele and Cosser were both there. Neither spoke.

"Ah—good morning," said Mark awkwardly.

Steele finished making a pencil note.

"What is it, Mr. Studdock?" he said without looking up.

"I came to see Cosser," said Mark, and then, addressing Cosser, "I've been thinking over the last section in that report—— "

"What report's this?" said Steele to Cosser.

"Oh, I thought," replied Cosser, with a little twisty smile at one corner of his mouth, "that it would be a good thing to put together a report on Cure Hardy. Mr. Studdock helped me."

"Well, never mind about that now," said Steele. "You can talk to Mr. Cosser about it some other time, Mr. Studdock."

"Look here," said Mark, "I think we'd better understand one another. Am I to take it that this report was simply a private hobby of Cosser's? And whose orders am I under?"

Steele, playing with his pencil, looked at Cosser.

"I asked you a question about my position, Mr. Steele," said Mark.

"I haven't time for this sort of thing," said Steele. "I know nothing about your position."

Mark turned on his heel and left the room, slamming the door behind him. He was going to see the Deputy Director.

At the door of Wither's room he hesitated for a moment because he heard voices from within. But he was too angry to wait. He knocked and entered without noticing whether the knock had been answered.

"My dear boy," said the Deputy Director, looking up but not quite fixing his eyes on Mark's face, "I am delighted to see you."

Mark noticed that there was a third person in the room, a man called Stone whom he had met the day before yesterday. Stone was standing in front of Wither's table rolling and unrolling a piece of blotting-paper with his fingers.

"Delighted to see you," repeated Wither. "All the more so because you—er—interrupted me in what I am afraid I must call a rather painful interview. As I was just saying to poor Mr. Stone when you came in, nothing is nearer to my heart than the wish that this great Institute should all work together like one family . . . the greatest unity of will and purpose, Mr. Stone, the freest mutual confidence . . . that is what I expect of my colleagues. But then as you may remind me, Mr.—ah—Studdock, even in family life there are occasionally strains and misunderstandings. And that is why, my dear boy, I am not at the moment quite at leisure—don't go, Mr. Stone. I have a great deal more to say to you."

" Perhaps I'd better come back later? " said Mark.

"Well, perhaps in all the circumstances . . . it is *your* feelings that I am considering, Mr. Stone . . . perhaps . . . the usual method of seeing me, Mr. Studdock, is to apply to my secretary and make an appointment. Not, you will understand, that I have the least wish to insist on any formalities. It is the waste of *your* time that I am anxious to avoid."

" Thank you, sir," said Mark. " I'll go and see your secretary."

The secretary's office was next door. Mark made an appointment for ten o'clock to-morrow, the earliest hour they could offer him. As he came out he ran into Fairy Hardcastle.

" Hullo, Studdock," said the Fairy. " Hanging round the D.D.'s office? That won't do, you know."

" I have decided," said Mark, " that I must either get my position definitely fixed or else leave the Institute."

She looked at him with an ambiguous expression and suddenly slipped her arm through his.

" Look, sonny," she said, " you drop all that, see? Come and have a talk."

" There's really nothing to talk about, Miss Hardcastle," said Mark. " Either I get a real job here, or I go back to Bracton."

To this the Fairy made no answer, and the steady pressure of her arm compelled Mark to go with her along the passage.

She brought him to her own offices on the second floor. The outer office was full of what he had already learned to call Waips, the girls of the Women's Auxiliary Institutional Police. The men of the force, though more numerous, were not often met with indoors, but Waips were constantly seen wherever Miss Hardcastle appeared. Far from sharing the masculine characteristics of their chief they were small and fluffy and full of giggles. Miss Hardcastle behaved to them as if she were a man, and addressed them in tones of half-breezy, half-ferocious gallantry. When they reached the inner office she made Mark sit down but remained standing herself.

"Cut it all out, Studdock," said Miss Hardcastle. "And whatever you do, don't go bothering the D.D."

"That might be very good advice, Miss Hardcastle," said Mark, "if I were committed to staying here. I've very nearly made up my mind to go home. Only I thought I'd just have a talk with him first, to make everything clear."

"Making things clear is the one thing the D.D. can't stand," replied Miss Hardcastle. "That's not how he runs the place. And mind you, he knows what he's about. It works, sonny. You needn't bother your head about all the Steeles and Cossers. Not one of them is going to be left when we get going."

"That's just the line Cosser took about Steele," said Mark, "and it didn't seem to do me much good when it came to the point."

"Do you know, Studdock," said Miss Hardcastle, "I've taken a fancy to you. Because if I hadn't, I'd be disposed to resent that last remark."

"I don't mean to be offensive," said Mark. "But— damn it all—look at it from my point of view."

"No good. You don't know enough yet for your point of view to be worth sixpence. You're being offered a chance. And there are only two alternatives, you know; to be in the N.I.C.E. or to be out of it. And I know which is going to be most fun."

"I *do* understand that," said Mark. "Give me a real place in the Sociological Department and I'll . . ."

"Rats! That whole Department is going to be scrapped. It had to be there at the beginning for propaganda purposes."

"But what assurance have I that I'm going to be one of their successors?"

"You aren't. The real work has nothing to do with all these departments. The kind of sociology we're interested in will be done by my people—the police."

"Then where do I come in?"

" If you'll trust me I can put you on to a bit of your real work—what you were brought here to do—straight away."

" What's that? "

" Alcasan."

" You mean the radiologist—the man who was guillotined? " asked Mark, who was completely bewildered.

The Fairy nodded.

" He's to be rehabilitated," she said. " Gradually. You begin with a quiet little article—not questioning his guilt, but just hinting that of course he *was* a member of their quisling government, and there was a prejudice against him. Then you follow it up in a day or two with an article of quite a different kind. Popular account of the value of his work. You can mug up the facts—enough for *that* kind of article—in an afternoon. By that time——"

" What on earth is the point of all this? "

" I'm telling you, Studdock. Alcasan is to be rehabilitated. Made into a martyr."

" But what for? "

" There you go again! You grumble about being given nothing to do, and as soon as I suggest a bit of real work you expect to have the whole plan of campaign told you before you do it. That's not the way to get on here. The great thing is to do what you're told. You don't seem to realise what we are. We're an army."

" Anyway," said Mark, " I didn't come here to write newspaper articles. And if I had, I'd want to know a good deal more about the politics of the N.I.C.E. before I went in for that sort of thing."

" Haven't you been told that it's strictly non-political? "

" I've been told so many things that I don't know whether I'm on my head or my heels," said Mark. " But I don't see how one's going to start a newspaper stunt without being political. Is it Left or Right papers that are going to print all this rot about Alcasan? "

" Both, honey, both," said Miss Hardcastle. " Don't you understand *anything*? Isn't it absolutely essential to keep a fierce Left and a fierce Right both on their toes and each terrified of the other? That's how we get things done. *Of course* we're non-political. The real power always is."

" Well," said Mark, " this is all very interesting, but it has nothing to do with me. I don't want to become a journalist at all : and if I did I should like to be an honest journalist."

"Very well," said Miss Hardcastle. "All you'll do is to help to ruin this country, and perhaps the human race. Besides dishing your own career."

The confidential tone in which she had been speaking up till now had disappeared and there was a threatening finality in her voice. The citizen and the honest man which had been awaked in Mark by the conversation, quailed a little: his other and far stronger self, the self that was anxious at all costs not to be placed among the outsiders, leaped up, fully alarmed.

"I don't mean," he said, "that I don't see your point. I was only wondering . . ."

"It's all one to me, Studdock," said Miss Hardcastle. "Go and settle it with the D.D. He doesn't *like* people resigning, but, of course, you can. He'll have something to say to Feverstone for bringing you here. We'd assumed you understood."

The mention of Feverstone brought sharply before Mark as a reality the plan, which had up till now been slightly unreal, of going back to Edgestow and satisfying himself with the career of a Fellow of Bracton. On what terms would he go back? Would he still be a member of the inner circle even at Bracton? And the salary of a mere don looked a poor thing after the dreams he had been dreaming for the last few days. Married life was already turning out more expensive than he had reckoned. Then came a sharp doubt about that two hundred pounds for membership of the N.I.C.E. club. But no—that was absurd.

"Well, obviously," he said in a vague voice, "the first thing is to see the D.D."

"You'd better run along now," said Miss Hardcastle. "Have a nice talk with the D.D. Be careful not to annoy the old man. He does so hate resignations."

The rest of that day he passed miserably enough, keeping out of people's way as much as possible lest his lack of occupation should be noticed. He wandered round to the back parts of the house, where the newer and lower buildings joined it. Here he was surprised by a stable-like smell and a medley of growls, grunts, and whimpers—all the signs, in fact, of a considerable zoo. At first he did not understand, but presently he remembered that an immense programme of vivisection, freed at last from Red Tape and from niggling economy, was one of the plans of the

N.I.C.E. He had not been particularly interested and had thought vaguely of rats, rabbits, and an occasional dog. The confused noises from within suggested something very different. As he stood there one great yawn-like howl arose, and then, as if it had set the key, all manner of trumpetings, bayings, screams, laughter even, which shuddered and protested for a moment and then died away into mutterings and whines. Mark had no scruples about vivisection. What the noise meant to him was the greatness and grandiosity of this whole undertaking from which, apparently, he was likely to be excluded. He *must* get the job: he must somehow solve the problem of Steele.

II

The first real fog of the autumn had descended on Belbury that morning. Mark ate his breakfast by artificial light, and neither post nor newspaper had arrived. It was a Friday, and a servant handed him his bill for the portion of a week which he had already spent in the Institute. He put it in his pocket after a hasty glance with a resolution that this, at any rate, should never be mentioned to Jane. Neither the total nor the items were of the sort that wives easily understand.

The odd half-hour which he had to wait before keeping his appointment with the Deputy Director passed slowly. No one spoke to him. He was glad when he was able to go and knock on Wither's door.

The conversation was not easy to begin because Wither said nothing. Mark, divided between his desire to make it clear that he had fully resolved to be left hanging about no longer and his equally keen desire not to lose the job if there were any real job going, did not perhaps speak very well. At all events the Deputy Director left him to run down—to pass into disjointed repetitions and thence into complete silence.

" So I think, sir, I'd better go," said Mark at last.

" You are Mr. Studdock I think ? " said Wither tentatively after another prolonged silence.

" Yes," said Mark impatiently. " I called on you with Lord Feverstone a few days ago. You gave me to understand that you were offering me a position on the——"

" One moment, Mr. Studdock," interrupted the Deputy

Director. " It is so important to be perfectly clear. You are no doubt aware that in certain senses it would be most unfortunate to speak of my offering anyone a post in the Institute. You must not imagine that I hold any kind of autocratic position, nor, on the other hand, that the relation between my own sphere of influence and the powers—their temporary powers, you understand—of the permanent committee are defined by any hard-and-fast system of—er—a constitutional, or even a constitutive, character. For example——"

" Then, sir, can you tell me whether anyone has offered me a post, and, if so, who ? "

" Oh," said Wither suddenly, changing both his position and his tone as if a new idea had struck him. " It was always understood that your co-operation with the Institute would be entirely acceptable—would be of the greatest value."

" Well, can I—I mean, oughtn't we to discuss the details ? I mean the salary for example and—who should I be working under ? "

" My dear friend," said Wither with a smile, " I do not anticipate that there will be any difficulty about the—er— the financial side of the matter. As for——"

" What would the salary be, sir ? " said Mark.

" Well, there you touch on a point which it is hardly for me to decide. I believe that members in the position which we had envisaged you as occupying usually draw some sum like fifteen hundred a year, allowing for fluctuations calculated on a very liberal basis. All questions of that sort will adjust themselves with the greatest ease."

" But when should I know, sir ? "

" You mustn't suppose, Mr. Studdock, that when I mention fifteen hundred I am at all excluding the possibility of some higher figure. I don't think any of us would . . ."

" I should be perfectly satisfied with fifteen hundred," said Mark. " I wasn't thinking of that. But—but——" The Deputy Director's expression became more and more courtly and confidential, so that when Mark finally blurted out, " I suppose there'd be a contract or something of the kind," he felt he had committed an unutterable vulgarity.

" Well," said the Deputy Director, fixing his eyes on the ceiling and sinking his voice to a whisper, " that is not exactly . . . it would, no doubt, be possible . . ."

"And that isn't the main point, sir," said Mark reddening. "Am I to work under Mr. Steele?"

"I have here a form," said Winter, "which has not, I believe, been ever actually used but which was designed for such agreements. You might care to study it at your leisure."

"But about Mr. Steele?"

At that moment a secretary entered and placed some letters on the table.

"Ah! The post at last!" said Wither. "Perhaps, Mr. Studdock, er—you will have letters of your own to attend to. You are, I believe, married?" A smile of fatherly indulgence overspread his face as he said these words.

"I'm sorry, sir," said Mark, "but about Mr. Steele? I should feel compelled to refuse any position which involved working under Mr. Steele."

"That opens up a very interesting question about which I should like to have a quite informal and confidential chat with you on some future occasion," said Wither. "For the moment, Mr. Studdock, I shall not regard anything you have said as final . . ." He became absorbed in the letter he had opened, and Mark, feeling that he had achieved enough for one interview, left the room. Apparently they did want him at the N.I.C.E. and were prepared to pay for him. He would fight it out about Steele later.

He came downstairs and found the following letter waiting for him.

BRACTON COLLEGE,
EDGESTOW,
Oct. 20th, 19—.

"My DEAR MARK,—We were all sorry to hear that you are resigning your Fellowship, but feel certain you've made the right decision as far as your own career is concerned. If you have not yet sent a formal resignation to N.O., I shouldn't be in any hurry to do so. If you wrote next term the vacancy would come up at the February meeting and we should have time to get ready a suitable candidate as your successor. Have you any ideas on the subject yourself? I was talking to James and Dick the other night about David Laird. No doubt you know his work: could you let me have a line about it, and about his more general qualifications? I may see him next week when I'm running over to Cambridge to dine with the Prime Minister and one or two others, and Dick might ask Laird. You'll have heard that we had rather a shindy here the other night. There was some sort of *fracas* between the new workmen and the local inhabitants. The N.I.C.E. police made the mistake of firing a few rounds over the heads of the crowd. We had the Henrietta Maria window smashed and stones came into Common Room. Glossop lost his head and wanted to go out and harangue the mob, but I managed to quiet him down.— Yours, G. C. CURRY."

At the first words of this letter a stab of fear ran through Mark. He tried to reassure himself. An explanation would be bound to put everything right. They couldn't shove a man out of his Fellowship simply on a chance word spoken by Lord Feverstone in Common Room. It came back to him with miserable insight that what he was now calling " a chance word " was exactly what he had learned, in the Progressive Element, to describe as " settling real business in private " or " cutting out the Red Tape ", but he tried to thrust this out of his mind. Then another thought struck him. A letter to Curry, saying plainly that he meant to stay at Bracton, would be shown to Feverstone. Feverstone would tell Wither. Such a letter could be regarded as a refusal of any post at Belbury. Well—let it be! He would give up this short-lived dream and fall back on his Fellowship. But how if that were impossible? The whole thing might have been arranged simply to let him fall between the two stools . . . then he and Jane left to sink or swim with not a *sou* between them. . . .

He rang the bell and ordered a large whisky. He must write a very careful and rather elusive letter. His first draft was, he thought, not vague enough: it could be used as a proof that he had abandoned all idea of a job at Belbury. But then, if it were too vague, it would do no good. Oh damn, damn, damn the whole thing. In the end, with the aid of the whisky and of a great many cigarettes, he produced the following:

THE NATIONAL INSTITUTE
for CO-ORDINATED EXPERIMENTS,
BELBURY.

Oct. 21st, 19—.

" MY DEAR CURRY,—Feverstone must have got me wrong. I never made the slightest suggestion of resigning my Fellowship and don't in the least wish to do so. As a matter of fact, I have almost made up my mind not to take a full-time job with the N.I.C.E. and hope to be back in College in a day or two. So be sure and contradict it if you hear anyone saying I am thinking of leaving Edgestow. I hope you'll enjoy your jaunt to Cambridge: what circles you do move in!—Yours, MARK G. STUDDOCK.

" *P.S.*—Laird wouldn't have done in any case. He got a third, and his only published work has been treated as a joke."

The relief of having finished the letter was only momentary, for almost as soon as he had sealed it the problem of how to pass the rest of this day returned to him. He decided to go and sit in his own room: but when he went up there he found the bed stripped and a vacuum cleaner in the middle of the floor. He came down and tried the lounge; the servants were tidying it. He looked into the library. It was empty but for two men who were talking with their heads close together. They stopped and looked up as soon as he entered, obviously waiting for him to go. In the hall he saw Steele himself standing by the notice-board and talking to a man with a pointed beard. Neither looked at Mark, but as he passed them they became silent. He opened the front door and looked out: the fog was thick, wet, and cold.

This day was so long to Mark that a faithful account of it would be unreadable.

Some time after lunch he met Stone. He knew by experience how dangerous it is to be friends with a sinking man or even to be seen with him: you cannot keep him afloat and he may pull you under. But his craving for companionship was now acute; against his better judgement he said, " Hullo ! "

Stone gave a start as if to be spoken to were almost a frightening experience. " Good afternoon," he said nervously and made to pass on.

And Mark did not answer because at that moment he saw the Deputy Director approaching. He was to discover during the next few weeks that no passage and no room at Belbury was safe from the prolonged indoor walks of the Deputy Director. They could not be regarded as a form of espionage, for the creak of Wither's boots and the dreary little tune which he was nearly always humming would have defeated any such purpose. One heard him quite a long way off. Often one saw him a long way off as well, staring vaguely towards one. Very slowly he came towards them, looked in their direction though it was not plain from his face whether he recognised them or not, and passed on.

Neither of the young men attempted to resume their conversation.

At tea Mark saw Feverstone and went at once to sit beside him. He knew that the worst thing a man in his position could do was to try to force himself on anyone, but he was now feeling desperate.

" I say, Feverstone," he began gaily, " I haven't had exactly what you'd call a glowing reception from Steele. But the D.D. won't hear of my leaving. And the Fairy seems to want me to write newspaper articles. What the hell *am* I supposed to be doing? "

Feverstone laughed long and loud.

" Because," concluded Mark, " I'm damned if I can find out. I've tried to tackle the old boy direct . . ."

" God ! " said Feverstone, laughing even louder.

" Well, how the devil is one to find out what's wanted if nobody offers any information? "

" Quite."

" Oh, and how on earth did Curry get the idea that I'm resigning my Fellowship? "

" Aren't you? "

" I never had the faintest notion of resigning it."

Feverstone's smile brightened and widened. " It doesn't make any odds, you know," he said. " If the N.I.C.E. want you to have a nominal job somewhere outside Belbury, you'll have one : and if they don't, you won't. Just like that."

" I'm merely trying to retain the Fellowship I already had. One doesn't want to fall between two stools."

" One doesn't *want* to."

" You mean? "

" Take my advice and get into Wither's good books again as soon as you can. I gave you a good start, but you seem to have rubbed him up the wrong way. And just between ourselves, I wouldn't be too thick with the Fairy : it won't do you any good higher up."

" In the meantime," said Mark, " I've written to Curry to explain that it's all rot about my resignation."

" No harm if it amuses you," said Feverstone, still smiling.

" Well, I don't suppose College wants to kick me out simply because Curry misunderstood something said by you."

"You *can't* be deprived of a Fellowship under any statute I know, except for gross immorality."

"Of course not. I didn't mean that. I meant not being re-elected when I come up for re-election next term."

"Oh. I see."

"And that's why I must rely on you to get that idea out of Curry's head."

"Me?"

"Yes."

"Why me?"

"Well—damn it all, Feverstone, you know perfectly well that there was no doubt about my re-election until you spoke a word in Curry's ear."

Feverstone eyed the muffin critically. "You make me rather tired," he said. "And I would advise you in talking to people here to adopt a more agreeable manner. Otherwise your life may be ' nasty, poor, brutish, and short '!"

"Short?" said Mark. "Is that a threat? Do you mean my life at Bracton or at the N.I.C.E.?"

"I shouldn't stress the distinction too much if I were you," said Feverstone.

And so Mark knew that if he lost the Belbury job he would lose his Fellowship at Bracton as well.

III

During these days Jane kept on going into Edgestow to find another "woman" instead of Mrs. Maggs. On one of these occasions she was delighted to find herself suddenly addressed by Camilla Denniston. Camilla had just stepped out of a car and next moment she introduced a tall, dark man as her husband. Jane saw that both the Dennistons were the sort of people she liked. She knew that Mr. Denniston had once been a friend of Mark's; and her first thought was to wonder why Mark's present friends were so inferior to those he once had.

"We were just coming to see you," said Camilla. "Look here, we have lunch with us. Let's drive you up to the woods beyond Sandown and all feed together in the car."

Jane thought this foggy day an odd choice for a picnic, but agreed.

They left the unfenced road beyond Sandown and went across grass and finally came to rest in a sort of little grassy bay with a fir thicket on one side and a group of beeches on the other. Then there was some unstrapping of baskets, and then sandwiches and sherry and hot coffee and cigarettes.

"Now," said Denniston at last, "I must tell you. Our little household, or whatever you like to call it, is run by a Mr. Fisher-King. At least that is the name he has recently taken. He had a sister in India, Mrs. Fisher-King. She has died and left him a large fortune on condition that he took the name. She was a friend of the great native Christian mystic whom you may have heard of—the Sura. And that's the point. The Sura had reason to believe that a great danger was hanging over the human race. And just before the end he became convinced that it would actually come to a head in this island. Mrs. Fisher-King handed over the problem to her brother. He was to collect a company to watch for this danger, and strike when it came."

Jane waited.

"The Sura said that when the time came we should find a seer: a person with second sight."

"Not that we'd *get* a seer, Arthur," said Camilla, "that a seer would turn up. Either we or the other side would get her."

"And it looks," said Denniston to Jane, "as if you were the seer."

"But please," said Jane, smiling, "I don't want to be anything so exciting."

Camilla turned to Jane and said, "I gathered from Grace Ironwood that you weren't quite convinced you *were* a seer. I mean you thought it might be ordinary dreams. Do you still think that?"

"It's all so strange and—*beastly*!" said Jane. Her habitual inner prompter was whispering, "Take care. Don't get drawn in. Don't commit yourself to anything." Then an impulse of honesty forced her to add: "As a matter of fact I've had another dream since then. And it turns out to have been true. I saw the murder—Mr. Hingest's murder."

"There you are," said Camilla. "Oh, you *must* come in. You must, you must. We've been wondering all this time exactly where the trouble is going to begin: and now you've seen something within a few miles of Edgestow. In

72

fact, we are apparently in the thick of it already—whatever it is."

"No, Cam, don't," said Denniston. "The Pendragon wouldn't like that. Mrs. Studdock must come in freely. You forget she knows practically nothing at all about us. And we can't tell her much until she has joined. We are, in fact, asking her to take a leap in the dark." He turned to Jane. "It *is* like that," he said, "like getting married, or becoming a monk. You can't know what it's like until you take the plunge." He did not perhaps know the complicated resentments and resistances which his choice of illustrations awoke in Jane.

"What exactly are you asking me to do?" she said.

"To come and see our chief, first of all. And then—well, to join. It would involve making certain promises to him. By the way, what view would Mark take about it?"

"Mark?" said Jane. "How does he come into it?"

"Would he object to your joining—putting yourself under the Head's orders and making the promises and all that?"

"Would he object?" asked Jane. "What on earth would it have to do with him?"

"Well," said Denniston, hesitating a little, "the Head—or the authorities he obeys—have rather old-fashioned notions. He wouldn't like a married woman to come in, if it could be avoided, without her husband's—without consulting——"

"Do you mean I'm to ask Mark's *permission*?" said Jane. The resentment which had been rising and ebbing for several minutes had now overflowed. All this talk of promises and obedience to an unknown Mr. Fisher-King had already repelled her. But the idea of this same person sending her back to get Mark's permission was the climax. For a moment she looked on Mr. Denniston with dislike. She saw him, and Mark, and the Fisher-King man simply as men—complacent, patriarchal figures making arrangements for women as if women were children or bartering them like cattle. ("And so the king promised that if anyone killed the dragon he would *give* him his daughter in marriage.") She was very angry.

"Arthur," said Camilla, "I see a light over there. Do you think it's a bonfire. Let's go for a little walk and look at the fire."

"Oh, do let's," said Jane.

They got out. It was warmer in the open than it had by now become in the car. The fire was big and in its middle life. They stood round it and chatted of indifferent matters for a time.

"I'll tell you what I'll do," said Jane presently. "I won't join your—your—whatever it is. But I'll promise to let you know if I have any more dreams of that sort."

"That is splendid," said Denniston. "And I think it is as much as we had a right to expect."

CHAPTER SIX

FOG

I

ANOTHER day dragged past before Mark was able to see the Deputy Director again. He went to him in a chastened frame of mind, anxious to get the job on almost any terms.

"I have brought back the Form, sir," he said.

"What Form?" asked the Deputy Director.

Mark found he was talking to a new and different Wither. The absent-mindedness was still there, but the courtliness was gone. He said he had understood that Mark had already refused the job. He could not, in any event, renew the offer. He spoke vaguely and alarmingly of strains and frictions, of injudicious behaviour, of the danger of making enemies, of the impossibility that the N.I.C.E. could harbour a person who appeared to have quarrelled with all its members in the first week. After he had hinted and murmured Mark into a sufficient state of dejection he threw him, like a bone to a dog, the suggestion of an appointment for a probationary period at six hundred a year. And Mark took it. He attempted to get answers even then to some of his questions. From whom was he to take orders? Was he to reside at Belbury?

Wither replied, "I think, Mr. Studdock, we have already mentioned elasticity as the keynote of the Institute. Unless you are prepared to treat membership as . . . er . . . a vocation rather than a mere appointment, I could not conscientiously advise you to come to us. There are no watertight compartments. I fear I could not persuade the committee to invent some cut-and-dried position in which you would discharge artificially limited duties and, apart from those, regard your time as your own. Pray allow me to finish, Mr. Studdock. We are, as I have said before, more like a family, or even, perhaps, like a single personality. You must make yourself useful, Mr. Studdock —generally useful. I do not think the Institute could allow anyone to remain in it who grudged this or that piece of service because it fell outside some function which he had chosen to circumscribe by a rigid definition. On the other hand, it would be quite equally disastrous . . . I mean for yourself, Mr. Studdock . . . quite equally disastrous if you allowed yourself to be distracted from your real work by unauthorised collaboration . . . or, worse still, inter-ference . . . with other members. Concentration, Mr. Studdock, concentration. If you avoid both the errors I have mentioned . . . ah, I do not despair of correcting on your behalf certain unfortunate impressions which, we must admit, your behaviour has already produced. No, Mr. Studdock, I can allow no further discussion. Good morn-ing, Mr. Studdock, good morning."

Mark reimbursed himself for the humiliation of this interview by reflecting that if he were not a married man he would not have borne it for a moment. When he went to tea he found that the reward for his submission had already begun. The Fairy signed to him to come and sit beside her.

"You haven't done anything about Alcasan yet?" she asked.

"No," said Mark, "I could come up and look at your materials this afternoon . . . at least as far as I know, for I haven't yet really found out what I'm supposed to be doing."

"Elasticity, sonny, elasticity," said Miss Hardcastle.

II

During the next few days the fog, which covered Edge-stow as well as Belbury, continued, and the grip of the N.I.C.E. on Edgestow was tightening. The disturbance in which the Bracton windows had been broken was taken little notice of in the London papers or even in the *Edgestow*

75

Telegraph. But it was followed by other episodes. There was an indecent assault in one of the mean streets down by the station. There were two "beatings up" in a public-house. There were increasing complaints of threatening and disorderly behaviour on the part of the N.I.C.E. workmen. Wherever one went one was jostled by crowds of strangers. To a little market town like Edgestow even visitors from the next county ranked as aliens: the day-long clamour of Northern, Welsh, and even Irish voices, the shouts, the cat-calls, the songs, the wild faces passing in the fog, were utterly detestable. "There's going to be trouble here" was the comment of many a citizen: and in a few days, "You'd think they *wanted* trouble." It is not recorded who first said, "We need more police." And then at last the *Edgestow Telegraph* took notice. A shy little article appeared suggesting that the local police were incapable of dealing with the new population.

Of all these things Jane took little notice. The dreams continued. There was one recurrent dream in which nothing exactly happened. She seemed indeed to be lying in her own bed. But there was someone who had drawn a chair up to the bedside and sat down to watch. He had a note-book in which he occasionally made an entry. Otherwise he sat still and attentive—like a doctor. She came to know his face infinitely well: the pince-nez, the well-chiselled, rather white features, and the pointed beard. And he must by now know hers equally well: it was certainly herself whom he appeared to be studying. Jane did not write about this to the Dennistons the first time it occurred. Even after the second she delayed until it was too late to post the letter that day. She wanted comfort, but she wanted it, if possible, without going out to St. Anne's and getting drawn into its orbit.

Mark meanwhile was working at the rehabilitation of Alcasan. "I'll put you on to the Captain," said the Fairy. "He'll show you the ropes." That was how Mark came to spend most of his working hours with her second-in-command, Captain O'Hara, a big white-haired man with a handsome face, talking in a Dublin accent. He claimed to be of ancient family and had a seat at Castlemortle. Mark did not really understand his explanations of the dossier, the Q Register, the Sliding File system, and what the Captain called "weeding". The whole selection of facts really remained in O'Hara's hands, and Mark found himself working merely as a writer. His journalism was a success. His articles and letters about Alcasan appeared in papers where he would never have had the *entrée* over his own signature: papers read by millions. He could not help feeling a little thrill of pleasurable excitement.

III

The pleasantest reward which fell to Mark for his obedience was admission to the library. This room, though nominally public, was in practice reserved for what one had learned, at school, to call "bloods" and, at Bracton, "the Progressive Element", and that was why, when Feverstone one evening sidled up to Mark and said, "What about a drink in the library?" Mark smiled and agreed and harboured no resentment for the last conversation he had had with Feverstone.

The circle in the library usually consisted of Feverstone, the Fairy, Filostrato, and—more surprising—Straik. It was balm to Mark's wounds to find that Steele never appeared there. One person whose frequent appearance he did not understand was the silent man with the pince-nez and the pointed beard, Professor Frost. The Deputy Director had a habit of drifting in and sauntering about, creaking and humming as usual. Sometimes he came up to the circle by the fire and listened and looked on: but he seldom said anything. He drifted away, and would return about an hour later and once more potter about the empty parts of the room and once more go away.

The least satisfactory member of the circle in Mark's eyes was Straik. Straik made no effort to adapt himself to the ribald and realistic tone in which his colleagues spoke. He never drank nor smoked. He would sit silent, nursing a threadbare knee. Then—perhaps once in the whole evening—something said would start him off; he would burst into loud and prolonged speech, threatening, denouncing, prophesying, talking, to Mark's great discomfort and bewilderment, about resurrection. "Neither an historical fact nor a fable, but a prophecy. All the miracles . . . shadows of things to come."

After a few evenings Mark ventured to walk into the library on his own; a little uncertain of his reception, yet

77

afraid that if he did not soon assert his right to the *entrée* this modesty might damage him. He knew that the error in either direction is equally fatal.

It was a success. Before he had closed the door behind him all had turned with welcoming faces and Filostrato had said " *Ecco* " and the Fairy, " Here's the very man." A glow of pleasure passed over Mark's whole body.

" How quick can you write two leading articles, Mark? " said Feverstone.

" Can you work all night? " asked Miss Hardcastle.

" I *have* done," said Mark. " What's it all about? "

" All are satisfied? " asked Filostrato. " That it—the disturbance—go forward at once, yes? "

" That's the joke of it," said Feverstone. " She's done her work too well."

" We cannot delay it if we wished," said Straik.

" What are we talking about? " said Mark.

" The disturbances at Edgestow," answered Feverstone.

" Oh. . . . Are they becoming serious? "

" They're going to become serious, sonny," said the Fairy. " And that's the point. The real riot was timed for next week. All this little stuff was only meant to prepare the ground. But it's been going on too well, damn it. The balloon will have to go up to-morrow, or the day after at latest."

" You mean you've *engineered* the disturbances? " said Mark.

" That's a crude way of putting it," said Feverstone.

" It makes no difference," said Filostrato. " This is how things have to be managed."

" Quite," said Miss Hardcastle. " It's always done. Anyone who knows police work will tell you. And as I say, the real thing—the big riot—must take place within the next forty-eight hours. In the meantime, you and I have to get busy about the account of the riot."

" But—what's it all for? "

" Emergency regulations," said Feverstone. " You'll never get the powers we want at Edgestow until the Government declares that a state of emergency exists there."

" Exactly," said Filostrato. " It is folly to talk of peaceful revolutions. Not that the *canaglia* would always resist— often they have to be prodded into it—but until there is

78

the disturbance, the firing, the barricades—no one gets powers to act effectively."

" And the stuff must be all ready to appear in the papers the very day after the riot," said Miss Hardcastle. " That means it must be handed in to the D.D. by six to-morrow morning."

" But how are we to write it to-night if the thing doesn't happen till to-morrow? "

Everyone burst out laughing.

" You'll never manage publicity that way, Mark," said Feverstone.

" No good, sonny," said Miss Hardcastle. " We've got to get on with it at once. Time for one more drink, and you and I'd better go upstairs and begin. We'll get them to give us devilled bones and coffee at two."

This was the first thing Mark had been asked to do which he himself, before he did it, clearly knew to be criminal. But the moment of his consent almost escaped his notice; certainly, there was no struggle, no sense of turning a corner. A few moments later he was trotting upstairs with the Fairy. They passed Cosser on the way. To think that he had once been afraid of Cosser!

IV

At four o'clock Mark sat in the Fairy's office re-reading the last two articles he had written—one for the most respectable of our papers, the other for a more popular organ. The first was as follows:

" While it would be premature to make any final comment on last night's riot at Edgestow, two conclusions seem to emerge from the first accounts with a clarity not likely to be shaken by sub-sequent developments. In the first place, the whole episode will administer a rude shock to any complacency which may still lurk among us as to the enlightenment of our own civilisation. It must, of course, be admitted that the transformation of a university town into a centre of national research cannot be carried out without some friction and some cases of hardship. But the Englishman has always had his own quiet and humorous way of dealing with frictions and has never showed himself unwilling, when the issue is properly put before him, to make sacrifices much greater than those small alterations of habit and sentiment which progress demands of the people of Edgestow. There is no suggestion that the N.I.C.E. has in any way exceeded its powers or failed in consideration and courtesy; and there is little doubt that the starting-point of the disturbances was some quarrel, probably in a public-house, between one of the N.I.C.E. workmen and some local Sir Oracle, and that this petty *fracas* was inflamed, if not exploited, by sectional interests or widespread prejudice.

" It is disquieting to be forced to suspect that the old distrust of planned efficiency and the old jealousy of what is called ' Bureau-cracy ' can be so easily revived; but the will of the nation is behind this magnificent ' peace-effort ', as Mr. Jules so happily described the Institute, and any ill-informed opposition which ventures to try conclusions with it will be, we hope gently, but certainly firmly, resisted.

" The second moral to be drawn from last night's events is a more cheering one. The original proposal to provide the N.I.C.E. with what is misleadingly called its own ' police force ' was viewed with distrust in many quarters. Our readers will remember that while not sharing that distrust, we extended to it a certain sym-pathy, but also insisted that the complexity of modern society rendered it an anachronism to confine the actual execution of the will of society to a body of men whose real function was the prevention and detection of crime: that the police, in fact, must be relieved sooner or later of that growing body of coercive func-tions which do not properly fall within their sphere. The so-called ' Police ' of the N.I.C.E.—who should rather be called its ' Sanitary Executive '—is the characteristically English solution. If any doubt as to the value of such a force existed, it has been amply set at rest by the episodes at Edgestow. The happiest relations seem to have been maintained throughout between the officers of the Institute and the National Police. As an eminent police officer observed to one of our representatives this morning, ' But for the N.I.C.E. Police, things would have taken quite a different turn.' If in the light of these events it is found con-venient to place the whole Edgestow area under the exclusive control of the Institutional ' police ' for some limited period, we do not believe that the British people will have the slightest objection."

The second said much the same with shorter words, more exclamation marks, and in a more truculent manner.

The more often he re-read the articles the better he liked them. It wasn't as if he were taken in by them himself. He was writing with his tongue in his cheek—a phrase that somehow comforted him by making the whole thing appear like a practical joke. And anyway, if he didn't do it, some-one else would. And all the while the child inside him whispered how splendid and how triumphantly grown up it was to be writing, with his tongue in his cheek, articles for great newspapers, against time, " with the printer's devil at the door " and all the inner ring of the N.I.C.E. depending on him, and nobody ever again having the least right to consider him a nonentity or cipher.

v

Jane stretched out her hand in the darkness but did not feel the table which ought to have been there at her bed's head. She discovered that she was not in bed, but standing. There was darkness all about her and intense cold. Groping, she touched uneven surfaces of stone. The place, whatever it was, did not seem large. She groped along one of the walls and struck her foot against something hard. She stooped down and felt. There was a platform or table of stone, about three feet high. And on it? Did she dare to explore? But it would be worse not to. Next moment she bit her lip to save herself from screaming, for she had touched a human foot; a naked foot, dead to judge by its coldness. To go on groping seemed the hardest thing she had ever done, but she was impelled to do it. The corpse was clothed in some very coarse stuff which was also uneven, as though it were heavily embroidered. It must be a very large man. On his chest the texture suddenly changed—as if the skin of some hairy animal had been laid over the coarse robe; then she realised that the hair really belonged to a beard. It was only a dream; she could bear it: but it was so dreary, as if she had slipped through a cleft in the present, down into some cold pit of the remote past. If only someone would come quickly and let her out. And immediately she had a picture of someone, someone bearded but also divinely young, someone golden and strong and warm coming with a mighty earth-shaking tread into that black place. At this point she woke.

She went into Edgestow immediately after breakfast to hunt for someone who would replace Mrs. Maggs. At the top of Market Street something happened which finally determined her to go to St. Anne's that very day. She came to a place where a big car was standing beside the pavement, an N.I.C.E. car. Just as she reached it a man came out of a shop, cut across her path to the car, and got in. He was so close to her that, despite the fog, she saw him very clearly. She would have known him, anywhere:

81

not Mark's face, not her own face in a mirror, was by now more familiar. She saw the pointed beard, the pince-nez, the face which somehow reminded her of a waxworks face. She had no need to think what she would do. Her body, walking quickly past, seemed of itself to have decided that it was heading for the station and thence for St. Anne's. It was something different from fear that drove her. It was a total revulsion from this man on all levels of her being.

The train was blessedly warm, her compartment empty, the fact of sitting down delightful. The slow journey through the fog almost sent her to sleep. She hardly thought about St. Anne's until she found herself there.

CHAPTER SEVEN

THE PENDRAGON

I

BEFORE she reached the Manor Jane met Mr. Denniston and told him her story as they walked. As they entered the house they met Mrs. Maggs.

"What? Mrs. Studdock! Fancy!" said Mrs. Maggs.

"Yes, Ivy," said Denniston, "and bringing great news. We must see Grace at once."

A few minutes later Jane found herself once more in Grace Ironwood's room. Miss Ironwood and the Dennistons sat facing her, and when Ivy Maggs brought in some tea she did not go away again, but sat down too.

"You need not mind Ivy, young lady," said Miss Ironwood. "She is one of our company."

There was a pause.

"We have your letter of the 10th," continued Miss Ironwood, "describing your dream of the man with the pointed beard sitting making notes in your bedroom. Perhaps I ought to tell you that he wasn't really there: at least, the Director does not think it possible. But he was really studying *you*. He was getting information about you from some other source which, unfortunately, was not visible to you in the dream."

"Will you tell us, if you don't mind," said Mr. Denniston, "what you were telling me as we came along?"

Jane told them about the dream of the corpse (if it was a corpse) in the dark place and how she had met the bearded man that morning in Market Street: and at once she was aware of having created intense interest.

Miss Ironwood opened a drawer and handed a photograph across to Jane and asked, "Do you recognise that?"

"Yes," said Jane in a low voice; "that is the man I dreamed of and the man I saw this morning in Edgestow."

It was a good photograph, and beneath it was the name Augustus Frost.

"In the second place," continued Miss Ironwood, "are you prepared to see the Director . . . *now*?"

"Well—yes, if you like."

"In that case, Camilla," said Miss Ironwood to Mrs. Denniston, "you had better go and tell him what we have just heard and find out if he is well enough to meet Mrs. Studdock."

The others rose and left the room.

"I have very little doubt," said Miss Ironwood, "that the Director will see you."

Jane said nothing.

"And at that interview," continued the other, "you will, I presume, be called upon to make a final decision."

Jane gave a little cough which had no other purpose than to dispel a certain air of unwelcome solemnity.

"And secondly," said Miss Ironwood, "I must ask you to remember that he is often in great pain."

"If Mr. Fisher-King is not well enough to see visitors . . .," said Jane vaguely.

"You must excuse me," said Miss Ironwood, "for impressing these points upon you. I am the only doctor in our company, and am responsible for protecting him as far as I can. If you will now come with me I will show you to the Blue Room."

She rose and held the door open for Jane. They passed out into the plain, narrow passage and thence up shallow steps into a large entrance hall whence a fine Georgian staircase led to the upper floors. On the first floor they found a little square place with white pillars where Camilla sat waiting for them. There was a door behind her.

"He will see her," she said to Miss Ironwood, getting up.

As Miss Ironwood raised her hand to knock on the door, Jane thought to herself, " Be careful. Don't get let in for anything. All these long passages and low voices will make a fool of you if you don't look out." Next moment she found herself going in. It was light—it seemed all windows. And it was warm—a fire blazed on the hearth. And blue was the prevailing colour. She was annoyed, and in a way ashamed, to see that Miss Ironwood was curtseying. " I won't," contended in Jane's mind with " I can't " : for she couldn't.

" This is the young lady, sir," said Miss Ironwood.

Jane looked; and instantly her world was unmade.

On a sofa before her, with one foot bandaged as if he had a wound, lay what appeared to be a boy, twenty years old.

On one of the long window-sills a tame jackdaw was walking up and down. Winter sunlight poured through the glass; apparently one was above the fog here. All the light in the room seemed to run towards the gold hair and the gold beard of the wounded man.

Of course he was not a boy—how could she have thought so? The fresh skin on his cheeks and hands had suggested the idea. But no boy could have so full a beard. And no boy could be so strong. It was manifest that the grip of those hands would be inescapable, and imagination suggested that those arms and shoulders could support the whole house. Miss Ironwood at her side struck her as a little old woman, shrivelled and pale—a thing you could have blown away.

Pain came and went in his face : sudden jabs of sickening pain. But as lightning goes through the darkness and the darkness closes up again and shows no trace, so the tranquillity of his countenance swallowed up each shock of torture. How could she have thought him young? Or old either? It came over her that this face was of no age at all. She had, or so she had believed, disliked bearded faces except for old men. But that was because she had long since forgotten the imagined Arthur of her childhood —and the imagined Solomon too. Solomon . . . for the first time in many years the bright solar blend of king and lover and magician which hangs about that name stole back upon her mind. For the first time in all those years she tasted the word *King* itself with all its linked associations of battle, marriage, priesthood, mercy, and power. Next

84

moment she was once more the ordinary social Jane, flushed and confused to find that she had been staring rudely (at least she hoped that rudeness would be the main impression) at a total stranger. But her world was unmade. Anything might happen now.

"Thank you, Grace," the man was saying. And the voice also seemed to be like sunlight and gold. "You must forgive me for not getting up, Mrs. Studdock," it said. "My foot is hurt."

And Jane heard her own voice saying, "Yes, sir," soft and chastened like Miss Ironwood's. She had meant to say, "Good morning, Mr. Fisher-King," in an easy tone. But her world was unmade: anything might happen now.

"Do you wish me to remain, sir?" said Miss Ironwood.

"No, Grace," said the Director, "I don't think you need stay. Thank you."

II

For a few minutes after Grace Ironwood had left them, Jane hardly took in what the Director was saying. It was not that her attention wandered: on the contrary, her attention was so fixed on him that it defeated itself.

"I—I beg your pardon," she said, wishing that she did not keep on turning red like a schoolgirl.

"I was saying," he answered, "that you have already done us the greatest service. We knew that one of the most dangerous attacks ever made upon the human race was coming very soon and in this island. We had an idea that Belbury might be connected with it. But we were not certain. That is why your information is so valuable. But in another way, it presents us with a difficulty. We had hoped you would be able to join us."

"Can I not, sir?" said Jane.

"It is difficult," said the Director, "you see, your husband is in Belbury."

Jane glanced up. It had been on the tip of her tongue to say "Do you mean that Mark is in any danger?" But she had realised that anxiety about Mark did not, in fact, make any part of the emotions she was feeling, and that to reply thus would be hypocrisy. It was a sort of scruple she had not often felt. "What do you mean?" she said.

85

"Why," said the Director, "it would be hard for the same person to be the wife of an official in the N.I.C.E. and also a member of my company."

"You mean you couldn't trust me?"

"I mean that, in the circumstances, you and I and your husband could not all be trusting one another."

Jane bit her lip in anger. Why should Mark and his affairs intrude themselves at such a moment?

"I must do what I think right, mustn't I?" she said softly. "I mean—if Mark—if my husband—is on the wrong side, I can't let that make any difference to what *I* do. Can I?"

"You are thinking about what is *right*?" said the Director. Jane started, and flushed. She had not been thinking about that.

"Of course," said the Director, "things might come to such a point that you would be justified in coming here, even against his will, even secretly. It depends on how close the danger is—to us all, and to you personally."

"I thought the danger was right on top of us now . . ."

"That is the question," said the Director, with a smile. "I am not allowed to be *too* prudent. I am not allowed to use desperate remedies until desperate diseases are really apparent. It looks as if you will have to go back. You will, no doubt, be seeing your husband again fairly soon. I think you must make at least one effort to detach him from the N.I.C.E."

"But how can I, sir?" said Jane. "What have I to say to him. He'd think it all nonsense." As she said it she wondered, "Did that sound cunning?" then, "*Was* it cunning?"

"No," said the Director. "And you must not mention me nor the company at all. We have put our lives in your hands. You must simply ask him to leave Belbury. You must put it on your own wishes."

"Mark never takes any notice of what I say," answered Jane.

"Perhaps," said the Director, "you have never asked anything as you will be able to ask this. Do you not *want* to save him as well as yourself?"

Jane ignored this question. She began speaking rapidly. "Don't send me back," she said. "I am all alone at home, with terrible dreams. It isn't as if Mark and I saw much of one another at the best of times. I am so unhappy. He won't care whether I come here or not."

" Are you unhappy *now*? " said the Director.

Suddenly she ceased at last to think how her words might make him think of her, and answered, " No. But," she added after a short pause, " it will be worse now, if I go back."

" Will it? "

" But is it really necessary? " she began. " I don't think I look on marriage quite as you do——"

" Child," said the Director, " it is not a question of how you or I look on marriage but how my Masters look on it,"

" They would never think of finding out first whether Mark and I believed in their ideas of marriage? "

" Well—no," said the Director with a curious smile. " They wouldn't think of doing that."

" And would it make no difference to them what a marriage was actually like . . . whether it was a success? Whether the woman loved her husband? " Jane had not intended to say this. " But I suppose you will say I oughtn't to have told you that," she added.

" My dear child," said the Director, " you have been telling me that ever since your husband was mentioned."

" Does it make no difference? "

" I suppose," said the Director, " it would depend on how he lost your love."

Jane was silent.

" I don't know," she said at last. " I suppose our marriage was just a mistake."

The Director said nothing.

" What would you—what would the people you are talking of—say about a case like that? "

" I will tell you if you really want to know," said the Director.

" Please," said Jane reluctantly.

" They would say," he answered, " that you do not fail in obedience through lack of love, but have lost love because you never attempted obedience."

Something in Jane that would normally have reacted to such a remark with anger was banished by the fact that the word obedience—but certainly not obedience to Mark— came over her, in that room, like a strange oriental perfume, perilous, seductive. . . .

" Stop it ! " said the Director sharply.

Jane stared at him, open-mouthed: the exotic fragrance faded away.

" You were saying, my dear? " resumed the Director.

" I thought love meant equality," she said.

" Ah, equality ! " said the Director. " Yes; we must all be guarded by equal rights from one another's greed, because we are fallen. Just as we wear clothes for the same reason. But the naked body should be there underneath the clothes. Equality is not the deepest thing, you know."

" I always thought that was just what it was. I thought it was in their souls that people were equal."

" You were mistaken; that is the last place where they are equal. Equality before the law, equality of incomes—that is very well. Equality guards life; it doesn't make it. It is medicine, not food."

" But surely in marriage . . .? "

" Worse and worse," said the Director. " Courtship knows nothing of it; nor does fruition. They never warned you. No one has ever told you that obedience—humility—is an erotic necessity. You are putting equality just where it ought not to be. As to your coming here, that may admit of some doubt. For the present, I must send you back. You can come out and see us. In the meantime, talk to your husband and I will talk to my authorities."

" When will you be seeing them? "

" They come to me when they please. But we've been talking too solemnly about obedience all this time. I'd like to show you some of its drolleries. You are not——"

He broke off sharply and a new look came into his eyes. At the same moment a new thought came into Jane's mind; an odd one. She was thinking of hugeness. Or rather, she was not thinking of it. She was, in some strange fashion, experiencing it. Something intolerably big, something from Brobdingnag, was pressing on her, was approaching, was almost in the room. She felt herself shrinking, suffocated, emptied of all power and virtue. She darted a glance at the Director which was really a cry for help, and that glance, in some inexplicable way, revealed him as being, like herself, a very small object. The whole room was a tiny place, a mouse's hole, and it seemed to her to be tilted aslant—as though the insupportable mass and splendour of this formless hugeness, in approaching, had knocked it askew. She heard the Director's voice.

"Quick," he said gently, "these are my Masters. You must leave me now. This is no place for us small ones, but I am inured. Go!"

III

During her homeward journey Jane was so divided that one might say there were three, if not four, Janes in the compartment.

The first was a Jane simply receptive of the Director, recalling every word and every look, and delighting in them—a Jane taken utterly off her guard and swept away on the flood-tide of an experience which she could not control. For she was trying to control it; that was the function of the second Jane. This second Jane regarded the first with disgust, as the kind of woman whom she had always particularly despised. To have surrendered without terms at the mere voice and look of this stranger, to have abandoned that prim little grasp on her own destiny, that perpetual reservation . . . the thing was degrading, uncivilised.

The third Jane was a new and unexpected visitant. Risen from some unknown region of grace or heredity, it uttered things which Jane had often heard before but which had never seemed to be connected with real life. If it had told her that her feelings about the Director were wrong, she would not have been very surprised. But it did not. It blamed her for not having similar feelings about Mark. It was Mark who had made the fatal mistake; she must be "nice" to Mark. The Director insisted on it. At the moment when her mind was most filled with another man there arose a resolution to give Mark much more than she had ever given him before, and a feeling that in so doing she would be really giving it to the Director. And this produced such a confusion of sensations that the whole inner debate became indistinct and flowed over into the larger experience of the fourth Jane, who was Jane herself.

This fourth and supreme Jane was simply in the state of joy. The other three had no power upon her, for she was in the sphere of Jove, amid light and music and festal pomp, brimmed with life and radiant in health, jocund and clothed in shining garments. She reflected with surprise how long it was since music had played any part in her life, and resolved to listen to many chorales by Bach on the gramophone that evening. She rejoiced also in her hunger and thirst and decided that she would make herself buttered toast for tea—a great deal of buttered toast. And she rejoiced also in the consciousness of her own beauty; for she had the sensation—it may have been false in fact, but it had nothing to do with vanity—that it was growing and expanding like a magic flower with every minute that passed. Her beauty belonged to the Director. It belonged to him so completely that he could order it to be given to another.

As the train came into Edgestow Station Jane was just deciding that she would not try to get a 'bus. She would enjoy the walk. And then—what on earth was all this? The platform, usually almost deserted at this hour, was like a London platform on a bank holiday. "Here you are, mate!" cried a voice as she opened the door, and half a dozen men crowded into her carriage so roughly that for a moment she could not get out. She found difficulty in crossing the platform. People seemed to be going in all directions at once—angry, rough, and excited people. "Get back into the train, quick!" shouted someone. "Get out of the station, if you're not travelling," bawled another voice. And from outside, beyond the station, came a great roaring noise like the noise of a football crowd.

IV

Hours later, bruised, frightened, and tired, Jane found herself in a street she did not even know, surrounded by N.I.C.E. policemen and a few of their females, the Waips. A couple of the men—one seemed to meet them everywhere except where the rioting was most violent—had shouted out, "You can't go down there, miss." But as they then turned their backs, Jane had made a bolt for it. They caught her. And that was how she found herself being taken into a lighted room and questioned by a uniformed woman with short grey hair, a square face, and an unlighted cheroot. The woman with the cheroot took no particular interest until Jane had given her name. Then Miss Hardcastle looked her in the face for the first time, and Jane felt quite a new sensation. She was already tired and frightened, but this was different. The face of the other woman affected her as the face of some men—fat men with small, greedy eyes and strange, disquieting smiles—had affected her when she was in her 'teens.

"Jane Studdock," said the Fairy. "You'll be the wife of my friend Mark." While she spoke she was writing something on a green form. "*That's* all right. Now, just one question, dear. What were you doing down here at this time of night?"

"I had just come off a train."

"And where had you been, honey?"

Jane said nothing.

"You hadn't been getting up to mischief while Hubby was away, had you?"

"Will you please let me go?" said Jane. "I want to get home. I am very tired and it's very late."

"But you're not going home," said Miss Hardcastle. "You're coming out to Belbury."

"My husband has said nothing about my joining him there."

Miss Hardcastle nodded. "That was one of his mistakes. But you're coming with *us*."

"What do you mean?"

"It's an arrest, honey," said Miss Hardcastle, holding out the piece of green paper on which she had been writing.

"O-oh!" screamed Jane suddenly, overcome with a sensation of nightmare, and made a dash for the door. A moment later she came to her senses and found herself held by the two policewomen.

"What a naughty temper!" said Miss Hardcastle playfully. "But we'll put the nasty men outside, shall we?" She said something and the policemen removed themselves.

Jane felt that a protection had been withdrawn from her. "Well," said Miss Hardcastle, addressing the two uniformed girls. "Let's see. Quarter to one . . . and all going nicely. I think, Daisy, we can afford a little stand-easy. Be careful, Kitty, make your grip under her shoulder a little tighter." While she was speaking Miss Hardcastle was undoing her belt. She removed the cheroot from her mouth, lit it, blew a cloud of smoke in Jane's direction, and addressed her. "Where had you been by that train?" she said.

And Jane said nothing; partly because she could not speak, and partly because she now knew beyond all doubt that these were the enemies whom the Director was fighting against, and one must tell them nothing. She heard Miss Hardcastle say, " I think, Kitty dear, you and Daisy had better bring her round here." The two women forced her round to the other side of the table, and she saw Miss Hardcastle sitting with her legs wide apart; long leather-clad legs projecting from beneath her short skirt. The women forced her on, with a skilled, quiet increase of pressure, until she stood between Miss Hardcastle's feet: whereupon Miss Hardcastle brought her feet together so that she had Jane's ankles pinioned between her own. And Miss Hardcastle stared at her, smiling and blowing smoke in her face.

" Do you know," said Miss Hardcastle at last, " you're rather a pretty little thing in your way."

There was another silence.

" Where had you been by that train? " said Miss Hardcastle.

Suddenly she leant forward and, after very carefully turning down the edge of Jane's dress, thrust the lighted end of the cheroot against her shoulder. After that there was another pause and another silence.

" Where had you been by that train? " said Miss Hardcastle.

How many times this happened Jane could never remember. But there came a time when Miss Hardcastle was talking not to her but to one of the women.

" What *are* you fussing about, Daisy? " she was saying.

" I was only saying, ma'am, it was five past one."

" How time flies, doesn't it, Daisy? Aren't you comfortable, Daisy? You're not getting tired, holding a little bit of a thing like her? "

" No, ma'am, thank you. But you did say, ma'am, you'd meet Captain O'Hara at one sharp."

" Captain O'Hara? " said Miss Hardcastle dreamily at first, and then louder, like one waking from a dream. Next moment she had jumped up and was putting on her belt. " Bless the girl! " she said. " Why didn't you remind me before? "

" You don't like us to interrupt, ma'am, sometimes, when you're examining," said the girl sulkily.

" Don't argue! " shouted Miss Hardcastle, wheeling

round and hitting her cheek a resounding blow with the palm of her hand. " Get the prisoner into the car."

A few seconds later (there seemed to be room for five in the car) Jane found herself gliding through the darkness. " Better go through the town as little as possible, Joe," said Miss Hardcastle's voice. " It'll be pretty lively by now." There seemed to be all sorts of strange noises and lights about. At places, too, there seemed to be a great many people. Then there came a moment when Jane found that the car had drawn up. " What the hell are you stopping for? " said Miss Hardcastle. For a second or two there was no answer from the driver except grunts and the noise of unsuccessful attempts to start up the engine. The street was empty but, to judge by the noise, it was near some other street which was very full and very angry. The man got out, swearing under his breath, and opened the bonnet of the car. Miss Hardcastle continued pouring abuse on him. The noise grew louder. Suddenly the driver straightened himself and turned his face towards Miss Hardcastle.

" Look here, miss," he said, " that's about enough, see? "

" Don't you try taking that line with me, Joe," said Miss Hardcastle, " or you'll find me saying a little word about you to the ordinary police."

" For the lord's sake speak to him nicely, ma'am," wailed Kitty. " They're coming. We'll catch it proper." And in fact men running, by twos and threes, had begun to trickle into the street.

" Foot it, girls," said Miss Hardcastle. " Sharp's the word. This way."

Jane found herself hustled out of the car and hurried along between Daisy and Kitty. Miss Hardcastle walked in front. The party darted across the street and up an alley on the far side.

The alley turned out to be a dead end. Miss Hardcastle stood still for a moment. Unlike her subordinates, she did not seem to be frightened, but only pleasantly excited.

The shouting in the street they had left had grown louder. Suddenly it became much louder still and angrier.

" They've caught Joe," said Miss Hardcastle. " If he can make himself heard he'll send them up here. Blast! This means losing the prisoner. Quick. We must go down into the crowd separately. Keep your heads. Try to get to

Billingham at the cross-roads. Ta-ta, Babs! The quieter you keep, the less likely we are to meet again."

Miss Hardcastle set off at once. Jane saw her stand for a few seconds on the fringes of the crowd and then disappear into it. The two girls hesitated and then followed. Jane sat down on a doorstep. She was deadly cold and a little sick. But, above all, tired; so tired she could drop asleep almost. . . .

She shook herself. There was complete silence all about her: she was colder than she had ever been before, and her limbs ached. "I believe I *have* been asleep," she thought. She put her hand in the pocket of the coat which Daisy and Kitty had flung round her and found a slab of chocolate. She was ravenous and began munching. Just as she finished a car drew up.

"Are you all right?" said a man, poking his head out.

"Were you hurt in the riot?" said a woman's voice from within.

The man stared at her and then got out. "I say," he said, "you don't look too good." Then he turned and spoke to the woman inside. The unknown couple made her sit in the car and gave her brandy. Where was her home?

And Jane, somewhat to her surprise, heard her own voice very sleepily answering, "The Manor, at St. Anne's."

"That's fine," said the man. "We have to pass it."

Then Jane fell asleep at once again, and awoke only to find herself entering a lighted doorway and being received by a woman in pyjamas and an overcoat who turned out to be Mrs. Maggs. But she was too tired to remember how she got to bed.

CHAPTER EIGHT

MOONLIGHT AT BELBURY

I

"I AM the last person, Miss Hardcastle," said the Deputy Director, "to wish to interfere with your—er—private pleasures. But, really! . . ." It was some hours before breakfast-time and he and the Fairy were standing in his study.

"She can't be far away," said Fairy Hardcastle. "We'll pick her up some other time. It was well worth trying. If I'd got out of her where she'd been—and I should have if I'd had a few minutes longer—why, it might have turned out to be enemy headquarters."

"It was hardly a suitable occasion—— " began Wither, but she interrupted him.

"We haven't so much time to waste, you know. You tell me Frost is already complaining that the woman's mind is less accessible. That means she's falling under the influence of the other side. Where'll we be if you lose touch with her mind before I've got her body locked up here?"

"I am always, of course," said Wither, "most ready and —er—interested to hear expressions of your own opinions and would not for a moment deny that they are, in certain respects, of course, if not in all, of a very real value. On the other hand, there are matters . . . The Head will, I fear, take the view that you have exceeded your authority. I do not say that I necessarily agree with him. But we must *all* agree——"

"Oh, cut it out, Wither!" said the Fairy, seating herself on the side of the table. "Try that game on the Steeles and Stones. It's no bloody good trying the elasticity stunt on me. It was a golden opportunity, running into that girl. If I hadn't taken it you'd have talked about lack of initiative. We've got to get the girl, haven't we?"

"But not by an arrest. If a mere arrest could have secured the—er—goodwill and collaboration of Mrs. Studdock, we should hardly have embarrassed ourselves with the presence of her husband."

"I couldn't tell that the bucking car was going to break down, could I?"

"I do not think," said Wither, "the Head could be induced to regard that as the only miscarriage. Once the slightest resistance on this woman's part developed, it was not, in my opinion, reasonable to expect success by the method you employed. I always deplore anything that is not perfectly humane: but that is quite consistent with the position that if more drastic expedients have to be used then they must be used thoroughly. *Moderate* pain, such as any ordinary degree of endurance can resist, is always a mistake. I should not be doing my duty if I failed to remind you that complaints from that quarter have already been made, though not, of course, minuted, as to your tendency to allow a certain—er—emotional excitement in the disciplinary side of your work to distract you from the demands of policy."

"You won't find anyone can do a job like mine well unless they get some kick out of it," said the Fairy sulkily. "Anyway, what does the Head want to see me *now* for? I've been on my feet the whole bloody night. I might be allowed a bath and some breakfast."

"The path of duty, Miss Hardcastle," said Wither, "can never be an easy one."

"Well, I must have something to drink before I go in."

Wither held out his hands in deprecation.

"Come on, Wither. I *must*," said Miss Hardcastle.

"You don't think he'll smell it?" said Wither.

"I'm not going in without it, anyway," said she.

The old man unlocked his cupboard and gave her whisky. Then the two left the study and went a long way, right over to the other side of the house where it joined on to the actual Blood Transfusion Offices. At last they came to a place where the lights were on and there was a mixture of animal and chemical smells, and then to a door which was opened to them after they had parleyed through a speaking-tube. Filostrato, wearing a white coat, confronted them in the doorway.

"Enter," said Filostrato. "He expect you for some time."

"Is it in a bad temper?" said Miss Hardcastle.

"You are to go in at once," said Filostrato, "as soon as you have made yourselves ready."

"Stop! Half a moment," said Miss Hardcastle suddenly.

"What is it? Be quick, please," said Filostrato.

"I'm going to be sick."

"You cannot be sick here. Go back. I will give you some X54 at once."

"It's all right now," said Miss Hardcastle. "It was only momentary. It'd take more than this to upset me."

"Silence, please," said the Italian. "Do not attempt to open the second door until my assistant has shut the first one behind you. Do not speak more than you can help. Do not say yes when you are given an order. The Head will assume your obedience. Do not get too close. Now!"

Long after sunrise there came into Jane's sleeping mind a sensation which, had she put it into words, would have sung, " Be glad thou sleeper and thy sorrow offcast. I am the gate to all good adventure." Sometime after this Mrs. Maggs came in and lit the fire and brought breakfast.

" It's ever so nice, us both being here, isn't it, Mrs. Studdock? " she said.

Shortly after breakfast came Miss Ironwood. She examined and dressed the burns, which were not serious.

" You can get up in the afternoon, if you like, Mrs. Studdock," she said. " What would you like to read? "

" I'd like *Mansfield Park*, please," said Jane, " and Shakespeare's *Sonnets*."

Having been provided with reading matter, she comfortably went to sleep again.

When Mrs. Maggs looked in at about four o'clock Jane said she would like to get up.

" All right, Mrs. Studdock," said Mrs. Maggs, " just as you like. I'll bring you along a nice cup of tea in a minute and then I'll get the bathroom ready for you. There's a bathroom next door almost, only I'll have to get that Mr. Bultitude out of it. He's that lazy, and he *will* sit there all day when it's cold."

As soon as Mrs. Maggs had gone, however, Jane decided to get up. She felt that her social abilities were quite equal to dealing with the eccentric Mr. Bultitude. Accordingly, she put on her coat, took her towel, and proceeded to explore; and that was why Mrs. Maggs, coming upstairs with the tea a moment later, saw Jane emerge from the bathroom with a white face and slam the door behind her.

" Oh dear! " said Mrs. Maggs, bursting into laughter. " I ought to have told you. Never mind. I'll soon have him out of that." She set the tea-tray down on the passage floor and turned to the bathroom.

" Is it safe? " asked Jane.

" Oh yes, he's *safe* alright," said Mrs. Maggs. With that she opened the bathroom door. Inside, sitting up on its hunkers beside the bath, was a great, snuffly, wheezy, beady-eyed, loose-skinned, gor-bellied brown bear, which, after a great many reproaches, exhortations, pushes, and blows from Mrs. Maggs, heaved up its enormous bulk and came slowly out into the passage. "Why don't you go out and take some exercise this lovely afternoon, you great lazy thing?" said Mrs. Maggs. "Don't be frightened, Mrs. Studdock. He'll let you stroke him."

Jane extended a hesitant and unconvincing hand to touch the animal's back, but Mr. Bultitude was sulking, and without a glance at Jane continued his slow walk along the passage to a point about ten yards away, where he quite suddenly sat down. Everyone on the floor below must have known that Mr. Bultitude had sat down.

"Is it really safe to have a creature like that loose about the house?" said Jane.

"Mrs. Studdock," said Ivy Maggs with solemnity, "if the Director wanted to have a tiger about the house it would be safe. There isn't a creature in the place that would go for another or for us once he's had his little talk with them. Just the same as he does with us. You'll see."

"If you would put the tea in my room . . ." said Jane rather coldly, and went towards the bathroom.

"Well," said Mrs. Maggs, "you'll find us in the kitchen, I expect, Mother Dimble and me and the rest."

"Is Mrs. Dimble staying in the house?" asked Jane with a slight emphasis on the *Mrs.*

"*Mother* Dimble we all call her here," said Mrs. Maggs. "And I'm sure she won't mind you doing the same."

When Jane had washed and dressed herself she set out to look for the inhabited rooms. When she reached the hall she saw at once where the back premises of the house must lie—down two steps and along a paved passage, and then, guided by voices and other sounds, to the kitchen itself.

A wide, open hearth glowing with burning wood lit up the comfortable form of Mrs. Dimble, who was seated at one side of it, apparently engaged in preparing vegetables. Mrs. Maggs and Camilla were doing something at a stove and in a doorway, which led to the scullery, a tall, grizzle-headed man, who wore gum-boots and seemed to have just come from the garden, was drying his hands.

"Come in, Jane," said Mother Dimble. "We're not expecting you to do any work to-day. This is Mr. Mac-Phee—who has no right to be here, but he'd better be introduced to you."

Mr. MacPhee, having finished the drying process and carefully hung the towel behind the door, advanced rather ceremoniously and shook hands with Jane. His own hand was very large and coarse in texture, and he had a shrewd, hard-featured face.

" I am very glad to see you, Mrs. Studdock," he said, in what Jane took to be a Scotch accent, though it was really that of an Ulsterman.

" Don't believe a word he says, Jane," said Mother Dimble. " He's your prime enemy. He doesn't believe in your dreams."

" Mrs. Dimble," said MacPhee, " I have repeatedly explained to you the distinction between a personal feeling of confidence and a logical satisfaction of the claims of evidence."

" Of course," said Jane vaguely, and a little confused. " I'm sure you have a right to your own opinions."

All the women laughed as MacPhee in a somewhat louder tone replied, " Mrs. Studdock, I have *no* opinions— on any subject in the world. I state the facts and exhibit the implications. If everyone indulged in fewer opinions " (he pronounced the word with emphatic disgust) " there'd be less silly talking and printing in the world."

" I know who talks most in this house," said Mrs. Maggs, somewhat to Jane's surprise.

The Ulsterman eyed the last speaker with an unaltered face while producing a small pewter box from his pocket and helping himself to a pinch of snuff.

" What are you waiting for, anyway ? " said Mrs. Maggs. " Women's day in the kitchen to-day."

" I was wondering," said MacPhee, " whether you had a cup of tea saved for me."

" And why didn't you come in at the right time, then ? " said Mrs. Maggs. Jane noticed that she talked to him much as she had talked to the bear.

" I was busy," said the other, seating himself at one end of the table ; and added after a pause, " trenching celery."

" What is ' women's day ' in the kitchen ? " asked Jane of Mother Dimble.

" There are no servants here," said Mother Dimble, " and we all do the work. The women do it one day and the men the next. . . . What ? . . . No, it's a very sensible arrangement. The Director's idea is that men and women can't do housework together without quarrelling."

"The cardinal difficulty," said MacPhee, "in collaboration between the sexes is that women speak a language without nouns. If two men are doing a bit of work one will say to the other, 'Put this bowl inside the bigger bowl which you'll find on the top shelf of the green cupboard.' The female for this is, 'Put that in the other one in there.' There is consequently a phatic hiatus."

"There's your tea now, and I'll go and get you a piece of cake," said Ivy Maggs, and left the room.

Jane took advantage of this to say to Mother Dimble in a lower voice, "Mrs. Maggs seems to make herself very much at home here."

"My dear, she *is* at home here."

"As a maid, you mean?"

"Well, no more than anyone else. She's here chiefly because her house has been taken from her. She had nowhere else to go."

"You mean she is . . . one of the Director's charities."

"Certainly that. Why do you ask?"

At that moment the door opened and a voice from behind it said, "Well, go in then, if you're going." Thus admonished, a very fine jackdaw hopped into the room, followed, firstly, by Mr. Bultitude and, secondly, by Arthur Denniston.

"Dr. Dimble's just come back, Mother Dimble," said Denniston. "But he's had to go straight to the Blue Room. And the Director wants you to go to him, too, MacPhee."

III

Mark sat down to lunch that day in good spirits. Everyone reported that the riot had gone off most satisfactorily, and he had enjoyed reading his own accounts of it in the morning papers. His morning, too, had involved a conversation with Frost, the Fairy, and Wither himself, about the future of Edgestow. All agreed that the Government would follow the almost unanimous opinion of the Nation (as expressed in the newspapers) and put it temporarily under the control of the Institutional Police. An emergency governor of Edgestow must be appointed. Feverstone was the obvious man. As a Member of Parliament he represented the Nation, as a Fellow of Bracton he represented the

University, as a member of the Institute he represented the Institute; the articles on this subject which Mark was to write that afternoon would almost write themselves. And Mark had (as he would have put it) " got to know " Frost. He knew that there is in almost every organisation some quiet, inconspicuous person whom the small fry suppose to be of no importance but who is really one of the main-springs. Even to recognise such people shows that one has made progress. There was, to be sure, a cold, fish-like quality about Frost which Mark did not like and something even repulsive about the regularity of his features. But the pleasures of conversation were coming, for Mark, to have less and less connection with his spontaneous liking of the people he talked to. He was aware of this change, and welcomed it as a sign of maturity.

Wither had thawed in a most encouraging manner. At the end of the conversation he had taken Mark aside, spoken vaguely but paternally of the great work he was doing, and finally asked after his wife. The D.D. hoped there was no truth in the rumour which had reached him that she was suffering from—er—some nervous disorder. " Who the devil has been telling him that? " thought Mark. " Because," said Wither, " it had occurred to me, in view of the great pressure of work which rests on you at present and the difficulty, therefore, of your being at home as much as we should all (for your sake) wish, that in *your* case the Institute might be induced . . . I am speaking in a quite informal way . . . that we should all be delighted to wel-come Mrs. Studdock here."

Until the D.D. said this Mark had not realised that there was nothing he would dislike so much as having Jane at Belbury. Her mere presence would have made all the laughter of the Inner Ring sound metallic, unreal; and what he now regarded as common prudence would seem to her, and through her to himself, mere flattery, back-biting, and toad eating. His mind sickened at the thought of trying to teach Jane that she must help to keep Wither in a good temper. He excused himself vaguely to the D.D., with profuse thanks, and got away as quickly as he could.

That afternoon, while he was having tea, Fairy Hard-castle came and leaned over the back of his chair and said:

" *You've* torn it, Studdock."

" What's the matter now, Fairy? " said he.

" I can't make out what's the matter with *you*. Have you made up your mind to annoy the Old Man? Because it's a dangerous game, you know."

" What on earth are you talking about? "

" Well, here we've all been working on your behalf, and this morning we thought we'd succeeded. He was talking about giving you the appointment originally intended for you and waiving the probationary period. Not a cloud in the sky: and then you have five minutes' chat with him, and in that time you've managed to undo it all."

" What the devil's wrong with him this time? "

" Well *you* ought to know! Didn't he say something about bringing your wife here? "

" Yes he did. What about it? "

" And what did you say? "

" I said not to bother about it . . . and, of course, thanked him very much and all that."

The Fairy whistled. " Don't you see, honey," she said, gently rapping Mark's scalp with her knuckles, " that you could hardly have made a worse bloomer? It was a most terrific concession for him to make. He's never done it to anyone else. He's burbling away now about lack of confidence. Says he's ' hurt '; takes your refusal as a sign that you are not really ' settled ' here."

" But that is sheer madness. I mean . . ."

" Why the blazes couldn't you tell him you'd have your wife here? "

" Isn't that my own business? "

" Don't you want to have her? You're not very polite to little wifie, Studdock. And they tell me she's a damned pretty girl."

At that moment the form of Wither, slowly sauntering in their direction, became apparent to both, and the conversation ended.

At dinner he sat next to Filostrato, and as they rose from the table he whispered in Mark's ear, " I would not advise the Library for you to-night. You understand? Come and have a little conversation in my room."

Mark followed him, glad that in this new crisis with the D.D. Filostrato was apparently still his friend. They went up to the Italian's sitting-room on the first floor. There Mark sat down before the fire, but his host continued to walk up and down the room.

"I am very sorry, my young friend," said Filostrato, "to hear of this new trouble between you and the Deputy Director. It must be stopped, you understand? If he invite you to bring your wife here why do you not bring her?"

"Well, really," said Mark, "I never knew he attached so much importance to it." His objection to having Jane at Belbury had been temporarily deadened by the wine he had drunk at dinner and the pang he had felt at the threat of expulsion from the library circle.

"It is of no importance in itself," said Filostrato. "But I have reason to believe it came not from Wither but from the Head himself."

"The Head? You mean Jules?"

"Jules?" said Filostrato. "Why do you speak of him? As for your wife, I attach no importance to it. What have I to do with men's wives? The whole subject disgusts me. But if they make a point of it . . . Look, my friend, the real question is whether you mean to be truly at one with us or no."

"I don't quite follow," said Mark.

"Do you want to be a mere hireling? But you have already come too far in for that. If you try to go back you will be as unfortunate as the fool Hingest. If you come really in—the world . . . bah, what do I say? . . . the universe is at your feet."

"But of course I want to come in," said Mark. A certain excitement was stealing over him.

"The Head will have all of you, and all that is yours—or else nothing. You must bring the woman in too. She also must be one of us."

This remark was a shock, yet at that moment, fixed with the little, bright eyes of the Professor, he could hardly make the thought of Jane real to himself.

"You shall hear it from the lips of the Head himself," said Filostrato suddenly.

"Is Jules *here*?" said Mark.

Filostrato turned sharply from him and flung back the window curtains; the full moon stared down upon them.

"There is a world for you, no?" said Filostrato. "There is cleanness, purity. Thousands of square miles of polished rock with not one blade of grass, not one fibre of lichen, not one grain of dust. Not even air."

"Yes. A dead world," said Mark, gazing at the moon.

"No!" said Filostrato. "No. There is life there."

"Do we *know* that?" asked Mark.

"Oh, *si*. Intelligent life. Under the surface. A great race, further advanced than we. A *pure* race. They have cleaned their world, broken free (almost) from the organic."

"But how——?"

"They do not need to be born and breed and die; only their common people, their *canaglia* do that. The Masters live on. They retain their intelligence: they can keep it artificially alive after the organic body has been dispensed with—a miracle of applied biochemistry. They do not need organic food. They are almost free of Nature, attached to her only by the thinnest, finest cord."

"Do you mean that all *that*," Mark pointed to the mottled white globe of the moon, "is their own doing?"

"Why not? If you remove all the vegetation, presently you have no atmosphere, no water."

"But what was the purpose?"

"Hygiene. Why should they have their world all crawling with organisms?"

"But how do we know all this?"

"The Head has many sources of information. I speak that you may know what can be done: what shall be done here. This Institute—*Dio mio*, it is for something better than housing and vaccinations and curing the people of cancer. It is for the conquest of death: or for the conquest of organic life, if you prefer. They are the same thing. It is to bring out of that cocoon of organic life which sheltered the babyhood of mind, the New Man, the man who will not die, the artificial man, free from Nature."

"And you think that some day we shall really find a means of keeping the brain alive indefinitely?"

"We have begun already. The Head himself . . ."

"Go on," said Mark. This at last was the real thing.

"The Head himself has already survived death, and you shall speak to him this night."

"Do you mean that Jules has died?"

"Bah! Jules is nothing. He is not the Head."

"Then who is?"

At this moment there was a knock on the door. Someone came in.

"Is the young man ready?" asked the voice of Straik.

" Oh yes.   You are ready, are you not, Mr. Studdock? "

" Do you mean really to join us, young man? " said Straik.   " The Head has sent for you.   Do you understand —*the Head*?   You will look upon one who was killed and is still alive.   The resurrection of Jesus in the Bible was a symbol: to-night you shall see what it symbolised.   This is real Man at last."

" What the devil are you talking about? " said Mark.

" My friend is quite right," said Filostrato.   " Our Head is the first of the New Men—the first that lives beyond animal life.   If Nature had her way his brain would now be mouldering in the grave.   But he will speak to you within this hour, and—a word in your ear—you will obey."

" But who *is* it? " said Mark.

" It is François Alcasan," said Filostrato.

" You mean the man who was guillotined? " gasped Mark.   Both the heads nodded.   Both faces were close to him: in that disastrous light they looked like masks hanging in the air.

" You are frightened? " said Filostrato.   " *Ahi*—if you were outside, if you were mere *canaglia*, you would have reason.   It is the beginning of all power."

" It is the beginning of Man Immortal and Man Ubiquitous," said Straik.   " It is what all the prophecies really meant."

" At first, of course," said Filostrato, " the power will be confined to a small number of individual men.   Those who are selected for eternal life."

" And you mean," said Mark, " it will then be extended to all men? "

" No," said Filostrato.   " I mean it will then be reduced to one man.   You are not a fool, are you, my young friend? All that talk about the power of Man over Nature is only for the *canaglia*.   You know, as I do, that Man's power over Nature means the power of some men over other men, with Nature as the instrument.   There is no such thing as Man— it is a word.   It is not Man who will be omnipotent, it is some one man, some immortal man.   Alcasan, our Head, is the first sketch of it.   The completed product may be some-one else.   It may be you.   It may be me."

" I don't understand, I don't understand," said Mark.

" But it is very easy," said Filostrato.   " We have found how to make a dead man live.   He was a wise man even in his natural life. He live now forever: he get wiser. Later, we make them live better—for at present this second life is probably not very agreeable. Later we make it pleasant for some—perhaps not so pleasant for others. For we can make the dead live whether they wish it or not. They cannot refuse the little present."

" And so," said Straik, " the lessons you learned at your mother's knee return. God will have power to give eternal reward and eternal punishment."

" God?" said Mark. " How does He come into it? I don't believe in God."

" But, my friend," said Filostrato, " does it follow that because there was no God in the past that there will be no God also in the future? "

" Don't you see," said Straik, " that we are offering you the unspeakable glory of being present at the creation of God Almighty? "

" And that little affair of the wife," added Filostrato. " You will do as you are told. One does not argue with the Head."

Mark had nothing now to help him but the rapidly ebbing exhilaration of the alcohol taken at dinner-time and some faint gleams of memory from hours during which the world had had a different taste from this exciting horror which now pressed upon him. On the other side was fear. What would they do to him if he refused now? And, aiding the fear, there was, even then, a not wholly disagreeable thrill at the thought of sharing so stupendous a secret.

" Yes," he said. " Yes—of course—I'll come."

They led him out. He stumbled, and they linked arms with him. The journey seemed long: passage after passage, doors to unlock, strange smells. Then Filostrato spoke through a speaking-tube and a door was opened to them. A young man in a white coat received them.

" Strip to your underclothes," said Filostrato. The opposite wall of the room was covered with dials. Numbers of flexible tubes came out of the floor and went into the wall just beneath the dials. The staring dial faces and the bunches of tubes beneath them, faintly pulsating, gave one the impression of looking at some creature with many eyes and many tentacles. When the three newcomers had removed their outer clothes, they washed their hands and faces, and Filostrato plucked white clothes for them out of a glass container with a pair of forceps. He gave them gloves and masks such as surgeons wear. He studied the dials. "Yes, yes," he said. "A little more air. Turn on the chamber air . . . slowly . . . to Full. Now air in the lock. A little less of the solution. Now."

CHAPTER NINE

THE SARACEN'S HEAD

I

" It was the worst dream I've had yet," said Jane next morning. She was in the Blue Room with the Director and Grace Ironwood. " I was in a dark room," said Jane, " with queer smells and a humming noise. Then the light came on, and for a long time I didn't realise what I was looking at. I thought I saw a face floating in front of me. A face, not a head, if you understand. That is, there was a beard and nose and coloured glasses, but there didn't seem to be anything above the eyes. Not at first. But as I got used to the light, I thought the face was a mask tied on to a kind of balloon. But it wasn't, exactly. . . . I'm telling this badly. What it really was, was a head (the rest of a head) which had had the top part of the skull taken off and then . . . then . . . as if something inside had boiled over. A great big mass which bulged out from inside what was left of the skull. Wrapped in some kind of composition stuff, but very thin stuff. You could see it twitch. I remember thinking, ' Oh, kill it. Put it out of its pain.' But only for a second, because I thought the thing was dead, really. It was green looking and the mouth was wide open and quite dry. And soon I saw that it wasn't floating. It was fixed up on some kind of bracket, and there were things hanging from it. From the neck, I mean. Yes, it had a neck, but nothing below: no shoulders or body. Only these hanging things. Little rubber tubes and bulbs and metal things."

" You're all right, Jane, are you? " said Miss Ironwood.

" Oh yes," said Jane, " as far as that goes. Only one somehow doesn't *want* to tell it. Well, quite suddenly, like when an engine is started, there came a puff of air out of its mouth, with a hard, dry, rasping sound. And then there came another, and it settled down into a sort of rhythm—*huff*, *huff*, *huff*—like an imitation of breathing. Then came a most horrible thing: the mouth began to dribble. Then it began working its mouth about and even licking its lips. It was like someone getting a machine into working order. Then three people came into the room, all dressed up in white, with masks on. One was a great fat man, and another was lanky and bony. The third was Mark. I knew his walk."

" I am sorry," said the Director.

" And then," said Jane, " all three of them stood in front of the Head. They bowed to it. You couldn't tell if it was looking at them because of its dark glasses. Then it spoke."

" In English? " said Grace Ironwood.

" No, in French."

" What did it say? "

" Well, my French wasn't quite good enough to follow it. It spoke in a queer way. With no proper expression."

" Did you understand any of what was said? "

" Not much. The fat man seemed to be introducing Mark to it. It said something to him. Then Mark tried to answer. I could follow him all right, his French isn't much better than mine."

" What did he say? "

" He said something about ' doing it in a few days if possible '."

" Was that all? "

" Very nearly. You see Mark couldn't stand it. I knew he wouldn't be able to: I saw he was going to fall. He was sick too. Then they got him out of the room."

All three were silent for a few seconds.

" Was that all? " said Miss Ironwood.

" Yes," said Jane. " That's all I remember. I think I woke up then."

The Director took a deep breath. " Well! " he said, glancing at Miss Ironwood, " it becomes plainer and plainer. We must hold a council this evening. Make all arrangements." He paused and turned to Jane. " I am afraid this is very bad for you, my dear," he said; " and worse for him."

" You mean for Mark, sir? "

" Yes. Don't think hardly of him. He is suffering. If we are defeated we shall all go down with him. If we win we will rescue him; he cannot be far gone yet. We are quite used to trouble about husbands here, you know. Poor Ivy's is in jail."

" In jail? "

" Oh yes—for ordinary theft. But quite a good fellow. He'll be all right again."

II

Mark woke next morning to the consciousness that his head ached all over . . . and then, as one of the poets says, he " discovered in his mind an inflammation swollen and deformed, his memory ". Oh, but it had been a nightmare, it must be shoved away, it would vanish away now that he was fully awake. It was an absurdity. A head without any body underneath. A head that could speak when they turned on the air and the artificial saliva with taps in the next room.

But he knew it was true. And he could not, as they say, " take it ". He was very ashamed of this, for he wished to be considered one of the tough ones.

Meantime he must get up. He must do something about Jane. Apparently he would *have* to bring her to Belbury. His mind had made this decision for him at some moment he did not remember. He must get her, to save his life. They would kill him if he annoyed them; perhaps behead him. . . .

It must be remembered that in Mark's mind hardly one rag of noble thought, either Christian or Pagan, had a secure lodging. His education had been neither scientific nor classical—merely "Modern". The severities both of abstraction and of high human tradition had passed him by: and he had neither peasant shrewdness nor aristocratic honour to help him. He was a man of straw, a glib examinee in subjects that require no exact knowledge (he had always done well on Essays and General Papers), and the first hint of a real threat to his bodily life knocked him sprawling.

He was late for breakfast, but that made little difference, for he could not eat. He drank several cups of black coffee and then went into the writing-room. Here he sat for a long time drawing things on the blotting-paper. This letter to Jane proved almost impossible now that it came to the point.

"Hullo, Studdock!" said the voice of Miss Hardcastle. "Writing to little wifie, eh?"

"Damn!" said Mark. "You've made me drop my pen."

Not since he had been bullied at school had he known what it was to hate and dread anyone as he now hated and dreaded this woman.

"I've got bad news for you, sonny," she said presently.

"What is it?"

She did not answer quite at once and he knew she was studying him.

"I'm worried about little wifie, and that's a fact," she said at last.

"What do you mean?"

"I looked her up," said Miss Hardcastle, "all on your account, too. I thought Edgestow wasn't too healthy a place for her to be at present."

"Can't you tell me what's wrong?"

"Don't shout, honey. It's only—well, I thought she was behaving pretty oddly when I saw her."

Mark well remembered his conversation with his wife on the morning he left for Belbury. A new stab of fear pierced him. Might not this detestable woman be speaking the truth?

"What did she say?" he asked.

"If there is anything wrong with her in that way," said the Fairy, "take my advice, Studdock, and have her over here at once. I wouldn't like to have anyone belonging to me popped into Edgestow Asylum. Specially now that we're getting our emergency powers. They'll be using the ordinary patients experimentally, you know. If you'll just sign this form I'll run over after lunch and have her here this evening."

"But you haven't given me the slightest notion what's wrong with her."

"She kept on talking about someone who'd broken into your flat and burned her with cigars. Then, most unfortunately, she noticed my cheroot, and, if you please, she identified *me* with this imaginary persecutor. Of course, after that I could do no good."

"I must go home at once," said Mark, getting up.

"Don't be a fool, lovey," said Miss Hardcastle. "You're in a damn dangerous position already. You'll about do yourself in if you're absent without leave now. Send me. Sign the form. That's the sensible way to do it."

"But a moment ago you said she couldn't stand you at any price."

"Oh, that wouldn't make any odds. I say, Studdock, you don't think little wifie could be jealous, do you?"

"Jealous? Of you?" said Mark with uncontrollable disgust.

"Where are you off to?" said the Fairy sharply.

"To see the D.D. and then home."

"Come back, Studdock," shouted the Fairy. "Wait! Don't be a bloody fool." But Mark was already in the hall. He put on his hat and coat, ran upstairs and knocked at the door of the Deputy Director's office.

There was no answer, but the door was not quite shut. He ventured to push it open a little farther, and saw the Deputy Director sitting with his back to the door. "Excuse me, sir," said Mark. "Might I speak to you for a few minutes." There was no answer. "Excuse me, sir," said Mark in a louder voice, but the figure neither spoke nor moved. Mark went in and walked round to the other side of the desk; but when he turned to look at Wither he caught his breath, for he thought he was looking into the face of a corpse. A moment later he recognised his mistake. In the stillness of the room he could hear the man breathing. He was not even asleep, for his eyes were open. He was not unconscious, for his eyes rested momentarily on Mark and then looked away. "I beg your pardon, sir," began Mark, and then stopped. The Deputy Director was not listening. What looked out of those pale, watery eyes was, in a sense, infinity—the shapeless and the interminable. The room was still and cold. It was impossible to speak to a face like that.

When at last Mr. Wither spoke, his eyes were fixed on some remote point beyond the window.

"I know who it is," said Wither. "Your name is Studdock. You had better have stayed outside. Go away."

Mark's nerve suddenly broke. All the slowly mounting fears of the last few days ran together into one fixed determination, and a few seconds later he was going downstairs three steps at a time. Then he was crossing the hall. Then he was out, and walking down the drive.

He was out of the grounds now: he was crossing the road. He stopped suddenly. Something impossible was happening. There was a figure before him; a tall, very tall, slightly stooping figure, sauntering and humming a little dreary tune; the Deputy Director himself. And in one moment all that brittle hardihood was gone from Mark's mood. He turned back. He stood in the road; this seemed to him the worst pain that he had ever felt. Then, tired, so tired that he felt his legs would hardly carry him, he walked very slowly back into Belbury.

III

Mr. MacPhee had a little room at the Manor which he called his office, and in this tidy but dusty apartment he sat with Jane Studdock before dinner that evening, having invited her there to give her what he called " a brief, objective outline of the situation ".

" I should premise at the outset, Mrs. Studdock," he said, " that I have known the Director for a great many years and that for most of his life he was a philologist. His original name was Ransom."

" Not Ransom's *Dialect and Semantics*? " said Jane.

" Aye. That's the man," said MacPhee. " Well, about six years ago—I have all the dates in a wee book there—came his first disappearance. He was clean gone—not a trace of him—for about nine months. And then one day what does he do but turn up again in Cambridge and go sick. And he wouldn't say where he'd been except to a few friends."

" Well? " said Jane eagerly.

" He said," answered MacPhee, producing his snuff-box and laying great emphasis on the word *said*, " He said he'd been to the planet Mars."

" You mean he said this . . . while he was ill? "

" No, no. He says so still. Make what you can of it, that's his story."

" I believe it," said Jane.

MacPhee selected a pinch of snuff.

" I'm giving you the facts," he said. " He told us he'd been to Mars, kidnapped, by Professor Weston and Mr.

Devine—Lord Feverstone as he now is. And by his own account he'd escaped from them—on Mars, you'll understand—and been wandering about there alone."

" It's uninhabited, I suppose? "

" We have no evidence except his own story. You are aware, Mrs. Studdock, that a man in complete solitude even on this earth—an explorer, for example—gets into remarkable states of consciousness."

" You mean he might have imagined things that weren't there? "

" I'm making no comments," said MacPhee. " I'm recording. By his accounts there are all kinds of creatures walking about there; that's maybe why he has turned this house into a sort of menagerie, but no matter for that. But he also says he met one kind of creature there which specially concerns us. He called them eldils."

" Were these things . . . well, intelligent? Could they talk? "

" Aye. They could talk. They were intelligent, forbye, which is not always the same thing."

" In fact these were the Martians? "

" That's just what they weren't, according to him. They were on Mars, but they didn't rightly belong there. He says they are creatures that live in empty space."

" But there's no air."

" I'm telling you his story. He says they don't breathe. He said also that they don't reproduce their species and don't die."

" What on earth are they like? "

" I'm telling you how he described them."

" Are they *huge*? " said Jane almost involuntarily.

" The point, Mrs. Studdock, is this. Dr. Ransom claims that he has received continual visits from these creatures since he returned to Earth. So much for his first disappearance. Then came the second. That time he said he'd been in the planet Venus—taken there by these eldils."

" Venus is inhabited by them, too? "

" You'll forgive me observing that this remark shows you have not grasped what I'm telling you. These creatures are not planetary creatures at all, though they may alight on a planet here and there; like a bird alighting on a tree. There's some of them, he says, are more or less permanently attached to particular planets, but they're not native there."

" They are, I gather, more or less friendly? "

" That is the Director's idea about them, with one exception."

" What's that? "

" The eldils that have for centuries concentrated on our own planet. We seem to have had no luck in our particular complement of parasites. And that, Mrs. Studdock, brings me to the point."

Jane waited. MacPhee's manner almost neutralised the strangeness of what he was telling her.

" The long and the short of it is," said he, " that this house is dominated either by the creatures I'm talking about or by a sheer delusion. It is by advices he thinks he has received from eldils that the Director has discovered the conspiracy against the human race; and it's on instructions from eldils that he's conducting the campaign—if you call it conducting! It may have occurred to you to wonder how any man thinks we're going to defeat a conspiracy by growing winter vegetables and training performing bears. It is a question I have propounded on more than one occasion. The answer is always the same: we're waiting for orders."

" From the eldils? It was them he meant when he spoke of his Masters? "

" It would be."

" But, Mr. MacPhee, I thought you said the ones on our planet were hostile."

" That's a good question," said MacPhee, " but it's not our own ones that the Director claims to be in communication with. It's his friends from outer space. Our own crew, the terrestrial eldils, are at the back of the whole conspiracy."

" You mean that the other eldils, out of space, come here —to this house? "

" That is what the Director thinks."

" But you must know whether it's true or not."

" How? "

" Have you seen them? "

" That's not a question to be answered Aye or No. I've seen a good many things in my time that weren't there or weren't what they pretended to be; rainbows and reflections and sunsets, not to mention dreams."

" You have seen something, then? "

"Aye. But we must keep an open mind. It might be an hallucination. It might be a conjuring trick . . ."

"By the Director?" asked Jane angrily. "Do you really expect me to believe that the Director is a charlatan?"

"I wish, ma'am," said MacPhee, "you could consider the matter without constantly using such terms as *believe*. Obviously, conjuring is one of the hypotheses that any impartial investigator must take into account. The fact that it is a hypothesis specially uncongenial to the emotions of this investigator or that, is neither here nor there."

"There's such a thing as loyalty," said Jane.

MacPhee looked up with a hundred Covenanters in his eyes.

"There is, ma'am," he said. "As you get older you will learn that it is a virtue too important to be lavished on individual personalities."

At that moment there was a knock at the door. "Come in," said MacPhee, and Camilla entered.

"Have you finished with Jane, Mr. MacPhee?" she said. "She promised to come out for a breath of air with me before dinner."

"Och, breath of air your grandmother!" said MacPhee with a gesture of despair. "Very well, ladies, very well. Away out to the garden. I doubt they're doing something more to the purpose on the enemy's side."

"He's been telling you?" said Camilla, as the two girls went together down the passage.

Moved by a kind of impulse which was rare to her experience, Jane seized her friend's hand as she answered "Yes!" Both were filled with some passion, but what passion they did not know. They came to the front door, and as they opened it a sight met their eyes which, though natural, seemed at the moment apocalyptic.

All day the wind had been rising, and they found themselves looking out on a sky swept almost clean. The air was intensely cold; the stars severe and bright. High above the last rags of scurrying cloud hung the Moon in all her wildness—the huntress, the untameable virgin, the spear-head of madness. The wildness crept into Jane's blood.

"That Mr. MacPhee . . ." said Jane, as they walked uphill to the summit of the garden, "how does he explain the Director's age?"

" Yes. That is what people are like who come back from the stars. Or at least from Perelandra. He will never grow a year or a month older again."

" Will he die? "

" He will be taken away, I believe. Back into Deep Heaven. It has happened to one or two people, perhaps about six, since the world began."

" What—what *is* he? "

" He's a man, my dear. And he is the Pendragon of Logres. This house, all of us here, are all that's left of Logres: all the rest has become merely Britain. Let's go right to the top. How it's blowing. They might come to him to-night."

IV

. That evening the Director held council in the Blue Room.

" Well," said Ransom, as Grace Ironwood concluded reading from her notes. " That is the dream, and everything in it seems to be objective."

" Objective? " said Dimble. " I don't understand, sir. You don't mean they could really have a thing like that? "

" What do you think, MacPhee? " asked Ransom.

" Oh aye, it's possible," said MacPhee. " They do it often in laboratories. You cut off a cat's head, maybe, and throw the body away. You can keep the head going for a bit if you supply it with blood at the right pressure."

" Do you mean, keep it *alive*? " said Dimble.

" *Alive* is ambiguous. It's what would be popularly called alive. But a human head—and consciousness—I don't know what would happen if you tried that."

" It has been tried," said Miss Ironwood. " A German tried it before the first war. With the head of a criminal. It failed. The head decayed in the ordinary way."

" Then this abomination," said Dr. Dimble, " is real—not only a dream."

" We have no evidence of that," said MacPhee. " I'm only stating the facts. What the girl has dreamed is possible."

" And what about this turban business," said Denniston, " this sort of swelling on top of the head? "

" Supposing the dream to be veridical," said MacPhee. " You can guess what it would be. Once they'd got it kept alive, the first thing that would occur to boys like them would be to increase its brain. They'd try all sorts of stimulants. And then, maybe, they'd ease open the skull-cap and just—well, just let it boil over, as you might say."

" Is it at all probable," said the Director, " that a hypertrophy like that would increase thinking power? "

" That seems to me the weak point," said Miss Ironwood. " I should have thought it just as likely to produce lunacy. But it *might* have the opposite effect."

"Then what we are up against," said Dimble, "is a criminal's brain swollen to superhuman proportions and experiencing a mode of consciousness which we can't imagine, but which is presumably a consciousness of agony and hatred."

" It's not certain," said Miss Ironwood, " that there would be very much actual pain."

" It tells us one thing straightaway," said Denniston.

" What's that? " asked MacPhee.

" That the enemy movement is international. To get that head they must have been hand-in-glove with at least one foreign police force."

" It tells us," said the Director, " that if this technique is really successful, the Belbury people have for all practical purposes discovered a way of making themselves immortal. It is the beginning of what is really a new species—the Chosen Heads who never die. They will call it the next step in evolution. And henceforward all the creatures that you and I call human are mere candidates for admission to the new species or else its slaves—perhaps its food."

" Mr. Director," said MacPhee. " You'll excuse me for speaking frankly. Your enemies have provided themselves with this Head. They have taken possession of Edgestow, and they're in a fair way to suspend the laws of England. And still you tell us it is not time to move. If you had taken my advice six months ago we would have had an organisation all over this island by now and maybe a party in the House of Commons. I know well what you'll say—that those are not the right methods. And maybe no. But if you can neither take our advice nor give us anything to do, what are we all sitting here for? Have you seriously considered sending us away and getting some other colleagues that you *can* work with? "

" Dissolve the Company, do you mean? " said Dimble.

"Aye, I do," said MacPhee.

The Director looked up with a smile. "But," he said, "I have no power to dissolve it."

"In that case," said MacPhee, "I must ask what authority you had to bring it together?"

"I never brought it together," said the Director. Then, after glancing round the company, he added: "There is some strange misunderstanding here! Were you all under the impression I had *selected* you? Were you?" he repeated, when no one answered.

MacPhee's stern features relaxed into a broad grin. "I see what you're driving at," he said. "We've all been playing blind-man's buff, I doubt. But I'll take leave to observe, Dr. Ransom, that you carry things a wee bit high. I don't just remember how you came to be called Director."

"I am the Director," said Ransom, smiling. "Do you think I would claim the authority I do if the relation between us depended either on your choice or mine? You never chose me. I never chose you. Even the great Oyéresu whom I serve never chose me. I came into their worlds by what seemed, at first, a chance; as you came to me—as the very animals in this house first came to it. You and I have not started or devised this: it has descended on us. It is, no doubt, an organisation: but we are not the organisers. And that is why I have no authority to give any one of you permission to leave my household."

MacPhee resumed his chair, and the Director continued.

"We have learned to-night," he said, "if not what the real power behind our enemies is doing, at least the form in which it is embodied at Belbury. We therefore know something about one of the two attacks which are about to be made on our race. But I'm thinking of the other."

"Meaning by that?" asked MacPhee.

"Meaning," said Ransom, "whatever is under Bragdon Wood. And I think that what is under it is that old man in a mantle whom Jane found in a dark hole in her dream."

"You're still thinking about *that*?" said the Ulsterman.

"I am thinking of almost nothing else," said the Director. "It may be the greater danger of the two. But what is certain is that the greatest danger of all is the junction of the enemies' forces. When the new power from Belbury joins up with the old power under Bragdon Wood, Logres—indeed Man—will be almost surrounded. For us everything turns on preventing that junction. That is the point at which we must be ready both to kill and die. But we cannot get into Bragdon and start excavating ourselves. There must be a moment when they find him—it. I have no doubt we shall be told in one way or another. Till then we must wait."

"I don't believe a word of all that other story," said MacPhee.

"I thought," said Miss Ironwood, "we weren't to use words like *believe*. I thought we were only to state facts and exhibit implications."

"If you two quarrel much more," said the Director, "I think I'll make you marry one another."

v

At the beginning the grand mystery for the Company had been why the enemy wanted Bragdon Wood. The land was unsuitable and Edgestow itself was not an obviously convenient place. By intense study in collaboration with Dr. Dimble the Director had at last come to a certain conclusion. They knew that Edgestow lay in what had been the very heart of ancient Logres, and that an historical Merlin had once worked in Bragdon Wood.

What exactly he had done there they did not know; but they had all, by various routes, come too far either to consider his art mere legend and imposture, or to equate it exactly with what the Renaissance called Magic. They thought that Merlin's art was the last survival of something older and different—something brought to Western Europe after the fall of Atlantis and going back to an era in which the general relations of mind and matter on this planet had been other than those we know. It had probably differed from Renaissance Magic profoundly. It had possibly (though this was doubtful) been less guilty: it had certainly been more effective.

But if the only possible attraction of Bragdon lay in its association with the last vestiges of Atlantean magic, this told the Company something else. It told them that the N.I.C.E., at its core, was not concerned solely with modern or materialistic forms of power. It told the Director, in fact, that there was Eldilic energy and Eldilic knowledge behind it.

Up to a certain point the Director had supposed that the powers for which the enemy hankered were resident in the mere site at Bragdon—for there is an old belief that locality itself is of importance in such matters. But from Jane's dream of the cold sleeper he had learned better. There was something under the soil of Bragdon, something to be discovered by digging. It was, in fact, the body of Merlin. What the eldils had told him about the possibility of such discovery was no wonder to them. In their eyes the normal Tellurian modes of engendering and birth and death and decay were no less wonderful than the countless other patterns of being which were continually present to their unsleeping minds. That a body should lie uncorrupted for fifteen hundred years did not seem strange to them; they knew worlds where there was no corruption at all. That its life should remain latent in it all that time was to them no more strange: they had seen innumerable different modes in which soul and matter could be combined and separated, separated without loss of reciprocal influence, combined without true incarnation, or brought together in a union as short, and as momentous, as the nuptial embrace. It was not as a marvel in natural philosophy, but as an information in time of war that they brought the Director their tidings. Merlin had not died. His life had been side-tracked, moved out of our one-dimensioned time, for fifteen centuries. But under certain conditions it would return to his body.

It was this that kept the Director wakeful, in the cold hours when the others had left him. There was no doubt now that the enemy had bought Bragdon to find Merlin: and if they found him they would re-awake him. The old Druid would inevitably cast in his lot with the new planners. A junction would be effected between two kinds of power which between them would determine the fate of our planet. Doubtless that had been the will of the Dark-Eldils for centuries. The sciences, good and innocent in themselves, had even in Ransom's own time begun to be subtly manœuvred in a certain direction. Despair of objective truth had been increasingly insinuated into the scientists; indifference to it, and a concentration upon power, had been the result. Babble about the *élan vital* and flirtations with pan-psychism were bidding fair to restore the *Anima Mundi* of the magicians. Dreams of the far future destiny of man were dragging up from its shallow and unquiet grave the old dream of Man as God. The very experiences of the pathological laboratory were breeding a conviction that the stifling of deep-set repugnances was the first essential for progress. And now all this had reached the stage at which its dark contrivers thought they could safely begin to bend it back so that it would meet that other and earlier kind of power. Indeed, they were choosing the first moment at which this could have been done. You could not have done it with nineteenth-century scientists. Their firm objective materialism would have excluded it from their minds; and their inherited morality would have kept them from touching dirt. MacPhee was a survivor from that tradition. It was different now. Perhaps few or none at Belbury knew what was happening: but once it happened, they would be like straw in fire. What should they find incredible, since they believed no longer in a rational universe? What should they regard as too obscene, since they held that all morality was a mere subjective by-product of the physical and economic situations of men? From the point of view which is accepted in hell, the whole history of our Earth had led up to this moment. There was now at last a real chance for fallen Man to shake off that limitation of his powers which mercy had imposed upon him as a protection from the full results of his fall. If this succeeded, hell would be at last incarnate.

CHAPTER TEN

THE CONQUERED CITY

I

Mark was called earlier than usual, and with his tea came a note. The Deputy Director sent his compliments and must ask Mr. Studdock to call on him *instantly* about a most urgent and distressing matter. Mark dressed and obeyed.

In Wither's room he found Wither and Miss Hardcastle. To Mark's surprise and relief Wither showed no recollection of their last meeting. Indeed, his manner was genial, even deferential, though extremely grave.

"Good morning, good morning, Mr. Studdock," he said. "It is with the greatest regret that I—er—in short, I would not have kept you from your breakfast unless I had felt that in your own interests you should be placed in possession of the facts at the earliest moment. I feel sure that as the conversation proceeds (pray be seated, Mr. Studdock) you will realise how very wise we have been in securing from the outset a police force—to give it that rather unfortunate name—of our own."

Mark licked his lips and sat down.

"My reluctance to raise the question," continued Wither, "would, however, be much more serious if I did not feel able to assure you—in *advance* you understand—of the confidence which we all feel in you and which I very much hoped " (here for the first time he looked Mark in the eyes) "you were beginning to reciprocate. We regard ourselves here as being so many brothers and—er—sisters: and shall all feel entitled to discuss the subject in the most informal manner possible."

Miss Hardcastle's voice suddenly broke in.

"You have lost your wallet, Studdock," she said.

"Yes. I have. Have you found it?"

"Does it contain three pounds ten, letters from a woman signing herself Myrtle, from the Bursar of Bracton, from G. Hernshaw, and a bill for a dress-suit from Simonds and Son, 32A Market Street, Edgestow?"

"Well, more or less so."

"There it is," said Miss Hardcastle. "No you don't!" she added as Mark made a step towards it. "None of that! This wallet was found beside the road about five yards away from Hingest's body."

"My God!" said Studdock. "You don't mean . . . the thing's absurd."

"I don't really think," said the Deputy Director, "that you need have the slightest apprehension that there is, at this stage, any radical difference between your colleagues and yourself as to the light in which this painful matter should be regarded. The question is really a constitutional one——"

"Constitutional?" said Mark angrily. "If I understand her, Miss Hardcastle is accusing me of murder."

Wither's eyes looked at him as if from an infinite distance. "Oh," said he, "I don't really think that does justice to Miss Hardcastle's position. That element in the Institute which she represents would be strictly *ultra vires* in doing anything of the kind within the N.I.C.E.—supposing, but purely of course for purposes of argument, that they wished, or should wish at a later stage, to do so—while in relation to the outside authorities her function——"

"But it's the outside authorities with whom I'm concerned, I suppose," said Mark. "As far as I can understand, Miss Hardcastle means I'm going to be arrested."

"On the contrary," said Wither. "This is precisely one of those cases in which you see the enormous value of possessing our own executive. I do not know if Miss Hardcastle has made it perfectly clear to you that it was her officers, and they only, who have made this—er—embarrassing discovery."

"What do you mean?" said Mark. "If Miss Hardcastle does not think there's a prima facie case against me, why am I being arraigned in this way at all? And if she does, how can she avoid informing the authorities?"

"My dear friend," said Wither in an antediluvian tone, "there is not the slightest desire on the part of the Committee to insist on defining, in cases of this sort, the powers of action of our own police, much less, what is here in question, their powers of inaction. I do not think anyone had suggested that Miss Hardcastle should be *obliged*—in any sense that limited her own initiative—to communicate to outside authorities any facts acquired by her staff in the course of their internal functioning within the N.I.C.E."

"Do I understand," said Mark, "that Miss Hardcastle thinks she has facts justifying my arrest for the murder of Mr. Hingest, but is kindly offering to suppress them?"

"You got it now, Studdock," said the Fairy.

"But that's not what I want," said Mark. This was not quite true. "I don't want that," he said, speaking rather too loud. "I'm innocent. I think I'd better go to the police—the *real* police, I mean—at once."

"If you *want* to be tried for your life," said the Fairy, "that's another matter."

"I want to be vindicated," said Mark. "The charge would fall to pieces at once. There was no conceivable motive. And I have an alibi. Everyone knows I slept here that night."

"There's always a *motive*, you know," said she, "for anyone murdering anyone. The police are only human. When the machinery's started they naturally want a conviction."

Mark assured himself he was not frightened.

"There's a letter you wrote," said the Fairy.

"What letter?"

"A letter to a Mr. Pelham, of your own College, dated six weeks ago, in which you say, ' I wish Bill the Blizzard could be moved to a better world.' "

Like a sharp physical pain the memory of that scribbled note came back to Mark. It was the sort of silly jocularity one used in the Progressive Element—the kind of thing that might be said a dozen times a day in Bracton about an opponent or even about a bore.

"You don't suppose," said Mark, " that anyone could take that letter to be meant seriously? "

"Ever tried to make a policeman understand anything? " said the Fairy. " I mean what you call a *real* policeman."

Mark said nothing.

"And I don't think the alibi is specially good," said the Fairy. "You were seen talking to Bill at dinner. You were seen going out of the front door with him when he left. You were not seen coming back. Nothing is known of your movements till breakfast-time next morning. If you had gone with him by car to the scene of the murder you would have had ample time to walk back and go to bed by about two-fifteen. Frosty night, you know. No reason why your shoes should have been muddy."

"If I might pick up a point made by Miss Hardcastle," said Wither, " this is a very good illustration of the immense importance of the Institutional Police. There are so many fine shades involved which, so long as they remain in our own family circle (I look upon the N.I.C.E., Mr. Studdock, as one great family), need develop no tendency to lead to any miscarriage of justice."

"You really advise me, sir," said Mark, " not to go to the police? "

"To the police? " said Wither as if this idea were completely new. " I don't think, Mr. Studdock, that anyone had quite contemplated your taking any irrevocable action of that sort. It might even be argued that by such an action you would be guilty—unintentionally guilty, I hasten to add—of some degree of disloyalty. You would, of course, be placing yourself outside our protection. . . ."

"That's the point, Studdock," said the Fairy. "Once you are in the hands of the police you are in the hands of the police."

The moment of Mark's decision passed by him without his noticing it.

"Then there's nothing to be done at present?" said Mark.

"No," said Wither. "No. No immediate action of any official character. It is, of course, very advisable that you should act, as I am sure you will, with the greatest prudence and—er—er—caution for the next few months. As long as you are with us, Scotland Yard would, I feel, see the inconvenience of trying to act unless they had a very clear case indeed."

"But, look here, damn it!" said Mark. "Aren't you hoping to catch the thief in a day or two? Aren't you going to do *anything*?"

"The thief?" said Wither. "There has been no suggestion so far that the body was rifled."

"I mean the thief who stole my wallet."

"Oh—ah—your wallet," said the other, very gently stroking his refined, handsome face. "I see. I understand, do I, that you are advancing a charge of theft against some person or persons unknown——"

"But, good God!" shouted Mark, "were you not assuming that someone stole it? Do you think I was there myself? Do *you* both think I am a murderer?"

"Please!" said the Deputy Director, "please, Mr. Studdock, you really must not shout. Quite apart from the indiscretion of it, I must remind you that you are in the presence of a lady. As far as I can remember, nothing has been said on our side about murder, and no charge of any sort has been made. My only anxiety is to make perfectly clear what we are all doing. I am sure Miss Hardcastle agrees with me."

"It's all one to me," said the Fairy. "Why Studdock should start bellowing at us because we are trying to keep him out of the dock, I don't know. But that's for him to decide. I've got a busy day and don't want to hang about here all morning."

"Really," said Mark, "I should have thought it was excusable to——"

"Pray compose yourself, Mr. Studdock," said Wither.

" As I said before, we look upon ourselves as one family, and nothing like a formal apology is required. We all understand one another and all dislike—er—scenes."

" I'm sorry if I was rude," said Mark. " What do you advise me to do? "

" Don't put your nose outside Belbury, Studdock," said the Fairy.

" I do not think Miss Hardcastle could have given you better advice," said Wither. " And now that Mrs. Studdock is going to join you here, this will not be a serious hardship. You must look upon this as your *home*, Mr. Studdock."

" Oh . . . that reminds me, sir," said Mark. " I'm not quite sure about having my wife here. As a matter of fact she's not in very good health——"

" But surely, in that case, you must be all the more anxious to have her here? "

" I don't believe it would suit her, sir."

The D.D.'s eyes wandered and his voice became lower.

" I had almost forgotten, Mr. Studdock," he said, " to congratulate you on your introduction to our Head. We all now feel that you are really one of us in a deeper sense. He is anxious to welcome Mrs. Studdock among us at the earliest opportunity."

" Why? " said Mark suddenly.

Wither looked at Mark with an indescribable smile.

" My dear boy," he said. " Unity, you know. The family circle. She'd—she'd be company for Miss Hardcastle! " Before Mark had recovered from this staggeringly new conception, Wither rose and shuffled towards the door. " You must be hungry for your breakfast," he said. " Don't let me delay you. Behave with the greatest caution. And —and "—here his face suddenly changed. The widely opened mouth looked all at once like the mouth of some animal. " And bring the girl. Do you understand? Get your wife," he added. " The Head . . . he's not patient."

II

As Mark closed the door behind him he immediately thought " Now! They're both in there together. Safe for a minute at least." Without even waiting to get his hat he walked briskly to the front door and down the drive.

Nothing but physical impossibility would stop him from going to Edgestow and warning Jane. After that he had no plans.

Now he was past the road; he was in the belt of trees. Scarcely a minute had passed since he had left the D.D.'s office and no one had overtaken him. But yesterday's adventure was happening over again. A tall, stooped, shuffling, creaking figure, humming a tune, barred his way. Mark had never fought. Ancestral impulses lodged in his body directed the blow which he aimed at this senile obstructor. But there was no impact. The shape had suddenly vanished.

Those who know best were never fully agreed as to the explanation of this episode. It may have been that Mark, both then and on the previous day, being overwrought, saw an hallucination. It may be that the appearance of Wither which haunted so many rooms and corridors of Belbury was, in one sense of the word, a ghost—one of those sensory impressions which a strong personality in its last decay can imprint, most commonly after death but sometimes before it, on the very structure of a building. Or it may, after all, be that souls who have lost the intellectual good do indeed receive in return, and for a short period, the vain privilege of thus reproducing themselves in many places as wraiths. At any rate the thing, whatever it was, vanished.

The path ran diagonally across a field in grass, now powdered with frost, and the sky was hazy blue. Then he went across a road, across a stream by a foot-bridge, and so into the frozen ruts of the lane that led him into Courthampton.

The first thing he saw as he came into the village street was a farm-cart. A woman and three children sat beside the man who was driving, and in the cart were piled chests of drawers, mattresses, and a canary in a cage. Immediately after it came a man and woman and child on foot wheeling a perambulator: it also was piled with small household property. After that came a family pushing a hand-cart, and then a heavily loaded trap, and then an old car. A steady stream of such traffic was passing through the village. Mark had never seen war: if he had he would have recognised at once the signs of flight, the message " Enemy behind ".

It took him a long time to get to the cross-roads by the pub, where he could find a glazed and framed table of buses. There would not be one to Edgestow till twelve-fifteen. He hung about, understanding nothing of what he saw. At eleven-thirty the pub opened. He went in and ordered a pint and some bread and cheese.

The bar was at first empty. During the next half-hour men dropped in one by one till about four were present. For some time they did not talk at all. Then a very little man with a face like an old potato observed to no one in particular, " I seen old Rumbold the other night." No one replied for five minutes, and then a very young man in leggings said, " I reckon he's sorry he ever tried it." It was only when the subject of Rumbold was thoroughly exhausted that the talk, very indirectly and by gradual stages, began to throw some light on the stream of refugees.

" Still coming out," said one man.

" Ah," said another.

" Can't be many left there by now."

" Don't know where they'll all get in, I'm sure."

Little by little the whole thing came out. These were the refugees from Edgestow. Some had been turned out of their houses, some scared by the riots, and still more by the restoration of order. Something like a terror appeared to have been established in the town.

" They tell me there were two hundred arrests yesterday," said the landlord.

" Ah," said the young man. " They're hard cases those N.I.C.E. police, every one of them. They put the wind up my old Dad proper, I tell 'ee." He ended with a laugh.

" 'Taint the police so much as the workmen by what I hear," said another. " They never ought to have brought those Welsh and Irish."

When the time came he had no difficulty in getting on to the bus, for all the traffic was going in the opposite direction. It put him down at the top of Market Street and he set out to walk up to the flat. The town wore a new expression. One house out of three was empty. About half the shops had their windows boarded up. As he gained height and came into the region of large villas with gardens he noticed that many of these had been requisitioned and bore white placards with the N.I.C.E. symbol—a muscular male nude grasping a thunderbolt. At every corner lounged or sauntered the N.I.C.E. police, helmeted, swinging their clubs, with revolvers in holsters on their black shiny belts.

Would Jane be in? He felt he could not bear it if Jane should not be in. It seemed cold and damp on the staircase: cold and damp and dark on the landing. "Ja-ane," he shouted as he unlocked the door of the flat: but he had already lost hope. As soon as he was inside the door he knew the place was uninhabited. A pile of unopened letters lay on the inside door-mat. There was not a tick of a clock. The bread in the cupboard was stale. There was a jug half full of milk, but the milk had thickened and would not pour. A splutter of unreasonable anger arose. Why the hell hadn't Jane told him she was going away? Or had someone taken her away? Perhaps there was a note for him. He took a pile of letters off the mantelpiece, but they were only letters he had put there himself to be answered. Then on the table he noticed an envelope addressed to Mrs. Dimble at her own house over beyond the Wynd. So that damned woman had been here! Those Dimbles had always, he felt, disliked him. They'd probably asked Jane to stay with them. Been interfering somehow, no doubt. He must go down to Northumberland and see Dimble.

The idea of being annoyed with the Dimbles occurred to Mark almost as an inspiration. To bluster a little as an injured husband in search of his wife would be a pleasant change from the attitudes he had recently been compelled to adopt.

III

"Come in," said Dimble in his rooms at Northumberland. "Oh, it's you, Studdock," he added as the door opened. "Come in."

"I've come to ask about Jane," said Mark. "Do you know where she is?"

"I can't give you her address, I'm afraid," said Dimble.

"Do you mean you don't know it?"

"I can't give it," said Dimble.

According to Mark's programme this was the point at which he should have begun to take a strong line. But he did not feel the same now that he was in the room. Dimble had always treated him with scrupulous politeness, and Mark had always felt that Dimble disliked him. This had not made him dislike Dimble. It had only made him uneasily talkative in Dimble's presence and anxious to please. Vindictiveness was by no means one of Mark's vices. For Mark liked to be liked. There was a good deal of the spaniel in him.

"What do you mean?" he asked. "I don't understand."

"If you have any regard for your wife's safety you will not ask me to tell you where she has gone," said Dimble.

"Safety from what?"

"Don't you know what has happened?"

"What's happened?"

"On the night of the riot the Institutional Police attempted to arrest her. She escaped, but not before they had tortured her."

"Tortured her? What do you mean?"

"Burned her with cigars."

"That's what I've come about," said Mark. "Jane—I'm afraid she is on the verge of a nervous breakdown. That didn't really happen, you know."

"The doctor who dressed the burns thinks otherwise."

"Great Scott!" said Mark. "So they really did? But, look here . . ."

Under the quiet stare of Dimble he found it difficult to speak.

"Why have I not been told about this outrage?" he shouted.

"By your colleagues?" asked Dimble drily. "It is an odd question to ask me. You ought to understand the workings of the N.I.C.E. better than I do."

"Why didn't *you* tell me? Why has nothing been done about it? Have you been to the police?"

"The Institutional Police?"

"No, the ordinary police."

"Do you really not know that there are no ordinary police left in Edgestow?"

"I suppose there are some magistrates."

"There is the Emergency Commissioner, Lord Feverstone. You seem to misunderstand. This is a conquered and occupied city."

"Then why, in Heaven's name, didn't you get on to me?"

"*You?*" said Dimble.

For one moment Mark saw himself exactly as a man like Dimble saw him. It almost took his breath away.

"Look here," he said. "You don't . . . it's too fantastic! You don't imagine I knew about it! You don't really believe I send policemen about to man-handle my own wife!"

Dimble said nothing and his face did not relax.

"I know you've always disliked me," said Mark. "But I didn't know it was quite as bad as that." And again Dimble was silent.

"Well," said Studdock, "there doesn't seem to be much more to say. I insist on being told where Jane is."

"Do you *want* her to be taken to Belbury?"

"I don't see why I should be cross-questioned in this way. Where is my wife?"

"I have no permission to tell you. She is not in my house nor under my care. If you still have the slightest regard for her happiness you will make no attempt to get into touch with her."

"Am I some sort of leper or criminal that I can't even be trusted to know her address?"

"Excuse me. You are a member of the N.I.C.E. who have already insulted, tortured, and arrested her. Since her escape she has been left alone only because your colleagues do not know where she is."

"And if it really was the N.I.C.E. police, do you suppose I'm not going to have a very full explanation out of them? Damn it, what do you take me for?"

"I can only hope that you have no power in the N.I.C.E. at all. If you have no power, then you cannot protect her. If you have, then you are identified with its policy. In neither case will I help you to discover where Jane is."

"This is fantastic," said Mark. "Even if I do happen to hold a job in the N.I.C.E. for the moment, you know *me*."

"I do *not* know you," said Dimble. "I have no conception of your aims or motives."

He seemed to Mark to be looking at him not with anger or contempt but with that degree of loathing which produces in those who feel it a kind of embarrassment. In reality Dimble was simply trying very hard not to hate, not to despise, and he had no idea of the fixed severity which this effort gave to his face.

"There has been some ridiculous mistake," said Mark.

" I'll make a row. I suppose some newly enrolled police-man got drunk or something. Well, he'll be broken. I——"

" It was the chief of your police, Miss Hardcastle herself, who did it."

" Very well. I'll break *her* then."

" Do you know Miss Hardcastle well? " asked Dimble.

Mark thought that Dimble was reading his mind and seeing there his certainty that he had no more power of calling Miss Hardcastle to account than of stopping the revolution of the Earth.

Suddenly Dimble's face changed, and he spoke in a new voice. " Have *you* the means to bring her to book? " he said. " Are you already as near the centre of Belbury as that? If so, then you have consented to the murder of Hingest, the murder of Compton. It is with your approval that criminals—honest criminals whose hands you are unfit to touch—are being taken from the jails to which British judges sent them and packed off to Belbury to undergo for an indefinite period, out of reach of the law, whatever tortures and assaults on personal identity you call Remedial Treatment. It is you who have driven two thousand families from their homes. It is you who can tell us why Place and Rowley have been arrested. And if you are as deeply in it as that, not only will I not deliver Jane into your hands, but I would not deliver my dog."

" Really—really," said Mark. " This is absurd. What have I ever done that you should make me responsible for every action that any N.I.C.E. official has taken—or is said to have taken in the gutter Press? "

" Gutter Press! What nonsense is this? Do you suppose I don't know that you have control of every paper in the country except one? And that one has not appeared this morning."

It may seem strange to say that Mark, having long lived in a world without charity, had nevertheless seldom met anger. Malice in plenty he had encountered, but it all operated by snubs and sneers and stabbing in the back. The eyes and voice of this elderly man had an effect on him which was unnerving. (At Belbury one used the words " whining " and " yapping " to describe any opposi-tion which Belbury aroused in the outer world.)

" I tell you I knew nothing about it," he shouted. " I'll

raise hell about it. I'll break the infernal bitch who did it, if it means breaking the whole N.I.C.E."

He knew that Dimble knew that he was now talking nonsense. Yet Mark could not stop.

" Sooner than put up with this," he shouted, " I'll leave the N.I.C.E."

" Do you mean that? " asked Dimble with a sharp glance. To Mark this glance appeared accusing and intolerable. In reality it had been a glance of awakened hope.

" I see you don't trust me," said Mark.

Dimble was a truthful man. " No," he said after a longish pause. " I don't quite."

Mark shrugged his shoulders and turned away.

" Studdock," said Dimble, " this is not a time for foolery, or compliments. It may be that both of us are within a few minutes of death. You have probably been shadowed into the college. And I, at any rate, don't propose to die with polite insincerities in my mouth. I don't trust you. Why should I? You are (at least in some degree) the accomplice of the worst men in the world. Your very coming to me this afternoon may be a trap."

" Don't you know me better than *that*? " said Mark.

" Stop talking nonsense! " said Dimble. " Stop posturing and acting, if only for a minute. They have corrupted better men than you or me before now. Straik was a good man once. Filostrato was at least a genius. Even Alcasan —yes, yes, I know who your Head is—was a plain murderer: something better than they have now made of him. Who are you to be exempt? "

Mark gaped.

" Nevertheless," continued Dimble, " knowing this— knowing that you may be only bait in the trap—I will take a risk. I will risk things compared with which both our lives are a triviality. If you seriously wish to leave the N.I.C.E., I will help you."

One moment it was like the gates of Paradise opening— then, at once, caution and the incurable wish to temporise rushed back. The chink had closed.

" I—I'd need to think that over," he mumbled. " It's a question affecting my whole future career."

" Your career! " said Dimble. " It's a question of damnation or—a last chance. But you must come at once."

"I don't think I understand," said Mark. "You keep on suggesting some kind of danger. What is it? And what powers have you to protect me—or Jane—if I do bolt?"

"I can offer you no security. There is no security for anyone now. I'm offering you a place on the right side. I don't know which will win."

"As a matter of fact," said Mark, "I *had* been thinking of leaving. But I must think it over. Supposing I look you up again to-morrow?"

"Do you know that you'll be able?"

"Or in an hour? Come, that's only sensible. Will you be here in an hour's time?"

"What can an hour do for you? You are only waiting in the hope that your mind will be less clear."

"But will you be here?"

"If you insist. But no good can come of it."

"I want to think. I want to think," said Mark, and left the room without waiting for a reply.

Mark had said he wanted to think: in reality he wanted alcohol and tobacco. And he wanted Jane, and he wanted to punish Jane for being a friend of Dimble, and he wanted never to see Wither again, and he wanted to creep back and patch things up with Wither somehow. He wanted to be admired for manly honesty among the Dimbles and also for realism and knowingness at Belbury. Damn the whole thing! Why had he such a rotten heredity? Why had his education been so ineffective? Why was the system of society so irrational? Why was his luck so bad?

It was raining as he reached the College lodge. Some sort of van seemed to be standing in the street outside, and there were three or four uniformed men in capes.

"Excuse me, sir," said one of the men. " I must ask for your name."

"Studdock," said Mark.

"Mark Gainsby Studdock," said the man, " it is my duty to arrest you for the murder of William Hingest."

IV

Dr. Dimble drove out to St. Anne's dissatisfied with himself, haunted with the suspicion that if he had been wiser, or more perfectly in charity with this very miserable young man, he might have done something for him.

"Here he is! Here's Dr. Dimble," shouted Ivy Maggs as he drove up to the front door of the Manor.

"Don't put the car away, Dimble," said Denniston.

"Oh Cecil!" said his wife; and he saw fear in her face.

A few moments later, blinking in the lighted kitchen, he saw that this was not to be a normal evening. The Director himself was there, seated by the fire. There were signs that everyone else had had an early supper, and Dimble found himself almost at once seated at the end of the table and being rather excitedly urged to eat and drink by his wife and Mrs. Maggs.

"Don't stop to ask questions, dear," said Mrs. Dimble. "Go on eating while they tell you. Make a good meal."

"You have to go out again," said Ivy Maggs.

"Yes," said the Director. "We're going into action at last. I'm sorry to send you out the moment you come in: but the battle has started."

"I have already repeatedly urged," said MacPhee, "the absurdity of sending out an older man like yourself, when here am I, a great strapping fellow sitting doing nothing."

"It's no good, MacPhee," said the Director, "you can't go. Put the other map on the table where Dimble can see it while he goes on with his meal. And now, Dimble. What was under Bragdon was a living Merlin. Yes, asleep, if you like to call it sleep. And nothing has yet happened to show that the enemy have found him. Last night Jane had the most important dream she's had. You remember that in an earlier dream she saw (or so I thought) the very place where he lay under Bragdon. But—and this is the important thing—it's not reached by a shaft and a stair. She dreamed of going through a long tunnel with a very gradual descent. Jane thinks she can recognise the entrance to that tunnel: under a heap of stones at the end of a copse with—what was it, Jane?"

"A white gate, sir. An ordinary five-barred gate with a cross-piece. But the cross-piece was broken off about a foot from the top. I'd know it again."

"You see, Dimble? There's a very good chance that this tunnel comes up *outside* the area held by the N.I.C.E."

"You mean," said Dimble, "that we can now get *under* Bragdon without going into Bragdon."

"Exactly. But that's not all. Apparently we are almost too late. He has waked already."

Dimble stopped eating.

"Jane found the place empty," said Ransom.

"You mean the enemy have already found him?"

"No. Not quite as bad as that. The place had not been broken into. He seems to have waked of his own accord."

"But what does it mean?"

"I think it means that the thing has been planned long, long ago," said the Director. "That he went into the parachronic state for the very purpose of returning at this moment."

"Is he *out*?" asked Dimble.

"He probably is by now," said the Director. "Tell him what it was like, Jane."

"It was the same place," said Jane. "The slab of stone was there, but no one lying on it; this time it wasn't quite cold. Then I dreamed about this tunnel . . . sloping up from the *souterrain*. And there was a man in the tunnel. A big man. Breathing heavily. At first I thought it was an animal. It got colder as we went up the tunnel. It seemed to end in a pile of loose stones. He was pulling them about just before the dream changed. Then I was outside, in the rain, at the white gate."

"It looks, you see," said Ransom, "as if they had not yet—or not then—established contact with him. Our only chance now is to meet this creature before they do."

"Bragdon is very nearly water-logged," put in MacPhee. "Where you'll find a dry cavity is a question."

"That's the point," said the Director. "The chamber must be under the high ground—the gravelly ridge on the south, where it slopes up to the Eaton Road. That's where you'll have to look for Jane's white gate. I suspect it opens on the Eaton Road. Or else that other road—the yellow one that runs up into the Y of Cure Hardy."

"We can be there in half an hour," said Dimble.

"I suppose it must be to-night?" said Mrs. Dimble shamefacedly.

"I am afraid it must, Margaret," said the Director. "Every minute counts."

"Of course. I see. I'm sorry," said Mrs. Dimble.

"And what is our procedure, sir?" said Dimble.

"The first question is whether he's *out*," said the Director. "He may take hours getting out."

" You'll need at least two strong men with picks——"
began MacPhee.

" It's no good, MacPhee," said the Director. " I'm not
sending you. But he may have powers we don't know. If
he's out, you must look for tracks. Thank God it's a muddy
night."

" If Jane is going, sir," said Camilla, " couldn't I go
too? "

" Jane has to go because she is the guide," said Ransom.
" You must stay at home. We in this house are all that is
left of Logres. You carry its future in your body. As I was
saying, Dimble, you must hunt. I do not think he can get
far. The country will be quite unrecognisable to him, even
by daylight."

" And . . . if we do find him, sir? "

" That is why it must be you, Dimble. Only you know
the Great Tongue. Even if he does not understand it he
will, I think, recognise it. That will teach him he is dealing
with Masters. There is a chance that he will think *you* are
the Belbury people. In that case you will bring him here at
once."

" And if not? "

" That is the moment when the danger comes. We do
not know what the powers of the old Atlantean circle were:
some kind of hypnotism probably covered most of it. Don't
be afraid: but don't let him try any tricks. Keep your
hand on your revolver. You too, Denniston."

" I'm a good hand with a revolver myself," said MacPhee.
" And why——? "

" You can't go, MacPhee," said the Director. " He'd
put *you* to sleep in ten seconds. The others are heavily pro-
tected and you are not. You understand, Dimble? Your
revolver in your hand, a prayer on your lips. Then, if he
stands, conjure him."

" What shall I say in the Great Tongue? "

" Say that you come in the name of God and all angels
and in the power of the planets from one who sits to-day
in the seat of the Pendragon, and command him to come
with you. Say it now."

And Dimble raised his head, and great syllables of words
came out of his mouth. Jane felt her heart leap and quiver;
it was as if the words spoke themselves through him from
some strong place at a distance—or as if they were not

words at all but present operations of God, the planets, and the Pendragon. For this was the language spoken before the Fall and beyond the Moon. Language herself, as she first sprang at Maleldil's bidding out of the molten quicksilver of the star called Mercury on Earth, but Viritrilbia in Deep Heaven.

"Thank you," said the Director. "And if he comes with you, all is well. If he does not—why then, Dimble, say your prayers and keep your will fixed in the will of Maleldil. I don't know what he will do. You can't lose your soul, whatever happens; at least, not by any action of his."

"Yes," said Dimble. "I understand."

"*You* are all right, Jane?"

"I think so, sir," said Jane.

"Do you place yourself in the obedience," said the Director, "in obedience to Maleldil?"

"Sir," said Jane, "I know nothing of Maleldil. But I place myself in obedience to you."

"It is enough for the present," said the Director. "This is the courtesy of Deep Heaven: that when you mean well, He always takes you to have meant better than you knew. It will not be enough for always. He is very jealous. He will have you for no one but Himself in the end. But for to-night, it is enough."

"This is the craziest business ever I heard of," said MacPhee.

CHAPTER ELEVEN

BATTLE BEGUN

I

"I can't see a thing," said Jane.

"This rain is spoiling the whole plan," said Dimble from the back seat. "Is this still Eaton Road, Arthur?"

"I think . . . yes, there's the toll-house," said Denniston, who was driving.

"I say!" said Jane suddenly. "Look! Look! What's that? Stop."

"I can't see a white gate," said Denniston.

" Oh, it's not that," said Jane. " Look over there."

" Do you mean that light? " said Denniston.

" Yes, of course, that's the fire."

" What fire? "

" It's the light," she said, " the fire in the hollow. Yes, I know: I never told Grace, or the Director. I'd forgotten that part of the dream till this moment. That was how it ended. It was the most important part. That was where I found *him*—Merlin, you know. Sitting by a fire in a little wood. After I came out of the place underground. Oh, come quickly! "

" What do you think, Arthur? " said Dimble.

" I think we must go wherever Jane leads," answered Denniston.

" Oh, do hurry," said Jane. " There's a gate here. It's only one field away."

All three of them crossed the road and opened the gate and went into the field. Dimble said nothing. He had, perhaps, a clearer idea than the others of what sort of things might happen when they reached the place.

Jane, as guide, went first, and Denniston beside her, giving her his arm and showing an occasional gleam of his torch on the rough ground. Dimble brought up the rear.

The change from the road to the field was as if one had passed from a waking into a phantasmal world. They realised that they had not really believed in Merlin till now. They had thought they were believing the Director in the kitchen; but they had been mistaken. Out here, with only the changing red light ahead and the black all round, one began to accept as fact this tryst with something dead and yet not dead, something exhumed from that dark pit of history which lies between the ancient Romans and the beginning of the English. " The Dark Ages," thought Dimble; how lightly one had read and written those words.

Suddenly all that Britain which had been so long familiar to him as a scholar rose up like a solid thing. He could see it all. Little dwindling cities where the light of Rome still rested—little Christian sites, Camalodunum, Kaerleon, Glastonbury—a church, a villa or two, a huddle of houses, an earthwork. And then, beginning a stone's-throw beyond the gates, the wet, tangled, endless woods; wolves slinking, beavers building, wide shallow marshes, dim horns and drummings, eyes in the thickets, eyes of men not only

Pre-Roman but Pre-British, ancient creatures, unhappy and dispossessed, who became the elves and ogres and wood-wooses of the later tradition. But worse than the forests, the clearings. Little strongholds with unheard-of kings. Little colleges and covines of Druids. Houses whose mortar had been ritually mixed with babies' blood.

Then came a check. They had walked right into a hedge. They had come to the end of a field. They went a long way out of their course before they found a gate. It would not open, and as they came down on the far side, after climbing it, they went ankle-deep into water.

Hitherto Jane had scarcely attempted to think of what might lie before them. As they went on, the real meaning of that scene in the kitchen began to dawn on her. He had told the men to bid good-bye to their wives. He had blessed them all. It was likely, then, that this—this stumbling walk on a wet night across a ploughed field—meant death. Jane was trying to see death in the new light of all she had heard since she left Edgestow. She had long ceased to feel any resentment at the Director's tendency, as it were, to dispose of her—to give her, at one time or in one sense, to Mark, and in another to Maleldil; never, in any sense, to keep her for himself. But Maleldil. Up to now she had not thought of Maleldil either. She did not doubt that the eldils existed; nor did she doubt the existence of this stronger and more obscure being whom they obeyed . . . whom the Director obeyed, and through him the whole household, even MacPhee. If it had ever occurred to her to question whether all these things might be the reality behind what she had been taught at school as " religion ", she had put the thought aside. But this time, if it was really to be death, the thought would not be put aside. Because, really, it now appeared that almost anything might be true. One might be in for anything. Maleldil might be, quite simply and crudely, God. There might be a life after death: a Heaven: a Hell. " But . . . this is unbearable," she thought, " I should have been told."

" Look out, Jane," said Denniston. " That's a tree."

" I—I think it's a cow," said Jane.

" No. It's a tree. Look. There's another."

" Hush," said Dimble. " This is Jane's little wood. We are very close now."

The ground rose in front of them for about twenty yards and there made an edge against the firelight. They walked slowly and quietly up to the edge and stopped. Below them a big fire of wood was burning at the bottom of a little dingle. There were bushes all about, whose changing shadows, as the flames rose and fell, made it difficult to see clearly. Beyond the fire there seemed to be some rude kind of tent made out of sacking and an upturned cart. In the foreground there was a kettle.

"Is there anyone here?" whispered Dimble to Denniston.

"Look!" said Jane suddenly. "There! When the flame blew aside."

"What?" said Dimble.

"Didn't you see him?"

"I thought I saw a man," said Denniston.

"I saw an ordinary tramp," said Dimble. "A man in modern clothes."

"What did he look like?"

"I don't know."

"We must go down," said Dimble.

"*Can* one get down?" said Denniston.

"Not this side," said Dimble. "It looks as if a sort of path came into it over there to the right."

Cautiously they began to skirt the lip of the hollow, stealing from tree to tree.

"Stop!" whispered Jane suddenly.

"What is it?"

"There's something moving."

"Where?"

"In there. Quite close."

"Wait a moment," said Denniston. "It's just there. Look!—damn it, it's only an old donkey!"

"That's what I said," said Dimble. "The man's a gypsy; a tinker or something. This is his donkey. Still, we must go down."

And in less than a minute all three walked down into the dingle and past the fire. And there was the tent, and a few miserable attempts at bedding inside it, and a tin plate, and some matches on the ground, and the dottle of a pipe, but they could see no man.

"What I can't understand, Wither," said Fairy Hardcastle, "is why you don't let me try my hand on the young pup. All these ideas of yours are so half-hearted—keeping him on his toes about the murder, arresting him, leaving him all night in the cells to think it over. Twenty minutes. of my treatment would turn his mind inside out. I know the type."

Miss Hardcastle was talking, at about ten o'clock that same wet night, to the Deputy Director in his study. There was a third person present—Professor Frost.

"I assure you, Miss Hardcastle," said Wither, fixing his eyes not on her but on Frost's forehead, "you need not doubt that your views on this, or any other matter, will always receive the fullest consideration. But you must excuse me for reminding you—not, of course, that I assume you are neglecting the point—that we need the woman—I mean, that it would be of the greatest value to welcome Mrs. Studdock among us—chiefly on account of the remarkable psychical faculty she is said to possess. In using the word *psychical*, I am not, you understand, committing myself to any particular theory."

"You mean these dreams?"

"It is very doubtful," said Wither, "what effect it might have on her if she were brought here under compulsion and then found her husband—ah—in the markedly, though no doubt temporarily, abnormal condition which we should have to anticipate as a result of your scientific methods of examination. One would run the risk of a profound emotional disturbance on her part."

"We have not yet had Major Hardcastle's report," said Professor Frost quietly.

"No good," said the Fairy. "He was shadowed into Northumberland. Only three possible people left the College after him—Lancaster, Lyly, and Dimble. I put them in that order of probability. Lancaster is a Christian, and a very influential man. He's in the Lower House of Convocation. He had a lot to do with the Repton Conference. He has a real stake in their side. Lyly is rather the same type, but less of an organiser. Both are dangerous men. Dimble is quite a different type. Except that he's a Christian, there isn't much against him. He's purely academic. Impractical . . . he'd be too full of scruples to be much use to them."

"You should tell Major Hardcastle that we have access to most of these facts already," said Professor Frost.

"Perhaps," said Wither, "in view of the late hour——"

"Well," said the Fairy, "I had to follow all three. With the resources I had at the moment. You'll realise young Studdock was seen setting off for Edgestow only by good luck. It was a bomb-shell. Half my people were already busy. I had to lay my hands on anyone I could get. I posted a sentry and had six others out of sight of the College, in plain clothes. As soon as Lancaster came out I told off the three best to keep him in sight. We may be on to something there. I sent the next two of my lads to deal with Lyly. Dimble came out last. I would have sent my last man to follow him, but a call came through at that moment from O'Hara, who wanted another car. So I sent my man up with the one hc had. Dimble can be got any time. He comes into college pretty regularly; and he's a nonentity."

"I do not quite understand," said Frost, "why you had no one inside the College to see what staircase Studdock went to."

"Because of your damned Emergency Commissioner," said the Fairy. "We're not *allowed* into colleges now, if you please. I said at the time that Feverstone was the wrong man. He's trying to play on both sides."

"I am far from denying," said Wither, "though without at all closing my mind to other possible explanations, that some of Lord Feverstone's measures may have been injudicious. It would be inexpressibly painful to me to suppose that——"

"Need we keep Major Hardcastle?" said Frost.

"Bless my soul!" said Wither. "How very right of you! I had almost forgotten, my dear lady, how tired you must be, and how very valuable your time is." He got up and held the door open for her.

"You don't think," said she, "that I ought to let the boys have just a *little* go at Studdock?"

And suddenly, as Wither stood with his hand on the doorhandle, the whole expression faded out of his face. Miss Hardcastle had the feeling that a mere mask of skin and flesh was staring at her. A moment later she was gone.

"I wonder," said Wither as he came back to his chair, "whether we are attaching too much importance to this Studdock woman."

"Allow me to remind you of the facts," said Frost. "The authorities had access to the woman's mind for only a very short time. They inspected only one important dream—which revealed, though with some irrelevancies, an essential element in our programme. That warned us that if the woman fell into the hands of any ill-affected persons who knew how to exploit her faculty, she would constitute a grave danger."

"Oh, to be sure, to be sure. I never intended to deny——"

"That was the first point," said Frost. "The second is that her mind became opaque to our authorities immediately afterwards. We know only one cause for such occultations. They occur when the mind in question has placed itself, by some voluntary choice, however vague, under the control of some hostile organism. The occultation, therefore, while cutting off our access to the dreams, also tells us that she has come under enemy influence. It also means that to find her would probably mean discovering the enemy's headquarters. Miss Hardcastle is probably right in maintaining that torture would soon induce Studdock to give up his wife's address. But as you pointed out, a round-up at their headquarters, an arrest, and the discovery of her husband here in the condition in which the torture would leave him, would produce psychological conditions in the woman which might destroy her faculty. That is the first objection. The second is, that an attack on enemy headquarters is very risky. They almost certainly have protection of a kind we are not prepared to cope with. And, finally, the man may not *know* his wife's address. In that case . . ."

"Oh," said Wither, "there is nothing I should more deeply deplore. Scientific examination (I cannot allow the word *Torture* in this context) in cases where the patient doesn't *know* the answer is always a mistake. As men of humanity we should neither of us . . . and then, if you go on, the patient naturally does not recover. . . ."

"There is, in fact, no way of implementing our instructions except by inducing Studdock to bring his wife here himself."

" Or else," said Wither, a little more dreamily than usual, " if it were possible, by inducing in him a much more radical allegiance to our side than he has yet shown. I am speaking, my dear friend, of a real change of heart."

" I was saying that he must be induced to send for the woman himself. That can be done in two ways. Either by supplying him with some motive on the instinctive level, such as fear of us or desire for her; or else by conditioning him to identify himself so completely with the Cause that he will understand the real motive for securing her person and act on it."

" Exactly . . . exactly," said Wither.

" Where is Studdock at present ? " said Frost.

" In one of the cells."

" Under the impression he has been arrested by the ordinary police ? "

" I presume he would be."

" And how are you proposing to act ? "

" We had proposed to allow the psychological results of the arrest to mature. I have ventured . . . of course, with every regard for humanity . . . to reckon on the value of some slight discomforts—he will not have dined, you understand. They have instructions to empty his pockets. One would not wish the young man to relieve any nervous tension by smoking."

" Of course. And what next ? "

" Well, I suppose some sort of examination. I am inclined to think that the appearance of examination by the ordinary police should be maintained a little longer. Then at a later stage will come the discovery that he is still in our hands. It would be well to let him realise only gradually that this by no means frees him from the—er—embarrassments arising out of Hingest's death. I take it that some fuller realisation of his inevitable solidarity with the Institute would then follow. . . ."

" The weakness is that you are relying wholly on fear."

" Fear," repeated Wither as if he had not heard the word before. " I do not quite follow the connection of thought. I can hardly suppose you are following the opposite suggestion, once made, if I remember, by Miss Hardcastle."

" What was that ? "

" Why," said Wither, " if I understand her aright she thought of taking scientific measures to render the society

145

of his wife more desirable to him. Some of the chemical resources . . ."

" You mean an aphrodisiac? "

Wither sighed gently and said nothing.

" That is nonsense," said Frost. " It isn't to his wife that a man turns under the influence of aphrodisiacs. But as I was saying, I think it is a mistake to rely wholly on fear. But there are other alternatives. There is desire."

" I am not sure that I am following you. You have rejected the idea of any medical or chemical approach."

" I was thinking of stronger desires."

Neither at this stage of the conversation nor at any other did the Deputy Director look much at the face of Frost. But either Frost or Wither—it was difficult to say which— had been gradually moving his chair, so that by this time the two sat with their knees almost touching.

" I had my conversation with Filostrato," said Frost. " I used expressions which must have made my meaning clear if he had any notion of the truth. His assistant, Wilkins, was present. The truth is, neither is really interested. What interests them is the fact that they have succeeded—as they think—in keeping the Head alive and getting it to talk. What it says does not really interest them. As to any question about what is really speaking, they have no curiosity."

" You are suggesting, if I understand," said Wither, " a movement towards Mr. Studdock along *those* lines. I need hardly say that I fully realise a certain disappointment which serious-minded people must feel with such colleagues as Filostrato."

" That is the point," said Frost. " One must guard against supposing that the political and economic dominance of England by the N.I.C.E. is more than a subordinate object: it is individuals we are really concerned with. A hard core of individuals really devoted to the cause—that is what we need and are under orders to supply. We have not succeeded so far in bringing many people in—really *in*."

" There is still no news from Bragdon Wood? "

" No."

" And you believe that Studdock might really be a suitable person? "

" You must not forget," said Frost, " that his value does not rest solely on his wife's clairvoyance. The couple are

146

eugenically interesting. And I think he can offer no resistance. The hours of fear in the cell, and then an appeal to desires that undercut the fear, will have an almost certain effect on a character of that sort."

"Of course," said Wither, "nothing is so much to be desired as the greatest possible unity. Any fresh individual brought into that unity would be a source of the most intense satisfaction—to—ah—all concerned. You need not doubt that I would open my arms to receive—to absorb— to assimilate this young man."

They were now sitting so close together that their faces almost touched, as if they had been lovers about to kiss. Suddenly there was a crash. *Who's Who* had fallen off the table, swept on to the floor as, with sudden, swift convulsive movement, the two old men lurched forward towards each other and sat swaying to and fro, locked in an embrace from which each seemed to be struggling to escape. And as they swayed and scrabbled with hand and nail, there arose, shrill and faint at first, a cackling noise that seemed in the end rather an animal than a senile parody of laughter.

III

When Mark was bundled out of the police waggon and left at length alone in a little lighted room, he had no idea that he was at Belbury. Nor would he have cared greatly if he had known, for the moment he was arrested he had despaired of his life. He was going to be hanged.

There came a sudden uprush of grisly details about execution, supplied long since by Miss Hardcastle.

Because he felt that he was choking, he looked round the cell for any sign of ventilation. There was, in fact, some sort of grating above the door. All else was white floor, white ceiling, white wall, without a chair or table or peg, and one hard white light in the centre of the ceiling.

Something in the look of the place now suggested to him for the first time the idea that he might be at Belbury and not in an ordinary police station. But the flash of hope aroused by this idea was so brief as to be instantaneous. What difference did it make whether Wither and Miss Hardcastle and the rest decided to get rid of him by handing him over to the ordinary police or by making away with him in private? They were all his enemies, playing upon his hopes and fears to reduce him to servility, certain to kill him if he broke away, and certain to kill him in the long run when he had served the purpose for which they wanted him. It appeared to him astonishing that he could ever have thought otherwise.

What a fool—a babyish, gullible fool—he had been! Why had he come to Belbury in the first instance? Ought not his first interview with the Deputy Director to have warned him. Feverstone's guffaw, that day he had called him an " incurable romantic ", came back to his mind. Feverstone . . . that was how he had come to believe in Wither: on Feverstone's recommendation. Apparently his folly went farther back. How on earth had he come to trust Feverstone? Jane, or Dimble, would have seen through him at once. He had " crook " written all over him. He was fit only to deceive puppets like Curry and Busby. But then, at the time when he first met Feverstone, he had not thought Curry and Busby puppets. With astonishment he remembered how he had felt about the Progressive Element at Bracton when he was first admitted to its confidence. Was there *no* beginning to his folly? Had he been a fool all through from the day of his birth? Even as a schoolboy, when he had ruined his work and half broken his heart trying to get into the society called Grip, and lost his only real friend in doing so? Even as a child, fighting Myrtle because she *would* go and talk secrets with Pamela next door?

There were no moral considerations at this moment in Mark's mind. He looked back on his life, not with shame but with a kind of disgust at its dreariness. He saw himself as a little boy in short trousers, hidden in the shrubbery beside the paling to overhear Myrtle's conversation with Pamela, and trying to ignore the fact that it was not at all interesting when overheard. He saw himself making believe that he enjoyed those Sunday afternoons with the athletic heroes of Grip, while all the time (as he now saw) he was almost homesick for one of the old walks with Pearson —Pearson whom he had taken such pains to leave behind. He saw himself in his teens laboriously reading rubbishy grown-up novels and drinking beer when he really enjoyed John Buchan and stone ginger. The hours that he had spent learning the slang of each new circle, the assumption of interest in things he found dull and of knowledge he did not possess, the sacrifice of nearly every person and thing he actually enjoyed, the miserable attempt to pretend that one *could* enjoy Grip, or the Progressive Element, or the N.I.C.E. —all this came over him with a kind of heartbreak. When had he ever done what he wanted? Mixed with the people whom he liked? Or even eaten and drunk what took his fancy? The concentrated insipidity of it all filled him with self-pity.

In his normal condition, explanations that laid on impersonal forces outside himself the responsibility for all this life of dust and broken bottles would have occurred at once to his mind and been at once accepted. None of these occurred to him now. He was aware that it was he himself who had chosen the dust and broken bottles, the heap of old tin cans, the dry and choking places.

An unexpected idea came into his head. This—this death of his—would be lucky for Jane. He now knew, for the first time, what he had secretly meant to do with Jane. If all had succeeded, if he had become the sort of man he hoped to be, she was to have been the great hostess. Well . . . it was lucky for Jane. She seemed to him, as he now thought of her, to have in herself deep wells and knee-deep meadows of happiness, rivers of freshness, enchanted gardens of leisure, which he could not enter but could have spoiled. She was one of those other people—like Pearson, like Denniston, like the Dimbles—who could enjoy things for their own sake. She was not like him. It was well that she should be rid of him. Of course she would get over it. She had tried to do her best, but she didn't really care for him. Nobody ever had, much.

At that moment came the sound of a key turning in the lock of the cell-door. Instantly physical terror rushed back upon him.

It was not a policeman who came in. It was a man whose pince-nez, as he glanced towards the light, became opaque windows concealing his eyes. Mark knew him at once and knew that he was at Belbury. It was not this that made him open his own eyes even wider and almost forget his terror in his astonishment. It was the change in the man's appearance—or rather the change in the eyes with which Mark saw him. In one sense everything about Professor Frost was as it had always been—the pointed beard, the extreme whiteness of forehead, and the bright Arctic smile. But Mark could not understand how he had ever managed to overlook something about the man so obvious that any child would have shrunk away from him and any dog would have backed into the corner with raised hackles and bared teeth. Death itself did not seem more frightening than the fact that only six hours ago he would in some measure have trusted this man, and made believe that his society was not disagreeable.

CHAPTER TWELVE

WET AND WINDY NIGHT

I

" WELL," said Dimble, " there's no one here."

" He was here a moment ago," said Denniston.

" You're sure you *did* see someone? " said Dimble.

" Hush! Listen! " said Jane.

" That's only the old donkey," said Dimble presently, " moving about at the top."

There was another silence.

" He seems to have been pretty extravagant with his matches," said Denniston, glancing at the trodden earth in the firelight. " One would expect a tramp——"

" On the other hand," said Dimble, " one would not expect Merlin to have brought a box of matches with him from the Fifth Century."

" I'm looking at this mud," said Denniston, who had been stooping and using his torch. Now he suddenly straightened himself. " Look," he said, " there have been several people here. Look. Can't you see, sir? "

" Aren't they our own footprints? " said Dimble.

" Some of them are pointing the wrong way. Look at that—and that."

" Might they be the tramp himself? " said Dimble. " If it was a tramp."

" He couldn't have walked up that path without our seeing him," said Jane.

" Come," said Dimble. " Let's follow them up to the top."

As they reached the lip of the hollow, mud changed into

grass under foot and the footprints disappeared. It had turned into a fine night: Orion dominated the whole sky.

II

The Deputy Director hardly ever slept. When it became necessary for him to do so, he took a drug, but the necessity was rare, for the mode of consciousness he experienced at most hours of day or night had long ceased to be exactly like what other men call waking. The manner and outward attitude which he had adopted half a century ago were now an organisation which functioned almost independently, like a gramophone. While the brain and lips carried on his work, and built up day by day for those around him the vague and formidable personality which they knew so well, his inmost self was free to pursue its own life. A detachment of the spirit not only from the senses but even from the reason was now his.

Hence he was still, in a sense, awake an hour after Frost had left him. His eyes were not shut. The face had no expression; the real man was far away, suffering, enjoying, or inflicting whatever such souls do suffer, enjoy, or inflict when the cord that binds them to the natural order is stretched out to its utmost. When the telephone rang at his elbow he took up the receiver without a start.

" This is Stone, sir," came a voice. " We have found the chamber."

" Yes."

" It was empty, sir."

" Are you sure, my dear Mr. Stone, that you have found the right place? It is possible . . ."

" Oh yes, sir. Stonework and some Roman brick. And a kind of slab in the middle, like an altar or a bed."

" And am I to understand there was no one there? No sign of occupation? "

" Well, sir, it seemed to us to have been recently disturbed."

" Pray be as explicit as possible, Mr. Stone."

" Well, sir, there was an exit—I mean a tunnel, leading out of it to the south. We went up this tunnel at once. It comes out about eight hundred yards away, outside the area of the wood. We got out to the open air. But something had been smashed-up there quite recently. It looked as if it had been done by explosives. As if the end of the tunnel had been walled up and had some depth of earth on top of it, and as if someone had recently blasted his way out."

"Continue, Mr. Stone. What did you do next?"

"I used the order you had given me, sir, to collect all the police available and have sent off search-parties for the man you described."

"I see. And how did *you* describe him to them?"

"Just as you did, sir: an old man with a long beard, probably in unusual clothes. It occurred to me at the last moment to add that he might have no clothes at all."

"Why did you add that, Mr. Stone?"

"Well, sir, I didn't know how long he'd been there, and I'd heard about clothes preserved in a place like that and falling to pieces as soon as the air was admitted. I hope you won't imagine for a moment that I'm trying to find out anything you don't choose to tell me. But I——"

"You were right, Mr. Stone," said Wither, "in thinking that anything remotely resembling inquisitiveness on your part might have the most disastrous consequences. And what did you instruct your search-parties to do on finding any such—er—person?"

"Well, sir, I sent my assistant, Father Doyle, with one party, because he knows Latin. And I gave Inspector Wrench the ring you gave me and put him in charge of the second. The best I could do for the third party was to see that it contained someone who knew Welsh."

"Well, Mr. Stone, I am, on the whole, and with certain inevitable reservations, moderately satisfied with your conduct of this affair. I believe that I may be able to present it in a favourable light to my colleagues. If only I could persuade—say Miss Hardcastle and Mr. Studdock—to share my appreciation of your very real qualities, you would need to have no apprehensions about your career or—ah—your security."

"But what do you want me to *do*, sir?"

"My dear young friend, there are only two errors which would be fatal to one placed in the peculiar situation which certain parts of your previous conduct have unfortunately created for you. On the one hand, anything like a lack of initiative or enterprise would be disastrous. On the other, the slightest approach to unauthorised action might have consequences from which even I could not protect you.

But as long as you keep quite clear of these two extremes, there is no reason (speaking unofficially) why you should not be safe."

Without waiting for a reply, he hung up the receiver.

III

"Oughtn't we to be nearly at the gate we climbed over?" said Dimble.

It was lighter now that the rain had stopped, but the wind had risen and was roaring about them. The branches of the hedge swayed and dipped and rose again as if they were lashing the bright stars.

"It's a good deal longer than I remembered," said Denniston.

"Hullo!" said Jane sharply. "What's this?"

All listened. Because of the wind, the unidentified noise which they were straining to hear seemed quite distant at one moment, and then, next moment, with shouts of "Look out!"—"Go away you great brute!" and the like, all were shrinking back into the hedge as the *plosh-plosh* of a horse cantering on soft ground passed close beside them. A cold gobbet of mud struck Denniston in the face.

"Oh, look! Look!" cried Jane. "Stop him. Quick!"

"Stop him?" said Denniston, who was trying to clean his face. "What on earth for?"

"Oh, shout out to him, Dr. Dimble," said Jane, in an agony of impatience. "Come on. Run! Didn't you see?"

"See what?"

"There's a man on his back," gasped Jane. She was tired and out of breath and had lost a shoe.

"A man?" said Denniston: and then, "By God, sir, Jane's right. Look, look there! Against the sky . . . to your left."

"We can't overtake him," said Dimble.

"Hi! Stop! Come back! Friends—*amis—amici*," bawled Denniston.

Dimble was not able to shout for the moment. And while he stood trying to get his breath all the others suddenly cried "Look" yet again: for high among the stars, looking unnaturally large and many legged, the shape of the horse appeared as it leaped a hedge some twenty yards away, and

153

on its back, with some streaming garment blown far out behind him in the wind, the great figure of a man. It seemed to Jane that he was looking back over his shoulder as though he mocked. Then came a splash and thud as the horse alighted on the far side; and then nothing but wind and starlight again.

IV

" You are in danger," said Frost, when he had finished locking the door of Mark's cell, " but you are also within reach of a great opportunity."

" I gather," said Mark, " I am at the Institute and not in a police station."

" Yes. That makes no difference to the danger. The Institute will soon have official powers of liquidation. It has anticipated them. Hingest and Carstairs have both been liquidated."

" If you are going to kill me," said Mark, " why all this farce of a murder charge? "

" Before going on," said Frost, " I must ask you to be objective. Resentment and fear are both chemical phenomena. Our reactions to one another are chemical phenomena. You must observe these feelings in yourself in an objective manner. Do not let them distract your attention from the facts."

" I see," said Mark. He was acting while he said it—trying to sound at once faintly hopeful and slightly sullen, ready to be worked upon. But within, his new insight into Belbury kept him resolved not to believe one word the other said, not to accept (though he might feign acceptance) any offer he made.

" The murder charge against you and the alternations in your treatment have been part of a programme with a well-defined end in view," said Frost. " It is a discipline through which everyone is passed before admission to the Circle."

Only a few days ago Mark would have swallowed any hook with that bait on it; and even now . . .

" I don't quite see the purpose of it," he said aloud.

" It is, again, to promote objectivity. A circle bound together by subjective feelings of mutual confidence and liking would be useless. Those are chemical phenomena.

They could all, in principle, be produced by injections. In so far as there must be social feelings between members of the circle it is, perhaps, better that they should be feelings of dislike. There is less risk of their being confused with the real *nexus*."

" The circle? " said Studdock, acting a tremulous eagerness. But it was perilously easy for him to act it.

" Yes," said Frost. " You have been selected as a possible candidate for admission. If you do not gain admission, or if you reject it, it will be necessary to destroy you."

" It—it seems rather a formidable decision," said Mark.

" That is merely a proposition about the state of your own body at the moment. If you please, I will go on to give you the necessary information. I must begin by telling you that neither the Deputy Director nor I are responsible for shaping the policy of the Institute."

" The Head? " said Mark.

" No. Filostrato and Wilkins are quite deceived about the Head. They have, indeed, carried out a remarkable experiment. But Alcasan's mind is not the mind we are in contact with when the Head speaks."

" Do you mean Alcasan is really . . . *dead*? "

" In the present state of our knowledge," said Frost, " that question has no meaning. But the cortex and vocal organs in Alcasan's head are used by a different mind. And now, attend carefully. You have probably not heard of macrobes."

" Microbes? " said Mark in bewilderment. " But of course——"

" I did not say *microbes*, I said *macrobes*. The formation of the word explains itself. Below the level of animal life we have long known that there are microscopic organisms. Their actual results on human life have, of course, made up a large part of history."

" Go on," said Mark. Ravenous curiosity was moving beneath his conscious determination to stand on guard.

" I have now to inform you that there are similar organisms *above* the level of animal life. When I say ' above ' I am not speaking biologically. I mean that they are more permanent, dispose of more energy, and have greater intelligence."

" They must be pretty nearly human, then."

" You have misunderstood me. When I said they transcended the animals, I was including the most efficient animal, Man. The *macrobe* is more intelligent than Man."

" But how is it in that case that we have had no communication with them? "

" It is not certain that we have not. But in primitive times it was opposed by prejudice. But though there has been little intercourse, there has been profound influence. Their effect on human history has been greater than that of the microbes, though equally unrecognised. The real causes of all the principal events are quite unknown to the historians."

" I think I'll sit down, if you don't mind," said Mark, resuming his seat on the floor.

" The vocal organs and brain taken from Alcasan," Frost continued, " have become the conductors of a regular intercourse between the macrobes and our own species. The circle to which you may be admitted is the organ of that co-operation between the two species which has created a new situation for humanity. The change is far greater than that which turned the sub-man into the man."

" These organisms, then," said Mark, " are friendly to humanity? "

" Friendship is a chemical phenomenon; so is hatred. Both of them presupposes organisms of our own type."

" I didn't mean ' friendly ' in that sense. I meant, were their aims compatible with our own? "

" What do you mean by our own aims? "

" Well—I suppose—the scientific reconstruction of the human race—the elimination of war and poverty—a fuller exploitation of nature—the preservation and extension of our species, in fact."

" I do not think this pseudo-scientific language really modifies the essentially subjective and instinctive basis of the ethics you are describing."

" Surely," said Mark, " one requires a large population for the full exploitation of nature, if for nothing else? And surely war is disgenic and reduces efficiency? "

" That idea is a survival from conditions which are rapidly being altered. A few centuries ago, a large agricultural population was essential; and war destroyed types which were then useful. But every advance in industry and agriculture reduces the number of work-people required. A large, unintelligent population is now a dead-weight. The importance of scientific war is that scientists have to be reserved. It was not the great technocrats of Koenigsberg or Moscow who supplied the casualties in the siege of Stalingrad. The effect of modern war is to eliminate retrogressive types, while sparing the technocracy and increasing its hold upon public affairs. In the new age, what has hitherto been merely the intellectual nucleus of the race is to become, by gradual stages, the race itself. You are to conceive the species as an animal which has discovered how to simplify nutrition and locomotion to such a point that the old complex organs and the large body which contained them are no longer necessary. The masses are therefore to disappear. The body is to become all head. The human race is to become all Technocracy."

" I see," said Mark. " I had thought that the intelligent nucleus would be extended by education."

" That is a pure chimera. The great majority of the human race cannot be educated. Even if they could, the day for a large population has passed. It has served its function as a kind of cocoon for Technocratic and Objective Man. Now, the macrobes, and the selected humans who co-operate with them, have no further use for it."

" The last two wars, then, were not disasters in your view? "

" On the contrary, they were simply the first two of the sixteen major wars which are scheduled to take place in this century."

Mark sat with his eyes fixed on the floor. He was occupied with the conflict between his resolution not to trust these men, and the terrible strength of an opposite emotion. For here, here surely at last (so his desire whispered him) was the true inner circle of all, the circle whose centre was outside the human race—the ultimate secret, the supreme power, the last initiation. The fact that it was almost completely horrible did not in the least diminish its attraction. Nothing that lacked the tang of horror would have been quite strong enough to satisfy the delirious excitement which now set his temples hammering.

A knocking which had been obscurely audible for some time now became so loud that Frost turned to the door. " Go away," he said, raising his voice. " What is the meaning of this impertinence? " The noise of someone shouting was heard, and the knocking went on. Frost's smile widened as he turned and opened the door. Instantly a piece of paper was put into his hand. As he read it, he started violently. Without glancing at Mark, he left the cell. Mark heard the door locked behind him.

V

"What friends those two are!" said Ivy Maggs. She was referring to Pinch the cat and Mr. Bultitude the bear. The latter was sitting up with his back against the warm wall by the kitchen fire. The cat, after walking to and fro with erected tail and rubbing herself against his belly, had finally curled up and gone to sleep between his legs.

Mrs. Dimble, who sat farther back in the kitchen, darning as if for dear life, pursed her lips a little as Ivy Maggs spoke. She could not go to bed. She wished they would all keep quiet.

"When we use the word Friends of those two creatures," said MacPhee, "I doubt we are being merely anthropomorphic. There's no evidence for it."

"What's she go making up to him for, then?" asked Ivy.

"Well," said MacPhee, "maybe there'd be a desire for warmth—she's away in out of the draught there. And likely enough some obscure transferred sexual impulses."

"Really, Mr. MacPhee," said Ivy with great indignation. "To say those things about two dumb animals! I'm sure I never did see Pinch——"

"I said *transferred*," interrupted MacPhee drily. "And anyway, they like the friction as a means of rectifying irritations set up by parasites. Now, you'll observe——"

"If you mean they have fleas," said Ivy, "you know as well as anyone they have no such thing."

"What do you think, sir?" added Ivy, looking at the Director.

"Me?" said Ransom. "I think MacPhee is introducing into animal life a distinction that doesn't exist there, and then trying to determine on which side of that distinction the feelings of Pinch and Bultitude fall. You've got to become human before physical cravings are distinguishable from affections—as you have to become spiritual before affections are distinguishable from charity. What is going

158

on in them isn't one or other of these things: it is one of Barfield's ' ancient unities '."

Mrs. Dimble leaned her head towards Camilla and said in a whisper, " I do wish Mr. MacPhee could be persuaded to go to bed. It's perfectly unbearable at a time like this."

" Was that only the wind? " said Grace Ironwood.

" It sounded to me like a horse," said Mrs. Dimble.

" Here," said MacPhee jumping up. " Get out of the way, Mr. Bultitude, till I get my gum boots. It'll be those two horses of Broad's again, tramping all over my celery. Why the man can't keep them shut up . . ."—he was bundling himself into his mackintosh as he spoke.

" My crutch, please, Camilla," said Ransom. " Come back, MacPhee. We will go to the door together, you and I. Ladies, stay where you are."

There was a look on his face which some of those present had not seen before. A moment later Ransom and Mac-Phee stood alone in the scullery. The back door was so shaking with the wind that they did not know whether someone were knocking or not.

" Now," said Ransom, " open it."

For a second MacPhee worked with the bolts. Then the storm flung the door against the wall and he was momentarily pinned behind it. Ransom, leaning forward on his crutch, saw in the light from the scullery, outlined against the blackness, a huge horse, all in a lather of sweat and foam, its yellow teeth laid bare, its ears flattened against its skull, and its eyes flaming. It had neither saddle, stirrup, nor bridle; but at that very moment a man leapt off its back. He seemed both very tall and very fat, almost a giant. His reddish-grey hair and beard were blown all about his face so that it was hardly visible; and it was only after he had taken a step forward that Ransom noticed his clothes—the ragged, ill-fitting khaki coat, baggy trousers, and boots that had lost the toes.

VI

In a great room at Belbury, where the fire blazed and wine and silver sparkled on side-tables, and a great bed occupied the centre of the floor, the Deputy Director watched while four men carried in a burden on a stretcher. As they removed the blankets and transferred the occupant of the stretcher to the bed, Wither's interest became intense. What he saw was a naked human body, alive, but apparently unconscious. He ordered the attendants to place hot-water bottles at its feet and raise the head with pillows; when they had withdrawn he drew a chair to the foot of the bed and sat down to study the face of the sleeper. The head was very large, though perhaps it looked larger than it was because of the unkempt beard and the tangled grey hair. For a quarter of an hour he sat thus: then the door opened and Professor Frost came in.

He walked to the bedside, bent down and looked closely into the stranger's face.

" Is he asleep? " whispered Wither.

" I think not. It is more like some kind of trance."

" You have no doubts, I trust? "

" Where did they find him? "

" Quarter of a mile from the entrance to the *souterrain*. They had the track of bare feet almost all the way."

" You will make provision about Stone? "

" Yes. But what do you think? "—he pointed with his eyes to the bed.

" I think it is he," said Frost. " The place is right. The nudity is hard to account for on any other hypothesis. The skull is the kind I expected."

" But the face? "

" Yes. There are certain traits which are a little disquieting."

" I could have sworn," said Wither, " that I knew the look of a Master—even the look of one who could be made into a Master. You understand me . . . one sees at once that Straik or Studdock might do; that Miss Hardcastle, with all her excellent qualities, would not."

" Yes. Perhaps we must be prepared for great crudities in . . . *him*. Who knows what the technique of the Atlantean Circle was really like? "

" Certainly, one must not be—ah—narrow-minded. One can suppose that the Masters of that age were not quite so sharply divided from the common people as we are. All sorts of emotional, and even instinctive, elements were perhaps still tolerated in the Great Atlantean which we have had to discard."

Instead of replying, Frost signalled to his companion. The Sleeper had opened his eyes.

As the seconds passed Wither's main impression of the face was its caution. But there was nothing intense or uneasy about it. It had an habitual, unemphatic defensiveness.

Wither rose to his feet, and cleared his throat.

" *Magister Merline*," he said, " *Sapientissime Britonum, secreti secretorum possessor, incredibili quodam gaudio afficimur quod te domum nostram accipere nobis—ah—contingit. Scito nos etiam haud imperitos esse magnae artis—et—ut ita dicam* . . ." [1]

But his voice died away. It was too obvious that the Sleeper was taking no notice of what he said. Was there, then, some error in his own pronunciation? But he felt by no means sure that this man could not understand him. The total lack of interest in his face suggested rather that he was not listening.

Frost took a decanter from the table and poured out a glass of red wine. He then returned to the bedside, bowed deeply, and handed it to the stranger. The latter sat up in bed, revealing a huge hairy chest and lean, muscular arms. His eyes turned to the table and he pointed. Frost went back to it and touched a different decanter. The stranger shook his head and pointed again.

" I think," said Wither, " that our very distinguished guest is trying to indicate the jug."

" It contains beer," said Frost.

" Well, it is hardly appropriate—still, perhaps, we know so little of the customs of that age . . ."

While he was still speaking Frost had filled a pewter mug with beer and offered it to their guest. For the first time a gleam of interest came into that cryptic face. The man snatched the mug eagerly, pushed back his disorderly moustache from his lips, drank, set it down, wiped his wet lips with the back of his hand, and heaved a long sigh. Then he turned his attention once more to the table.

For about twenty minutes the two old men fed him. All sorts of delicacies had been provided, but the stranger devoted his attention entirely to cold beef, chicken, pickles, bread, cheese, and butter. The butter he ate neat, off the end of a knife. He took the chicken bones in both hands,

[1] " Master Merlin, wisest of the Britons, possessor of the secret of secrets; it is with inexpressible pleasure that we embrace the opportunity of—ah—welcoming you in our house. You will understand that we also are not unskilled in the Great Art, and, if I may say so . . ."

placing them under the pillow when he had done. When he had eaten, he signalled for a second pint of beer, drank it at two long draughts, wiped his mouth on the sheet and his nose on his hand, and seemed to be composing himself for further slumber.

" *Ah—er—domine,*" said Wither, " *nihil magis mihi displiceret quam tibi ullo modo—ah—molestum esse. Attamen, venia tua . . .*" [1]

But the man was taking no notice at all. Frost and Wither exchanged enquiring glances.

" There is no approach to this room, is there," said Frost, " except through the next one? "

" No," said Wither.

" Let us go out there and discuss the situation. We can leave the door ajar."

VII

When Mark found himself left suddenly alone by Frost, his first sensation was an unexpected lightness of heart. In the very midst of his fears, a strange sense of liberation had sprung up. The relief of no longer trying to win these men's confidence, the shuffling off of miserable hopes, was almost exhilarating. He might lose the fight. But at least it was now his side against theirs. And he could talk of " his side " now. Already he was with Jane and with all she symbolised.

The approval of one's own conscience is a very heady draught; and specially for those who are not accustomed to it. Within two minutes Mark had passed from that first sense of liberation to a conscious attitude of courage, and thence into unrestrained heroics. It wasn't everyone, after all, who could have resisted an invitation like Frost's. An invitation that beckoned you right across the frontiers of human life . . . a touch on that infinitely secret cord which was the real nerve of all history. How it would have attracted him once!

Would have attracted him once. . . . Suddenly, like a thing that leaped to him across infinite distances with the speed of light, desire (salt, black, ravenous, unanswerable desire)

[1] " Ah—er—sir—nothing would be farther from my wish than to be in any way troublesome to you. At the same time, with your pardon . . ."

162

took him by the throat. The merest hint will convey to those who have felt it the quality of the emotion which now shook him, like a dog shaking a rat: for others, no description perhaps will avail. Many writers speak of it in terms of lust: a description illuminating from within, misleading from without. It has nothing to do with the body. But it is in two respects like lust. For like lust, it disenchants the universe. Everything else that Mark had ever felt— love, ambition, hunger, lust itself—appeared to have been mere milk and water, toys for children. The infinite attraction of this dark thing sucked all other passions into itself. But it was like lust in another respect also. It is idle to point out to the perverted man the horror of his perversion: while the fierce fit is on, that horror is the very spice of his craving. It is ugliness itself that becomes, in the end, the goal of his lechery; beauty has long since grown too weak a stimulant. And so it was here. These creatures of which Frost had spoken—and he did not doubt now that they were locally present with him in the cell—breathed death on the human race and on all joy. Not despite this but because of this, the terrible gravitation sucked and tugged and fascinated him towards them. The image of Wither's face rose to his memory; and this time he did not merely loathe it. He noted, with shuddering satisfaction, the signs it bore of a shared experience between them.

At the same moment it came back to him that he would probably be killed. As soon as he thought of that, he became once more aware of the cell. He blinked his eyes. What had he been thinking and feeling while he forgot death?

Gradually he realised that he had sustained some sort of attack, and that he had put up no resistance; and with that realisation a new kind of dread entered his mind. Though he was theoretically a materialist, he had all his life believed quite inconsistently and even carelessly in the freedom of his own will. When he had resolved some hours ago to trust the Belbury crew no farther, he had taken it for granted that he would be able to do what he resolved. It had never occurred to him that his mind could thus be changed for him in an instant of time, beyond recognition. If that sort of thing could happen . . . It was unfair. Here was a man trying to do what was obviously the right thing—the thing that Jane and the Dimbles would have approved of. You might have expected that when a man behaved in that way the universe would back him up. Yet the very moment you tried to be good, the universe let you down. That was what you got for your pains.

The cynics, then, were right. But at this thought, he stopped sharply. Some flavour that came with it had given him pause. Was this the other mood beginning again? Oh, not that, at any price! He clenched his hands. No, no, no! He could not stand this much longer. " Oh, don't, don't let me go back into it! " he said; and then louder, " Don't, don't! " All that could be called himself went into that cry; and the dreadful consciousness of having played his last card began to turn slowly into a sort of peace. There was nothing more to be done. Unconsciously he allowed his muscles to relax. His young body was very tired by this time, and even the hard floor was grateful to it. The cell also seemed to be somehow emptied and purged, as if it, too, were tired after the conflicts it had witnessed—emptied like a sky after rain, tired like a child after weeping. He fell asleep.

CHAPTER THIRTEEN

THEY HAVE PULLED DOWN DEEP HEAVEN ON THEIR HEADS

I

" STAND! Stand where you are and tell me your name and business," said Ransom.

The ragged figure on the threshold tilted its head a little sideways like one who cannot quite hear. The inner door, between the scullery and the kitchen, clapped to with a loud bang, isolating the three men from the women. The stranger took a pace farther into the room.

" *Sta*," said Ransom in a great voice. " *In nomine Patris et Filii et Spiritus Sancti, dic mihi qui sis et quam ob causam venias.*" [1]

The Stranger raised his hand and flung back the dripping

[1] " Stand. In the name of the Father and the Son and the Holy Ghost, tell me who you are and why you come."

hair from his forehead. The light fell full on his face, from which Ransom had the impression of an immense quietness.

His eyes rested on Ransom for a second with no particular interest. Then he turned his head to his left, to where the door was flung back almost against the wall. MacPhee was concealed behind it.

" Come out," said the Stranger, in Latin. What surprised Ransom was the fact that MacPhee immediately obeyed. He did not look at Ransom but at the Stranger. Then, unexpectedly, he gave an enormous yawn. The Stranger turned to the Director.

" Fellow," he said in Latin, " tell the Lord of this House that I am come."

" I am the Master here," said Ransom, in the same language.

" To be sure! " answered the Stranger. " And yonder whipper-snapper (*mastigia*) is without doubt your Bishop." He did not exactly smile, but a look of disquieting amusement came into his keen eyes.

" Tell your master that I am come," he repeated.

Ransom looked at him without the flicker of an eyelid.

" Do you really wish," he said at last, " that I call upon my Masters? "

" A daw that lives in a hermit's cell has learned before now to chatter book-Latin," said the other. " Let us hear your calling, mannikin (*homuncio*)."

" I must use another language for it," said Ransom.

" A daw could have Greek also in its bill."

" It is not Greek."

" Let us hear your Hebrew, then."

" It is not Hebrew."

" Nay," answered the other, " if you come to the gabble of barbarians, it will go hard, but I shall out-chatter you. Here is excellent sport."

" It may happen to seem to you the speech of barbarians," said Ransom, " for it is long since it has been heard. Not even in Numinor was it heard in the streets."

The Stranger gave no start, and his face remained as quiet as before, if it did not become quieter; but he spoke with a new interest.

" Your Masters let you play with dangerous toys," he said. " Tell me, slave, what is Numinor? "

"The true West," said Ransom.

"Well . . ." said the other. Then, after a pause, he added, "You see, I have already crossed the threshold."

"I value that at a straw," said Ransom. "Shut the door, MacPhee," he added in English. But MacPhee had sat down and was fast asleep.

"What is the meaning of this foolery?" said Ransom, looking sharply at the Stranger.

"If you are indeed the Master of this house, you have no need to be told. Do not fear; your horse-boy will be none the worse."

"This shall be seen to shortly," said Ransom. "In the meantime, I do not fear your entering the house. I have more cause to fear your escaping. Shut the door if you will, for you see my foot is hurt."

The Stranger swept back his left hand and slammed the door to. "Now," he said, "what of these Masters of yours?"

"My Masters are the Oyéresu."

"Where did you hear that name?" asked the Stranger. "Or, if you are truly of the College, why do they dress you like a slave?"

"Your own garments," said Ransom, "are not those of a druid."

"That stroke was well put by," answered the other. "Since you have knowledge, answer me three questions, if you dare."

"I will answer them if I can. But as for daring, we shall see."

The Stranger mused for a few seconds; then, speaking in a slightly sing-song voice, he asked the following question:

"Who is called Sulva? What road does she walk? Why is the womb barren on one side? Where are the cold marriages?"

Ransom replied, "Sulva is she whom mortals call the Moon. She walks in the lowest sphere. Half of her orb is turned towards us and shares our curse. On this side the womb is barren and the marriages cold. There dwell an accursed people, full of pride and lust. There when a man takes a maiden in marriage they do not lie together, but each lies with a cunningly fashioned image of the other, made to move and to be warm by devilish arts, for real flesh will not please them, they are so dainty (*delicati*) in their dreams of lust. Their real children they fabricate by vile arts in a secret place."

"You have answered well," said the Stranger. "I thought there were but three men in the world that knew this question. But my second may be harder. Where is the ring of Arthur the King? What Lord has such a treasure in his house?"

"The ring of the King," said Ransom, "is on Arthur's finger where he sits in the land of Abhalljin, beyond the seas of Lur in Perelandra. For Arthur did not die; but Our Lord took him to be in the body till the end, with Enoch and Elias and Moses and Melchisedec the King Melchisedec is he in whose hall the steep-stoned ring sparkles on the forefinger of the Pendragon."

"Well answered," said the Stranger. "In my college it was thought that only two men in the world knew this. But as for my third question, no man knew the answer but myself. Who shall be Pendragon in the time when Saturn descends from his sphere? In what world did he learn war?"

"In the sphere of Venus I learned war," said Ransom. "In this age Lurga shall descend. I am the Pendragon."

When he had said this he took a step backwards, for the big man had begun to move and there was a new look in his eyes. Slowly, ponderously, yet not awkwardly, as though a mountain sank like a wave, he sank on one knee; and still his face was almost on a level with the Director's.

II

"This throws a quite unexpected burden on our resources," said Wither to Frost, where they both sat in the outer room with the door ajar. "I must confess I had not anticipated any serious difficulty about language."

"We must get a Celtic scholar at once," said Frost. "Ransom would be the man to advise us if he were available."

"I met him once," said Wither, half closing his eyes. "He was a man whose penetrations might have been of infinite value, if he had not embraced the cause of reaction. It is a saddening reflection——"

"Of course," said Frost, interrupting him. "Straik knows modern Welsh. His mother was a Welsh woman."

"It would certainly be much more satisfactory," said Wither, "if we could, so to speak, keep the whole matter in the family. There would be something very disagreeable—about introducing a Celtic expert from outside."

"The expert would, of course, be provided for as soon as we could dispense with his services," replied Frost. "It is the waste of time that is the trouble. What progress have you made with Straik?"

"Oh, really excellent," said the Deputy Director. "Indeed I am almost a little disappointed. I had been thinking that it would be specially fitting and—ah—gratifying if your pupil and mine could be initiated together. We should both, I am sure, have felt . . . But, of course, if Straik is ready some time before Studdock, I should not feel myself entitled to stand in his way."

"I was thinking," said Frost, "that there must be some-one on duty here. He may wake at any moment. Our pupils—Straik and Studdock—could take it in turns. There is no reason why they should not be useful even before their full initiation."

"You think Mr.—ah—Studdock is far enough on?"

"It doesn't matter," said Frost. "What harm can he do? He can't get *out*. We only want someone to watch."

III

MacPhee found himself violently waked by someone shaking his shoulder. He suddenly perceived that he was cold and his left foot was numb. Then he saw Denniston's face looking into his own. The scullery seemed full of people—Denniston and Dimble and Jane. They appeared extremely bedraggled, torn, and muddy and wet.

"Are you all right?" Denniston was saying. "I've been trying to wake you for several minutes."

"All right?" said MacPhee, swallowing once or twice and licking his lips. "Aye, I'm all right." Then he sat upright. "There's been a—a man here," he said.

"What sort of a man?" asked Dimble.

"Well," said MacPhee, "as to that . . . it's not just so easy . . ."

The others exchanged glances. Next moment MacPhee jumped to his feet.

"Lord save us!" he exclaimed. "He had the Director

here. Quick! It was some kind of impostor or spy. I know now what's wrong with me. I've been hypnotised. There was a horse, too."

This last detail had an immediate effect on his hearers. Denniston flung open the kitchen door and the whole party surged in after him. The four women sat fast asleep. Mr. Bultitude, stretched out on his side across the hearth, slept also.

"They're all right," said MacPhee from behind. "It's just the same as he did to me. We've no time to wake them. Get on."

They passed from the kitchen into the flagged passage. To all of them except MacPhee the silence of the house seemed intense after their buffeting in the wind and rain. The lights as they switched them on successively revealed empty rooms and empty passages which wore the abandoned look of indoor midnight.

"Now for upstairs," said Dimble.

"The lights are on upstairs," said Jane, as they all came to the foot of the staircase.

"Excuse me," said Dimble to MacPhee, "I think perhaps I'd better go first."

Up to the first landing they were in darkness; on the second and last the light from the first floor fell. Looking down on them from the balustrade were two men, one clothed in sweepy garments of red and the other in blue. It was the Director who wore blue, and for one instant a thought that was pure nightmare crossed Jane's mind. The two robed figures looked to be two of the same sort . . . and what, after all, did she know of this Director? And there they were, the pair of them, talking their secrets, the man who had been dug up out of the earth and the man who had been in outer space. . . . All this time she had hardly looked at the Stranger. Next moment she noticed his size. The man was monstrous. And the two men were allies. And the Stranger was speaking and pointing at her as he spoke.

She did not understand the words: but Dimble did, and heard Merlin saying in what seemed to him a rather strange kind of Latin:

"Sir, you have in your house the falsest lady of any at this time alive."

And Dimble heard the Director answer, "Sir, you are

mistaken. She is doubtless like all of us a sinner: but the woman is chaste."

"Sir," said Merlin, "know well that she has done in Logres a thing of which no less sorrow shall come than came of the stroke that Balinus struck. For, sir, it was the purpose of God that she and her lord should between them have begotten a child by whom the enemies should have been put out of Logres for a thousand years."

"She is but lately married," said Ransom. "The child may yet be born."

"Sir," said Merlin, "be assured that the child will never be born, for the hour of its begetting is passed. Of their own will they are barren: I did not know till now that the usages of Sulva were so common among you. For a hundred generations in two lines the begetting of this child was prepared; and unless God should rip up the work of time, such seed, and such an hour, in such a land, shall never be again."

"Enough said," answered Ransom. "The woman perceives that we are speaking of her."

"It would be great charity," said Merlin, "if you gave order that her head should be cut from her shoulders; for it is a weariness to look at her."

Dimble thrust Jane behind him and called out, "Ransom! What in heaven's name is the meaning of this?"

MacPhee, who had followed the Latin even less than Jane, broke into the conversation.

"Dr. Ransom," he said. "I don't know who the big man is and I'm no Latinist. But I know well that you've kept me under your eye all this night against my own will, and allowed me to be hypnotised. It gives me little pleasure, to see yourself dressed up like something out of a pantomime and standing there hand-in-glove with that shaman, or priest, or whatever he is. He need not look at me the way he's doing. I'm not afraid of him. And as for my own life and limb—if you have changed sides after all that's come and gone, I don't know that I've much more use for either. But I'm not going to be made a fool of. We're waiting for an explanation."

The Director looked down on them in silence for a few seconds.

"Has it really come to this?" he said. "Does not one of you trust me?"

"I do, sir," said Jane suddenly.

"Well," said the Director, after a pause, "we have all been mistaken. So has the enemy. This man is Merlinus Ambrosius. They thought that if he came back he would be on their side. I find he is on ours. You, Dimble, ought to realise that this was always a possibility."

"That is true," said Dimble. "I suppose it was—well, the look of the thing. And his appalling blood-thirstiness."

"I have been startled by it myself," said Ransom. "But after all we had no right to expect that his penal code would be that of the nineteenth century. I find it difficult, too, to make him understand that I am not an absolute monarch."

"Is—is he a Christian?" asked Dimble.

"Yes," said Ransom. "As for my clothes, I have for once put on the dress of my office to do him honour. In his days men did not, except for necessity, go about in shapeless sacks of drab."

"Do I understand, Dr. Ransom," said MacPhee, "that you are asking us to accept this person as a member of our organisation?"

"I am afraid," said the Director, "I cannot put it that way. He *is* a member."

"What enquiries have been made into his credentials?"

"It would be hard," said the Director, "to explain to you my reasons for trusting Merlinus: but no harder than to explain to him why, despite appearances which might be misunderstood, I trust you." There was just the ghost of a smile about his mouth as he said this. Then Merlin spoke to him again in Latin and he replied. After that Merlin addressed Dimble.

"The Pendragon tells me," he said, "that you accuse me for a fierce and cruel man. It is a charge I never heard before. A third part of my substance I gave to widows and poor men. I never sought the death of any but felons and heathen Saxons. As for the woman, she may live, for me. I am not master in this house. Even that gallows bird (*crucarius*) beside you—I mean you, fellow; you with the face like sour milk and the voice like a saw in a hard log and the legs like a crane's—even that cut-purse (*sector zonarius*), though I would have him to the gatehouse, yet the rope should be used on his back, not his throat."

"Mr. Director," said MacPhee, when Merlin had finished, "I would be obliged if——"

"Come," said the Director suddenly, "we have none of us slept to-night. Arthur, will you come and light a fire for our guest in the big room at the north end? And would someone wake the women? Ask them to bring him up refreshments. A bottle of Burgundy and whatever you have cold. And then, all to bed."

IV

"We're going to have difficulties with that new colleague of ours," said Dimble. He was alone with his wife in their room at St. Anne's late on the following day.

"I felt that at lunch, you know," said his wife. "It was silly not to have realised that he wouldn't know about forks. But what surprised me even more (after the first shock) was how—well, how *elegant* he was without them."

"Oh, the old boy's a gentleman in his own way—anyone can see that. But . . . well, I don't know. I suppose it's all right."

"What happened at the meeting?"

"Well, everything had to be explained. We'd a job to make him understand that Ransom isn't the king of this country. And then we had to break it that we weren't the British, but the English—what he'd call Saxons."

"I see."

"And then MacPhee had to choose that moment for embarking on an explanation of the relations between Scotland and Ireland and England. MacPhee imagines he's a Celt when, apart from his name, there's nothing Celtic about him any more than about Mr. Bultitude. By the way Merlinus made a prophecy about Mr. Bultitude."

"Oh! What was that?"

"He said that before Christmas this bear would do the best deed that any bear had done in Britain except some other bear that none of us had heard of. He keeps on saying things like that. As if something like a camera shutter opened at the back of his mind and closed again immediately."

"He and MacPhee didn't quarrel again?"

"Not exactly. I think Merlinus has concluded that he is the Director's fool."

" Did you get down to actual business? "

" Well, in a way," said Dimble. " We were all at cross purposes, you see. The business about Ivy's husband being in prison came up, and he seemed to imagine us just riding off and taking the County Jail by storm. That's the sort of thing one was up against."

" Cecil," said Mrs. Dimble suddenly. " Is he going to be any use? "

" He's going to be able to *do* things, if that's what you mean."

" What sort of things? " asked his wife.

" The universe is so very complicated," said Dr. Dimble.

His wife waited as those wait who know by long experience the mental processes of the person who is talking to them.

" I mean," said Dimble, in answer to the question she had not asked, " if you dip into any college, or school, or parish— anything you like—at a given point in its history, you always find that there was a time before that point when there was more elbow-room and contrasts weren't so sharp; and that there's going to be a time after that point when there is even less room for indecision and choices are more momentous. Good is always getting better and bad getting worse: the possibilities of neutrality are always diminishing. The whole thing is sorting itself out all the time, coming to a point, getting sharper and harder."

" Like Browning's line: ' Life's business being just the terrible choice.' "

" Exactly! But not only in questions of moral choice. Everything is getting more different from everything else. Evolution means species getting less and less like one another. Minds get more spiritual, matter more material. Poetry and prose draw farther apart."

" Yes? "

" Well, about Merlin. Were there possibilities for a man of that age which there aren't for a man of ours? The earth itself was more like an animal. Mental processes were more like physical actions. And there were—well, Neutrals, knocking about."

" Neutrals? "

" I don't mean, of course, that anything can be a *real* neutral. There might be things neutral in relation to us."

" You mean eldils—angels? "

173

" Well, the word *angel* rather begs the question. Even the Oyéresu aren't exactly angels in the same sense as our guardian angels. There used to be things on this earth pursuing their own business. They weren't ministering spirits sent to help humanity, but neither were they enemies preying upon us . . . all the gods, elves, dwarfs, water-people, *fate, longaevi*."

" You think there are things like that? "

" I think there were. I think there was room for them then, but the universe has come more to a point. Not all rational things perhaps. Some would be mere wills inherent in matter, hardly conscious. More like animals. Others—but I don't really know. At any rate, that is the sort of situation in which one got a man like Merlin."

" It sounds rather horrible."

" It was *rather* horrible. I mean even in Merlin's time, though you could still use that sort of life in the universe innocently, you couldn't do it safely. The things weren't bad in themselves, but they were already bad for us. They withered the man who dealt with them. Not on purpose. They couldn't help doing it. Merlinus is withered. That quietness of his is just a little deadly, like the quiet of a gutted building."

" Cecil, do you feel quite comfortable about the Director's using a man like this? Doesn't it look a *little* bit like fighting Belbury with its own weapons? "

" No. I *had* thought of that. Merlin is the reverse of Belbury. He is the last vestige of an old order in which matter and spirit were, from our point of view, confused. For him every operation on Nature is a kind of personal contact. After him came the modern man to whom Nature is a machine to be worked, and taken to bits if it won't work as he pleases. Finally come the Belbury people, who take over that view unaltered and simply want to increase power by tacking on to it the aid of spirits—extra-natural, anti-natural spirits. They thought the old *magia* of Merlin, which worked in with the spiritual qualities of Nature, loving and reverencing them and knowing them from within, could be combined with the new *goeteia*—the brutal surgery from without. No. In a sense, Merlin represents what we've got to get back to in some different way."

" Good gracious! " said Mrs. Dimble, " there's six o'clock.

174

I'd promised Ivy to be in the kitchen at quarter to. There's no need for *you* to move, Cecil."

v

Merlin and the Director were meanwhile talking in the Blue Room. The Druid was still robed, and beneath the robe had surprisingly little clothing, for the warmth of the house was to him excessive and he found trousers uncomfortable. His loud demands for oil after his bath had involved some shopping in the village, which had produced, by Denniston's exertions, a tin of brilliantine. Merlinus had used it freely so that the sweet, sticky smell filled the room. That was why Mr. Bultitude had pawed so insistently at the door that he was finally admitted and now sat as near the magician as he could get. He had never smelled such an interesting man before.

" Sir," said Merlin, in answer to the question which the Director had just asked him, " I give you great thanks. I cannot, indeed, understand the way you live, and your house is strange. You give me a bath such as the Emperor himself might envy, but no one attends me to it: a bed softer than sleep, but when I rise from it I find I must put on my own clothes as if I were a peasant. I lie in a room with windows of pure crystal, but I lie in it alone, with no more honour than a prisoner in a dungeon. In all the house there is warmth and softness and silence that might put a man in mind of paradise terrestrial ; but no musicians, no perfumes, no high seats, not a hawk, not a hound. You live neither like a lord nor a hermit. Sir, I tell you these things because you have asked me. They are of no importance. Now that none hears us save the last of the seven bears of Logres, it is time we open counsels."

He glanced at the Director's face as he spoke.

" Does your wound pain you ? " he asked.

Ransom shook his head.

" Sir," said Merlinus in a softer voice, " I could take all the anguish from your heel as though I were wiping it out with a sponge. Give me but seven days to go in and out and up and down and to and fro, to renew old acquaintance. These fields and I, this wood and I, have much to say to one another."

He was leaning forward so that his face and the bear's

175

were almost side by side. The druid's face had a strangely animal appearance: not sensual nor fierce, but full of the patient, unarguing sagacity of a beast.

"You might find the country much changed," said Ransom.

"No," said Merlin. "Not much changed." Merlin was like something that ought not to be indoors. Bathed and anointed though he was, a sense of mould, gravel, wet leaves, weedy water hung about him. One might have believed that he listened continually to a murmur of evasive sounds; rustling of mice and stoats, the small shock of falling nuts, creaking of branches, the very growing of grass. The bear had closed its eyes. The room was heavy with a sort of floating anaesthesia. "Through me," said Merlin, "you can suck up from the Earth oblivion of all pains."

"Silence," said the Director sharply. The magician started and straightened himself. Even the bear opened its eyes again.

"No," said the Director. "God's glory, do you think you were dug out of the earth to give me a plaster for my heel? We have drugs that could cheat the pain as well as your magic, if it were not my business to bear it to the end. I will hear no more of that."

"I hear and obey," said the magician. "But I meant no harm. If not to heal your wound, yet for the healing of Logres, you will need my commerce with field and water."

Again that sweet heaviness, like the smell of hawthorn.

"No," said the Director, "that cannot be done any longer. The soul has gone out of the wood and water. Oh, I dare say you could awake them—a little. But it would not be enough. Your weapon would break in your hands. For the Hideous Strength confronts us, and it is as in the days when Nimrod built a tower to reach heaven."

"Hidden it may be," said Merlinus, "but not *changed*. Leave me to work, Lord. I will wake it."

"No," said the Director, "I forbid it. Whatever of spirit may still linger in the earth has withdrawn fifteen hundred years farther away from us since your time. You shall not lift your little finger to call it up. It is in this age utterly unlawful." He leaned forward and said in a different voice, "It never was *very* lawful, even in your day. Remember, when we first knew that you would be awaked,

176

we thought you would be on the side of the enemy. And because Our Lord does all things for each, one of the purposes of your reawakening was that your own soul should be saved."

Merlin sank back into his chair. The bear licked his hand.

"Sir," he said, "if I am not to work in that fashion, then you have taken into your house a silly bulk of flesh, for I am no longer much of a man of war."

"Not that way either," said Ransom. "No power that is merely earthly will serve against the Hideous Strength."

"Then let us all to prayers," said Merlinus.

"Certainly, to prayers," said Ransom, "now and always. But that was not what I meant. There are celestial powers: created powers, not in this Earth, but in the Heavens."

Merlinus looked at him in silence.

"You know well what I am speaking of," said Ransom. "Did not I tell you when we first met that the Oyéresu were my masters?"

"Of course," said Merlin. "And that was how I knew you were of the college. Is it not our password?"

"A password?" exclaimed Ransom, with a look of surprise. "I did not know that."

"But . . . but," said Merlinus, "if you knew not the password, how did you come to say it?"

"I said it because it was true."

The magician licked his lips which had become very pale.

"True as the plainest things are true," repeated Ransom; "true as it is true that you sit here with my bear beside you."

Merlin spread out his hands.

"Suffer me to speak," he said at last, "for I am in the hollow of your hand. I had heard of it in my own days—that some had spoken with the gods. Blaise, my Master, knew a few words of that speech. Yet these were, after all, powers of Earth. For—I need not teach you, you know more than I—it is not the very Oyéresu, the true powers of heaven, whom the greatest of our craft meet, but only their earthly wraiths. Only the earth-Venus, the earth-Mercurius: not Perelandra herself, not Viritrilbia ——"

"I am not speaking of the wraiths," said Ransom. "I

have stood before Mars himself in the sphere of Mars and before Venus herself in the sphere of Venus."

" But, Lord," said Merlin, " how can this be? Is it not against the Seventh Law? "

" What law is that? " asked Ransom.

" Has not our Fair Lord made it a law for Himself that He will not send down the Powers to mend or mar in this earth until the end of all things? Or is this the end? "

" It may be the beginning of the end," said Ransom, " I know nothing of that. Maleldil may have made it a law not to send down the Powers. But if men by enginery and natural philosophy learn to fly into the Heavens, and come, in the flesh, among the heavenly powers and trouble them, He has not forbidden the Powers to react. For all this is within the natural order. A wicked man came flying, by a subtle engine, to where Mars dwells in Heaven and to where Venus dwells, and took me with him captive. And there I spoke with the true Oyéresu face to face."

Merlin inclined his head.

" And so the wicked man brought about the thing he least intended. For now there was one man in the world—even myself—who was known to the Oyéresu and spoke their tongue, neither by God's miracle nor by magic from Numinor, but naturally, as when two men meet in a road. Our enemies had taken away from themselves the protection of the Seventh Law. That is why Powers have come down, and in this chamber where we are now discoursing Malacandra and Perelandra have spoken to me."

Merlin's face became paler.

" I have become a bridge," said Ransom.

" Sir," said Merlin, " if they put forth their power, they will unmake middle earth."

" Their naked power, yes," said Ransom. " That is why they will work only through a man."

The magician drew one large hand across his forehead.

" Through a man whose mind is opened to be so invaded," said Ransom; " one who by his own will once opened it. I take Our Fair Lord to witness that if it were my task I would not refuse it. But he will not suffer a mind that still has its virginity to be so violated. And through a black magician's mind their purity neither can nor will operate. One who has dabbled . . . in the days when dabbling had not begun to be evil, or was only just beginning . . . also a Christian and a penitent. A tool (I must speak plainly) good enough to be so used and not too good. In all these western parts of the world there was only one man who had lived in those days and could still be recalled. You . . ."

He stopped, shocked at what was happening. The huge man had risen from his chair. From his horribly opened mouth there came a yell that seemed to Ransom utterly bestial, though it was only the yell of Celtic lamentation. All the Roman surface in Merlinus had been scraped off.

" Silence ! " shouted Ransom. " Sit down. You put us both to shame."

As suddenly as it had begun the frenzy ended. Merlin resumed his chair. To a modern it seemed strange that, having recovered his self-control, he did not show the slightest embarrassment at his temporary loss of it.

" Do not think," said Ransom, " that for me either it is child's play to meet those who will come down for your empowering."

" Sir," faltered Merlin, " you have been in Heaven. You have looked upon their faces before."

" Not on all of them," said Ransom. " Greater spirits will descend this time. We are in God's hands. It may unmake us both. There is no promise that either you or I will save our lives or our reason."

Suddenly the magician smote his hand upon his knee.

" *Mehercule !* " he cried. " Are we not going too fast? If the Powers must tear me in pieces to break our enemies, God's will be done. But is it yet come to that? This Saxon king of yours who sits at Windsor, now—is there no help in him? "

" He has no power in this matter."

" Then is he not weak enough to be overthrown? "

" I have no wish to overthrow him. In the order of Logres I may be Pendragon, but in the order of Britain I am the King's man."

" Is it, then, his great men—the counts and legates and bishops—who do the evil and he does not know of it? "

" It is—though they are not exactly the sort of great men you have in mind."

" But what of the true clerks? Is there no help in them? It cannot be that *all* your priests and bishops are corrupted."

" The Faith itself is torn in pieces since your day and

179

speaks with a divided voice. Even if it were made whole, the Christians are but a tenth part of the people. There is no help there."

"Then let us seek help from over sea. Is there no Christian prince in Neustria or Ireland who would come in and cleanse Britain if he were called?"

"There is no Christian prince left."

"Then we must go to him whose office is to put down tyrants and give life to dying kingdoms. We must call on the Emperor."

"There is no Emperor."

"No Emperor . . ." began Merlin, and then his voice died away. Presently he said, "This is a cold age in which I have awaked. If all this west part of the world is apostate, might it be lawful, in our great need, to look farther . . . beyond Christendom? Should we not find some even among the heathen who are not wholly corrupt? There were tales in my day of some such: men who knew not the articles of our most holy Faith but who worshipped God as they could and acknowledged the Law of Nature. Sir, I believe it would be lawful to seek help even there—beyond Byzantium. I know not where—Babylon, Arabia, or Cathay."

Ransom shook his head. "The poison was brewed in these West lands, but it has spat itself everywhere by now. However far you went you would find the machines, the crowded cities, the empty thrones, the false writings: men maddened with false promises and soured with true miseries, cut off from Earth their mother and from the Father in Heaven. The shadow of one dark wing is over all Tellus."

"Is it, then, the end?" asked Merlin.

"And this," said Ransom, ignoring the question, "is why we have no way left save the one I have told you. The Hideous Strength holds all this Earth in its fist. If of their own evil will they had not broken the frontier and let in the celestial Powers, this would be their moment of victory. Their own strength has betrayed them. They have gone to the gods who would not have come to them, and pulled down Deep Heaven on their heads. Therefore they will die. For though you search every cranny to escape, now that you see all crannies closed, you will not disobey me."

Slowly there crept back into Merlin's white face that

almost animal expression, earthy and healthy with a glint of half-humorous cunning.

"Well," he said, "if the earths are stopped the fox faces the hounds. But had I known who you were at our first meeting I think I would have put the sleep on you as I did on your Fool."

"I am a very light sleeper since I have travelled in the Heavens," said Ransom.

CHAPTER FOURTEEN

"REAL LIFE IS MEETING"

I

MARK did not know whether it was minutes or hours later that he found himself once more awake, once more confronting Frost, and still fasting. The Professor came to ask if he had thought over their recent conversation. Mark, who judged that some show of reluctance would make his final surrender more convincing, replied that he did not quite understand what one stood to gain by co-operation with the Macrobes. He saw that the motives on which most men act were mere products of the animal organism. But he did not yet see what was to be substituted for these irrational motives. On what ground henceforward were actions to be justified or condemned?

"The question," said Frost, "is meaningless. It presupposes a means-and-end pattern of thought which descends from Aristotle, who was merely hypostatising elements in the experience of an iron-age, agricultural community. Motives are not the causes of action but its by-products. When you have attained real objectivity you will recognise *all* motives as subjective epiphenomena. You will then have no motives and you will find that you do not need them."

"I see," said Mark. The philosophy which Frost was expounding was by no means unfamiliar to him. He recognised it as the logical conclusion of thoughts which he had always hitherto accepted and which at this moment he found himself irrevocably rejecting. The knowledge

181

that his own assumptions led to Frost's position combined with what he saw in Frost's face and had experienced in this cell, effected a complete conversion. All the philosophers and evangelists in the world might not have done the job so neatly.

"And that," continued Frost, " is why a systematic training in objectivity must be given to you. It is like killing a nerve. That whole system of instinctive preferences, whatever ethical, aesthetic, or logical disguise they wear, is to be simply destroyed."

After that Frost took Mark from the cell and gave him a meal in some neighbouring room. When the meal was over Frost led him to the ante-room of the Head and he was stripped and re-clothed in surgeon's overalls and a mask. Then he was brought into the presence of the gaping and dribbling Head. Frost took not the slightest notice of it. He led him across the room to an arched door in the far wall.

Here he paused and said, " Go in. You will speak to no one of what you find here. I will return presently."

The room, at first, was an anti-climax. It appeared to be an empty committee room with a long table, eight or nine chairs, some pictures, and (oddly enough) a large step-ladder in one corner. There were no windows; it was lit by an electric light which produced, better than Mark had ever seen it produced before, the illusion of a cold, grey place out of doors.

A man of trained sensibility would have seen at once that the room was ill proportioned, not grotesquely but sufficiently to produce dislike. Mark felt the effect without analysing the cause, and the effect grew as time passed. Sitting staring about him, he next noticed the door. The point of the arch was not in the centre; the thing was lopsided. Once again, the error was not gross. The thing was near enough to the true to deceive you for a moment and to go on teasing the mind after the deception had been unmasked. He turned and sat with his back to it . . . one mustn't let it become an obsession.

Then he noticed the spots on the ceiling; little round black spots at irregular intervals on the pale mustard-coloured surface. He determined that he would not fall into the trap of trying to count them. They would be hard to count, they were so irregularly placed. Or weren't they? They suggested some kind of pattern. Their peculiar ugliness consisted in the fact that they kept on suggesting it and then frustrating expectation. He realised that this was another trap. He fixed his eyes on the table. He got up and began to walk about. He had a look at the pictures.

Some belonged to a school with which he was familiar. There was a portrait of a young woman who held her mouth wide open to reveal the fact that the inside of it was thickly overgrown with hair. It was very skilfully painted in the photographic manner so that you could feel that hair. There was a giant mantis playing a fiddle while being eaten by another mantis, and a man with corkscrews instead of arms bathing in a flat, sadly coloured sea beneath a summer sunset. But most of the pictures were not of this kind. Mark was a little surprised at the predominance of scriptural themes. It was only at the second or third glance that one discovered certain unaccountable details. Who was the person standing between the Christ and the Lazarus? And why were there so many beetles under the table in the Last Supper? What was the curious trick of lighting that made each picture look like something seen in delirium? When once these questions had been raised the apparent ordinariness of the pictures became like the ominous surface innocence at the beginning of certain dreams. Every fold of drapery, every piece of architecture, had a meaning one could not grasp but which withered the mind.

He understood the whole business now. Frost was not trying to make him insane; at least not in the sense Mark had hitherto given to the word "insanity". To sit in the room was the first step towards what Frost called objectivity—the process whereby all specifically human reactions were killed in a man so that he might become fit for the fastidious society of the Macrobes. Higher degrees in the asceticism of anti-nature would doubtless follow: the eating of abominable food, the dabbling in dirt and blood, the ritual performances of calculated obscenities. They were playing quite fair with him—offering him the same initiation through which they themselves had passed.

After an hour this long, high coffin of a room began to produce on Mark an effect which his instructor had probably not anticipated. As the desert first teaches men to love water, or as absence first reveals affection, there rose up against this background of the sour and the crooked some kind of vision of the sweet and the straight. Something else—something he vaguely called the " Normal "—apparently existed. He had never thought about it before. But there it was—solid, massive, like something you could touch, or eat, or fall in love with. It was all mixed up with Jane and fried eggs and soap and sunlight and the rooks cawing at Cure Hardy. He was not thinking in moral terms at all; or else (what is much the same thing) he was having his first deeply moral experience.

While it was still at its height Frost returned. He led Mark to a bedroom where a fire blazed and an old man lay in bed. The light gleamed on glasses and silver, and Frost told him that he must remain here till relieved and must ring up the Deputy Director if the patient spoke or stirred. He himself was to say nothing; indeed, it would be useless, for the patient did not understand English.

Frost retired. Mark glanced round the room. He was reckless now. Do or die for it, he was going to have a meal. Perhaps a smoke first.

" Damn! " he said as he put his hand into his pocket and found it empty. At the same moment he noticed that the man in the bed had opened his eyes and was looking at him. " I'm sorry," said Mark, " I didn't mean——" and then stopped.

The man sat up in bed and jerked his head towards the door.

" Ah? " he said enquiringly.

" I beg your pardon," said Mark.

" Ah? " said the man again. " Foreigners, eh? "

" You *do* speak English, then? " said Mark.

" Ah! " said the man. After a pause of several seconds he said, " Guv'ner! " Mark looked at him. " Guv'ner," repeated the patient with great energy, " you ha'nt got such a thing as a bit of baccy about you? Ah? "

II

" I think that's all we can do for the present," said Mother Dimble. " We'll do the flowers this afternoon." She was speaking to Jane, and both were in what was called the Lodge—a little stone house beside the garden door at which Jane had been first admitted to the Manor. Mrs. Dimble and Jane had been preparing it for the Maggs family. For Mr. Maggs's sentence expired to-day, and Ivy had gone off by train on the previous afternoon to spend the night with an aunt in the town where he was imprisoned and to meet him at the prison gates.

In Mrs. Dimble's hands the task became something between a game and a ritual. It woke in Jane memories of sixteenth century epithalamions—old superstitions, jokes, and sentimentalities about bridal beds and bowers. Mother Dimble, for all her nineteenth-century propriety, struck her this afternoon as being herself an archaic person.

Ivy had discussed her own story with Jane only the day before. Mr. Maggs had stolen some money from the laundry that he worked for. He had done this before he met Ivy and at a time when he had got into bad company. Since he and Ivy had started going out together he had gone " as straight as straight "; but the little crime had been unearthed and come out of the past to catch him. Jane had said very little during the telling of this story. Ivy had not seemed conscious of the purely social stigma attaching to petty theft and a term of imprisonment, so that Jane would have had no opportunity to practise, even if she had wished, that almost technical " kindness " which some people reserve for the sorrows of the poor. On the other hand, she was given no chance to be revolutionary or speculative—to suggest that theft was no more criminal than all wealth was criminal. Ivy seemed to take traditional morality for granted. She had been " ever so upset " about it. It seemed to matter a great deal in one way, and not to matter at all in another. It had never occurred to her that it should alter her relations with her husband—as though theft, like ill health, were one of the normal risks one took in getting married.

Mrs. Dimble went back to the house presently to fetch some little nicety which would put the finishing touch to the bedroom in the Lodge. Jane, feeling a little tired, knelt on the window-seat and put her elbows on the sill and her chin in her hands. The sun was almost hot. The thought of going back to Mark if Mark were ever rescued from Belbury was one which her mind had long accepted; it was not horrifying, but flat and insipid. She must, of course, be very different with him when they met again.

But it was that " again " which so took the savour out of the good resolution—like going back to a sum one had already got wrong. " If they met again . . ." she felt guilty at her lack of anxiety. Almost at the same moment she found that she was a little anxious. Hitherto she had always somehow assumed that Mark would come back. The possibility of his death now presented itself. She had no direct emotions about herself living afterwards; she just saw the image of Mark dead, that face dead, in the middle of a pillow, that whole body rigid, those hands and arms (for good and ill so different from all other hands and arms) stretched out straight and useless like a doll's. She felt very cold. Yet the sun was hotter than ever, almost impossibly hot for the time of year. It was very still, too, so still that she could hear the movements of a bird hopping along the path outside the window. This path led to the door in the garden wall. The bird hopped on to the threshold of that door, and on to someone's foot. For now Jane saw that someone was sitting just inside the door. This person was only a few yards away, and she must have been very quiet for Jane not to have noticed her.

A flame-coloured robe, in which her hands were hidden, covered this person from the feet to where it rose behind her neck in a kind of high ruff-like collar, but in front it was so low or open that it exposed her large breasts. Her skin was darkish and Southern and glowing, almost the colour of honey. Some such dress Jane had seen worn by a Minoan priestess on a vase from Cnossus. The head, poised motionless on the muscular pillar of her neck, stared straight at Jane. It was a red-cheeked, wet-lipped face, with black eyes—almost the eyes of a cow—and an enigmatic expression. It was not by ordinary standards at all like the face of Mother Dimble; but Jane recognised it. It was Mother Dimble's face with something left out, and the omission shocked Jane. " It is brutal," she thought, for its energy crushed her; but then she half changed her mind and thought, " It is I who am weak, trumpery." " It is mocking me," she thought, but then once more changed her mind and thought, " It is ignoring me. It doesn't see me." She tried to look aside from the face—succeeded—and saw for the first time that there were other creatures present—a whole crowd of ridiculous little men: fat dwarfs in red caps with tassels on them, gnome-like little men, insufferably familiar, frivolous, and irrepressible. There was no doubt that they, at any rate, were mocking her; nodding, mimicking, standing on their heads, turning somersaults. Jane was not yet frightened; partly because the warmth of the air made her feel drowsy. Her main feeling was indignation. A suspicion which had crossed her mind before now returned with irresistible force; the suspicion that the real universe might be simply silly. It was closely mixed up with the memories of that grown-up laughter—loud, careless, masculine laughter on the lips of bachelor uncles—which had often infuriated her in childhood.

The giantess rose. They were all coming at her. With a great glow and a noise like fire the flame-robed woman and the dwarfs were in the room with her. The strange woman had a torch in her hand. It burned with terrible, blinding brightness, crackling, and sent up a cloud of dense black smoke, and a sticky, resinous smell. " If they're not careful," thought Jane, " they'll set the house on fire." The outrageous little men began making hay of the room. In a few seconds the bed was a mere chaos, the sheets on the floor, the pillows hurtling through the air, feathers flying everywhere. " Look out! Look out, can't you?" shouted Jane, for the giantess was beginning to touch various parts of the room with her torch. She touched a vase on the mantelpiece. Instantly there rose from it a streak of colour which Jane took for fire. She was just moving to try to put it out when she saw that the same thing had happened to a picture on the wall. It happened faster and faster all round her. The very top-knots of the dwarfs were now on fire. But just as the terror of this became unbearable, Jane noticed that what was curling up from everything the torch had touched was not flame after all, but vegetation. Ivy and honeysuckle were growing up the legs of the bed, red roses were sprouting from the caps of the little men, and from every direction huge lilies rose to her knees and waist, shooting out their yellow tongues at her.

" Jane! Jane! " said the voice of Mrs. Dimble suddenly. " What on earth is the matter? "

Jane sat up. The room was empty, but the bed had all been pulled to pieces.

" Are you ill, child? " asked Mother Dimble.

" I must see the Director at once," said Jane. " It's all right. Don't bother. I can get up by myself . . . really."

III

Mr. Bultitude's mind was as furry and as unhuman as his body. He did not remember the provincial zoo from which he had escaped during a fire, nor his first snarling and terrified arrival at the Manor, nor the stages whereby he had learned to love and trust its inhabitants. He did not know that he loved and trusted them now. He did not know that they were people, nor that he was a bear. Everything that is represented by the words *I* and *Me* and *Thou* was absent from his mind. When Mrs. Maggs gave him a tin of golden syrup, he did not recognise either a giver or a recipient. His loves might, if you wished, be all described as cupboard loves. But if by a cupboard love you meant something cold or calculating you would be quite misunderstanding the beast's sensations. He was no more like a human egoist than he was like a human altruist. There was no prose in his life. The appetencies which a human might disdain as cupboard loves were for him quivering aspirations which absorbed his whole being, infinite yearnings, stabbed with the threat of tragedy and shot through with the colours of Paradise. One of our race, if plunged for a moment in the warm, trembling, iridescent pool of that pre-Adamite consciousness, would have emerged believing that he had grasped the absolute: for states below reason and states above it have a superficial resemblance. But fathoms deeper than any memory can take us, right down in the central warmth and dimness, the bear lived all its life.

To-day an unusual thing had happened to him—he had got into the garden without being muzzled. He was always muzzled out of doors, not because there was any fear of his becoming dangerous but because of his partiality for fruit and for the sweeter kinds of vegetables. But to-day the precaution had been forgotten and the bear had passed a very agreeable morning investigating the turnips. Now —in the early afternoon—he had approached the garden wall. There was a chestnut tree within the wall which the bear could easily climb, and from its branches he could drop down on the far side. He was standing looking up at this tree. Mrs. Maggs would have described his state of mind by saying, "He knows perfectly well he's not allowed out of the garden." That was not how it appeared to Mr. Bultitude. He had no morals: but the Director had given him certain inhibitions. A mysterious reluctance arose, a clouding of the emotional weather, when the wall was too close; but mixed with this there was an opposite impulse to get beyond that wall. If the pressure behind this impulse could be translated into human terms at all, it would appear more like a mythology than a thought. One met bees in the garden. The bees all went away, over the wall. And to follow bees was the obvious thing to do. There was a sense in the bear's mind—one could hardly call it a picture—of green lands beyond the wall, and hives, and bees the size of sparrows, and there, walking, trickling, oozing to meet one, something or someone stickier, sweeter, than honey itself.

Three times Mr. Bultitude turned away from the tree and the wall, but each time he came back. Then, very cautiously and quietly, he began to climb the tree. When he got up into the fork he sat there for a long time. He sat there for nearly half an hour. Sometimes his mind wandered from the point and once he nearly went to sleep. In the end he got down on the outside of the wall. When he found that the thing had really happened he became so frightened that he sat still at the bottom of the grassy bank on the very edge of the road.

A motor van came into sight. It was driven by a man in the livery of the N.I.C.E., and another man in the same livery sat beside him.

"Hullo . . . I say!" said the second man. "Pull up, Sid. What about *that*?"

"What?" said the driver.

"Haven't you got eyes in your head?" said the other.

"Gor," said Sid, pulling up. "A bloody great bear. I say—it couldn't be our own bear, could it?"

"Get on," said his mate. "She was in her cage all right this morning."

"You don't think she could have done a bunk? There'd be hell to pay for you and me. . . ."

"She couldn't have got here if she *had* done a bunk. Bears don't go forty miles an hour. But hadn't we better pinch this one?"

" We haven't got no orders," said Sid.

" No. And we haven't failed to get that blasted wolf either, have we? "

" Wasn't our fault."

" Course it wasn't our fault. But the boss won't take no notice of that. It's get on or get out at Belbury."

" Get out? " said Sid. " I wish to hell I knew how to."

Len spat over the side and there was a moment's silence.

" Anyway," said Sid presently, " what's the good of taking a bear back? "

" Well, isn't it better than coming back with nothing? " said Len. " I know they want another one. And here it is free."

" All right," said Sid ironically, " if you're so keen on it, just hop out and ask him to step in."

" Dope," said Len.

" Not on my bit of dinner, you don't," said Sid.

" You're a bucking good mate to have," said Len, groping in a greasy parcel. " It's a good thing for you I'm not the sort of chap who'd split on you."

" You done it already," said the driver. " I know all your little games."

Len produced a sandwich and dabbed it with some strong-smelling liquid from a bottle. When it was saturated, he opened the door and went a pace forward, about six yards from the bear. He threw the sandwich to it.

Quarter of an hour later Mr. Bultitude lay on his side, unconscious and breathing heavily. They had no difficulty in tying up his mouth and all four paws, but they had great difficulty in lifting him into the van.

IV

Mark's waking life was now divided between periods by the Sleeper's bedside and periods in the room with the spotted ceiling. The training in objectivity which took place in the latter cannot be described; the details would be unprintable and had, indeed, a kind of nursery fatuity about them which is best ignored. There indeed lay the horror—to perform petty obscenities which a silly child might have thought funny under the unchangingly serious inspection of Frost, with a stop watch and a note-book and all the ritual of experiment. And day by day, as the process went on, that idea of the Straight or the Normal which had occured to him during his first visit to this room, grew stronger and more solid in his mind till it became a kind of mountain. He had never before known what an Idea meant.

The other thing that helped to save him was the Man in the Bed. Mark's discovery that he really could speak English had led to a curious acquaintance with him. It can hardly be said that they conversed. The man was so very allusive and used gesture so extensively that Mark's less sophisticated modes of communication were almost useless. Thus when Mark explained that he had no tobacco, the man had slapped an imaginary tobacco pouch on his knees at least six times and struck an imaginary match about as often, each time jerking his head sideways with a look of such relish as Mark had seldom seen on a human face. Then Mark went on to explain that though " they " were not foreigners, they were extremely dangerous people and that probably the Stranger's best plan would be to preserve his silence.

" Ah," said the Stranger, jerking his head again, " don't get nothing out of me. I tell 'ee. Don't get nothing out of me. Eh? I tell 'ee. You and me knows. Ah? " and his look embraced Mark in such an apparently gleeful conspiracy that it warmed the heart.

Believing this matter to be now sufficiently clear, Mark began, " But, as regards the future——"

" Ah," said the man. " Foreigners. Eh? "

" No, no," said Mark. " I told you they weren't. They seem to think *you* are, though. And that's why——"

" That's right," interrupted the man. " I know. Foreigners, I call them. I know."

" I've been trying to think out some sort of plan," said Mark.

" Ah," said the man approvingly, " I got a plan."

" What is it? "

" Ah," said the man, winking at Mark with infinite knowingness and rubbing his belly.

" Go on. What is it? " said Mark.

" How'd it be," said the man. " How'd it be if you and I made ourselves a nice bit of toasted cheese? "

" I mean a plan for escape," said Mark.

"Ah," replied the man. "My old Dad, now. He never had a day's illness in his life."

"It's a remarkable record," said Mark.

"Ah. You may say so," replied the other. "On the road all his life. Never had a stomach-ache. And what did he attribute his health to?" He prounced the word *attribute* with great relish, laying the accent on the first syllable.

Mark was about to reply when the man indicated by a gesture that the question was purely rhetorical.

"He attributed his health," continued the speaker, "to eating toasted cheese. Keeps the water out of the stomach, that's what it does. Makes a lining."

In several interviews Mark endeavoured to discover something of the Stranger's own history and particularly how he had been brought to Belbury. This was not easy, for though the tramp's conversation was very autobiographical, it was filled almost entirely with accounts of conversations in which he had made stunning repartees whose points remained wholly obscure. But by repeated and cautious questioning, he couldn't help getting the idea that the tramp had been made to give up his clothes to a total stranger and then put to sleep. He never got the story in so many words. As for the identity or appearance of the person who had taken his clothes, nothing whatever could be made out. The nearest Mark ever got to it, after hours of talk and deep potations, was some such statement as "Ah. He was a one!" or "He was a kind of—eh? *You* know?" or "That was a customer, that was."

Throughout the man's conversation, gusto was the most striking characteristic. He never passed any kind of moral judgement on the various things that had been done to him in the course of his career, nor did he ever try to explain them. Much that was unjust and more that was simply unintelligible seemed to be accepted not only without resentment but with a certain satisfaction provided only that it was striking. Even about his present situation he showed very much less curiosity than Mark would have thought possible. It did not make sense, but then the man did not expect things to make sense. He deplored the absence of tobacco and regarded the "Foreigners" as very dangerous people: but the main thing, obviously, was to eat and drink as much as possible while the present conditions lasted.

Every now and then their *tête-à-tête* was interrupted. Frost or Wither or both would come in introducing some stranger who addressed the tramp in an unknown language, failed completely to get any response, and was ushered out again. The tramp's habit of submission to the unintelligible, mixed with a kind of animal cunning, stood him in good stead during these interviews. It would never have occurred to him to undeceive his captors by replying in English. Undeceiving was an activity wholly foreign to his mind. For the rest, his expression of tranquil indifference, varied occasionally by extremely sharp looks but never by the least sign of anxiety or bewilderment, left his interrogators mystified.

And then, one day, there came an interview that was different.

v

" It sounds like a mythological picture by Titian come to life," said the Director, when Jane had described her experience in the lodge.

" Yes, but . . ." said Jane, and stopped. " I see," she began again, " it was very like that. As if the air were on fire. But I always thought I liked Titian. I suppose I wasn't really taking the pictures seriously enough."

" You didn't like it when it came out into real life? "

Jane shook her head.

" Was it real, sir? " she asked presently. " Are there such things? "

" Yes," said the Director, " it was real enough. Oh, there are thousands of things within this square mile that I don't know about yet. And I dare say that the presence of Merlinus brings out certain things. And you yourself . . . you are a seer. You were perhaps bound to meet her. She's what you'll get if you won't have the other."

" How do you mean, sir? " said Jane.

" You said she was a little like Mother Dimble. So she is. But Mother Dimble with something left out. Mother Dimble is friends with all that world as Merlinus is friends with the woods and rivers. But he isn't a wood or a river himself. She has not rejected it, but she has baptized it. You are not a Christian wife; neither are you a virgin. You have put yourself where you must meet

193

that Old Woman and you have rejected all that has happened to her since Maleldil came to Earth. So you get her raw—untransformed, demoniac. And you don't like it."

"You mean," said Jane slowly, "I've been repressing something."

The Director laughed; just that loud, assured, bachelor laughter which had often infuriated her on other lips.

"Yes," he said. "But don't think I'm talking of Freudian repressions. He knew only half the facts. I'm afraid there's no niche in the world for people that won't be either Pagan or Christian. Just imagine a man who was too dainty to eat with his fingers and yet wouldn't use forks!"

His laughter rather than his words had reddened Jane's cheeks. Her female dream of finding a man who "really understood" was being insulted. Some knowledge of a world beyond nature she had already gained from living in his house, but she had been conceiving this world as "spiritual" in the negative sense—as some neutral, or democratic, vacuum where differences disappeared, where sex and sense were not transcended but simply taken away.

"No," said the Director, "there is no escape. If it were a virginal rejection of the male, He would allow it. Such souls can by-pass the male and go on to meet something far more masculine, higher up, to which they must make a yet deeper surrender. But your trouble has been what old poets called *Daungier*. We call it Pride. You are offended by the masculine itself: the loud, irruptive, possessive thing—the gold lion, the bearded bull—which breaks through hedges and scatters the little kingdom of your primness as the dwarfs scattered the carefully made bed. The male you could have escaped, for it exists only on the biological level. But the masculine none of us can escape. What is above and beyond all things is so masculine that we are all feminine in relation to it. You had better agree with your adversary quickly."

"You mean I shall have to become a Christian?" said Jane.

"It looks like it," said the Director.

Playing for time, she asked. "Who was that Huge Woman?"

"I'm not sure," said the Director. "But I think I can

194

make a guess. Did you know that all the planets are represented in each? "

" No, sir. I didn't."

" Apparently they are. There is no Oyarsa in Heaven who has not got his representative on Earth. And there is no world where you could not meet a little unfallen partner of our own black Archon, a kind of other self. That is why there was an Italian Saturn as well as a heavenly one, and a Cretan Jove as well as an Olympian. What concerns you more, there is a terrestrial as well as a celestial Venus—Perelandra's wraith as well as Perelandra."

" And you think . . .? "

" I do: I have long known that this house is deeply under her influence. There is even copper in the soil. Also—the earth-Venus will be specially active here at present. For it is to-night that her heavenly archetype will really descend."

" I had forgotten," said Jane.

" You will not forget it once it has happened. All of you had better stay together. Do not come upstairs. To-night I will bring Merlin before my masters, all five of them—Viritrilbia, Perelandra, Malacandra, Glund, and Lurga. He will be opened. Powers will pass into him."

" What will he *do*, sir? "

The Director laughed. " The first step is easy. The enemies at Belbury are already looking for experts in archaic western dialects, preferably Celtic. We shall send them an interpreter! Yes, by the splendour of Christ, we will send them one."

There was a sudden knock on the door and Grace Ironwood entered.

" Ivy is back, sir," she said. " I think you'd better see her. She never saw her husband. The sentence is over, but they haven't released him. He's been sent on to Belbury for remedial treatment. Apparently it does not require a sentence from a court. . . . She is in great distress."

VI

Jane had gone into the garden to think. She accepted what the Director had said, yet it seemed to her nonsensical. " Religion " ought to mean a realm in which her haunting female fear of being treated as a thing, an object of barter

195

and desire and possession, would be set permanently at rest, and what she called her " true self " would soar upwards and expand in some freer and purer world. For still she thought that " Religion " was a kind of exhalation or a cloud of incense, something steaming up from specially gifted souls towards a receptive heaven. Then, quite sharply, it occurred to her that the Director never talked about Religion, nor did the Dimbles nor Camilla. They talked about God. They had no picture in their minds of some mist steaming upward: rather of strong, skilful hands thrust down to make and mend, perhaps even to destroy. Supposing one were a *thing* after all—a thing designed and invented by Someone Else and valued for qualities quite different from what one had decided to regard as one's true self? Supposing all those people who, from the bachelor uncles down to Mark and Mother Dimble, had infuriatingly found her sweet and fresh when she wanted them to find her also interesting and important, had all along been simply right and perceived the sort of thing she was? Supposing Maleldil on this subject agreed with them and not with her? For one moment she had a ridiculous and scorching vision of a world in which God Himself would never understand, never take her with full seriousness. Then, at one particular corner of the gooseberry patch, the change came.

What awaited her there was serious to the degree of sorrow and beyond. There was no form nor sound. The mould under the bushes, the moss on the path, and the little brick border were not visibly changed. But they were changed. A boundary had been crossed. She had come into a world, or into a Person, or into the presence of a Person. Something expectant, patient, inexorable, met her with no veil or protection between. In the closeness of that contact she perceived at once that the Director's words had been entirely misleading. This demand which now pressed upon her was not, even by analogy, like any other demand. It was the origin of all right demands and contained them. In its light you could understand them: but from them you could know nothing of it. There was nothing, and never had been anything, like this. And now there was nothing except this. Yet also, everything had been like this: only by being like this had anything existed. In this height and depth and breadth the little idea of herself which she had hitherto called *me* dropped down and vanished, unfluttering, into bottomless distance, like a bird in space without air. The name *me* was the name of a being whose existence she had never suspected, a being that did not yet fully exist but which was demanded. It was a person (not the person she had thought) yet also a thing—a made thing, made to please Another and in Him to please all others—a thing being made at this very moment, without its choice, in a shape it had never dreamed of. And the making went on amidst a kind of splendour or sorrow or both, whereof she could not tell whether it was in the moulding hands or in the kneaded lump.

Words take too long. To be aware of all this and to know that it had already gone made one single experience. It was revealed only in its departure. The largest thing that had ever happened to her had, apparently, found room for itself in a moment of time too short to be called time at all. Her hand closed on nothing but a memory, and as it closed, without an instant's pause, the voices of those who have not joy rose howling and chattering from every corner of her being.

"Take care. Draw back. Keep your head. Don't commit yourself," they said. And then more subtly, from another quarter, "You have had a religious experience. This is very interesting. Not everyone does. How much better you will now understand the seventeenth-century poets!" Or from a third direction, more sweetly, "Go on. Try to get it again. It will please the Director."

But her defences had been captured, and these counter-attacks were unsuccessful.

CHAPTER FIFTEEN

THE DESCENT OF THE GODS

I

ALL the house at St. Anne's was empty, but for two rooms. In the kitchen, drawn a little closer than usual about the fire and with the shutters closed, sat Dimble and MacPhee and Denniston and the women. Removed from them by many a long vacancy of stair and passage, the Pendragon and Merlin were together in the Blue Room.

If anyone had gone up to the lobby outside the Blue Room, he would have found something other than fear that barred his way—an almost physical resistance. If he had succeeded in forcing his way forward against it, he would have come into a region of tingling sounds that were clearly not voices though they had articulation: and if the passage were quite dark he would probably have seen a faint light, not like fire or moon, under the Director's door. I do not think he could have reached the door itself unbidden. Already the whole house would have seemed to him to be tilting and plunging like a ship in a Bay of Biscay gale. He would have been horribly compelled to feel this earth not as the base of the universe but as a ball spinning and rolling onwards, both at delirious speed, and not through emptiness but through some densely inhabited and intricately structured medium. He would have known sensuously, until his outraged senses forsook him, that the visitants in that room were in it not because they were at rest but because they glanced and wheeled through the packed reality of heaven (which men call empty space) to keep their beams upon this spot of the moving earth's hide.

The Druid and Ransom had begun to wait for these visitors soon after sundown. Ransom was on his sofa. Merlin sat beside him, his hands clasped, his body a little bent forward. Sometimes a drop of sweat trickled coldly down his grey cheek. He had at first addressed himself to kneel, but Ransom forbade him. "See thou do it not!" he had said. "Have you forgotten that they are our fellow-servants?" The windows were uncurtained, and all the light that there was in the room came thence: frosty red when they began their waiting, but later star-lit.

Long before anything happened in the Blue Room the party in the kitchen had made their ten-o'clock tea. It was while they sat drinking it that the change occurred. Up till now they had instinctively been talking in subdued voices, as children talk in a room where their elders are busied about some august incomprehensible matter, a funeral, or the reading of a will. Now of a sudden they all began talking loudly at once, each, not contentiously but delightedly, interrupting the others. A stranger coming into the kitchen would have thought they were drunk, not soddenly but gaily drunk: would have seen heads bent close together, eyes dancing, an excited wealth of gesture. What they said, none of the party could afterwards remember. Dimble maintained that they had been chiefly engaged in making puns. MacPhee denied that he had ever, even that night, made a pun, but all agreed that they had been extraordinarily witty. If not plays upon words, yet certainly plays upon thoughts, paradoxes, fancies, anecdotes, theories laughingly advanced, yet, on consideration, well worth taking seriously, had flowed from them and over them with dazzling prodigality. Even Ivy forgot her great sorrow. Mother Dimble always remembered Denniston and her husband as they had stood, one on each side of the fireplace, in a gay intellectual duel, each capping the other, each rising above the other, up and up, like birds or aeroplanes in combat. Never in her life had she heard such talk—such eloquence, such toppling structures of double meaning, such sky-rockets of metaphor and allusion.

A moment after that and they were all silent. Calm fell, as suddenly as when one goes out of the wind behind a wall. They sat staring upon one another, tired and a little self-conscious.

Upstairs this first change had had a different operation. There came an instant at which both men braced themselves. Ransom gripped the side of his sofa: Merlin set his teeth. A rod of coloured light, whose colour no man can name or picture, darted between them: no more to see than that, but seeing was the least part of their experience. Quick agitation seized them: a kind of boiling and bubbling in mind and heart which shook their bodies also. It went to a rhythm of such fierce speed that they feared their sanity must be shaken into a thousand fragments. And then it seemed that this had actually happened. But it did not matter: for all the fragments —needle-pointed desires, brisk merriments, lynx-eyed thoughts—went rolling to and fro like glittering drops and reunited themselves. It was well that both men had some knowledge of poetry. The doubling, splitting, and recombining of thoughts which now went on in them would have been unendurable for one whom that art had not already instructed in the counterpoint of the mind, the mastery of doubled and trebled vision. For Ransom, whose study had been for many years in the realm of words, it was heavenly pleasure. He found himself sitting within the very heart of language, in the white-hot furnace of essential speech. All fact was broken, splashed into cataracts, caught, turned inside out, kneaded, and reborn as meaning. For the lord of Meaning himself, the herald, the messenger, the slayer of Argus, was with them: the angel that spins nearest the sun, Viritrilbia, whom men call Mercury and Thoth.

Down in the kitchen drowsiness stole over them after the orgy of speaking had come to an end. Jane, having nearly fallen asleep, was startled by her book falling from her hand, and looked about her. How warm it was . . . how comfortable and familiar. She had always liked wood fires, but to-night the smell of the logs seemed more than ordinarily sweet. She began to think it was sweeter than it could possibly be, that a smell of burning cedar or of incense pervaded the room. It thickened. Fragrant names hovered in her mind—nard and cassia's balmy smells and all Arabia breathing from a box: even something more subtly sweet, perhaps maddening—why not forbidden?—but she knew it was commanded. She was too drowsy to think deeply how this could be. The Dimbles were talking together, but in so low a voice that the rest could not hear. Their faces appeared to her transfigured. She could no longer see that they were old—only mature, like ripe fields in August, serene and golden with the tranquillity of fulfilled desire. On her other side, Arthur said something in Camilla's ear. There too . . . but as the warmth and sweetness of that rich air now fully mastered her brain, she could hardly bear to look on them: not through envy (that thought was far away) but because a sort of brightness flowed from them that dazzled her, as if the god and goddess in them burned through their bodies and through their clothes and shone before her in a young double-natured nakedness of rose-red spirit that overcame her. And all about them danced (as she half saw) not the gross and ridiculous dwarfs which she had seen that afternoon but grave and ardent spirits, bright winged, their boyish shapes smooth and slender like ivory rods.

In the Blue Room also Ransom and Merlin felt about this time that the temperature had risen. The windows, they did not see how or when, had swung open; but the temperature did not drop, for it was from without that the warmth came. Through the bare branches, across the ground which was once more stiffening with frost, a summer breeze was blowing into the room, but the breeze of such a summer as England never has. Laden like heavy barges that glide nearly gunwale under, laden so heavily you would have thought it could not move, laden with ponderous fragrance of night-scented flowers, sticky gums, groves that drop odours, and with cool savour of midnight fruit, it stirred the curtains, it lifted a letter that lay on the table, it lifted the hair which had a moment before been plastered on Merlin's forehead. The room was rocking. They were afloat. A tingling and shivering as of foam and breaking bubbles ran over their flesh. Tears ran down Ransom's cheeks. He alone knew from what seas and what islands that breeze blew. Merlin did not: but in him also the inconsolable wound with which man is born waked and ached at this touching. Low syllables of prehistoric Celtic self-pity murmured from his lips. These yearnings and fondlings were, however, only the forerunners of the goddess. As the whole of her virtue seized, focused, and held that spot of the rolling earth in her long beam, something harder, shriller, more perilously ecstatic, came out of the centre of all the softness. Both the humans trembled —Merlin because he did not know what was coming, Ransom because he knew. And now it came. It was fiery, sharp, bright, and ruthless, ready to kill, ready to die, outspeeding light: it was Charity, not as mortals imagine it, not even as it has been humanised for them since the Incarnation of the Word, but the trans-lunary virtue, fallen upon them direct from the Third Heaven, unmitigated. They were blinded, scorched. They thought it would burn their bones. They could not bear that it should continue. They could not bear that it should cease. So Perelandra, triumphant among planets, whom men call Venus, came and was with them in the room.

Down in the kitchen MacPhee sharply drew back his chair so that it grated on the tiled floor like a pencil squeaking on a slate. "Man!" he exclaimed, "it's a shame for us to be sitting here looking at the fire. If the Director hadn't got a game leg himself, I'll bet you he'd have found some other way for us to go to work."

Camilla's eyes flashed towards him. "Go on!" she said, "go on!"

" What do you mean, MacPhee? " said Dimble.

" He means fighting," said Camilla.

" They'd be too many for us, I'm afraid," said Arthur Denniston.

" Maybe so! " said MacPhee. " But maybe they'll be too many for us this way, too. But it would be grand to have one go at them before the end. To tell you the truth, I sometimes feel I don't greatly care what happens. But I wouldn't be easy in my grave if I knew they'd won and I'd never had my hands on them."

" Oh," said Camilla, " if one could have a charge in the old style. I don't mind anything once I'm on a horse."

" I can't understand it," said Dimble. " I'm not like you, MacPhee. I'm not brave. But I was just thinking as you spoke that I don't feel afraid of being killed and hurt as I used to do. Not to-night."

" We may be, I suppose," said Jane.

" As long as we're all together," said Mother Dimble. " It might be . . . no, I don't mean anything heroic . . . it might be a *nice* way to die." And suddenly all their faces and voices were changed. They were laughing again, but it was a different kind of laughter. Their love for one another became intense. Each, looking on all the rest, thought, " I'm lucky to be here. I could die with these." But MacPhee was humming to himself:

" King William said, Be not dismayed, for the loss of one commander."

Upstairs it was, at first, much the same. Merlin saw in memory the wintry grass on Badon Hill, the long banner of the Virgin fluttering above the heavy British-Roman cataphracts, the yellow-haired barbarians. He heard the snap of the bows, the *click-clack* of steel points in wooden shields, the cheers, the howling, the ringing of struck mail. He remembered also the evening, fires twinkling along the hill, frost making the gashes smart, starlight on a pool fouled with blood, eagles crowding together in the pale sky. And Ransom, it may be, remembered his long struggle in the caves of Perelandra. But all this passed. Something tonic and lusty and cheerily cold, like a sea-breeze, was coming over them. There was no fear any-where: the blood inside them flowed as if to a marching-song. They felt themselves taking their places in the ordered rhythm of the universe, side by side with punctual seasons and patterned atoms and the obeying Seraphim. Under the immense weight of their obedience their wills stood up straight and untiring like caryatides. Eased of all fickleness and all protestings they stood; gay, light, nimble, and alert. They had outlived all anxieties; care was a word without meaning. To live was to share without effort this processional pomp. Ransom knew, as a man knows when he touches iron, the clear, taut splendour of that celestial spirit who now flashed between them: vigilant Malacandra, captain of a cold orb, whom men call Mars and Mavors, and Tyr who put his hand in the wolf-mouth. Ransom greeted his guests in the tongue of heaven. But he warned Merlin that now the time was coming when he must play the man. The three gods who had already met in the Blue Room were less unlike humanity than the two whom they still awaited. In Viritrilbia and Venus and Malacandra were represented those two of the Seven genders which bear a certain analogy to the biological sexes, and can therefore be in some measure understood by men. It would not be so with those who were now preparing to descend. These also doubtless had their genders, but we have no clue to them. These would be mightier energies: ancient eldils, steersmen of giant worlds which have never from the beginning been subdued to the sweet humiliations of organic life.

"Stir the fire, Denniston, for any sake. That's a cold night," said MacPhee in the kitchen.

"It must be cold outside," said Dimble.

All thought of that; of stiff grass, hen-roosts, dark places in the middle of woods, graves. Then of the sun's dying, the earth gripped, suffocated, in airless cold, the black sky lit only with stars. And then, not even stars: the heat-death of the universe, utter and final blackness of nonentity from which Nature knows no return. Another life? "Possibly," thought MacPhee. "I believe," thought Denniston. But the old life gone, all its times, all its hours and days, gone. Can even Omnipotence *bring back*? Where do years go, and why? Man never would understand it.

Saturn, whose name in the heavens is Lurga, stood in the Blue Room. His spirit lay upon the house, or even on the whole earth, with a cold pressure such as might flatten

the very orb of Tellus to a wafer. Matched against the
lead-like burden of his antiquity, the other gods themselves
perhaps felt young and ephemeral. It was a mountain
of centuries sloping up from the highest antiquity we can
conceive, up and up like a mountain whose summit never
comes into sight, not to eternity where the thought can
rest, but into more and still more time, into freezing wastes
and silence of unnameable numbers. It was also strong
like a mountain: its age was no mere morass of time where
imagination can sink in reverie, but a living, self-remem-
bering duration which repelled lighter intelligences from
its structure as granite flings back lighter waves, itself unwithered
and undecayed, but able to wither any who approached it
unadvised. Ransom and Merlin suffered a sensation of
unendurable cold: and all that was strength in Lurga
became sorrow as it entered them. Yet Lurga in that room
was overmatched. Suddenly a greater spirit came—one
whose influence tempered and almost transformed to his
own quality the skill of leaping Mercury, the clearness of
Mars, the subtler vibration of Venus, and even the numbing
weight of Saturn.

In the kitchen his coming was felt. No one afterwards
knew how it happened, but somehow the kettle was put
on, the hot toddy was brewed. Arthur—the only musician
among them—was bidden to get out his fiddle. The chairs
were pushed back, the floor cleared. They danced. What
they danced no one could remember. It was some round
dance, no modern shuffling: it involved beating the floor,
clapping of hands, leaping high. And no one, while it
lasted, thought himself or his fellows ridiculous. It may,
in fact, have been some village measure, not ill-suited to
the tiled kitchen: the spirit in which they danced it was
not so. It seemed to each that the room was filled with
kings and queens, that the wildness of their dance expressed
heroic energy, and its quieter movements had seized the
very spirit behind all noble ceremonies.

Upstairs his mighty beam turned the Blue Room into a
blaze of lights. Before the other angels a man might sink;
before this he might die, but if he lived at all he would
laugh. If you had caught one breath of the air that came
from him, you would have felt yourself taller than before.
Though you were a cripple, your walk would have become
stately: though a beggar, you would have worn your rags

magnanimously. Kingship and power and festal pomp and courtesy shot from him as sparks fly from an anvil. The ringing of bells, the blowing of trumpets, the spreading out of banners are means used on earth to make a faint symbol of his quality. It was like a long sunlit wave, creamy-crested and arched with emerald, that comes on nine feet tall, with roaring and with terror and unquenchable laughter. It was like the first beginning of music in the halls of some king so high and at some festival so solemn that a tremor akin to fear runs through young hearts when they hear it. For this was great Glund-Oyarsa, King of Kings, through whom the joy of creation principally blows across these fields of Arbol, known to men in old times as Jove and under that name, by fatal but not inexplicable misprision, confused with his Maker—so little did they dream by how many degrees the stair even of created being rises above him.

At his coming there was holiday in the Blue Room. The two mortals, momentarily caught up into the *Gloria* which those five excellent Natures perpetually sing, forgot for a time the lower and more immediate purpose of their meeting. Then they proceeded to operation. Merlin received the powers into him.

He looked different next day. Partly because his beard had been shaved: but also, because he was no longer his own man. No one doubted that his final severance from the body was near. Later in the day MacPhee drove him off and dropped him in the neighbourhood of Belbury.

II

Mark had fallen into a doze in the tramp's bedroom that day, when he was startled, and driven suddenly to collect himself, by the arrival of visitors. Frost came in first. Two others followed. One was the Deputy Director: the other was a man whom Mark had not seen before.

This person was dressed in a rusty cassock and carried in his hand a wide-brimmed black hat such as priests wear in many parts of the Continent. He was a very big man, and the cassock perhaps made him look bigger. He was clean shaven, revealing a large face with heavy and complicated folds in it, and he walked with his head a little bowed. Mark decided that he was a simple soul, probably

205

an obscure member of some religious order who happened to be an authority on some even more obscure language. It was rather odious to see him between those two birds of prey—Withers effusive and flattering on his right and Frost, on his left, waiting with scientific attention but also, as Mark could see, with a certain cold dislike, for the result of the new experiment.

Wither talked to the stranger for some moments in a language which Mark recognised as Latin. "A priest, obviously," thought Mark. "But I wonder where from? Wither knows most of the ordinary languages. Would the old chap be a Greek?" The stranger took a step nearer to the bed and spoke two syllables in a low voice. For a second or two the tramp seemed to be afflicted with a shivering fit; then, slowly, but with continuous movement, as when the bows of a ship come round in obedience to the rudder, he rolled round and lay staring up into the other's face. From certain jerkings of his head and hands and from certain attempts to smile, Mark concluded that he was trying to say something, probably of a deprecatory and insinuating kind. What next followed took his breath away. The stranger spoke again: and then, with much facial contortion, mixed with coughs and stammers and spluttering and expectoration, there came out of the tramp's mouth, in a high unnatural voice, syllables, words, a whole sentence, in some language that was neither Latin nor English. All this time the stranger kept his eyes fixed on those of the tramp.

The stranger spoke again. This time the tramp replied at much greater length and seemed to manage the unknown language a little more easily, though his voice remained quite unlike that in which Mark had heard him talking for the last few days. At the end of his speech he sat up in bed and pointed to where Wither and Frost were standing. The stranger appeared to ask him a question. The tramp spoke for the third time.

At this reply the stranger started back, crossed himself several times, and exhibited every sign of terror. He turned and spoke rapidly in Latin to the other two, caught up his skirts, and made a bolt for the door. But the scientists were too quick for him. For a few minutes all three were wrangling there, Frost's teeth bared like an animal's, and the loose mask of Wither's face wearing, for once, a quite unambiguous expression. The old priest was being threatened. Shaking his head and holding out his hands, he came timidly back to the bedside. The tramp, who had relaxed during the struggle at the door, suddenly stiffened again and fixed his eyes on this frightened old man as if awaiting orders.

More words in the unknown language followed. The tramp once more pointed at Wither and Frost. The stranger turned and spoke to them in Latin, apparently translating. Wither and Frost looked at one another as if each waited for his fellow to act. What followed was pure lunacy. With infinite caution, wheezing, and creaking, down went the whole shaky senility of the Deputy Director, down on to its knees: and half a second later with a jerky, metallic movement Frost got down beside him. When he was down he suddenly looked over his shoulder to where Mark was standing. "Kneel," he cried, and instantly turned his head. Mark never could remember whether he simply forgot to obey this order or whether his rebellion dated from that moment.

The tramp spoke again, always with his eyes fixed on those of the man in the cassock. And again the latter translated, and then stood aside. Wither and Frost began going forward on their knees till they reached the bedside. The tramp's hairy, dirty hand with its bitten nails was thrust out to them. They kissed it. Then it seemed that some further order was given them. Wither was gently expostulating in Latin against this order. He kept on indicating Frost. The words *venia tua* [1] (each time emended to *venia vestra*) recurred so often that Mark could pick them out. But apparently the expostulation was unsuccessful: a few moments later Frost and Wither had both left the room.

As the door shut, the tramp collapsed like a deflated balloon. He rolled himself to and fro on the bed muttering, "Gor', blimey. Couldn't have believed it. It's a knock-out. A fair knock-out." But Mark had little leisure to attend to this. He found that the stranger was addressing him, and though he could not understand the words, he looked up. Instantly he wished to look away again and found that he could not. A moment later he fell into his chair and slept.

[1] "With your kind permission "; or, "If you will pardon me."

" It is . . . er . . . profoundly perplexing," said the Deputy Director, as soon as they found themselves outside the door.

" It certainly looked," continued Frost, " as if the man in the bed were being hypnotised and the Basque priest were in charge of the situation."

" And how on your hypothesis would a Basque priest come to invent the story that our guest was Merlinus Ambrosius? "

" That is the point. If the man in the bed is *not* Merlinus, then someone else, someone quite outside our calculations, namely the priest, knows our whole plan."

" And that, my dear friend, is why the retention of both these persons and a certain extreme delicacy in our attitude to both is required."

" They must, of course, be detained."

" I would hardly say *detained*. It has implications . . . the most cordial welcome, the most meticulous courtesy . . ."

" Do I understand that you had always pictured Merlinus entering the Institute as a Dictator rather than a colleague? "

" As to that," said Wither, " my conception had always been elastic. It would be a very real grief to me if I thought you were allowing any misplaced sense of your own dignity . . . ah, in short, provided he *is* Merlinus . . ."

" Where are you taking us at the moment? "

" To my own apartments. The request was that we should provide our guest with some clothes."

" There was no request. We were ordered."

The Deputy Director made no reply. When both men were in his bedroom and the door was shut, Frost said, " You do not seem to realise the dangers. We must take into account the possibility that the man is not Merlinus. And if he is not, then the priest knows things he ought not to know. And where did you get the priest from? "

" I think that is the kind of shirt which would be most suitable," said Wither, laying it on the bed. " The suits are in here. The . . . ah . . . clerical personage said he had come in answer to our advertisement."

" What do you propose to do? "

" We will, of course, consult the Head at once. I use that term, you understand, purely for convenience."

" But how can you? Have you forgotten that this is

the night of the inaugural banquet, and that Jules is coming down? He may be here in an hour. You will be dancing attendance on him till midnight."

Wither had indeed forgotten. But the realisation of this troubled him more than it would have troubled another. It was like the first breath of winter—the first crack in that great secondary self which he had built up to carry on the business of living while he floated far away on the frontiers of ghosthood.

"You have to consider at once," said Frost, "what to do with these two men this very evening."

"Which reminds me that we have already left them alone—and with Studdock, too—for over ten minutes. We must go back."

"And without a plan?" enquired Frost.

"We must be guided by circumstances," said Wither.

They were greeted on their return by a babble of imploring Latin from the man in the cassock. "Let me go," he said; "I entreat you do not do violence to a harmless old man. I will tell nothing—God forgive me—but I cannot stay here. This man who says he is Merlinus come back from the dead—he is a diabolist, a worker of infernal miracles. Look! Look what he did to the poor young man." He pointed to where Mark lay unconscious in his chair.

"Silence!" said Frost in the same language, "and listen. If you do what you are told, no harm will come to you. If you do not, you will be destroyed."

The man whimpered.

Suddenly, not as if he wished to but as if he were a machine that had been worked, Frost kicked him. "Get on," he said.

The end of it was that the tramp was washed and dressed. When this had been done, the man in the cassock said, "He is saying that he must now be taken through your house and shown the secrets."

"Tell him," said Wither, "that it will be a very great pleasure and privilege——"

But here the tramp spoke again. "He says," translated the big man, "first that he must see the Head and the beasts and the criminals who are being tormented. Secondly, that he will go with one of you alone. With you, sir," and here he turned to Wither.

"I will allow no such arrangement," said Frost in English.

"My dear Frost," said Wither, "this is hardly the moment . . . and *one* of us must be free to meet Jules."

Wither thought that Frost had intended to say something but had grown afraid. In reality, Frost found it impossible to remember any words. Perhaps it was due to the shifts from Latin to English which had been going on. Nothing but nonsense syllables would occur to his mind. He had long known that his intercourse with the beings he called macrobes might have effects on his psychology which he could not predict. In a dim way the possibility of complete destruction was never out of his thoughts. Now, it seemed to be descending on him. He reminded himself that fear was only a chemical phenomenon. For the moment, clearly, he must step out of the struggle, come to himself, and make a new start later in the evening. For, of course, this could not be final. At worst it could only be the first hint of the end. Probably he had years of work before him. He would outlast Wither. He stood aside, and the tramp, accompanied by the real Merlin and the Deputy Director, left the room.

Frost had been right in thinking that the aphasia would be only temporary. As soon as they were alone he found no difficulty in saying, as he shook Mark by the shoulder, "Get up. What do you mean by sleeping here? Come with me to the Objective Room."

IV

Before proceeding to their tour of inspection Merlin demanded robes for the tramp, and Wither dressed him as a Doctor of Philosophy of the University of Edgestow. Thus arrayed, walking with eyes half shut, the bewildered tinker was led upstairs and downstairs and through the zoo and into the cells. Now and then his face underwent a spasm as if he were trying to say something; but he never succeeded in producing any words except when the real Merlin asked him a question and fixed him with his eye.

Meanwhile, in the Objective Room, something like a crisis had developed. As soon as they arrived there Mark saw that the table had been drawn back. On the floor lay a crucifix, almost life-size, a work in the Spanish tradition, ghastly and realistic. "We have half an hour to pursue our exercises," said Frost. Then he instructed Mark to trample on it and insult it in other ways.

Now, whereas Jane had abandoned Christianity in early childhood, along with fairies and Santa Claus, Mark had never believed it at all. At this moment, therefore, it crossed his mind for the first time that there might conceivably be something in it. Frost, who was watching him carefully, knew perfectly well that this might be the result of the present experiment. But he had no choice. Whether he wished it or not, this sort of thing was part of the initiation.

" But, look here," said Mark.

"What is it?" said Frost. "Pray be quick."

"This," said Mark, "this is all surely a pure superstition."

"Well?"

"Well, if so, what is there objective about stamping on the face? Isn't it just as subjective to spit on a thing like this as to worship it?"

"That is superficial. If you had been brought up in a non-Christian society, you would not be asked to do this. Of course it is a superstition: but it is that particular superstition which has pressed upon our society for many centuries. It can be experimentally shown that it still forms a dominant system in the subconscious of many whose conscious thought appears to be wholly liberated. An explicit action in the reverse direction is therefore a necessary step towards complete objectivity. We find in practice that it cannot be dispensed with."

Mark was surprised at the emotions he was undergoing. He did not regard the image with anything like a religious feeling. Most emphatically it did not belong to that idea of the Straight or Normal which had, for the last few days, been his support. The horrible vigour of its realism was, indeed, as remote from that Idea as anything else in the room. That was one source of his reluctance. To insult even a carved image of such agony seemed abominable. But it was not the only source. With the introduction of this Christian symbol the whole situation had altered, and become incalculable. His simple antithesis of the Normal and the Diseased had obviously failed to take something into account. Why was the crucifix there? Why were more than half the poison-pictures religious?

"Pray make haste," said Frost.

He was on the verge of obeying and getting the whole silly business over, when the defencelessness of the figure deterred him. Not because its hands were nailed and helpless, but because they were only made of wood and therefore even more helpless, because the thing, for all its realism, was inanimate and could not in any way hit back, he paused. The unretaliating face of a doll—one of Myrtle's dolls—which he had pulled to pieces in boyhood had affected him in the same way.

"What are you waiting for, Mr. Studdock?" said Frost.

Mark was aware of rising danger. Obviously, if he disobeyed, his last chance of getting out of Belbury alive might be gone. Even of getting out of this room. He was himself, he felt, as helpless as the wooden Christ. As he thought this, he found himself looking at the crucifix in a new way —neither as a piece of wood nor a monument of superstition but as a bit of history. Christianity was nonsense, but one did not doubt that the man had lived and had been executed thus by the Belbury of those days. And that, as he suddenly saw, explained why this image, though not itself an image of the Straight or Normal, was yet in opposition to crooked Belbury. It was a picture of what happened when the Crooked met the Straight—what would happen to him if he remained straight. It was, in a more emphatic sense than he had understood, a *cross*.

"Do you intend to go on with the training or not?" said Frost. His eye was on the time. He knew that Jules must have very nearly reached Belbury, and that he might be interrupted at any moment. He had chosen this time for this stage in Mark's initiation partly in obedience to an unexplained impulse (such impulses grew more frequent with him every day), but partly because he wished, in the uncertain situation which had now arisen, to secure Mark at once. He and Wither and possibly (by now) Straik were the only full initiates in the N.I.C.E. On them lay the danger of making any false step in dealing with the man who claimed to be Merlin and with his mysterious interpreter. For him who took the right steps there was a chance of ousting all the others. He knew that Wither was waiting eagerly for any slip on his own part. Hence it seemed to him of the utmost importance to bring Mark as soon as possible beyond that point after which there is no return, and the disciple's allegiance both to the macrobes and to the teacher who has initiated him becomes a matter of psychological necessity.

" Do you not hear what I am saying? " he asked.

Mark was thinking, and thinking hard. Christianity was a fable. It would be ridiculous to die for a religion one did not believe. This Man himself, on that very cross, had discovered it to be a fable, and had died complaining that the God in whom he trusted had forsaken him—had, in fact, found the universe a cheat. But this raised a question that Mark had never thought of before. Was *that* the moment at which to turn against the Man? If the universe was a cheat, was that a good reason for joining its side? Supposing the Straight was utterly powerless, always and everywhere certain to be mocked, tortured, and finally killed by the Crooked, what then? Why not go down with the ship? He began to be frightened by the very fact that his fears seemed to have vanished. They had been a safeguard . . . they had prevented him, all his life, from making mad decisions like that which he was now making as he turned to Frost and said, " It's all bloody nonsense, and I'm damned if I do any such thing."

When he said this he had no idea what might happen next. Then he saw that Frost was listening, and he began to listen himself. A moment later the door opened. The room seemed suddenly full of people—a man in a red gown (Mark did not recognise the tramp) and the huge man in the black gown and Wither.

v

In the great drawing-room at Belbury a singularly uncomfortable party was by now assembled. Horace Jules, Director of the N.I.C.E., had arrived about half an hour before. Conversation was hanging fire.

Conversation with Mr. Jules was always difficult, because he insisted on regarding himself not as a figure-head but as the real Director of the Institute, and even as the source of most of its ideas. And since, in fact, any science he knew was that taught him at the University of London over fifty years ago, it was not, in fact, possible to talk to him about most of the things the Institute was really doing. That was why the absence of the Deputy Director was so disastrous; Wither alone was master of a conversational style that exactly suited Jules.

Jules was a cockney, a very little man, whose legs were so short that he had unkindly been compared to a duck. He had a turned-up nose and a face in which some original *bonhomie* had been much interfered with by years of good living and conceit. His novels had first raised him to fame and affluence; later, as editor of the weekly called *We Want to Know*, he had become such a power in the country that his name was really necessary to the N.I.C.E.

" And as I said to the Archbishop," observed Jules, " you may not know, my lord, said I, that modern research shows the temple at Jerusalem to have been about the size of an English village church."

" God ! " said Feverstone to himself, where he stood silent on the fringes of the group.

" Have a little more sherry, Director," said Miss Hardcastle.

" Well, I don't mind if I do," said Jules. " It's not at all bad sherry, though I think I could tell you of a place where we could get something better. And how are you getting on, Miss Hardcastle, with your reforms of our penal system ? "

" Making real headway," she replied. " I think——"

" What I always say," remarked Jules, interrupting her, " is, why not treat crime like any other disease ? What you want to do is to put the man on the right lines—give him a fresh start—give him an interest in life. I dare say you've been reading a little address I gave at Northampton."

" I agreed with you," said Miss Hardcastle.

" That's right," said Jules. " I tell you who didn't, though. Old Hingest—and by the by, that was a queer business. You never caught the murderer, did you ? Very last time I met him one or two of us were talking about juvenile offenders, and do you know what he said ? He said, ' The trouble with these courts for young criminals nowadays is that they're always binding them over when they ought to be bending them over.' Not bad, was it ? Still, as Wither said—and, by the way, where *is* Wither ? "

" I think he should be here any moment now," said Miss Hardcastle.

" I think," said Filostrato, " he have a breakdown with his car. He will be desolated, Mr. Director, not to have given you the welcome."

" Oh, he needn't bother about that," said Jules, " though I did think he'd be here when I arrived. You're looking very well Filostrato. I'm following your work. I look upon you as one of the makers of mankind."

" Yes, yes," said Filostrato, " that is the real business. Already we begin——"

" I try to help you all I can on the non-technical side," said Jules. " It's a battle I've been fighting for years. The whole question of our sex-life. What I always say is that once you get the whole thing out into the open, you don't have any more trouble. I want every boy and girl in the country——"

" God ! " said Feverstone to himself.

" Forgive me," said Filostrato, who, being a foreigner, had not yet despaired of trying to enlighten Jules. " But that is not precisely the point."

At this moment the clock struck a quarter.

" I say," asked Jules, " what time is this dinner at ? "

" At quarter to eight," said Miss Hardcastle.

" You know," said Jules, " this fellow Wither really ought to be here. I mean to say. It isn't the kind of thing a chap expects, is it ? "

" *Ecco,*" said Filostrato. " Someone come."

It was indeed Wither who entered the room, in company which Jules had not expected, and Wither's face had certainly good reason to look even more chaotic than usual. He had been bustled round his own institute as if he were a kind of footman. He had not even been allowed to have the supply of air turned on for the Head when they made him take them into the Head's room. And " Merlin " (if it was Merlin) had ignored it. Worst of all, it had gradually become clear to him that this intolerable incubus and his interpreter fully intended to be present at dinner. No one could be more keenly aware than Wither of the absurdity of introducing to Jules a shabby old priest who couldn't speak English, in charge of what looked like a somnambulist chimpanzee dressed up as a Doctor of Philosophy. To tell Jules the real explanation—even if he knew which was the real explanation—was out of the question. It was a minor nuisance that ever since their visit to the Objective Room he had been compelled to have both Frost and Studdock in attendance. Nor did it mend matters that as they approached Jules, and all eyes were fixed upon them, the pseudo-Merlin collapsed into a chair, muttering, and closed his eyes.

"My dear Director," began Wither, a little out of breath, "this is one of the happiest moments of my life. It has been most unfortunate that I was called away. A remarkable coincidence . . . another very distinguished person has joined us at the very same moment. A foreigner . . ."

"Oh," interrupted Jules in a slightly rasping voice, "who's he?"

"Allow me," said Wither, stepping a little to one side.

"Do you mean *that*?" said Jules. The supposed Merlin sat with his arms hanging down on each side of the chair, his eyes closed, his head on one side, and a weak smile on his face. "Is he drunk? Or ill? And who is he, anyway?"

"He is, as I was observing, a foreigner," began Wither.

"Well, that doesn't make him go to sleep the moment he is introduced to me, does it?"

"Hush!" said Wither, drawing Jules a little out of the group. "There are circumstances—it would be very difficult to go into it here—I have been taken by surprise. Our distinguished guest has, I admit, certain eccentricities, and . . ."

"But who is he?" persisted Jules.

"His name is . . . er . . . Ambrosius. Dr. Ambrosius, you know."

"Never 'eard of him," snapped Jules.

"Very few of us have heard of him *yet*," said Wither. "But everyone will have heard of him soon. That is why, without in the least . . ."

"And who's *that*?" asked Jules, indicating the real Merlin. "He looks as if he were enjoying himself."

"Oh, that is merely Dr. Ambrosius's interpreter."

"Interpreter? Can't he talk English?"

"Unfortunately not. He lives rather in a world of his own."

"And can't you get anyone except a priest to act for him? We don't want that sort of thing here at all. And who are *you*?"

The last question was addressed to Straik, who had thrust

216

his way up to the Director. "Mr. Jules," he said, fixing the latter with a prophetic eye, "I am the bearer of a message to you which you must hear. I——"

"Shut up," said Frost.

"Really, Mr. Straik, really," said Wither. They shouldered him aside.

"Now look 'ere, Mr. Wither," said Jules, "I tell you straight I'm very far from satisfied. Here's *another* parson. I don't remember the name of any such person coming before me, and it wouldn't have got past me if it had done, see? It seems to me you've been making appointments behind my back and turning the place into a kind of seminary. And that's a thing I won't stand. Nor will the British people."

"I know. I know," said Wither. "I understand your feelings exactly. I am eager and waiting to explain the situation to you. In the meantime, perhaps, as Dr. Ambrosius seems slightly overcome and the dressing-bell has just sounded . . . oh, I beg your pardon. This *is* Dr. Ambrosius."

The tramp, to whom the real magician had recently turned, was now risen from his chair, and approaching Jules, held out his hand sulkily. Dr. Ambrosius, looking over Jules's shoulder and grinning in an inexplicable fashion, seized it and shook it, as if absent-mindedly, some ten or fifteen times. His breath, Jules noticed, was strong and his grip horny. He was not liking Dr. Ambrosius.

CHAPTER SIXTEEN

BANQUET AT BELBURY

I

IT was with great pleasure that Mark found himself once more dressing for dinner. He got a seat with Filostrato on his right and an inconspicuous newcomer on his left. Even Filostrato seemed human compared with the two initiates, and to the newcomer his heart positively warmed. He noticed with surprise the tramp sitting at the high table between Jules and Wither, but did not often look in that direction, for the tramp, catching his eye, had imprudently raised his glass and winked at him. The strange priest stood patiently behind the tramp's chair. Nothing of importance happened until the King's health had been drunk and Jules rose to make his speech.

For the first few minutes anyone glancing down the long tables would have seen what we always see on such occasions: the placid faces of *bons viveurs* whom food and wine had placed in a contentment which no amount of speeches could violate, the patient faces of diners who had learned how to pursue their own thoughts while attending just enough to respond wherever a laugh or a rumble of assent was obligatory, the fidgety faces of young men unappreciative of port and hungry for tobacco, the over-elaborate attention on the powdered faces of women who knew their duty to society. But if you had gone on looking down the tables you would presently have seen a change. You would have seen face after face look up and turn in the direction of the speaker. You would have seen first curiosity, then fixed attention, then incredulity. Finally, you would have noticed that the room was utterly silent, without a cough or a creak, that every eye was fixed on Jules, and soon every mouth opened in something between fascination and horror.

To different members of the audience the change came differently. To Frost it began at the moment when he heard Jules end a sentence with the words " as gross an anachronism as to trust to calvary for salvation in modern war ". *Cavalry*, thought Frost. Why couldn't the fool mind what he was saying. Perhaps—but hallo! what was this? Jules seemed to be saying that the future density of mankind depended on the implosion of the horses of Nature. " He's drunk," thought Frost. Then, crystal clear in articulation, beyond all possibility of mistake, came " The madrigore of verjuice must be talthibianised."

Wither was slower to notice what was happening. He had never expected the speech to have any meaning as a whole, and for a long time the familiar catchwords rolled on in a manner which did not disturb the expectation of his ear. Then he thought: " Come! That's going too far. Even they must see that you can't talk about accepting the challenge of the past by throwing down the gauntlet of the future." He looked cautiously down the room. All

was well.   But it wouldn't be if Jules didn't sit down pretty
soon.   In that last sentence there were surely words he
didn't know.   What the deuce did he mean by *aholibate*?
He looked down the room again.   They were attending
too much, always a bad sign.   Then came the sentence,
" The surrogates esemplanted in a continual of porous
variations."

Mark did not at first attend to the speech at all.   Once
or twice some phrase made him want to smile.   What first
awoke him to the real situation was the behaviour of those
who sat near him.   He was aware of their increasing stillness.   He noticed that everyone except himself had begun
to attend.   He looked up and saw their faces.   And then
first he really listened.   " We shall not," Jules was saying,
" we shall not till we can secure the erebation of all pros-
tundiary initems."   He looked round again.   Obviously
it was not he who was mad—they had all heard the gibberish.   Except possibly the tramp, who looked as solemn as a
judge.   He had never heard a speech from one of these
real toffs before, and would have been disappointed if he
could understand it.   Nor had he ever before drunk
vintage port, and though he did not much like the taste,
he had been working away like a man.

Wither had not forgotten that there were reporters
present.   That in itself did not matter much.   If anything
unsuitable appeared in to-morrow's paper, it would be
child's play for him to say that the reporters were drunk
or mad and break them.   On the other hand, he might
let the story pass.   Jules was a nuisance, and this might be
as good an opportunity as any other for ending his career.
But this was not the immediate question.   Wither was
wondering whether he should wait till Jules sat down or
whether he should rise and interrupt him with a few
judicious words.   He did not want a scene.   Glancing at
his watch, he decided to wait two minutes more.   Almost
as he did so he knew that he had misjudged it.   An intolerable falsetto laugh rang out; some fool of a woman had got
hysterics.   Immediately Wither touched Jules on the arm
and rose.

" Eh?   Blotcher   bulldoo? "   muttered   Jules.   But
Wither, laying his hand on the little man's shoulder, quietly
but with all his weight, forced him into a sitting position.
Then Wither cleared his throat.   He knew how to do that

so that every eye in the room turned immediately to look at him. The woman stopped screaming Wither looked down the room for a second or two in silence, feeling his grip on the audience. He saw that he already had them in hand. There would be no more hysterics. Then he began to speak.

They ought to have all looked more and more comfortable as he proceeded; and there ought soon to have been murmurs of grave regret for the tragedy which they had just witnessed. That was what Wither expected. What he actually saw bewildered him. The same too attentive silence which had prevailed during Jules's speech had returned. The woman began to laugh again—or no, this time it was two women. Cosser bolted from the room.

The Deputy Director could not understand this, for to him his own voice seemed to be uttering the speech he had resolved to make. But the audience heard him saying, " Tidies and fulgemen—I sheel foor that we all—er—most steeply rebut the defensible, though, I trust, lavatory, aspasia which gleams to have selected our redeemed inspector this deceiving. It would—ah—be shark, very shark, from anyone's debenture . . ."

The woman who had laughed rose hastily from her chair. The man next to her heard her murmur, " Vood wooloo." He took in the meaningless syllables and her unnatural expression at one moment. Both for some reason infuriated him. He rose to help her to move back her chair with one of those gestures of savage politeness which often, in modern society, serve instead of blows. He wrenched the chair, in fact, out of her hand. She screamed, tripped, and fell. The man on the other side of her saw the first man's expression of fury. " Bot are you blammit? " he roared, leaning towards him. Four or five people in that part of the room were now up. They were shouting. There was movement elsewhere. Several men were making for the door. " Bundlemen, bundlemen," said Wither sternly, in a much louder voice.

He was not even heard. At least twenty people present were at that very moment attempting to do the same thing. To each of them it seemed plain that things were just at that stage when a word or so of plain sense, spoken in a new voice, would restore the whole room to sanity. As a result fresh gibberish in a great variety of tones rang out from several places at once. Frost was the only one of the leaders who attempted to say nothing. Instead he pencilled a few words on a slip of paper, beckoned to a servant, and made him understand by signs that it was to be given to Miss Hardcastle.

By the time the message was put into her hands the clamour was universal. Miss Hardcastle smoothed out the paper and stooped her head to read. The message ran: *Blunt frippers intantly to pointed bdeluroid. Purgent. Cost.*

Miss Hardcastle had known before she got the message that she was three parts drunk. She had expected and intended to be so: she knew that later on in the evening she would go down to the cells and do things. There was a new prisoner there—a little fluffy girl of the kind the Fairy enjoyed—with whom she could pass an agreeable hour. The tumult of gibberish did not alarm her: she found it exciting. Apparently Frost wanted her to take some action. She decided that she would. She rose and walked the whole length of the room to the door, locked it, put the key in her pocket, and then turned to survey the company. She noticed for the first time that neither the supposed Merlin nor the Basque priest were anywhere to be seen. Wither and Jules, both on their feet, were struggling with each other. She set out towards them.

So many people had now risen that it took her a long time to reach them. All semblance of a dinner-party had disappeared: it was more like the scene at a London terminus on a bank holiday. Everyone was trying to restore order, but everyone was unintelligible, and everyone, in the effort to be understood, was talking louder and louder. She shouted several times herself. She even fought a good deal before she reached her goal.

There came an ear-splitting noise and after that, at last, a few seconds of dead silence. Mark noticed first that Jules had been killed: only secondly that Miss Hardcastle had shot him. After that it was difficult to be sure what happened. The stampede and the shouting may have concealed a dozen reasonable plans for disarming the murderess, but it was impossible to concert them. She fired again and again. It was the smell more than anything else which recalled the scene to Mark in later life: the smell of the shooting mixed with the sticky compound smell of blood and port and Madeira.

Suddenly the confusion of cries ran all together into one

thin, long-drawn noise of terror. Everyone had become *more* frightened. Something had darted across the floor between the two long tables and disappeared under one of them. Perhaps half the people present had not seen what it was—had only caught a gleam of black and tawny. But Mark had recognised it. It was a tiger.

For the first time that evening everybody realised how many hiding-places the room contained. The tiger might be under any of the tables. It might be in any of the deep bay windows, behind the curtains. There was a screen across one corner of the room, too.

It is not to be supposed that even now none of the company kept their heads. With loud appeals to the whole room or with urgent whispers to their immediate neighbours they tried to stem the panic, to arrange an orderly retreat from the room, to indicate how the brute could be lured or scared into the open and shot. The doom of gibberish frustrated their efforts. They could not arrest the two movements which were going on. The majority had not seen Miss Hardcastle lock the door : they were pressing towards it, to get out at all costs. A large minority, on the other hand, knew that the door was locked. There must be another door ; they were pressing to the opposite end of the room to find it. The whole centre of the room was occupied by the meeting of these two waves—a huge scrum, at first noisy with efforts at explanation, but soon, as the struggle thickened, silent except for the sound of labouring breath, kicking or trampling feet, and meaningless muttering.

Four or five of these combatants lurched heavily against a table, pulling off the cloth in their fall and with it all the fruit-dishes, decanters, glasses, plates. Out of that confusion with a howl of terror broke the tiger. It happened so quickly that Mark hardly took it in. He saw the hideous head, the cat's snarl of the mouth, the flaming eyes. He heard a shot—the last. Then the tiger had disappeared again. Something fat and white and bloodied was down among the feet of the scrummers. Mark could not recognise it at first, for the face, from where he stood, was upside down, and the grimaces disguised it until it was quite dead. Then he recognised Miss Hardcastle.

Wither and Frost were no longer to be seen. There was a growling close at hand. Mark turned, thinking he had located the tiger. Then he caught out of the corner of his eye a glimpse of something smaller and greyer. He thought it was an Alsatian. If so, the dog was mad. It ran along the table, its tail between its legs, slavering. A woman, standing with her back to the table, turned, saw it, tried to scream, next moment went down as the creature leaped at her throat. It was a wolf. " Ai—ai!! " squealed Filostrato, and jumped on the table. Something else had darted between his feet. Mark saw it streak across the floor and enter the scrum and wake that mass of inter-locked terror into new and frantic convulsions. It was some kind of snake.

Above the chaos of sounds which now awoke—there seemed to be a new animal in the room every minute—there came at last one sound in which those still capable of understanding could take comfort. *Thud—thud—thud*; the door was being battered from the outside. It was a huge folding door, a door by which a small locomotive could almost enter, for the room was made in imitation of Versailles. Already one or two of the panels were splintering. The noise maddened those who had made that door their goal. It seemed also to madden the ani-mals. As if in imitation a great gorilla leaped on the table where Jules had sat and began drumming on its chest. Then, with a roar, it jumped down into the crowd.

At last the door gave. Both wings gave. The passage, framed in the doorway, was dark. Out of the darkness there came a grey snaky something. It swayed in the air : then began methodically to break off the splintered wood on each side and make the doorway clear. Then Mark saw distinctly how it swooped down, curled itself round a man—Steele, he thought—and lifted him bodily high off the floor. After that, monstrous, improbable, the huge shape of the elephant thrust its way into the room. It stood for a second with Steele writhing in the curl of its trunk and then dashed him to the floor. It trampled him. After that it raised head and trunk again and brayed horribly, then plunged straight forward into the room, trumpeting and trampling—continuously trampling like a girl treading grapes, heavily and soon wetly trampling in a pash of blood and bones, of flesh, wine, fruit, and sodden table-cloth. Then everything went black and Mark knew no more.

When Mr. Bultitude came to his senses he had found himself in a dark place full of unfamiliar smells. The smells were, on the whole, promising. He perceived that food was in the neighbourhood and—more exciting—a female of his own species. There were a great many other animals about too, apparently, but that was irrelevant. He decided to go and find both the female bear and the food. It was then he discovered that walls met him in three directions and bars in the fourth: he could not get out. This, combined with an inarticulate want for the human companionship to which he was accustomed, gradually plunged him into depression. Sorrow such as only animals know—huge seas of disconsolate emotion with not one little raft of reason to float on—drowned him fathoms deep. In his own fashion he lifted up his voice and wept.

And yet, not far away from him, another captive was almost equally engulfed. Mr. Maggs, seated in a little white cell, chewed steadily on his great sorrow as only a simple man can chew. An educated man in his circumstances would have been thinking how this new idea of cure instead of punishment, so humane in seeming, had in fact deprived the criminal of all rights and by taking away the *name* punishment made the *thing* infinite. But Mr. Maggs thought all the time simply of one thing: that this was the day he had counted on all through his sentence, that he had expected by this time to be having his tea at home with Ivy (she'd have got something tasty for him the first night) and that it hadn't happened. He sat quite still. About once in every two minutes a single large tear trickled down his cheek. He wouldn't have minded so much if they'd let him have a packet of fags.

It was Merlin who brought release to both. He had left the dining-room as soon as the curse of Babel was well fixed upon the enemies. No one saw him go. Wither had heard his voice calling loud and intolerably glad above the riot of nonsense, " *Qui Verbum Dei contempserunt, eis auferetur etiam verbum hominis.*" [1] After that he did not see

[1] " They that have despised the Word of God, from them shall the word of man also be taken away."

him again, nor the tramp either. Merlin had gone and spoiled his house. He had liberated beasts and men. The animals that were already maimed he killed with instantaneous power, swift as the mild shafts of Artemis. To Mr. Maggs he had handed a written message. It ran as follows:

" DEAREST TOM,—I do hope your well and the Director here is one of the right sort and he says to come as quick as you can to the Manor of St. Anne's. And dont go through Edgestow Tom whatever you do but come any way you can I should think some-one had give you a Lift. No more now. Lots of love ever your own IVY."

The other prisoners he let go where they pleased. The tramp, finding Merlin's back turned on him for a second, made his escape, first into the kitchen and thence, reinforced with all the edibles his pockets would hold, into the wide world.

The beasts, except for one donkey who disappeared about the same time as the tramp, Merlin sent to the dining-room, maddened with his voice and touch. But he retained Mr. Bultitude. Even without the brilliantine there was that in Merlin which exactly suited the bear. He laid his hand on its head and whispered in its ear, and its dark mind filled with excitement; long forbidden and forgotten pleasures were suddenly held out to it. Down the long, empty passages of Belbury it padded behind them. Saliva dripped from its mouth and it was beginning to growl. It was thinking of warm, salt tastes, of the pleasant resistances of bone, of things to crunch and lick and worry.

III

Mark felt himself shaken; then the cold shock of water dashed in his face. With difficulty he sat up. The room was empty except for the bodies of the distorted dead. The unmoved electric light glared down on hideous con-fusion—food and filth, spoiled luxury and mangled men, each more hideous by reason of the other. It was the supposed Basque priest who had roused him. " *Surge, miselle,*" [1] he said, helping Mark to his feet. Mark rose; he had some cuts and bruises and his head ached. He

---

[1] " Get up, wretched boy."

looked with bewilderment on the face of the stranger and found that a letter was being put into his hand. " Your wife awaits you ", it ran, " at the Manor at St. Anne's on the Hill. Come by road as best you can. Do not go near Edgestow.—A. DENNISTON." Merlin laid a hand on his shoulder, and impelled him over all the tinkling and slippery havoc to the door. His fingers sent a prickly sensation through Mark's skin. He was led down to the cloakroom, made to fling on a coat and hat (neither were his own) and thence out under the stars, bitter cold and two o'clock in the morning, Sirius bitter green, a few flakes of dry snow beginning to fall. He hesitated. The stranger, with his open hand, struck him on the back; Mark's bones ached at the memory as long as he lived. Next moment he found himself running as he had never run since boyhood; not in fear, but because his legs would not stop. When he became master of them again he was half a mile from Belbury, and looking back, he saw a light in the sky.

IV

Wither was not killed in the dining-room. He knew all the possible ways out of the room, and before the coming of the tiger he had slipped away. He understood what was happening, not perfectly, yet better than anyone else. He saw that the Basque interpreter had done the whole thing. And, by that, he knew that powers more than human had come down to destroy Belbury; only one in the saddle of whose soul rode Mercury himself could thus have unmade language. And this told him something worse. It meant that his own dark Masters had been out in their calculations. They had talked of a barrier, had assured him that nothing from outside could pass the Moon's orbit. All their polity was based on the belief that Tellus was blockaded. Therefore he knew that everything was lost.

It is incredible how little this knowledge moved him. It could not, because he had long ceased to believe in knowledge itself. He had passed from Hegel into Hume, thence through Pragmatism, and thence through Logical Positivism, and out at last into the complete void. The indicative mood now corresponded to no thought that his mind could entertain. Now, even the imminence of his own ruin could not wake him. The last moments before damnation are not always dramatic. Often the man knows that some still possible action of his own will could yet save him. But he cannot make this knowledge real to himself. With eyes wide open, seeing that the endless terror is just about to begin and yet (for the moment) unable to feel terrified, he watches, not moving a finger for his own rescue, while the last links with joy and reason are severed, and drowsily sees the trap close upon his soul. So full of sleep are they at the time when they leave the right way.

Straik and Filostrato were also still alive. They met in one of the cold, lighted passages, so far from the dining-room that the noise of the carnage was but a faint murmur. Filostrato was hurt, his right arm badly mauled. They did not speak—both knew that the attempt would be use-less—but walked on side by side. Filostrato was intending to get round to the garage by a back way: he thought that he might still be able to drive, in a fashion, at least as far as Sterk.

As they rounded a corner they saw what they had expected never to see again—the Deputy Director, stooped, creaking, pacing, humming his tune. Filostrato did not want to go with him, but Wither, as if noticing his wounded condition, offered him an arm. Filostrato tried to decline it: nonsense syllables came from his mouth. Wither took his left arm firmly; Straik seized the other, the mauled arm. Squealing and shivering with pain, Filostrato ac-companied them perforce. But worse awaited him. He was not an initiate, he knew nothing of the Dark Eldils. He believed that his skill had really kept Alcasan's brain alive. Hence, even in his pain, he cried out with horror when he found the other two drawing him through the ante-room of the Head and into the Head's presence with-out pausing for any of those antiseptic preparations which he had always imposed on his colleagues. He tried vainly to tell them that one moment of such carelessness might undo all his work. But this time it was in the room itself that his conductors began undressing. And this time they took off all their clothes.

They plucked off his, too. When the right sleeve, stiff with blood, would not move, Wither got a knife from the ante-room and ripped it. In the end, the three men stood naked before the Head. Then the high ridge of terror from which Filostrato was never again to descend, was reached; what he thought impossible began to happen. No one had read the dials, adjusted the pressures or turned on the air and the artificial saliva. Yet words came out of the dry mouth of the dead man's head. " Adore ! " it said.

Filostrato felt his companions forcing his body forwards, then up again, then forwards and downwards a second time. He was compelled to bob up and down in rhythmic obeisance, the others meanwhile doing the same. Almost the last thing he saw on earth was the skinny folds on Wither's neck shaking like the wattles of a turkey-cock. Almost the last thing he heard was Wither beginning to chant. Then Straik joined in. Then, horribly, he found he was singing himself—

> " Ouroborindra !
> Ouroborindra !
> Ouroborindra ba-ba-hee ! "

But not for long. " Another," said the voice, " give me another head." Filostrato knew at once why they were forcing him to a certain place in the wall. He had devised it all himself. In the wall that separated the Head's room from the ante-chamber there was a little shutter. When drawn back it revealed a window in the wall, and a sash to that window which could fall quickly and heavily. But the sash was a knife. The little guillotine had not been meant to be used like this! They were going to murder him uselessly, unscientifically! If he were doing it to one of them, all would have been different; everything would have been prepared weeks beforehand—the temperature of both rooms exactly right, the blade sterilised, the attachments all ready to be made almost before the head was severed. He had even calculated what changes the terror of the victim would probably make in his blood-pressure: the artificial blood-stream would be arranged accordingly, so as to take over its work with the least possible breach of continuity. His last thought was that he had under-estimated the terror.

The two initiates, red from top to toe, gazed at each other, breathing heavily. Almost before the fat dead legs and buttocks of the Italian had ceased quivering, they were driven to begin the ritual again—

"Ouroborindra!
Ouroborindra!
Ouroborindra ba-ba-hee!"

The same thought struck both of them at one moment—
"It will ask for another." And Straik remembered that
Wither had that knife. He wrenched himself free from
the rhythm with a frightful effort: claws seemed to be
tearing his chest from inside. As Straik bolted, Wither was
already after him. Straik reached the ante-room, slipped
in Filostrato's blood. Wither slashed repeatedly with his
knife. He had not strength to cut through the neck, but
he had killed the man. He stood up, pains gnawing at
his old man's heart. Then he saw the Italian's head lying
on the floor. It seemed to him good to pick it up and carry
it into the inner room: show it to the original Head. He
did so. Then he realised that something was moving in
the ante-room. Could it be that they had not shut the
outer door? He could not remember. He put down his
burden and stepped towards the door between the rooms.
A great bear, rising to its hind legs as he came in sight of
it, met him in the doorway—its mouth open, its eyes
flaming, its forepaws spread out as if for an embrace. Was
this what Straik had become? He knew (though even
now he could not attend to it) that he was on the very
frontier of a world where such things could happen.

v

No one that night had been cooler than Feverstone. He
was neither an initiate like Wither nor a dupe like Filostrato. He knew about the macrobes, but it wasn't the
sort of thing he was interested in. He saw at a very
early stage that something was going wrong. One had
to guess how far wrong. Was this the end of Belbury?
If so, he must get back to Edgestow and work up the
position he had already prepared for himself as the pro-
tector of the University against the N.I.C.E. On the other
hand, if there were any chance of figuring as the man who
had saved Belbury at a moment of crisis, that would be
definitely the better line. He would wait as long as it was
safe. He found a hatch through which hot dishes were
passed from the kitchen passage into the dining-room.
He got through it and watched the scene. He thought he

could pull and bolt the shutter in time if any dangerous animal made for the hatch. He stood there during the whole massacre, something like a smile on his face, smoking endless cigarettes and drumming with his hard fingers on the sill of the hatch. When it was all over he said to himself, "Well, I'm damned!" It had certainly been a most extraordinary show.

The beasts had all streaked away somewhere. He worked his way to the back of the house and into the garage; there were far fewer cars there than he had expected. Apparently other people had had the idea of getting away while the going was good, and his own car had been stolen. He felt no resentment, and set about finding another of the same make. It took him a longish time, and when he had found one he had considerable difficulty in starting her up. It was after two o'clock when he got going.

Just before he started he had the odd impression that someone had got into the back of the car behind him. "Who's that?" he asked sharply. He decided to get out and see. But to his surprise his body did not obey this decision: instead it drove the car out of the garage into the road. Snow was falling. He found he could not turn his head and could not stop driving. He was going ridiculously fast, too, in this damned snow. He had no choice. He'd often heard of cars being driven from the back seat, but now it seemed to be really happening. Then he found he had left the road. The car, still at a reckless speed, was bumping and leaping along what was called Gipsy Lane or (by the educated) Wayland Street—the old Roman Road from Belbury to Edgestow, all grass and ruts. "Here! What the devil am I doing?" thought Feverstone. "Am I tight? I'll break my neck at this game if I don't look out!" But on the car went as if driven by one who thought this track an excellent road and the obvious route to Edgestow.

VI

Frost had left the dining-room a few minutes after Wither. He did not know where he was going or what he was about to do. For many years he had theoretically believed that all which appears in the mind as motive or intention is merely a by-product of what the body is doing. But for the last year or so—since he had been initiated—he had begun to taste as fact what he had long held as theory. Increasingly, his actions had been without motive. He did this and that, he said thus and thus, and did not know why. His mind was a mere spectator. He could not understand why that spectator should exist at all. He resented its existence, even while assuring himself that resentment also was merely a chemical phenomenon. The nearest thing to a human passion which still existed in him was a sort of cold fury against all who believed in the mind. There were not, and must not be, such things as men.

Thus the Frost whose existence Frost denied watched his body go into the ante-room, watched it pull up sharply at the sight of a naked and bloodied corpse. The chemical reaction called shock occurred. Frost stooped, turned the body over, and recognised Straik. A moment later his flashing pince-nez and pointed beard looked into the room of the Head itself. He hardly noticed that Wither and Filostrato lay there dead. His attention was fixed by something more serious. The bracket where the Head ought to have been was empty: the metal ring twisted, the rubber tubes tangled and broken. Then he noticed a head on the floor: stooped and examined it. It was Filostrato's. Of Alcasan's head he found no trace, unless some mess of broken bones beside Filostrato's were it.

Still not asking what he would do, or why, Frost went to the garage. He came up with as many petrol tins as he could carry. He piled all the inflammables he could think of together in the Objective Room. Then he locked the outer door of the ante-room. Something compelled him to push the key into the speaking-tube which communicated with the passage. When he had pushed it as far in as his fingers could reach, he took a pencil from his pocket and pushed with that. He heard the clink of the key falling on the floor outside. That tiresome illusion, his consciousness, was screaming in protest: his body had no power to attend to those screams. Like the clockwork figure he had chosen to be, his stiff body, now terribly cold, walked back into the Objective Room, poured out the petrol and threw a lighted match into the pile. Not till then did his controllers allow him to suspect that death itself might not cure the illusion of being a soul—nay, might prove the entry into a world where that illusion raged infinite and unchecked. Escape for the soul, if not for the body, was offered him. He became able to know (and simultaneously refused the knowledge) that he had been wrong from the beginning, that souls and personal responsibility existed. He half saw: he wholly hated. The torture of the burning was hardly fiercer than his hatred of that. With one supreme effort he flung himself back into his illusion. In that attitude eternity overtook him.

CHAPTER SEVENTEEN

VENUS AT ST. ANNE'S

I

DAYLIGHT came with no visible sunrise as Mark was climbing to the highest ground in his journey. The snow-shower was just then coming to its end in a flurry of larger and slower flakes. A big lorry, looking black and warm in that landscape, overtook him. The man put out his head. " Going Birmingham way, mate? " he asked.

" Roughly," said Mark. " At least I'm going to St. Anne's."

" Where's that, then? " said the driver.

" Up on the hill behind Pennington," said Mark.

" Ah," said the man, " I could take you to the corner. Save you a bit."

Mark got in beside him.

It was mid-morning when the man dropped him at a corner beside a little country hotel. The snow had all lain, and there was more in the sky, and the day was extremely silent. Mark went into the little hotel and found a kind elderly landlady. He had a hot bath and a capital breakfast, and then went to sleep in a chair before a roaring fire. He did not wake till about four. " I suppose I must get on soon," he said to himself.

His slight reluctance to do so did not proceed from weariness—he felt, indeed, perfectly rested and better than he had felt for several weeks—but from a sort of shyness.

He was going to see Jane: and Denniston: and (probably) the Dimbles as well. In fact, he was going to see Jane in what he now felt to be her proper world. But not his. Everything about them was different. They could not even fling themselves into chairs without suggesting by the very posture of their limbs a certain lordliness, a leonine indolence. There was elbow-room in their lives, as there had never been in his. They were Hearts: he was only a Spade. Still, he must be getting on. . . . Of course, Jane was a Heart. He must give her her freedom. It would be quite unjust to think that his love for her had been basely sensual. Love, Plato says, is the son of Want. Mark's body knew better than his mind had known till recently, and even his sensual desires were the true index of something which he lacked and Jane had to give. When she had first crossed the dry and dusty world which his mind inhabited she had been like a spring shower; in opening himself to it he had not been mistaken. He had gone wrong only in assuming that marriage, by itself, gave him either power or title to appropriate that freshness. As he now saw, one might as well have thought one could buy a sunset by buying the field from which one had seen it.

He rang the bell and asked for his bill.

II

That same afternoon Mother Dimble and the three girls were upstairs in the big room which occupied nearly the whole top floor of one wing at the Manor, and which the Director called the Wardrobe. If you had glanced in you would have thought for one moment that they were not in a room at all but in some kind of forest—a tropical forest glowing with bright colours. In fact, they were standing amidst a collection of robes of state—dozens of robes which hung, each separate, from its little pillar of wood.

"That would do beautifully for you, Ivy," said Mother Dimble, lifting with one hand the folds of a vividly green mantle over which thin twists and spirals of gold played in a festive pattern. "Come, Ivy," she continued, "don't you like it? You're not still fretting about Tom, are you? Hasn't the Director told you he'll be here to-night or to-morrow midday at the latest?"

Ivy looked at her with troubled eyes.

" 'Tisn't that," she said. "Where'll the Director himself be?"

"But you can't want him to stay, Ivy," said Camilla, "not in continual pain. And his work will be done—if all goes well at Edgestow."

"He has longed to go back to Perelandra," said Mother Dimble. "He's—sort of home-sick. Always, always . . . I could see it in his eyes."

"Will that Merling man come back here?" asked Ivy.

"I don't think so," said Jane. "I don't think either he or the Director expected him to. And then my dream last night. It looked as if he was on fire . . . I don't mean burning, you know, but light—all sorts of lights in the most curious colours shooting out of him and running up and down him. That was the last thing I saw: Merlin standing there like a kind of pillar and all those dreadful things happening all round him. And you could see in his face that he was a man used up to the last drop—that he'd fall to pieces the moment the powers let him go."

"We're not getting on with choosing our dresses for to-night."

"What is it made of?" said Camilla, fingering and then smelling the green mantle. It was a question worth asking. It was not in the least transparent, yet all sorts of lights and shades dwelled in its rippling folds, and it flowed through Camilla's hands like a waterfall. Ivy became interested.

"Gor!" she said, "however much a yard would it be?"

"There," said Mother Dimble as she draped it skilfully round Ivy. Then she said, "Oh!" in genuine amazement. All three stood back from Ivy, staring at her with delight. The commonplace had not exactly gone from her form and face: the robes had taken it up, as a great composer takes up a folk-tune and tosses it like a ball through his symphony and makes of it a marvel, yet leaves it still itself. A "pert fairy" or "dapper elf", a small though perfect sprightliness, stood before them: but still recognisably Ivy Maggs.

"Isn't that like a man!" exclaimed Mrs. Dimble. "There's not a mirror in the room."

"I don't believe we were meant to see ourselves," said Jane. "He said something about being mirrors enough to one another."

234

"I would just like to see what I'm like at the back," said Ivy.

"Now, Camilla," said Mother Dimble, "there's no puzzle about you. This is obviously your one."

"Oh, do you think *that* one?" said Camilla.

"Yes, of course," said Jane.

"You'll look ever so nice in that," said Ivy.

It was a long slender thing which looked like steel in colour, though it was soft as foam to the touch. It wrapped itself close about her loins and flowed out in a glancing train at her heels. "Like a mermaid," thought Jane: and then "Like a Valkyrie."

"I'm afraid," said Mother Dimble, "you must wear a coronet with that one."

"Wouldn't that be rather . . .?"

But Mother Dimble was already setting it on her head. That reverence (it need have nothing to do with money value) which nearly all women feel for jewellery hushed three of them for a moment. There were, perhaps, no such diamonds in England. The splendour was fabulous, preposterous.

"What are you all staring at?" asked Camilla, who had seen but one flash as the crown was raised in Mrs. Dimble's hands and did not know that she stood "like starlight, in the spoils of provinces".

"Treasure of Logres, dears, treasure of Logres," said Mrs. Dimble. "Perhaps from beyond the Moon or before the flood. Now, Jane."

Jane could see nothing specially appropriate in the robe which the others agreed in putting on her. But when she saw the others all clap their hands, she submitted. Indeed, it did not now occur to her to do otherwise, and the whole matter was forgotten a moment later in the excitement of choosing a robe for Mother Dimble.

"Something quiet," she said. "I'm an old woman, and I don't want to be ridiculous."

"This wouldn't do at all," said Camilla, walking down the long row of hanging splendours, herself like a meteor as she passed. "That's lovely," she said, "but not for you. And oh!—look at that."

"Here! Oh, do come and look! Come here," cried Ivy.

"Oh! Yes, yes, indeed," said Jane.

"Certainly," said Camilla.

"Put it on, Mother Dimble," said Ivy. "You know you got to." It was of that almost tyrannous flame colour which Jane had seen in her vision down in the lodge, but differently cut, with fur about the great copper brooch that clasped the throat, with long sleeves and hangings from them. And there went with it a many-cornered cap. And they had no sooner clasped the robe than all were astonished. For now this provincial wife, this respectable and barren woman with grey hair and double chin, stood before them, not to be mistaken, as a kind of priestess or sybil, the servant of some prehistoric goddess of fertility— an old tribal matriarch, mother of mothers, grave, formidable, and august. A long staff, curiously carved as if a snake twined up it, was apparently part of the costume: they put it in her hand.

"Am I awful?" said Mother Dimble, looking in turn at the three silent faces.

Jane took up the old lady's hand and kissed it. "Darling," she said, "*aweful*, in the old sense, is just what you *do* look."

"What are the men going to wear?" asked Camilla suddenly.

"*They* can't very well go in fancy dress, can they?" said Ivy. "Not if they're cooking and bringing things in and out all the time. And I must say if this is to be the last night and all I do think we ought to have done the dinner, anyway. Let them do as they like about the wine. And I don't believe Mr. MacPhee ever roasted a bird in his life, whatever he says."

"You needn't be in the least worried about the dinner, girls," said Mother Dimble. "He will do it very well. Let's go and enjoy ourselves. How very warm it is in here."

"'s lovely," said Ivy.

At that moment the whole room shook from end to end.

"What on earth's that?" said Jane.

"If the war was still on I'd have said it was a bomb," said Ivy.

"Come and look," said Camilla, who had regained her composure sooner than any of the others and was now at the window which looked west towards the valley of the Wynd. "Oh, look!" she said again. "No. It's not

fire. And it's not searchlights. And it's not forked
lightning. Ugh! . . . there's another shock. And there
. . . Look at that. It's as bright as day there beyond the
church. What am I talking about, it's only three o'clock.
It's brighter than day. And the heat!"

" It has begun," said Mother Dimble.

III

At about the same time that morning when Mark had
climbed into the lorry, Feverstone, not much hurt but a
good deal shaken, climbed out of the stolen car. That car
had ended its course upside down in a deep ditch, and
Feverstone reflected that things might have been worse—
it might have been his own car. The snow was deep in
the ditch, and he was very wet. As he stood up and looked
about him he saw that he was not alone. A tall and massive
figure in a black cassock was before him, about five yards
distant. Its back was towards him, and it was already
walking steadily away. " Hi!" shouted Feverstone.
The other turned and looked at him in silence for a second
or two; then it resumed its walk. Feverstone felt he had
never liked the look of anyone less. Nor could he, in his
broken and soaking pumps, follow the four-mile-an-hour
stride of those booted feet. The black figure came to a
gate, there stopped and made a whinnying noise. He
was apparently talking to a horse across the gate. Next
moment (Feverstone did not quite see how it happened)
the man was over the gate and on the horse's back and off
at a canter across a wide field that rose milk-white to the
sky-line.

Feverstone had no idea where he was, but clearly the
first thing to do was to reach a road. It took him much
longer than he expected. It was not freezing now, and
deep puddles lay hidden beneath the snow in many places.
At the bottom of the first hill he came to such a morass that
he was driven to abandon the track and try striking across
the fields. The decision was fatal. It kept him for two
hours looking for gaps in hedges and trying to reach things
that looked like roads from a distance but turned out to be
nothing of the sort. He had always hated the country and
always hated weather, and he was not at any time fond of
walking.

237

Near twelve o'clock he found a road. Here, thank heavens, there was a fair amount of traffic, both cars and pedestrians, all going one way. The first three cars took no notice of his signals. The fourth stopped. " Quick, in you get," said the driver.

" Going to Edgestow? " asked Feverstone, his hand on the door.

" Good Lord, no ! " said the other. " *There's* Edgestow !" —and he pointed behind him—" if you want to go *there*." The man seemed surprised and excited.

There was nothing for it but walking. Every vehicle was going away from Edgestow, none going towards it. We have, naturally, hardly any first-hand evidence for what happened in Edgestow that afternoon and evening. But we have plenty of stories as to how so many people came to leave it at the last moment. Behind all the exaggerations there remains the undoubted truth that a quite astonishing number of citizens did. One had had a message from a dying father; another had decided quite suddenly, and he couldn't just say why, to go and take a little holiday; another went because the pipes in his house had been burst by the frost and he thought he might as well go away till they were put right. Not a few had gone because of some trivial event which seemed to them an omen—a dream, a broken looking-glass, tea-leaves in a cup. Omens of a more ancient kind had also revived during this crisis. One had heard his donkey, another her cat, say " as clear as clear ", " *Go away*." And hundreds were still leaving for the old reason—because their houses had been taken from them, their livelihood destroyed, and their liberties threatened by the Institutional Police.

It was at about four o'clock that Feverstone found himself flung on his face. That was the first shock. They continued, increasing in frequency, during the hours that followed—horrible shudderings, and soon heavings, of the earth, and a growing murmur of widespread subterranean noise. The temperature began to rise. Snow was disappearing in every direction, and at times he was knee-deep in water. Haze from the melting snow filled the air. When he reached the brow of the last steep descent into Edgestow he could see nothing of the city : only fog through which extraordinary coruscations of light came up to him. Another shock sent him sprawling. He now decided not to go down: he would turn and follow the traffic—work over to the railway line and try to get to London.

He was already a few paces down the hill when he made this decision, and he turned at once. But instead of going up he found he was still descending. As if he were in shale on a mountain slope, the ground slipped away backwards where he trod on it. When he arrested his descent he was thirty yards lower. He began again. This time he was flung off his feet, rolled head over heels, stones, earth, grass, and water pouring over him and round him in riotous confusion. It was as when a great wave overtakes you while you are bathing, but this time it was an earth wave. He got to his feet once again; set his face to the hill. Behind him the valley seemed to have turned into Hell. The pit of fog had been ignited and burned with blinding violet flame, water was roaring somewhere, buildings crashing, mobs shouting. The hill in front of him was in ruins— no trace of road, hedge, or field, only a cataract of loose raw earth. It was also far steeper than it had been. His mouth and hair and nostrils were full of earth. The slope was growing steeper as he looked at it. The ridge heaved up and up. Then the whole wave of earth rose, arched, trembled, and with all its weight and noise poured down on him.

IV

"Why Logres, sir?" said Camilla.

Dinner was over at St. Anne's and they sat at their wine in a circle about the dining-room fire, all diversely splendid: Ransom crowned, at the right of the hearth, Grace Ironwood in black and silver opposite him. It was so warm that they had let the fire burn low, and in the candlelight the court dresses seemed to glow of themselves.

"Tell them, Dimble," said Ransom. "I will not talk much from now on."

"Are you tired, sir?" said Grace. "Is the pain bad?"

"No, Grace," he replied, "it isn't that. But now that it's so very nearly time for me to go, all this begins to feel like a dream. A happy dream, you understand: all of it, even the pain. I want to taste every drop. I feel as though it would be dissolved if I talked much."

"I suppose you *got* to go, sir?" said Ivy.

"My dear," said he, "what else is there to do? I have not grown a day or an hour older since I came back from Perelandra. There is no natural death to look forward to. The wound will only be healed in the world where it was got."

"All this has the disadvantage of being clean contrary to the observed laws of Nature," observed MacPhee.

"It is not contrary to the laws of Nature," said Grace Ironwood. "The laws of the universe are never broken. Your mistake is to think that the little regularities we have observed on one planet for a few hundred years are the real unbreakable laws; whereas they are only the remote results which the true laws bring about more often than not."

"And that," said Denniston, "is why nothing in Nature is *quite* regular. There are always exceptions."

"Not many exceptions to the law of death have come my way," observed MacPhee.

"And *how*," said Grace with much emphasis, "how should *you* expect to be there on more than one such occasion? Were you a friend of Arthur's or Barbarossa's? Did you know Enoch or Elijah?"

"Do you mean," said Jane, "that the Director . . . the Pendragon . . . is going where they went?"

"He will be with Arthur, certainly," said Dimble. "I can't answer for the rest. There are people who have never died. We do not yet know why. We know a little more than we did about the How. There are many places in the universe where an organism can last practically for ever. Where Arthur is, we know."

"Where?" said Camilla.

"In the Third Heaven, in Perelandra. In Aphallin, the distant island. Perhaps alone . . .?" He hesitated and looked at Ransom, who shook his head.

"And that is where Logres comes in, is it?" said Camilla. "Because he will be with Arthur?"

"It all began," said Dimble, "when we discovered that the Arthurian story is mostly true history. There was a moment in the sixth century when something that is always trying to break through into this country nearly succeeded. Logres was our name for it—it will do as well as another. And then . . . gradually we began to see all English history in a new way. We discovered the haunting."

"What haunting?" asked Camilla.

240

"How something we may call Britain is always haunted by something we may call Logres. Haven't you noticed that we are two countries? After every Arthur, a Mordred; behind every Milton, a Cromwell: a nation of poets, a nation of shopkeepers; the home of Sidney—and of Cecil Rhodes. Is it any wonder they call us hypocrites? But what they mistake for hypocrisy is really the struggle between Logres and Britain."

He paused and took a sip of wine before proceeding.

"It was long afterwards," he said, "after the Director had returned from the Third Heaven, that we were told a little more. Ransom was summoned to the bedside of an old man then dying in Cumberland. His name would mean nothing to you if I told it. That man was the Pendragon, the successor of Arthur and Uther and Cassibelaun. Then we learned the truth. There has been a secret Logres in the very heart of Britain all these years; an unbroken succession of Pendragons. That old man was the seventy-eighth from Arthur: our Director received from him the office and the blessing; to-morrow we shall know, or to-night, who is to be the eightieth. Some of the Pendragons are well known to history, though not under that name. Others you have never heard of. But in every age they and the little Logres which gathered round them have been the fingers which gave the tiny shove or the almost imperceptible pull, to prod England out of the drunken sleep or to draw her back from the final outrage into which Britain tempted her."

"This new history of yours," said MacPhee, "is a wee bit lacking in documents."

"It has plenty," said Dimble with a smile. "But you do not know the language they're written in. When the history of these last few months comes to be written in *your* language, and printed, and taught in schools, there will be no mention in it of you and me, nor of Merlin and the Pendragon and the Planets. And yet in these months Britain rebelled most dangerously against Logres and was defeated only just in time."

"Aye," said MacPhee, "and it could be right good history without mentioning you and me or most of those present. I'd be greatly obliged if anyone would tell me what we *have* done—always apart from feeding the pigs and raising some very decent vegetables."

"You have done what was required of you," said the Director. "You have obeyed and waited. It will often happen like that. But don't jump to conclusions. You may have plenty of work to do before a month is passed. Britain has lost a battle, but she will rise again."

"So that, meanwhile, is England," said Mother Dimble. "Just this swaying to and fro between Logres and Britain?"

"Yes," said her husband. "Don't you feel it? The very quality of England. If we've got an ass's head it is by walking in a fairy wood. We've heard something better than we can do, but can't quite forget it . . . can't you see it in everything English—a kind of awkward grace, a humble, humorous imcompleteness? How right Sam Weller was when he called Mr. Pickwick an angel in gaiters! Everything here is either better or worse than——"

"Dimble!" said Ransom. Dimble, whose tone had become a little impassioned, stopped and looked towards him. He hesitated and (as Jane thought) almost blushed before he began again.

"You're right, sir," he said with a smile. "I was forgetting what you have warned me always to remember. This haunting is no peculiarity of ours. Every people has its own haunter. There's no nonsense about a chosen nation. We speak about Logres because it is *our* haunting, the one we know about."

"All this," said MacPhee "seems a very roundabout way of saying that there's good and bad men everywhere."

"It's not a way of saying that at all," answered Dimble. "You see, MacPhee, if one is thinking simply of goodness in the abstract, one soon reaches the fatal idea of something standardised—some common kind of life to which all nations ought to progress. Of course there are universal rules to which all goodness must conform. But that's only the grammar of virtue. It's not there that the sap is. He doesn't make two blades of grass the same: how much less two saints, two nations, two angels. The whole work of healing Tellus depends on nursing that little spark, on incarnating that ghost, which is still alive in every real people, and different in each. When Logres really dominates Britain, when the goddess Reason, the divine clearness, is really enthroned in France, when the order of Heaven is really followed in China—why, then it will be spring. But meantime, our concern is with Logres. We've got Britain down, but who knows how long we can hold her down? Edgestow will not recover from what is happening to her to-night. But there will be other Edgestows."

"I wanted to ask about Edgestow," said Mother Dimble. "Aren't Merlin and the eldils a trifle . . . well, *wholesale*. Did *all* Edgestow deserve to be wiped out?"

"Who are you lamenting?" said MacPhee. "The jobbing town council that'd have sold their own wives and daughters to bring the N.I.C.E. to Edgestow?"

"Well, I don't know much about them," said she. "But in the university. Even Bracton itself. We all knew it was a horrible College, of course. But did they really mean any great harm with all their fussy little intrigues? Wasn't it more *silly* than anything else?"

"Och aye," said MacPhee. "They were only playing themselves. Kittens letting on to be tigers. But there was a real tiger about, and their play ended by letting her in. It'll learn them not to keep bad company."

"Well, then, the fellows of other colleges. What about Northumberland and Duke's?"

"I know," said Denniston. "One's sorry for a man like Churchwood. I knew him well; he was an old dear. All his lectures were devoted to proving the impossibility of ethics, though in private life he'd have walked ten miles rather than leave a penny debt unpaid. But all the same . . . was there a single doctrine practised at Belbury which hadn't been preached by some lecturer at Edgestow? Oh, of course, they never thought anyone would *act* on their theories! But it was their own child coming back to them: grown up and unrecognisable, but their own."

"I'm afraid it's all true, my dear," said Dimble. "*Trahison des clercs*. None of us are quite innocent."

"You are all forgetting," said Grace, "that nearly everyone, except the very good (who were ripe for fair dismissal) and the very bad, had already left Edgestow. But I agree with Arthur. Those who have forgotten Logres sink into Britain. Those who call for Nonsense will find that it comes."

At that moment she was interrupted. A clawing and whining noise at the door had become audible.

"Open the door, Arthur," said Ransom. A moment later the whole party rose to its feet with cries of welcome, for the new arrival was Mr. Bultitude.

"Oh, I never *did*," said Ivy. "The pore thing! I'll just take him down to the kitchen and get him something to eat. Wherever have you been, you bad thing? Eh? Just look at the state you're in."

v

For the third time in ten minutes the train gave a violent lurch and came to a standstill. This time the shock put all the lights out.

"This is really getting a bit too bad," said a voice in the darkness. The four other passengers in the compartment recognised it as belonging to the well-informed man who had told everyone where they ought to change and why one now reached Sterk without going through Stratford.

Still the train did not move. The noise of two men quarrelling in a neighbouring compartment became audible.

Suddenly a shock flung them all together in the darkness. It was as if the train, going at full speed, had been unskilfully pulled up.

"It's all right," said the well-informed man in a loud, calm voice. "Putting on another engine."

"Hullo!" said someone. "We're moving."

Slow and grunting, the train began to go.

Once more a violent shock hit them. It was worse than the last one. For nearly a minute everything seemed to be rocking and rattling.

"This is outrageous!" exclaimed the well-informed man, opening the window. "There's some sort of light ahead," said he.

"Signal against us?" asked another.

"No. Not a bit like that. The whole sky's lit up. Like a fire, or like searchlights."

Another shock. And then, far away in the darkness, vague disastrous noise. The train began to move again, still slowly, as if it were groping its way.

About half an hour later the lighted platform of Sterk slowly loomed alongside.

"Station Announcer calling," said a voice. "Please keep your seats for an important announcement. Slight earthquake shock and floods have rendered the line to

244

Edgestow impassable. No details available. Passengers for Edgestow are advised . . ."

The well-informed man, who was Curry, got out. Such a man always knows all officials, and in a few minutes he was standing by the fire in the ticket collector's office.

"Well, we don't exactly know yet, Mr. Curry," said the man. "There's been nothing coming through for about an hour. It's very bad, you know. They're putting the best face on it they can. There's never been an earthquake like it in England from what I can hear. And there's the floods, too. No, sir, I'm afraid you'll find nothing of Bracton College. All that part of the town went almost at once. I don't know what the casualties'll be. I'm glad I got my old Dad out last week."

Curry always in later years regarded this as one of the turning-points of his life. He had not up till then been a religious man. But the word that now instantly came into his mind was "Providential". He'd been within an ace of taking the earlier train: and if he had . . . The whole College wiped out! It would have to be rebuilt. There'd be a complete new set of Fellows, a new Warden. It was Providential again that some responsible person should have been spared. The more he thought of it, the more fully Curry realised that the whole shaping of the future college rested with the sole survivor. It was almost like being a second founder. Providential—providential.

VI

Ivy Maggs, it will be remembered, had left the dining-room for the purpose of attending to Mr. Bultitude's comfort. It therefore surprised everyone when she returned in less than a minute with a wild expression on her face.

"Oh, come quick, someone. Come quick!" she gasped. "There's a bear in the kitchen."

"A bear, Ivy?" said the Director. "But of course——"

"Oh, I don't mean Mr. Bultitude, sir. There's a strange bear; another one."

"Indeed!"

"And it's eaten up all what was left of the goose, and now it's lying along the table eating everything as it goes along and wriggling from one dish to another and a-breaking all the crockery. Oh, do come quick!"

245

"And what is Mr. Bultitude doing?"

"Well, that's what I want someone to come and see. He's carrying on something dreadful sir. I never see anything like it. First of all he stood lifting up his legs in a funny way as if he thought he could dance. But now he's got up on the dresser on his hind legs making the awfullest noise—squeaking like—and he's put one foot into the plum pudding and he's got his head mixed up in the string of onions, and I can't do *nothing* with him, really I can't."

"This is very odd of Mr. Bultitude. You don't think, my dear, that the stranger might be a *she* bear?"

"Oh, don't say that, sir!" exclaimed Ivy with extreme dismay.

"I think that's the truth, Ivy. I strongly suspect that this is the future Mrs. Bultitude."

"Oh dear, what *shall* we do?" said Ivy.

"I am sure Mr. Bultitude is quite equal to the situation," replied the Director.

"No doubt, no doubt," said MacPhee. "But not in our kitchen."

"Ivy, my dear," said Ransom, "you must be firm. Go into the kitchen and tell the strange bear I want to see her. You wouldn't be afraid, would you?"

"Afraid? I'll show her who's the Director here."

"What's the matter with that jackdaw?" said Dr. Dimble. The bird had hitherto been asleep on Ransom's shoulder.

"I think it's trying to get out," said Denniston. "Shall I open the window?"

"It's warm enough, anyway," said the Director. And as the window was opened the daw hopped out and there was a scuffle and a chattering just outside.

"Another love affair," said Mrs. Dimble. "It sounds as if Jack had found a Jill. . . . What a delicious night!" she added. For as the curtain swelled and lifted over the open window, all the freshness of a midsummer night seemed to be blowing into the room. At that moment, a little farther off, came a sound of whinnying.

"Hullo!" said Denniston, "the old mare is excited, too."

"That's a different horse," said Denniston.

"It's a stallion," said Camilla.

"This," said MacPhee with great emphasis, "is becoming indecent!"

"On the contrary," said Ransom, "decent, in the old sense, *decens*, fitting, is just what she is. Venus herself is over St. Anne's."

"She comes more near the Earth than she was wont," quoted Dimble, "to make men mad."

"She is nearer than any astronomer knows," said Ransom. "The work is done, the other gods have withdrawn. She waits, and when she returns to her sphere I will ride with her."

Suddenly in the semi-darkness Mrs. Dimble's voice cried sharply, "Look out! Look out! Cecil! I'm sorry. I can't stand bats." *Cheep cheep* went the voices of the two bats as they flickered to and fro above the candles.

"You'd better go, Margaret," said the Director. "You and Cecil had better both go. I shall be gone very soon now. There is no need of long good-byes."

"I really think I *must* go," said Mother Dimble. "I can't stand bats."

"Comfort Margaret, Cecil," said Ransom. "No. Do not stay. Seeing people off is always folly."

"You mean us to go, sir?" said Dimble.

"Go, my dear friends. *Urendi Maleldil.*"

He laid his hands on their heads: Cecil gave his arm to his wife and they went.

"Here she is, sir," said Ivy Maggs, re-entering the room a moment later, flushed and radiant. A bear waddled at her side, its cheeks sticky with gooseberry jam. "And— oh, sir?" she added.

"What is it, Ivy?" said the Director.

"Please, sir, it's poor Tom. It's my husband. And if you don't mind——"

"You've given him something to eat and drink, I hope?"

"Well, yes, I have. I give him the cold pie and the pickles (he always was a great one for pickles) and the cheese and a bottle of stout, and I've put the kettle on so as we can make ourselves—so as he can make himself a nice cup of tea. And he's enjoying it ever so, sir, and he said would you mind him not coming up to say how d'you do because he never was much of a one for company if you take my meaning."

The strange bear had been standing with its eyes fixed on the Director. He laid his hand on its flat head. "*Urendi Maleldil,*" he said. "You are a good bear. Go

247

to your mate—but here he is," for at that moment the door, which was already ajar, was pushed farther open to admit the face of Mr. Bultitude. "Take her, Bultitude. But not in the house. Jane, open the other window, the French window. It is like a night in July." The window swung open and the two bears went out into the warmth and the wetness. Everyone noticed how light it had become.

"Are those birds all daft that they're singing at quarter to twelve?" asked MacPhee.

"No," said Ransom. "They are sane. Now, Ivy, you want to go and talk to Tom. Mother Dimble has put you both in the little room half-way up the stairs, not in the lodge after all."

"Oh, sir," said Ivy, and stopped.

"Of course you want to go," he said. "Why, he's hardly had time to see you in your new dress yet. Don't cry. Go and heal this man. *Urendi Maleldil*—we shall meet again."

"What's all yon squealing?" said MacPhee. "I hope it's not the pigs. There's already as much carrying on about this house and garden as I can stand."

"I think it's hedgehogs," said Grace Ironwood.

"That last sound was somewhere in the house," said Jane.

"Listen!" said the Director, and for a short time all were still. Then his face relaxed into a smile. "It's the mice behind the wainscot," he said. "There are revels there, too."

"I suppose," said MacPhee drily, "I suppose we may think ourselves lucky that no giraffes, hippopotami, elephants, or the like have seen fit to—God almighty, what's that?" For as he spoke, a long grey flexible tube came in between the swaying curtains and helped itself to a bunch of bananas.

"In the name of Hell, where's all them beasts coming from?" he said.

"They are the liberated prisoners from Belbury," said the Director. "Perelandra is all about us, and Man is no longer isolated. We are now as we ought to be—between the angels who are our elder brothers and the beasts who are our jesters, servants, and playfellows."

Whatever MacPhee was attempting to say in reply was drowned by an ear-splitting noise from beyond the window.

"Elephants! Two of them," said Jane weakly. "Oh, the celery! And the rose beds!"

"By your leave, Mr. Director," said MacPhee sternly, "I'll just draw these curtains. You seem to forget there are ladies present."

"No," said Grace Ironwood in a voice as strong as his, "there will be nothing unfit for anyone to see. Draw them wider. How light it is! Brighter than moonlight: almost brighter than day. A great dome of light stands over the whole garden. Look! The elephants are dancing. How high they lift their feet. And they go round and round. How ceremonial they are! It is like a minuet of giants."

"They are moving away," said Camilla.

"They will be as private as human lovers," said the Director. "They are not common beasts."

"I think," said MacPhee, "I'll away down to my office and cast some accounts. There'd better be one man about the place keep his head. Good night, ladies."

"Good-bye, MacPhee," said Ransom.

"No, no," said MacPhee, standing well back but extending his hand. "You'll speak none of your blessings over me. If ever I take to religion, it won't be your kind. My uncle was Moderator of the General Assembly. But there's my hand. What you and I have seen together . . . but no matter for that. You . . . you and I . . . but there are the ladies crying. I'm away this minute. Why would a man want to lengthen it? God bless you, Dr. Ransom. Ladies, I'll wish you a good night."

"Open all the windows," said Ransom. "The vessel in which I must ride is now almost within the air of this World."

"It is growing brighter every minute," said Denniston.

"Can we be with you to the very end?" said Jane.

"Child," said the Director, "you should not stay till then."

"Why, sir?"

"You are waited for."

"Me, sir?"

"Yes. Your husband is waiting for you in the lodge. It was your own marriage chamber that you prepared. Should you not go to him?"

"Must I go *now*?"

" If you leave the decision with me, it is now that I would send you."

" Then I will go, sir. But—but—am I a bear or a hedgehog? "

" More. But not less. Go in obedience and you will find love. You will have no more dreams. Have children instead. *Urendi Maleldil*."

VII

Long before he reached St. Anne's, Mark had realised that either he himself or else the world about him was in a strange condition. The journey took longer than he expected, but that was perhaps accounted for by one or two mistakes that he made. Much harder to explain was the horror of light to the west, over Edgestow, and the throbbings and bouncings of the earth. Then came sudden warmth and torrents of melted snow. Everything became a mist: and then, as the lights in the west vanished, this mist grew softly luminous in a different place—above him, as though the light rested on St. Anne's. He had the curious impression that things of very diverse shapes and sizes were slipping past him in the haze—animals, he thought. But in spite of all perplexities, he was conscious of extreme well-being. His mind was ill at ease, but as for his body—health and youth and pleasure seemed to be blowing towards him from the cloudy light upon the hill.

His mind was not at ease. He knew that he was going to meet Jane, and something was beginning to happen to him which ought to have happened to him far earlier. That same laboratory outlook upon love which had forestalled in Jane the humility of a wife, had forestalled in him, during what passed for courtship, the humility of a lover. Or if there had ever arisen in him at some wiser moment the sense of " Beauty too rich for us, for earth too dear," he had put it away from him. Now, belated, after all favours had been conceded, the unexpected misgiving was coming over him. He tried to shake it off. They were married, weren't they? And they were sensible, modern people? What could be more natural, more ordinary?

But then certain moments of unforgettable failure in their short married life rose in his imagination. He had thought often enough of what he called Jane's " moods ".

This time at last he thought of his own clumsy importunity. Inch by inch all the lout and clod-hopper in him was revealed to his own reluctant inspection; the coarse male boor blundering in where great lovers, knights, and poets would have feared to tread. How had he dared? Her driven snow, her sacrosanctity, the very style of all her movements . . . how had he dared? The very thoughts that crossed her face from moment to moment, all of them beyond his reach, made (had he but had the wit to see it) a hedge about her which such as he should never have had the temerity to pass.

All this, which should have been uneasy joy, was torment to him, for it came too late. He was discovering the hedge after he had plucked the rose. How had he dared? And who that understood could forgive him? He knew now what he must look like in the eyes of her friends and equals. Seeing that picture, he grew hot to the forehead.

Well, he would release her. She would be glad to be rid of him. It would now almost have shocked him to believe otherwise. Ladies in some noble and spacious room, discoursing in cool ladyhood together, with exquisite gravity or silver laughter—how should they *not* be glad when the intruder had gone?—the loud-voiced or tongue-tied creature, all boots and hands, whose true place was in the stable. What he had called her coldness seemed now to be her patience. Whereof the memory scalded.

Suddenly the diffused light brightened and flushed. He looked up and perceived a great lady standing by a doorway in a wall. It was not Jane, not like Jane. It was larger, almost gigantic. It was not human, though it was like a woman divinely tall, part naked, part wrapped in a flame-coloured robe. Light came from it. It was opening the door for him. He did not dare disobey. (" Surely," he thought, " I must have died ") and he went in : found himself in some place of sweet smells and bright fires, with food and wine and a rich bed.

VIII

And Jane went out of the big house with the Director's kiss upon her lips and his words in her ears, across the wet lawn (birds were everywhere) and down all the time, down to the lodge, descending the ladder of humility. First she thought of the Director, then she thought of Maleldil. And she thought of children, and of pain and death. And she thought of Mark and of all his sufferings. She came to the lodge and was surprised to see it dark and the door shut. As she stood with one hand on the latch, a thought came to her. How if Mark did not want her—not to-night, nor in that way, nor any time, nor in any way? How if Mark were not there, after all? Then she noticed that the window was open. Clothes were piled on a chair inside the room so carelessly that they lay over the sill: the sleeve of a shirt—Mark's shirt—even hung over down the outside wall. And in all this damp, too. How like Mark! Obviously it was time she went in.

Arthur Hailey

The book that remained for over six months on the American bestseller list, now filmed with a star-studded cast —

HOTEL 5/-

Against the background of a great New Orleans hotel move the characters — tycoons of the hotel industry, guests, and staff; men and women, young and old, dedicated and amoral — sealing their own destinies in five days of dramatic change.

'Compulsively readable' DAILY EXPRESS

THE FINAL DIAGNOSIS 5/-

The engrossing story of a young pathologist and his efforts to restore the standards of a hospital controlled by an ageing, once brilliant doctor. 'Probably the best and most potentially popular medical novel since *Not as a Stranger*' NEW YORK TIMES BOOK REVIEW

Arthur Hailey and John Castle

FLIGHT INTO DANGER 3/6

High over Canada a crippling emergency strikes an airliner — on the ground, helpless observers wait and pray . . . A brilliant novel of suspense in the air that enthralled millions as a TV play.

Science Fiction in PAN

Rosemary's Baby 5/-

IRA LEVIN

The book that topped US and British
bestseller lists for months and is now a
terrifying Paramount picture, starring
Mia Farrow, John Cassavetes and
Ralph Bellamy.

'At last I have got my wish. I am ridden
by a book that plagues my mind and
continues to squeeze my heart with
fingers of bone. I swear that Rosemary's
Baby is the most unnerving story I've
read.'
KENNETH ALLSOP, EVENING NEWS

'The pay-off is so fiendish, it made me
sweat. Diabolically good.'
PETER PHILLIPS, SUN

'... if you read this book in the dead of
night, do not be surprised if you feel the
urge to keep glancing behind you.'
QUEEN

'a darkly brilliant tale of modern deviltry
that, like James' *Turn of the Screw*,
induces the reader to believe the
unbelievable. I believed it and was
altogether enthralled.'
TRUMAN CAPOTE

A SELECTION OF
POPULAR READING IN PAN

☐	**PRIDE AND PREJUDICE** Jane Austen	3/6
☐	**INHERITANCE** Phyllis Bentley	7/6
☐	**SHOOTING SCRIPT** Gavin Lyall	5/-
☐	**WUTHERING HEIGHTS** Emily Brontë	3/6
☐	**THE SOUND OF THUNDER** Wilbur A. Smith	6/-
☐	**ONE OF OUR SUBMARINES** Edward Young (illus.)	5/-
☐	**ROSEMARY'S BABY** Ira Levin	5/-
☐	**EAGLE DAY** Richard Collier (illus.)	6/-
☐	**THE MAN WITH THE GOLDEN GUN** Ian Fleming	3/6
☐	**THE SPY WHO LOVED ME** Ian Fleming	3/6
☐	**THE MAGUS** John Fowles	8/6
☐	**FRUIT OF THE POPPY** Robert Wilder	5/-
☐	**I CAN SEE YOU BUT YOU CAN'T SEE ME**	
	Eugene George	5/-
☐	**THE ROOM UPSTAIRS** Monica Dickens	5/-
☐	**A SENTENCE OF LIFE** Julian Gloag	6/-
☐	**ON FORSYTE 'CHANGE** John Galsworthy	5/-
☐	**FAR FROM THE MADDING CROWD**	
	Thomas Hardy	5/-
☐	**THE RELUCTANT WIDOW** Georgette Heyer	5/-
☐	**FREDERICA** Georgette Heyer	5/-
☐	**STRANGERS ON A TRAIN** Patricia Highsmith	5/-
☐	**STORIES MY MOTHER NEVER TOLD ME (Part I)**	
	Alfred Hitchcock	3/6
☐	**YOUNG BESS** Margaret Irwin	5/-
☐	**THE DEEP BLUE GOOD-BYE** John D. MacDonald	3/6
☐	**THE LIFE OF IAN FLEMING**	
	John Pearson (illus.)	7/6
☐	**SHAMELADY** James Mayo	3/6
☐	**MADONNA OF THE SEVEN HILLS** Jean Plaidy	5/-
☐	**ROUND THE BEND** Nevil Shute	5/
☐	**THE BOSTON STRANGLER** Gerold Frank	7/6

**Obtainable from all booksellers and newsagents. If you
have any difficulty, please send purchase price plus 6d.
postage to PO Box 11, Falmouth, Cornwall.**

**I enclose a cheque/postal order for selected titles ticked
above plus 6d. per book to cover packing and postage.**

NAME ....

ADDRESS ....

....